THE LITTLE
VILLAGE SCHOOL

THE LITTLE VILLAGE SCHOOL

Gervase Phinn

WINDSOR
PARAGON

First published 2011
by Hodder & Stoughton
This Large Print edition published 2012
by AudioGO Ltd
by arrangement with
Hodder & Stoughton Ltd

Hardcover   ISBN: 978 1 445 87112 7
Softcover   ISBN: 978 1 445 87113 4

British Library Cataloguing in Publication Data available

Printed and bound in Great Britain by
MPG Books Group Limited

I should like to record the debt of gratitude that I owe to my editors, Carolyn Mays and Rowena Webb, and to my literary agent Luigi Bonomi, for their patient good humour, invaluable encouragement and wise advice.

CHAPTER ONE

'She was wearing red shoes!' gasped the caretaker, incomprehension creeping across his face.

'With silver heels,' added the school secretary, nodding and pursing her lips.

'With silver heels?' the caretaker repeated.

'That's what I said, Mr Gribbon. She was wearing red shoes with silver heels and black lacy stockings. Not the sort of outfit I would have thought suitable for someone coming for an interview for a head teacher's position.'

The caretaker shook his head like a tetchy little dog. 'Well, I never did. Red shoes with silver heels. You wouldn't credit it.'

It was the end of the school day, and the caretaker and Mrs Scrimshaw, the school secretary, were in the small office discussing the day's events. A new head teacher had just been appointed to Barton-in-the-Dale Parochial Primary School, a somewhat controversial appointment by all accounts.

The school secretary sat stiffly at her desk; the caretaker leant idly against the doorframe. Mrs Scrimshaw looked up at the clock on the wall and made a small clucking noise with her tongue. She was obliged to wait until all the staff and pupils were off the premises, and there was still a child in the entrance waiting to be collected, so she couldn't get off home. For her to remain in her office after school each afternoon was something Miss Sowerbutts, the head teacher, had insisted upon. 'In case there is an urgent telephone call

1

from a parent or the Education Office,' she had told her. Mrs Scrimshaw couldn't for the life of her understand why it was the head teacher who was out of the door a minute after the bell sounded for the end of school, and herself who had to remain, but she didn't say anything. No one argued with Miss Sowerbutts.

Mrs Scrimshaw, having locked the desk drawers and tidied the pens for a third time, covered the typewriter and put on her coat, glancing up at the clock again. It was a ritual performed each day but it was particularly galling to have to stay that Friday afternoon because she had a Women's Institute meeting that evening. Dr Hawksley-Pratt was to give a talk on 'Facing and Surviving a Life Threatening Disease', a presentation guaranteed to attract a large audience, and she had been asked to be in the chair.

In the thirty minutes after school the caretaker frequently called in to see her, usually to grumble about something or other. Mr Gribbon was a tall, gaunt man with a hard beak of a nose and the glassy protuberant eyes of a large fish. He was brusque and direct in his manner. The school secretary sometimes considered telling the caretaker, whom she found garrulous and self-opinionated and who spent most of his life complaining, to stop his moaning and get on with his work, but she bit her tongue. It was important, she thought, to keep on the right side of him. Caretakers could be extremely useful at times, but they could also be very difficult if crossed.

Mrs Scrimshaw peered over the top of her unfashionable horn-rimmed spectacles, brushed a strand of mouse-coloured hair from her forehead and nodded again. 'And she had earrings the size of onion rings and bright blonde hair,' she disclosed.

The caretaker sucked in his breath and blew out noisily. 'I've never heard the like,' he said, jangling the bunch of keys in his overall pocket.

'Well, you can imagine the reaction of Miss Sowerbutts when she caught sight of her sitting with the others in the corridor outside her room, red shoes, short skirt, black stockings and all,' continued the school secretary, smiling at the memory. 'She had a face like a smacked bottom, as my mother was wont to say.'

'And you say she got the job then, Mrs Scrimshaw, the woman with the red shoes?'

'Yes, she did,' the school secretary told him, before adding, 'Of course, there wasn't much to choose from. Between you and me there were very few applicants for the post.'

'Really?'

'Well, you would expect that, wouldn't you,' the secretary said, in a confidential tone of voice. 'There were only six applications for the job and two of those were completely unsuitable. I mean, it's difficult these days getting good applicants for primary headships in small village schools.'

'And that dreadful report from them poker-faced school inspectors must have put a lot of people off,' observed the caretaker. 'I mean, they'd not be queuing up to come to a place which got that sort of write-up and where parents are sending their kids to other schools.'

'Actually, the report never got a mention in the information I sent out to the candidates,' divulged the secretary. 'I don't think any of the candidates was aware of it. I suppose the governors wanted to

3

keep it under wraps.'

'Aye, well, the new head teacher will find out soon enough,' said the caretaker grimly, 'and she'll have a job on her hands and no mistake.'

'Yes, she will,' agreed Mrs Scrimshaw, glancing up at the clock again.

The caretaker sniffed noisily. ''Course, I came out of the report not too badly. They said the premises were clean and well kept, as I recall, despite the fact it's an old building in need of a lot of work. Something I've been saying for years, not that Miss Sowerbutts ever listens.'

Mrs Scrimshaw gave a slight smile. She had read the school inspectors' report in some detail, and the section on the state of the premises had hardly been as positive as the caretaker maintained —it had contained a number of issues that needed addressing. There was the question of the cockroaches, for a start. The insects crawled out from under the skirting-boards in the night. Many times she had arrived in the morning to discover several of the large black beetles wriggling on their backs in their death throes after the caretaker had sprinkled that dreadful-smelling white powder down the corridor. She had asked him more times than she could remember not to lure the revolting insects out from under the skirting-boards. They weren't doing any harm, so why didn't he just leave them be? She didn't say anything about that or the other recommendations of the inspectors, but turned her attention back to the appointment of the new head teacher.

'Of course, it wasn't a unanimous decision, you know,' she revealed.

'No?'

4

The school secretary lowered her voice conspiratorially. 'Evidently the governors were split. Dr Stirling wanted to re-advertise the position, from what I gathered, but the major, with the help of that objectionable councillor with the fat face and the red nose, the officious man from the Education Office and the vicar, pushed it through. He said the school needed a new head teacher straight away to get things moving.'

The caretaker gave a dismissive grunt.

'They had the interviews in Miss Sowerbutts' office and, of course, me being next door, I couldn't help but overhear what was going on,' said the school secretary airily. 'There were raised voices on a number of occasions.'

'Really?'

'Dr Stirling got quite hot under the collar, which is not like him at all,' confided the school secretary. 'He's usually such a placid, easy-going sort of man.'

'I must see him about my back,' said the caretaker, stretching theatrically. 'It's playing me up again. It's not been right since I moved them bins.'

When had his back ever been right, thought the school secretary. He'd been complaining about his wretched back ever since he'd started at the school a good ten years ago. She said nothing, but put on a sympathetic expression.

'Well, they couldn't have picked anyone more different from the present head teacher,' observed the caretaker. 'And that's the honest truth.'

The school secretary thought for a moment of the present incumbent, Miss Hilda Sowerbutts, dressed in her thick pleated tweed skirt, crisp white blouse buttoned up to her thin neck, heavy tan brogues and that silly knitted hat like a tea-cosy

5

perched on top of her head. She allowed herself another small smile. She tried to imagine her wearing red shoes, a short skirt and black lacy stockings. Yes, the new head teacher was certainly very different.

'So what did she have to say?' asked the caretaker, rubbing his chin thoughtfully.

'I beg your pardon?' asked the secretary, returning from her reverie.

'Miss Sowerbutts. What did she have to say about the appointment?'

'Nothing,' Mrs Scrimshaw told him. She brushed another loose strand of hair away from her face. 'I was taking the candidates a cup of coffee before the interviews when Miss Sowerbutts walks down the corridor, stares at them for a moment, gives this dry little smile, nods and then leaves the school, telling me she'll be back when the interviews are over. I mean, it was embarrassing. She never spoke to them. I didn't know where to look. When she got back to the school after the governors had appointed, she never said a word, not one word. Never asked who got the job or anything. Went into her office, closed the door and carried on as normal. Then she was out of the door when the bell sounded for end of school as if her life depended upon it. Of course, she was not best pleased that the governors hadn't seen fit to involve her in the appointment, that's why she was in such a black mood. They never showed her the shortlist, you know, although I have an idea she went into my drawer and looked through the applications, and they didn't ask her opinion or invite her to sit in on the interviews.'

'That must have stuck in her craw,' remarked the

caretaker, sniffing again.

'Oh, it did,' said the school secretary. 'She went off alarmingly the week before when she met the Chairman of Governors. She gave the major a piece of her mind and no mistake. I couldn't help but overhear because they raised their voices in the corridor. Well, she raised *her* voice. He didn't get so much as a word in.'

Mrs Scrimshaw had left the office door slightly ajar at the time of the major's visit, the better to hear the heated exchange. The chairman of the governing body, Major C. J. Neville-Gravitas, late of the Royal Engineers, had informed Miss Sowerbutts that it was not really appropriate for her to take part in the appointment process, and this had not been received very well at all. The head teacher had argued with him, of course, but to no avail. He had explained that, although he personally had no objection to her sitting in on the interviews, Mr Nettles, the representative of the Local Education Authority, had raised an objection and was adamant that she should not attend.

Miss Sowerbutts had responded angrily when it had been suggested that on the day of the interviews she might welcome the candidates, show them around the school and keep them company during the morning.

'I think not,' she had told him icily.

'Well, what did she expect?' said the caretaker now. 'I mean, after that damning report from the school inspectors, she'd be the very last person to take any advice from. I mean, let's face it, Mrs Scrimshaw, she's well past her sell-by date, is Miss Sowerbutts. She was teaching in this school when I was a lad. She should have retired years ago.

School's been going from bad to worse; parents complaining, children leaving to go to other schools like nobody's business, behaviour not all it should be and poor standards to boot, and her walking round the school with a face like a death mask.'

'You don't need to tell me, Mr Gribbon,' said the secretary. 'I've read the school inspectors' report as well.'

Yes, thought the caretaker, and she hadn't come out of it with flying colours either. Hadn't the inspectors said something about more efficiency, better record-keeping and greater attention to detail in the school office?

'So how did Miss Brakespeare take it then?' he asked. 'I suppose as the deputy head teacher she thought she was in with a chance of getting the job.'

'I think she found it a bit of a relief not to have got it, to be honest,' replied the school secretary. 'I'm pretty certain Miss Sowerbutts pushed her into applying. I don't wish to be unkind, but I guess they only interviewed Miss Brakespeare to fill up the numbers, and she would have been very upset had she not been called for interview having applied.'

'I don't want to be unkind, either,' said the caretaker, jangling the heavy bunch of keys in his pocket, 'but, let's face it, she hadn't a cat in hell's chance of getting the job. I mean, she's a nice enough woman, but if truth be told, she's another one who's well past her sell-by date and to be fair she'd not be up to it. I mean, I've been into some of her assemblies and the woman could bore for Britain. What was it that school inspector described her as? Dull and dreary, wasn't it?'

'No, no, he didn't single anyone out,' the school secretary told him, 'although it did say in the

8

report that some of the teaching in the juniors lacked vitality and could be more interesting and challenging. I think he might have been referring to Miss Brakespeare, because the other two teachers seemed to have got good enough reports by all accounts. No, the inspector's target was Miss Sowerbutts rather than her. He said the senior management was "lacklustre" and the school "moribund" and there were "serious weaknesses which needed addressing urgently".'

'I'd like to have been a fly on the wall when Miss Sowerbutts heard that little lot,' chuckled the caretaker, jangling his keys again. 'I can just picture her face. When she puts on that expression of hers, she could freeze soup in pans.'

'Anyway,' continued the school secretary, 'I think Miss Brakespeare was relieved not to have got the job, if truth be told. As you know, I'm not a one for gossip, but I don't think she or anybody else really thought she was in with a chance. I guess she didn't want it anyway, what with having that disabled mother to look after and her near retirement. She came into the office after the interviews in quite a jolly mood. As I said, if you want my opinion she only applied for the post because Miss Sowerbutts pushed her into it. You know how forceful she can be.'

'Tell me about it,' muttered the caretaker. 'So did you meet her then, the new head teacher?'

'Yes,' replied the school secretary. 'She seemed very pleasant and chatty and certainly had more about her than the other candidates. She popped into the office after the interview to say she looked forward to working with me and would be calling in to the school next week to look around and meet

9

people. She was a bit put out when she said she'd like to have a word with Miss Sowerbutts before she left and I told her that the head teacher wasn't on the premises.' A self-satisfied look came across Mrs Scrimshaw's face. 'Actually, she said that in her opinion the school secretary is a vital cog in the educational machine and, as I said, she looked forward to working with me.'

'Did she mention anything about the school, then?' asked the caretaker.

Mrs Scrimshaw knew exactly what he meant, fishing for compliments, but feigned ignorance. 'In what way?' she asked.

'Well, the state of the building. Did she mention anything about that?'

'No, she didn't,' replied the school secretary pointedly.

'I spent most of the weekend giving the place a good once-over,' moaned the caretaker petulantly, 'so that it would look nice and clean for the interviews. I would have thought some mention would have been made of that. I spend half my life getting a sheen on that parquet floor and sorting out the problem with the cockroach infestation, and what credit do I get?'

'She did make a point of having a word with Miss Brakespeare,' continued the school secretary mischievously, enjoying the caretaker's clear irritation at not getting a mention. 'She told her how she hoped they could work together.'

The caretaker laughed in a mirthless way. 'Huh. I'll tell you this, Miss Brakespeare will have to buck her ideas up now, by the sound of it.'

'Yes, I guess she will,' agreed the secretary. And so will you, she thought to herself. 'The school needs a fresh start,' she said, 'and this new woman will no doubt give it, although I wonder how parents and people in the village will react. She'll not be everyone's idea of a head teacher.'

'No,' agreed the caretaker, rubbing his jaw and sniffing again. 'Red shoes with silver heels. I just hope she doesn't start walking on my parquet floor with her silver heels. It's taken me an age to get it to the state it's in.'

The school secretary allowed herself another small smile. The state of the parquet floor in the school hall, she thought, was the least of the caretaker's worries. 'One wonders, of course,' she said, 'why someone so well qualified and already a very successful head teacher in a large city primary school should want to move to a village in the middle of the country. I saw her references and they were very good, very good indeed. I mean, there's a drop in salary for a start, then the cost of moving house.'

'Is she married then?' asked the caretaker.

'Well, she's "Mrs" on the application form,' the school secretary told him.

'Perhaps her husband's got a job in the area,' suggested the caretaker. 'She might—'

'Well, no,' interrupted Mrs Scrimshaw. 'I had to copy the application forms and the references for the governors and I couldn't help but notice that where it asked for marital status she had written, "Single".'

'She must be divorced, then?'

'Appears so, unless she's a widow.'

'Well, it's a bit of a mystery and no mistake,' said the caretaker.

'It is indeed,' agreed the school secretary

11

thoughtfully. 'It is indeed.'

A small voice could be heard in the corridor.

'Excuse me, Mr Gribbon, I'm sorry to interrupt your conversation but may I have a quick word with Mrs Scrimshaw?'

The caretaker moved away from the door to let a small boy into the office. He was a bright-eyed, rosy-cheeked child of about or eight or nine, his hair cut in the short-back-and-sides style and with a neat parting. Unlike the other junior boys in the school, who wore jumpers in the school colours, open-necked white shirts and long grey flannel trousers, this child was attired in a smart blue blazer, a hand-knitted pullover, grey shorts held up by an elastic belt with a snake clasp, a white shirt and tie, long grey stockings and sensible shoes. He could have been a schoolboy of the 1950s.

'Hasn't your mother arrived to collect you yet, Oscar?' asked the school secretary irritably.

'No, not yet, Mrs Scrimshaw,' replied the child cheerfully, 'but I am sure she will be here directly. She has a great many commitments on Fridays and she said she would be a little late.' He had a curiously old-fashioned way of speaking.

'Yes, well, I have to get home,' Mrs Scrimshaw told him sharply, glancing at the clock on the wall yet again. 'I really shouldn't have to wait around until your mother decides to collect you. I'm going out this evening and I wanted to be off promptly.'

'Anywhere nice?' asked the child cheerily, oblivious to the implied criticism of his mother.

Mrs Scrimshaw sighed impatiently. There was a slight raise of the eyebrow and a brief lift of the chin. 'Perhaps I ought to give your mother a ring,' she said.

12

'She'll be on her way,' the child told her. 'Friday is when she does her counselling and she sometimes runs a little late.'

'Well, what do you want, Oscar?' asked Mrs Scrimshaw.

'I just wanted a quick word with you about the new head teacher,' replied the boy.

'Oh yes,' said the school secretary, exchanging a glance with the caretaker.

'Miss Sowerbutts told us yesterday in assembly that the governors would be appointing a new head teacher today,' said the boy cheerfully.

'That's right.'

'And she said we had to be on our very best behaviour.'

'Did she?'

'And that whoever gets the job,' continued the boy, 'will probably be calling in at the school some time next week to meet the teachers and the children and to have a look around.'

'Well, what about it, Oscar?' asked Mrs Scrimshaw.

'Well, it occurred to me,' said the child, 'that it would be a really good idea to make a big poster that we could put in the entrance hall to greet our new head teacher for when he or she visits. It would make them feel welcome, don't you think? I could do it over the weekend. I've just been given some paints for my birthday by my Uncle Julian. And I could write a poem of welcome.'

Mrs Scrimshaw exchanged glances again with her colleague. He rolled his eyes and jangled his keys. 'I think you would need to ask Miss Sowerbutts about that, Oscar,' said the school secretary, imagining the expression on the face of the head teacher when such an idea was suggested.

'Well, I could do the poster and the poem and bring them in on Monday,' persisted the boy, 'and run it past her.'

The school secretary knew exactly what Miss Sowerbutts would think. The head teacher had been in a terrible mood all day, having been obliged to vacate her room for the interviews in which she had not been involved. The last thing she would want was a big poster and a poem welcoming her successor.

'I think that's a very good idea, Oscar,' said the school secretary. 'You run it past her on Monday. Now why don't you go and wait in the entrance for your mother and read your book.'

'So, did the governors pick a new head teacher, Mrs Scrimshaw?' asked the boy without moving.

'Off you go, Oscar,' the school secretary told him with a tight smile of dismissal. 'You'll find out soon enough.'

'It's just that I could put her name—or it could be the man of course—on my poster,' the child told her.

'Go on! Off you go!' said the caretaker sharply. 'And do as you're told.'

'Actually I'm glad I've seen you, Mr Gribbon,' said the boy, ignoring the instruction. 'I've noticed that one or two of the paving slabs on the school drive have cracked and could be a health and safety hazard.'

'Have you indeed?' The caretaker grimaced.

'A bit sticks up in places. I nearly tripped over and I could have hurt myself,' continued the boy.

'Well, you should look where you're going then, shouldn't you?' said the caretaker.

14

'It's just that if someone does trip up and falls over they could break a bone and then the school could get into a lot of trouble. My father was telling my mother at breakfast this morning about someone in the office where he works who slipped on the wet floor and broke her leg and she's taking the company to court. He said she could get a lot of money in compensation. I think it would be a really good idea, Mr Gribbon, if you replaced those paving slabs.'

The caretaker opened his mouth to reply but the boy smiled widely and said, 'Well, I think I can see my mother at the school gates. I'll get off then.'

'Goodbye, Oscar,' sighed the school secretary, slowly shaking her head.

'Oh, goodbye, Mrs Scrimshaw,' the boy replied. He turned to the caretaker. 'Goodbye, Mr Gribbon, and you won't forget about the broken paving slabs, will you?'

'Now look here, young man—' started the caretaker, scowling, but before he could complete the sentence the child was out of the door.

'I do hope the lady in the red shoes is our new head teacher,' shouted the boy from the corridor. 'She looked nice.'

*　　　*　　　*

Miss Hilda Sowerbutts, to avoid being there at the time of the interviews, had left the school that morning before the first candidate had been called into her room to face the appointment panel. She was curious to see the candidates, though, so she had looked them over as they sat in the corridor but had said nothing. They were a motley group,

15

she thought to herself. She had left the school and arrived back after the candidates and governors had departed at lunchtime, had not asked Mrs Scrimshaw who had been offered the position, and had closeted herself in her room for the remainder of the day. At the sound of the bell signalling the end of school she strode down the path, seething malevolently like a giant wasp, without saying 'Good afternoon' to the school secretary and ignoring the school caretaker, who attempted to catch her attention as she rattled through the gate. She was furious with the governors, of course, but Mrs Scrimshaw had annoyed her with the excessive attention she had paid to the candidates and by the obsequious way she had followed the Chairman of Governors around like some fussy little lapdog.

Miss Sowerbutts walked briskly through the village, past the village store and post office and the Blacksmith's Arms, to arrive at her small cottage at the end of the high street. After pouring herself a large extra dry sherry, she sat in the small tidy living room simmering. To be treated like this by the governors after all her years of loyal service to the school, to be slighted in such a way, was quite unforgivable. When the Chairman of Governors had informed her the week before that she was not to be involved in the interviewing process, she had, for one of those rare moments in her life, been lost for words.

'So, you see, Miss Sowerbutts,' the major had said, tugging nervously at his moustache, 'it was felt by the governing body that it would be for the best if you distanced yourself, so to speak. We thought it appropriate if you were not involved.'

'Distance myself?' she had said when she had

found her voice. She had stiffened, her face rigid. 'Not be involved?'

'That's right,' he had told her with a contrived smile. 'To leave the appointment in the hands of the governors, if you follow my drift.'

'No, Major!' she had snapped. She had prickled with irritation. 'I am afraid I do not follow your drift. Might I remind you that I have been head teacher in this school for twenty years?' She had tensed with indignation. Her tone of voice had been glacial. 'Furthermore, I have taught at Barton-in-the-Dale for thirty. Does that not mean anything?' The major had felt it politic not to reply. He had stared at her glassily. 'I guess it does not,' she had informed him coldly.

'It's a tad delicate, Miss Sowerbutts,' the major had started, smiling awkwardly, and then had begun again to tug at his moustache. 'You see—'

'Please allow me to finish,' she had interrupted, with exaggerated disdain. 'I should have thought that my opinion would count for something and at the very least my advice would have been sought.'

'You see,' the major had tried to explain, 'the representative of the Local Education Authority, Mr Nettles, felt very strongly that it might be for the best if you were not involved. As far as I am concerned, I have no objection to your being party to the appointment, indeed I suggested the same, but one has to take the advice of Mr Nettles. After all, he has attended many interviews and does guide us in these matters. As he was at pains to point out, he is the *locum tenent*—'

'The what?' Miss Sowerbutts had asked, sharply, her eyes slitted to contain her anger.

'He stands in for the Director of Education,' the

17

major had endeavoured to explain, 'there to advise us and see that things are done properly. I am told it is not usual for head teachers to sit in on the appointment of their successors.'

'Then you have been sadly misinformed, by this *local tenement* or whatever he styles himself,' she had told the major testily, her mouth dry with resentment. 'If it is not usual for head teachers to sit in on the appointment of their successors, then why was Mr Whyman sitting in on the interview for the headship at Tanbeck Wood Primary School last year?'

'Ah, yes, well,' the major had blustered. 'I think that was something of an exception to the rule, if you follow my drift. There were special circumstances at Tanbeck Wood, I gather, in that particular situation.'

'Which were?' she had asked tartly. The question was like a pistol shot.

'I beg your pardon?'

'What were these "special circumstances"?' she had demanded, emphasising the last two words.

'I'm not privy to that, Miss Sowerbutts,' the major had told her feebly.

'Really? Well, I should be very interested to know what they were,' she had persisted.

'You would have to have a word with Mr Nettles about that,' the major had replied, glancing at his watch to avoid her Medusa stare. How he had longed to be somewhere else.

'So, then, I am not even to see the application forms or give an opinion about who I think should be on the shortlist?' There had been a wary resentful look in her eyes. 'Is that what you are saying?'

'We . . . we . . . felt . . . Mr Nettles felt, that is,' the major had told her, thinking to himself that it would have been easier to face a squad of battle-hardened soldiers than tackle this woman, 'that it is better if you are not involved in the appointment.'

'Well, Major, let me tell you,' she had said, a look of distaste passing over her features, 'and I hope you will convey this back to the governors and to this Mr Nettles, that I feel personally and profoundly insulted. In my considered opinion you have not treated me with the proper respect and attention. I feel betrayed and I am extremely angry.'

'I am sorry you feel this way,' the Chair of Governors had said. 'Although you will not participate in the actual appointment, I do hope you will be involved to the extent of meeting the candidates, showing them around the school and answering any questions they may ask.'

Miss Sowerbutts had stared at him coldly. 'I think not,' she had said.

The major had departed with his tail between his legs.

On the day of the interviews Miss Sowerbutts, on arriving home, looked out over her neat little garden, the smooth green lawn, carefully trimmed hedges and tidy borders she so carefully tended. She bristled with suppressed anger as she recalled the disagreeable meeting with the major. Lifting the sherry glass to her lips, she emptied the contents in one great gulp.

The phone rang.

'Yes?' she answered sharply.

'It's me,' a small voice came down the line. It was the deputy head teacher. 'I didn't get a chance to

19

see you after school and I just wanted—'

'Did you get it?' Miss Sowerbutts asked quickly.

'No.'

'No!'

'The woman in the red shoes got it, a Mrs Devine.'

Miss Sowerbutts received the news with a face as hard as a diamond. 'Well, I think it is disgraceful,' she said angrily. 'Disgraceful!'

'She seems very nice,' Miss Brakespeare told her hesitantly. 'She was very pleasant and took the time to have a word with me after the interviews.'

Miss Sowerbutts did not listen as she tried to take in the shocking news. 'I just cannot believe it.'

'It might be for the best,' Miss Brakespeare said. She sounded almost cheerful.

'I'll see you tomorrow, Miriam,' said Miss Sowerbutts, and without a word of commiseration, she banged down the receiver.

What was surprising to her was that the deputy head teacher had not sounded at all disappointed that she had not got the job, in fact she had sounded not only resigned to the fact but distinctly light-hearted.

Miss Sowerbutts was not the sort of woman to let things lie. She considered herself well-respected in the village, indeed held in awe by many, and believed that she still had a deal of influence in many different circles. If the major and this woman with the red shoes and the black stockings thought they were in for an easy ride, then they had another think coming.

CHAPTER TWO

The Reverend Atticus, rector of Barton, surveyed his tea, which had just been placed before him, through the thin lenses of small steel-framed spectacles. In the centre of the plate was a weeping chunk of boiled ham, half a hard-boiled egg with a blob of sickly-looking mayonnaise on top, two circles of dry cucumber, a radish, an over-ripe tomato and a fan-shaped piece of wilting lettuce edged in brown.

'Is there something the matter with your tea, Charles?' asked the vicar's wife.

She was a plain woman with a long oval face and skin the colour of the wax candles on the altar in the church, but her redeeming features were the most striking jade green eyes and her soft Titian hair.

'No, no, my dear,' the vicar replied, raising a smile. I am sure someone starving somewhere in the world would be glad of this repast, he thought, but it looked deeply unappetising to him. Of course, he didn't say anything but picked up his knife and fork. 'I was just thinking,' he said.

'About what?' asked his wife, spearing a radish.

'Oh, what I might make the theme of my sermon on Sunday.'

'Well, I hope you will make it a great deal shorter than last week's sermon,' his wife said rather petulantly. 'It went on for far too long. And I do wish you wouldn't spend so much time talking outside the church after the service. The Yorkshire pudding tasted like cardboard when we eventually

21

sat down to eat.' She crunched on the radish.

His wife's culinary efforts frequently tasted like cardboard, thought the vicar, but he remained silent and poked the tomato to the side of his plate as if it were some insect that had crawled out of the lettuce.

'I mean,' continued his wife, 'how many in the congregation understand or indeed are remotely interested in what you say?'

The comment stung. 'One hopes that they take in something, my dear,' replied her husband. He stared out of the window at the pale green pastures, dotted with grazing sheep and criss-crossed by grey stone walls, that rolled upwards to the great whaleback hills and gloomy grey clouds in the distance. The scene had a cold and eerie beauty about it. He recalled a snatch of text: 'I will lift up mine eyes unto the hills, from whence cometh my help.'

'Are you listening, Charles?' asked his wife.

'Indeed, my dear,' he replied.

'It is a fact that most of the women come to church to show off their new hats and to exchange village gossip, and that the men come to talk about farming after the service,' observed his wife, cutting the piece of the insipid ham on her plate into stamp-sized squares.

'That's a trifle unkind,' said the vicar, with a gentle reproof in his voice.

'Oh, Charles, really,' said his wife in an exasperated tone. 'You sound so "holier than thou" at times. "A trifle unkind." You always have to look for the good in people, don't you?'

It was true that the vicar always looked for the good in others, tried to be fair and see the other person's point of view. It was in his nature. 'I'm a priest, my dear,' he reminded her. 'I think that is what priests are supposed to do.'

Mrs Atticus stared at her husband unblinkingly. 'Please don't patronise me, Charles.' She posted a piece of ham in her mouth and chewed slowly. They ate in silence for a while. 'Of course, you would have been much more than a mere priest if you had a bit more ambition,' she said. The vicar bit his lip. 'My father, the bishop, always made his sermons short and sweet,' she continued, prior to posting another square of meat into her mouth. 'The church was invariably full when he spoke.'

Here we go again, thought the vicar, forcing a piece of tasteless lettuce into his mouth. He'd thought it would not be long before the sainted bishop arose in his wife's conversation. He had never really got on with his wife's father. He could picture the narrow, bony face set in an expression of severe sanctity, and the wild bushy eyebrows that frequently arched with disapproval. He could hear the deep, resonant voice dripping with condescension and recall the searing blue eyes which had frequently rested upon him when they had disagreed.

The Reverend Atticus knew, soon after his marriage to the bishop's daughter, that he was something of a disappointment as a son-in-law. But she had taken to this rather serious and intense young man when she had first met him at one of her father's soirées and had been attracted by his warm, attentive manner and kindly eyes. The young clergyman was not a handsome man in any conventional sense, but, unlike some of the young clerics who fluttered and flattered around

23

her father, Charles Atticus had a thoughtful intelligent face and was his own man. Indeed, when the others at the clerical get-togethers talked inconsequentially, he had tried to debate with the bishop a number of ecclesiastical matters that had been troubling him. She had rather taken to the man who had the temerity to stand up to her father. The bishop had stroked his hand over his high bald dome and had told the young curate irritably that this was neither the time nor the place to be arguing points of theology.

For his part, the young Charles Atticus was drawn to the striking, almond-shaped green eyes and golden auburn hair of this pale-skinned young woman who introduced herself as the bishop's daughter. They had talked for most of the evening and he had been invigorated by her company.

She reminded of him of the Pre-Raphaelite figure that featured in the painting adorning his tutor's rooms at Oxford. Sadly, he thought, over the years, that lovely, interesting woman had become increasingly dissatisfied with her lot, more critical and tetchy and certainly more outspoken. She'd dreamed of ending her days in the bishop's palace, surrounded by her children. Sadly he recalled the time when they had come to realise at last that they would never be blessed with children. His wife more than he had felt the great sense of loss.

'And, of course,' continued his wife now, 'my father spoke in the sort of plain and simple language that people understood. I do think your sermons are way above their heads, with all these biblical quotations, classical references and theological opinions. You are not lecturing to divinity students.'

'I do try to stimulate some thought in those who hear me,' said the vicar, having succeeded in swallowing the lettuce.

'My father, though you did not share his stance on a number of theological matters, imagined that you might go far in the Church when you married me,' she said. 'He said you had a good mind and had great potential if you could only be less serious and more sociable and mix with the right people. Yes, and I too thought you might go far.'

'So you constantly keep reminding me, my dear,' said the vicar, smiling tolerantly. He gazed, frowning, at the view through the window and another quotation came to mind. 'A low voice is an excellent thing in a woman,' it ran. Was that in the Bible, he thought, or was it Shakespeare?

'Well, he did. He was an archdeacon by the time he reached thirty-five and a bishop when he was forty-six. You are as well qualified as he was, went to same college at Oxford and were very highly thought of. All my friends at university thought you were destined for high office. I think it is very short-sighted of the Church to pass you over for the dean's position in favour of that sanctimonious little man with the wire-rimmed spectacles and the loud voice.'

'I hardly think I was "passed over",' the vicar told her, smiling awkwardly. 'Dr Peacock is very good-humoured and kindly when you get to know him and he works extremely hard.'

'You see, there you go again, Charles, always looking for the good in people and rarely agreeing with my opinions. Dr Peacock lives up to his name. He is full of his own importance, strutting about the cathedral in his fancy cassock, and his wife is the

25

same. And as for referring to herself as Mrs Dean . . . How ridiculous.'

'I am very content here,' said the vicar.

'Well, I am not content here,' his wife retorted. 'I imagined that you would at the very least have been offered the dean's position when it came up, but it went to him, fussy, shrill-voiced little man that he is, who no doubt ingratiated himself with the bishop.'

The Reverend Atticus raised his eyes heavenwards and the snatch of verse again came to mind: 'I will lift up mine eyes unto the hills, from whence cometh my help.' Of course, no help was forthcoming. He sighed inwardly and examined his plate. He had never revealed to his wife that the present bishop had tried to persuade him that his name should be put forward for the said position, and that in every likelihood he would have been offered it; or that he had told the bishop he was honoured, but he was quite content to be the vicar of the small rural parish of Barton-in-the-Dale.

His wife, having consumed her salad and placed her knife and fork together on her plate, dabbed at the corners of her mouth. 'And then there's the bishop,' she said.

'And what about the bishop, my dear?' enquired the vicar, predicting what she was about to impart.

'"Call me Bill," he says, with that irritating laugh of his and his hearty handshake and happy-clappy services. The confirmation service was like a revivalist meeting, all that loud singing and clapping. It was like the Methodists. All they needed were tambourines.'

'I think they are actually called timbrels,' said the vicar, 'and it's the Salvation Army that—'

'Whatever!' snapped his wife testily. 'My father

26

must have spun in his grave when they saw fit to elevate such a man.'

'A merry heart doeth good as medicine,' observed the vicar.

'I beg your pardon?' asked his wife.

'The Song of Solomon,' murmured her husband.

His wife gave a weary sigh.

He prayed to himself: Dear Lord, give her patience and charity. He was saddened by his wife's resentful words and by the fact that he had not lived up to her expectations. 'You are not at all happy today, are you, Marcia?' he asked, putting down his knife and fork and resting his white, well-cared-for hands on the table with priestly precision.

'No, Charles, I am not,' she replied.

'Has something upset you?' he asked.

'If you really want to know, it's this village that has upset me. I can't walk down the high street without a curtain moving, I can't say anything in the doctor's surgery without it being broadcast around the whole neighbourhood, and I can't purchase an item from the village shop without all and sundry knowing what we are having for tea. I get stopped by parishioners all the time asking about church functions and services, and what are we doing about the Harvest Festival and the Summer Fête, and when is the next meeting of the Mothers' Union. And I am always the vicar's wife and expected to behave like someone they consider a vicar's wife should behave like. People seem to forget that I am a person in my own right.' She bit her lip momentarily and looked down at her empty plate. 'It's so very claustrophobic here. I imagined that when the dean's position came up we would be moving from this incestuous little village to that

27

lovely Georgian house in the cathedral precinct and be at the centre of the city, meet different and interesting people and have something of a life.'

The vicar rubbed his forehead. 'I am sorry you feel this way, Marcia,' he said. 'My one ambition was to be a country parson and serve a small community and hopefully to make some difference to people's lives. It was never my intention to climb up some ecclesiastical ladder. I am not an ambitious man. I have never wanted all the trappings and the responsibilities of a dean or an archdeacon or a bishop. You knew that when you married me.'

'Yes, Charles, you may be very happy being just a country parson but what about me?' She dabbed her eyes with her napkin. 'What sort of life is this for me?'

'Perhaps if you involved yourself in the life of the village a little more,' he suggested, with a harassed look on his face.

'You mean become a Morris dancer?' she said. 'Attend the local history society meetings? Join the Countrywomen's club? The WI? I don't think so.'

The couple sat in silence for while.

'I have not managed to do a dessert,' said the vicar's wife, sniffing. 'I have been very busy with other things this afternoon.'

The vicar decided it was judicious not to enquire what exactly his wife had been so busy with that afternoon. It certainly wasn't polishing the brasses or arranging the altar flowers in the church.

'We appointed the new head teacher at the school this morning,' he said, changing the subject and trying to sound cheerful.

'Well, I hope you picked someone different from the present incumbent,' replied his wife. 'That sour-faced woman should have gone years ago.'

The vicar thought for a moment and recalled the surprise on the faces of his fellow governors when this attractive blonde-haired woman with the red shoes and the black stockings had walked through the door at the interviews that morning. As soon as she spoke he had been immediately impressed by her confident manner, her sensible views on education and her obvious enthusiasm and good humour.

'Are you listening, Charles?' asked his wife. 'I said I hope you have picked someone different from the present incumbent.'

'Oh yes,' he replied, 'the new appointment is very different, very different indeed.'

'That head teacher who's at the school at the moment is a most disagreeable woman,' the vicar's wife informed him. 'And before you spring to her defence and tell me she has all these good points and I shouldn't be so unkind, I have not heard one person in the village say a good word about her.'

'I was about to say,' said the vicar, 'that Miss Sowerbutts does have something of a joyless disposition and a somewhat disconcerting countenance, I have to admit.'

'In simple language, Charles,' said his wife, 'she's a miserable, bad-tempered gorgon of a woman. I don't think I've ever seen her smile. She walks about the village with a permanent scowl. One good thing that came out of that inspection of the school was getting her to retire. It's a pity that it had to be the inspectors and not the governors who had to get rid of her. One wonders what you governors are for. I mean, you should have grasped the nettle years ago.'

The vicar sighed with weary sufferance and felt it better not to pursue this line of conversation. He could have told his wife that the governors had discussed a number of times the possibility of suggesting to Miss Sowerbutts that she might consider retiring early, when parents began to move their children to other schools, but that they had discovered it was extremely difficult to remove a head teacher—unless of course he or she ran off with the dinner money or interfered with a child.

'So what's the new head teacher like?' asked his wife.

'She's a very amiable and experienced person,' the vicar told her. 'Extremely well qualified and with excellent references. She's at present the head teacher of a large and very successful inner-city primary, which received a glowing report from the school inspectors. I feel certain she will change the school for the better.'

'One wonders,' said the vicar's wife, 'if she is so well qualified and experienced, why on earth she would want to leave a thriving and successful school and come to a backwater like Barton-in-the-Dale.'

That very thing had in fact been raised by one of the governors on the appointment panel, but the vicar said nothing and turned his attention to the circles of cucumber on his plate.

*   *   *

The governors had convened in Miss Sowerbutts' room for the interviews at nine o'clock that morning: the Chairman, Major C. J. Neville-Gravitas, RE (Retd); the Reverend Atticus, rector of Barton; Mr Nettles, an education officer from

30

County Hall; Dr Stirling, a local GP; Mrs Pocock, a parent governor; Mrs Bullock, a foundation governor and Councillor Cyril Smout, the Local Education Authority representative.

The head teacher's room, in contrast to the rest of the school, was bright, comfortable and well furnished. There was an occasional table and two easy chairs, a pale shag-pile carpet, long pale drapes at the window, and it had its own small private toilet. The room was dominated by a large desk. There were filing cupboards and cabinets of various sorts, an expensive-looking bookcase, and the walls, which were plain and the colour of soured cream, were decorated with colourful prints. With so many people clustered uncomfortably around the head teacher's desk it had been cramped, hot and airless. There being no staff-room, the four candidates, who had arrived at 8.30, had either wandered around the school or waited seated in the corridor outside until they were called, in turn, to be interviewed.

'It's a rum do, is this,' Councillor Smout announced, leaning back expansively on his chair, stretching his fat legs underneath the desk and sucking in his teeth. He was a broad individual with an exceptionally thick neck, a vast florid face and small darting eyes. His face seemed set in a permanent frown. His stomach pushed forcefully against his waistcoat, revealing a show of white shirt and the top of his trousers. 'T'head teacher clearing off like that. She shot out of that door like a rabbit wi' t'runs. Walked straight past me in t'corridor she did, wi'out a by-your-leave and with a mouth like a torn pocket.'

'She is rather upset that she was not invited to

31

sit in on the interview,' the chairman told him. 'I'm afraid she is not best pleased with the governors, if you follow my drift. I had quite a contretemps with her last week.'

'A what?' Mrs Bullock asked, craning her neck in the major's direction.

'A difference of opinion, Mrs Bullock,' the chairman said loudly.

'As I have been at pains to point out, Mr Chairman,' the education officer explained, 'there was no question whatsoever of Miss Sowerbutts being invited to sit on the appointment panel. It would be quite out of the question, particularly under the circumstances.'

'Well, she was not best pleased,' the major informed them, 'and she was extremely belligerent with me.'

'I can't see why she should be miffed,' the councillor said. 'I should 'ave thought that what with that critical report and all, she would 'ave wanted to keep 'er 'ead down.' He flicked through the papers in front of him. 'Any road, Mr Chairman, can we get on? I've a meeting of t'Parks and Recreation Committee this afternoon. I shouldn't think this'll tek too long. I mean, it's not as if we've got a reight good field to choose from, is it?'

'That is to be expected, councillor,' the education officer remarked. 'There is often a paucity of applications for head teacher posts at the small schools, and the salary is not that attractive. I guess also that those who live in the area and know the school will have got wind of the inspectors' report. That, no doubt, will have put some people off.'

'Do I take it that in the details sent to the

candidates the findings in the school inspectors' report were not revealed?' the vicar asked.

'We felt it prudent not to mention it,' the education officer told him.

'I think it would have been fair-minded to do so,' the Reverend Atticus said, clearly displeased. 'It seems to me that those who have applied for the post should at the very least have been informed—'

'Could we please resist talking persistently and tediously about the school report?' the major asked, sighing. 'We have discussed what the inspectors had to say in great detail at the last two meetings. I for one have heard quite enough about the report. It is surely time to move on and to appoint someone who will take the school forward and breathe fresh life into it.'

'Quite right, Mr Chairman,' Councillor Smout agreed. 'We were on t'edge of a precipice after what them inspectors said about t'school, but, as you've just said, we now need to move forward wi' confidence. Let's get cracking or we'll be 'ere all day.'

'And I do think, Reverend Atticus,' the education officer added, 'that it would be unwise to mention the report to the candidates. We really do not want any withdrawals. It is imperative that we appoint someone today.'

'I don't agree,' the vicar retorted. 'I think it is "imperative", to use your word, that they *do* know about the inspectors' report and what they will be taking on, and I for one will most certainly be mentioning it.'

'I really think that would be rather rash,' replied the education officer. 'I feel it is best not to raise the matter.'

33

'You may feel that, Mr Nettles,' said the vicar, 'but I do not, and furthermore I shall—'

'Could we please make a start?' the major barked, thinking that at this rate he would never make his round of golf that afternoon.

'I don't think Miss Brakespeare should get the job,' Mrs Pocock declared suddenly in a fierce and determined voice. 'She teaches my Ernest and he says she's rubbish. He says the lessons—'

'Let us not discount anyone at this stage,' Mr Nettles interrupted pompously. 'Since all these applicants have been called for interview, we must at least have the opportunity of hearing what they have to say. We must be very careful to follow the correct procedures and practices. And,' he added pointedly, looking directly at Mrs Pocock over the spectacles perched on the end of his nose, 'we have to be extremely careful how we refer to the candidates.'

'Well, I'm telling you now,' the parent governor told him sharply and meeting his gaze defiantly, 'I'm not voting for her!'

'Look,' the chairman said, drawing a deep exasperated breath, 'let us see what each of the candidates has to say and then we can make a decision.'

'I've made my decision when it comes to Miss Brakespeare,' Mrs Pocock said stubbornly, 'and I'm not going to change it.'

The major sighed. 'Let's get on with it, shall we?'

The first candidate, Miss Brakespeare, the deputy head teacher, proved singularly unimpressive and it was clear that her heart was not in her application. She arrived for the interview in a creased blue cotton suit a size too small, dark stockings and sensible sandals. Her hair was scraped back in a style that was a good twenty years out of date, and there was not a trace of any make-up. She smiled a great deal, sighed a great deal and nodded a great deal, but said very little. When asked if she would accept the position were it offered, she replied that she would need to think about it.

The second candidate, a thin woman with a pained expression and whose eyes, like those of some nocturnal tree-climbing creature, were magnified alarmingly behind thick-rimmed glasses, explained that she was looking for a quieter, less stressful life at a little country school. She had a tight little mouth and a strident voice, and spent most of the interview evading the questions and complaining about the dreadful behaviour of the children she taught at the moment and the decline in standards, particularly in literacy.

When the vicar mentioned the negative school report, the education officer sighed noisily and looked to the chairman. The major shrugged but remained silent. The candidate's mouth tightened.

'Negative school report,' she repeated. 'I wasn't aware of that.'

'The school recently received a rather critical report from the school inspectors,' the vicar told her. 'We are looking for someone who will take the school forward and make significant improvements. It will be a demanding but an exciting opportunity.'

'I see,' said the candidate, clearly perturbed. She stared at him blankly for a moment. 'Well, that was not made clear in the information sent out.' She awaited a response, but no one on the governing body decided to elaborate. The candidate folded her hands together in a slow, controlled manner. 'Well, bearing in mind this critical report of which I was not aware, I shall have to reconsider whether or not I want the position. Of course, should I decide to accept the post, were it offered, I would have to negotiate the salary and I would want the governors to meet a number of my requirements.'

'Well, that puts 'er out of t'runnin',' observed Councillor Smout after the woman had left the room. 'She's a carbon copy of t'head teacher we've got at t'moment. Out o' frying pan, into t'fire, if we was to appoint 'er.'

The penultimate applicant was a tall, pale-faced man in his late twenties with an explosion of wild, woolly ginger hair, a small goatee beard and a permanently surprised expression.

'Do take a seat,' the chairman told him, gesturing to a hard-backed chair facing the crescent of governors. The young man sat, crossed his legs, leaned back, folded his hands on his lap and smiled widely at the panel. It was clear to all from the major's expression that the Chairman of Governors was less than impressed with the outfit this candidate was wearing: a crumpled linen jacket which looked as if it had been left out in the rain and dried before an open fire, crushed strawberry corduroy trousers, a pink shirt and a wildly colourful and clumsily knotted tie. It could not have been more different from the major's own attire: dark blue barathea blazer with brash gold buttons, pressed grey trousers, crisp white shirt, and regimental tie fixed with a small gold pin and tied in a tight knot under the chin.

'Now, Mr Cuthberton,' the major asked, 'could you tell us why you applied for this position?'

The candidate uncrossed his legs, leaned forward earnestly in his chair, steepled his hands and launched into what was clearly a carefully prepared monologue.

When the vicar, much to the education officer's disapproval, raised the question of the inspectors' report again, the young man smiled and assured the panel that he was 'up for a challenge'. He then sat back and re-crossed his legs.

'Don't you feel you are a little young for this position?' asked Mrs Pocock.

The candidate hunched his shoulders and folded his arms across his chest. He looked heavenwards as if waiting for some divine inspiration before answering.

'Well,' he replied after a long pause, 'what I lack in experience, I certainly have in enthusiasm and commitment.' He seemed very pleased with his answer and clearly saw no need to elaborate.

Councillor Smout asked the stock question he always asked at head teacher appointments: 'So, what makes a good head teacher, then?'

This was a question the candidate had clearly been expecting, for he uncrossed his arms and legs, sat upright and delivered a statement which he had rehearsed. He concluded: 'And so, it goes without saying, a head teacher should be dynamic, dedicated and hard-working.'

'Well, why bother sayin' it then?' remarked Councillor Smout under his breath.

When this applicant had left the room the chairman shook his head. 'I was not keen on that chappie, I have to say. Not the sort of person we want for this school.'

'In what way?' the vicar asked. 'I felt he was a

very personable young man.'

'Well, vicar,' the chairman replied, lowering his voice, 'without putting a finer point on it, I think he bats from the pavilion end, if you follow my drift.'

'He what?' Mrs Bullock asked, tapping her hearing aid.

'I said I think he bats from the pavilion end, Mrs Bullock,' the chairman repeated loudly.

'I don't see the relevance of where he plays cricket,' she replied.

'No, I mean he's the other way inclined,' the major told her, 'if you follow my drift.'

'You mean you think this young man is a homosexual?' the vicar stated bluntly.

'A homo what?' Mrs Bullock asked.

'Well, I think it's pretty clear that the man is, what shall I say, of that particular inclination,' the major replied. 'I have nothing personally against people like that but I don't feel he is right for the school. I mean—'

'The candidate's predilection is not of any relevance,' Mr Nettles interrupted. 'Someone's sexual orientation is not an issue.'

'Well, I think—' the major started.

'Indeed, Mr Chairman,' Mr Nettles continued, 'this candidate cannot be ruled out merely because you are of the opinion that he is gay. There are clear guidelines which we are obliged to follow regarding discrimination on the grounds of gender, ethnicity, disability and sexual orientation. The fact that this candidate might be gay—'

'Who's gay?' Mrs Bullock asked.

'Mr Nettles is quite right on this occasion,' the vicar said. 'It is singularly out of order, Mr Chairman, for you to express your prejudices. It is quite unacceptable. Furthermore, it is mere supposition that this candidate is gay.'

'Who's gay?' Mrs Bullock asked again.

'Look,' Councillor Smout said tetchily, 'we're not gerrin anyweer 'ere. This man could 'ave two 'eads and a tail for all I care, provided that 'e's a good 'ead teacher. To be frank I din't take to 'im neither and not because of what t'major 'as said. He 'asn't t'experience, didn't answer t'questions and never looked me in t'eye and I've never trusted a man wi' a beard, it's a way of hiding summat—like an 'edge around a garden.'

'Well, that would have put Jesus out of the running for this post,' the vicar remarked in a voice hardly audible.

'And as I've said, I din't like t'woman with the big glasses who wanted more money,' the councillor continued. 'All she wanted was to come 'ere for an easy life and sit on her backside until retirement.'

'Well, I'm not voting for Miss Brakespeare,' the parent governor piped up. 'And I quite liked the man in the pink shirt.'

'Mrs Pocock,' the education officer said, his face becoming flushed with irritation, 'you must see all the candidates and then make up your mind.'

'Well,' Mrs Pocock retorted, 'the major has just said that he didn't like the man in the pink shirt and Councillor Smout didn't take to the woman with the big glasses, so I can't see why I can't say who I don't like and I don't like Miss Brakespeare and I am not voting for her.'

'Could we please move on?' the major pleaded.

The final candidate, an attractive woman in her late thirties, wearing a tailored grey suit, cream blouse, black stockings and red shoes with silver heels, brought the chatter of the governors to an abrupt halt when she walked through the door.

'Good morning,' she said cheerfully.

The major moved forward in his chair, stroked his moustache and smiled widely. 'Good morning,' he said. 'Do take a seat, Mrs er . . .'

'Devine,' she told him, returning the smile. Her eyes were clear and steady. 'Elisabeth Devine.'

There was an expression of absolute wonder on the major's face, as if he had discovered a rare and beautiful butterfly on a leaf.

The last candidate had considerable presence and gave an outstanding interview, answering the questions clearly, fully and confidently and looking each of the governors in the eye.

Councillor Smout asked his stock question: 'What makes a good head teacher, then?'

'Someone who believes that all children matter,' she told him, 'and that includes the bright and the talented, those with special educational needs and the damaged, disaffected and ill-favoured. The good head teacher never writes a child off. I think the good head teacher is keen and enthusiastic, respectful of children's backgrounds and culture, somebody who has a vision that a school should be cheerful and welcoming and optimistic, where children love to learn and learn to love. She is a leader who involves the governors, staff, parents and to some extent the pupils in the decisions and values their contributions, who manages with openness and fairness and has a sense of humour, indeed a sense of fun. Shall I continue?' she asked.

'No, no,' Councillor Smout said. He had sat throughout her answer as if transfixed, his legs apart, his arms comfortably crossed over his chest, his head tilted a little to the side and his mouth open. 'That's quite sufficient, thank you.'

The vicar then mentioned the inspectors' report. 'You are perhaps not aware, Mrs Devine, that this school has received a particularly critical report from the school inspectors. In the light of this are you still disposed to be considered for the post?'

The candidate was clearly surprised with the revelation but she had realised, she told him, having looked around the school and spoken to the deputy head teacher, that there were problems which needed addressing. She went on to say that she really wanted the post and that she would welcome the opportunity of working with the governors and staff in turning things around. Looking at Mr Nettles, she smiled and told him she assumed the Education Office would give her a deal of support in making the necessary changes.

'Of course,' the education officer assured her, in the tone of one humouring a child.

'Do we need to vote on this?' the chairman asked when Mrs Devine had left the room. 'It seems to me the last candidate is head and shoulders above the rest.'

There were grunts of agreement and nods of the heads. The one dissenting voice came from Dr Stirling, who, apart from asking each of the candidates a short question, spoke for the first time.

'I will grant you, Mr Chairman, that the last candidate was extremely impressive,' he said. 'Rather too impressive, perhaps. Mrs Devine is clearly in a different league from the other applicants, none of whom I think is suitable for this position, but what I would ask is this: why is she wishing to come here? She is aware, as she has said, that the school has problems and has been told it has received a highly critical report from Her Majesty's Inspectors. She also, having spoken to the deputy head teacher, probably knows we are losing children by the week. She comes with excellent references, is already a head teacher of a large and successful school, she is highly qualified and very experienced and on a considerably higher salary than we are offering. Why should she want to come to a small village school which is experiencing real difficulties? I am not altogether comfortable about appointing her. Those of you who are acquainted with me know well enough that I am not by nature a suspicious person, but there is something here that I think is not quite right. I feel we should re-advertise the position.'

'You should have asked 'er why she applied for the post then, Dr Stirling,' Councillor Smout said.

'I assumed that the chairman would be asking that question,' the doctor replied. 'He asked that of all the other candidates.'

The major had indeed intended to ask that question, but his mind had been elsewhere when faced with such an attractive and assured woman.

'There may be many reasons why Mrs Devine might wish to come here,' the vicar argued. 'For example, perhaps there is nothing left for her to do at her present school and she wishes to take on a fresh challenge.'

'Or she's looking for a quiet life in the country, like the other candidate,' observed the doctor.

'I think that is quite unfounded, Dr Stirling,' said the vicar. 'Mrs Devine is fully aware that this school is experiencing some difficulties. As I recall, she said as much in her interview. Didn't she say she would welcome the opportunity of turning things around?'

'An' if she were looking for a quiet life in t'country,' added Councillor Smout, 'she'd 'ave backed out when she were told about t'report by vicar 'ere.'

'Well, I thought she gave an excellent performance,' said the major.

'A what?' asked Mrs Bullock.

'Perhaps you have made my point, Mr Chairman,' the doctor said. 'It was indeed something of a performance. Rather too polished for my liking.'

'She might be escaping an abusive husband,' Mrs Pocock commented. 'You read about it all the time. My sister, Noreen, left her husband because he couldn't keep his hands off of her. I mean Mrs Devine says that she's single on her application form and yet she's married.'

'Or has been,' the major added.

'Who's a has-been?' Mrs Bullock enquired.

'Well, I for one think she's t'ideal replacement for Miss Sowerbutts,' Councillor Smout said, wishing to escape the small cramped room and have a substantial lunch before the meeting of the Parks and Recreation Committee. 'She's a striking-looking woman with a lot about 'er. What do you think, Mr Nettles?'

'I think Mrs Devine seems eminently suitable,' replied the education officer.

'Mr Chairman—' Dr Stirling started.

'No, Dr Stirling,' the Chairman told him, holding up a hand, 'I think we have decided and we have to get it sorted out today.' He turned to the education officer. 'I think I am right, aren't I, Mr Nettles?'

43

The education officer nodded. 'I am going to put it to the vote. Now all those in favour—'

'Mr Chairman!' Dr Stirling interrupted angrily. 'I really must insist that we give this greater consideration. First, we have not discussed the other candidates in any detail or considered the alternative of re-advertising the post.'

'You've already said yourself, Dr Stirling,' Councillor Smout remarked loudly, 'that none of t'others is up to scratch as far as you're concerned, so what's t'point of considering 'em, eh?'

'Nevertheless—' the doctor began.

'Dr Stirling,' the education officer said in a deeply patronising voice, 'as the representative of the Director of Education, here to advise the governors, I feel it incumbent upon me to point out that we need to expedite the matter of appointing with some urgency. The school requires a new head teacher and it would take a great deal of time and further effort to set the process in motion again. And, I feel I need to point out, it is highly unlikely that we will attract any better field than the one we have seen today. It appears you are the only dissenting voice, so I think, as the Chairman has suggested, that the governors should put it to a vote.'

And so it was that Mrs Elisabeth Devine was appointed the new head teacher of Barton-in-the-Dale Parochial Primary School.

CHAPTER THREE

Mrs Sloughthwaite, proprietor of the Barton-in-the-Dale village store and post office, stood at the door of her shop the morning after the interviews for the new head teacher. It was a bright, sunny summer Saturday, and Mrs Sloughthwaite, a round, red-faced woman with a large fleshy nose, pouchy cheeks and a great bay window of a bust, hoped the good weather would encourage visitors to the village. Tourists passing through on their way to more picturesque spots sometimes stopped to patronise her shop, and she enjoyed passing the time of day and regaling them with a potted history of the place—though nothing of great import had happened there.

Prince Rupert, on his way to Marston Moor to fight Oliver Cromwell, was reputed to have stayed at the Blacksmith's Arms, and it was said that Emily Brontë once spent a weekend at Limebeck House, but these were probably fanciful tales. There had been the fire up at the rectory a century before, when the rural dean, a seasoned drinker and notorious gambler, had set himself and the building alight, and the time during the last war when Mr Osbaldiston had discovered a German pilot hiding in his barn and handed him over to the Home Guard at the point of a pitchfork, but that was about it.

The village had a timeless quality about it that suited Mrs Sloughthwaite. Former inhabitants long since dead and buried in St Christopher's churchyard, were they to be resurrected, would recognise it immediately, for little had changed. And this is how Mrs Sloughthwaite and the villagers of Barton-in-the-Dale wanted it. Change was regarded with deep suspicion, for it inevitably meant a change for the worse. The Parish Council, supported by the older and more vociferous residents and the few commuters who wished to escape the hectic life of the city after a hard day's work, actively discouraged any sort of development, wishing to preserve the peaceful and unhurried lifestyle. Newcomers were regarded by Mrs Sloughthwaite from a distance at first, and their behaviour was meticulously observed until she had decided whether or not they were acceptable to her. Should she take a dislike to a person, not only would the unfortunate recipient of her displeasure get yesterday's bread but their character would be well and truly traduced over the counter later on.

Mrs Sloughthwaite looked down the high street and breathed in noisily. She waved to Mrs Siddall, setting up her fruit and vegetable stall outside the greengrocer's, and to Mr Farringdon, who stood at the door of his hardware shop, broom held like a bayonet over his chest ready for a charge. Mrs Sloughthwaite had lived here all her life, and she loved this village with its surrounding scattered conifer plantations, pale stone and pantile-roofed cottages, the old walls of greenish white limestone enclosing the solid Norman church with its square tower spearing the sky, the black yews and elms in the graveyard, the two pubs and the proud monument built in honour of the second Viscount Wadsworth, a long-dead local squire. Nothing of any real note happened here, but that was the way she liked it—predictable and undisturbed, well away from the noise and the bustle of town and city life. Mind you, she thought, folding her arms under her substantial bosom, there was a bit of interesting news. A new head teacher had been appointed up at the school. A glimmer of private amusement passed across her face as she thought of Miss Sowerbutts, the present holder of the post. That long beak of a nose had been well and truly put out of joint, or so she had heard.

It was as if the very thought of the said woman had conjured her up, for there she stood, body stiffly upright and wearing that silly knitted hat and mothball-scented skirt, with a battered canvas shopping bag hanging loosely from her arm.

'I take it you are open?' asked Miss Sowerbutts, without a smile.

'Oh, I didn't see you there, Miss Sowerbutts,' replied the shopkeeper in an overly friendly way. She smiled insincerely at the customer with the curled lip, hooded brow and heavy, judgemental eyes. 'I was in a world of my own. Yes, indeed we are open.' She moved out of the doorway to let the first customer of the day pass into the shop, following her and smoothing her hands down the front of her nylon overall. 'I was miles away.' She positioned herself behind the counter. 'It's a beautiful day, isn't it?'

'Yes, indeed,' replied Miss Sowerbutts, scanning the shelves.

'I love this time of year when all the buds come out and the flowers appear. June is my favourite month, although I have to say—'

'Are these the only biscuits you have?' interrupted Miss Sowerbutts stiffly.

'I'm afraid so. We don't have much call for any

47

others. The custard creams are nice and there's a Venetian selection box which is very popular.'

'They are not to my taste,' replied the customer. 'I don't have a sweet tooth. I want rich tea or plain digestives. I shall have to go into town next week.'

Suit yourself, you miserable old crone, thought Mrs Sloughthwaite. It wouldn't hurt her to be pleasant once in a while. That face of hers could have been hacked out of wood with a blunt axe.

'I gather they've appointed the new head teacher up at the school,' said the shopkeeper casually. It was a carefully and cleverly aimed provocation. She had heard from Mrs Pocock how displeased Miss Sowerbutts had been at not being consulted in the appointment of her successor and how she had stormed out of the school without even meeting her.

'Yes, so I hear,' was the murmured reply. The thin smile conveyed little more than feigned interest. 'I'll take a jar of that coffee, the special roasted blend.'

Mrs Sloughthwaite reached up to the shelf behind her. 'Yes, Mrs Pocock called in for her order yesterday afternoon and said the governors had appointed.'

'Did she? I'll have a packet of brown sugar as well.'

'Very colourful character by all accounts.'

'Who is?'

'The new head teacher.'

'Well, I wouldn't know,' Miss Sowerbutts told her with quick indifference. 'I've not met her. Are those scones freshly baked? The ones I had last week were on the stale side. You might mention that to your supplier.'

'These are fresh as a daisy,' replied the shopkeeper, with the fixed and artificial smile she had perfected over the years when faced with an objectionable customer. 'You'll be able to put your feet up now, won't you, and enjoy your retirement,' she added. It was a comment guaranteed to annoy.

Miss Sowerbutts stiffened, fixing Mrs Sloughthwaite with a piercing stare. 'Retirement?' she repeated.

'Well, now that you've finished at the school you'll have time on your hands, I should imagine.' The shopkeeper's smile was a mask on her face.

'Mrs Sloughthwaite,' Miss Sowerbutts replied with a bleak smile, 'I am not the sort of person who puts her feet up and I will most certainly not have time on my hands. I shall be as busy as ever.' She dug into her canvas bag for her purse. 'I'll leave the scones,' she said. 'How much for the coffee and the sugar?'

*   *   *

Marcia Atticus was digging in the herbaceous borders of the rectory garden when she caught sight of the lone figure wandering among the gravestones, pausing here and there to examine the inscriptions on the weathered stones. The visitor was a striking-looking woman with bright blonde hair, dressed in a stylish cream raincoat and a pale silk scarf of eau-de-Nil.

'Are you looking for someone in particular?' asked the vicar's wife, leaning over the low stone wall that surrounded the rectory garden.

Elisabeth turned and smiled broadly. 'No, I was just looking. I find epitaphs fascinating. Some are

49

quite small and rather sweet but others are so huge and elaborate, like that huge marble mausoleum in the centre of the graveyard. It dwarfs every other.'

'It was meant to,' the vicar's wife told her. 'That's the tomb of the notorious Dean Joseph Steerum-Slack. He was quite an unpleasant and outrageous character by all accounts. Spent most of his time hunting and drinking and gambling. Burnt the rectory to the ground with himself and his dogs inside during the last century. The Reverend Steerum-Slack was the only notable figure the village has ever had. He was larger than life when he was alive and he certainly intended to be larger than life when he was dead and never to be forgotten—hence that ridiculously over-the-top monstrosity with more Latin on it than in a Roman missal. He designed it himself, and left sufficient money in his will to have it erected. If it was up to me, I'd knock the thing down.'

Elisabeth smiled. 'Are you the vicar?' she asked.

'Gracious me, no!' exclaimed Mrs Atticus. 'I'm his wife. My husband closets himself away on Saturday mornings to write his sermons. He spends hours in his study, working out what he will say on the Sunday. It's a pity so few seem to listen to or indeed understand him.' There was a hint of disapproval in her voice.

'I am sure that is not the case,' replied Elisabeth diplomatically.

'Oh, but it is,' the vicar's wife confided. 'My husband feels he should give everyone the full benefit of his extensive knowledge, but I fear it falls upon stony ground.'

'It's a beautiful church, and so peaceful here,' said Elisabeth, changing the subject tactfully.

'A little too peaceful for my liking,' said Mrs Atticus, smiling ruefully.

'And your garden is quite delightful. I've never seen such a variety of plants.'

'One tries one's best. It's such an effort keeping the lawn in this condition. The dandelion seeds blow over from the graveyard. Such a nuisance. I do so wish Mr Massey would do something about the weeds. He is supposed to keep it tidy but he spends most of his time in the Blacksmith's Arms and comes and goes as he pleases.'

'Is the church open?' asked Elisabeth.

'Oh yes, my husband never locks it. I have told him that one day when the brass candlesticks disappear from the altar, and the poor box goes missing, he will finally decide to lock the door. My husband is a very trusting man. He tends to see the good in everyone.'

'Well, he is a priest, after all,' Elisabeth commented. 'I think that is what priests are supposed to do.'

'That is exactly what he says,' said the vicar's wife wryly. 'And, speak of the devil—if you will pardon the expression—here he comes.'

The Reverend Atticus emerged from the rectory, rubbing together his long white hands. He was a tall man with a thin-boned face, skin as smooth as parchment, high arching brows and a long prominent nose. When she had first set eyes upon him at her interview the day before, Elisabeth had thought he had the appearance of someone who was likely to be a severe and uncompromising individual, but he had proved very different. As soon as he had opened his mouth, she decided that she liked the Reverend Atticus, with his soft

51

voice and solicitous and kindly manner. Unlike the stony-faced doctor who never said a word and the bellicose, red-faced councillor with the loud voice, the Reverend Atticus had smiled a great deal throughout her interview and listened attentively to her answers. He had been the first to extend a hand to congratulate her when she had been offered the job, and he had expressed the hope that she would settle into the school and be happy in her new role. She had met his type before: honest and courteous, an other-worldly man of calm and calming disposition. The clergyman's smile broadened when he caught sight of her talking to his wife.

'Ah,' he said breezily, addressing his wife, 'you have become acquainted with our new head teacher, my dear?'

'Oh!' exclaimed Mrs Atticus. 'I didn't realise.'

'I'm Elisabeth Devine,' said Elisabeth, extending a hand across the wall.

Marcia Atticus removed a gardening glove. 'I'm very pleased to meet you,' she said.

'I thought I would spend a day in the village, have a look around and get a feel for the place,' Mrs Devine explained. 'It's quite a delightful spot, so unspoilt and tranquil.'

'We like it,' replied the vicar, glancing at his wife. 'Don't we, my dear?'

His wife gave a small and unconvincing smile, but didn't reply.

'I'm just about to have an interlude from writing tomorrow's sermon,' continued the cleric cheerfully. 'I'm considering the Parable of the Lost Sheep. Sheep always go down well in this part of the world. I feel sure my wife would enjoy a cup of coffee and a break from her labours in the garden.

Perhaps you might like to join us, Mrs Devine?'

'I wouldn't want to put you to any trouble,' replied Elisabeth.

'Oh, no trouble,' replied the vicar. He had the gentle look of a domesticated cat.

'Then I should very much like to join you,' she said.

'Good, good,' cooed the vicar.

The rectory was an unprepossessing building that had been erected in the late nineteenth century to replace an imposing grey stone Georgian mansion. With its shiny red brick walls, greasy grey slate roof, small square windows, towers and turrets and enveloping high black iron fence, the building resembled more of a workhouse than a vicarage. Inside it was cool and unwelcoming, with its black and white patterned tiles in the hallway, plain off-white walls, high ceilings and heavy oak doors. The place smelt of old wood and lavender floor polish.

'Come through into the sitting room, Mrs Devine,' urged the vicar. 'It's a little more homely than the drawing room. My wife will entertain you while I get the coffee.'

Elisabeth wondered what the drawing room could look like when she followed Mrs Atticus into a sombre and spartan space with heavy old-fashioned furniture, dark faded carpet and thick, plain green curtains. Her eyes were immediately drawn to a large watercolour painting of St Christopher's church which hung above the mantelpiece. It was one of the rare bits of colour.

'So what brings you to Barton-in-the-Dale?' asked the vicar's wife, gesturing to her visitor to take a seat in a heavy and threadbare armchair.

53

Elisabeth Devine did not know the questioner sufficiently well to confide in her why she had decided to leave such a comfortable, well-paid and rewarding position in the city to move to a small village in the Yorkshire Dales. She knew that whatever she divulged would spread like wildfire throughout the small community. It was best, she thought, to be evasive.

'Oh, I felt like a change,' she replied, casually. 'City life has become increasingly hectic and noisy and I decided it was time to move on.'

Mrs Atticus stared for a moment at her visitor, studying her carefully. Those penetrating pale blue eyes of hers, she thought, revealed nothing. She was certain there was more to it than merely a change of scenery and the desire for a quiet life. 'You will certainly find it very quiet here,' she said. 'Things move very slowly in Barton-in-the-Dale. It's a very close-knit community and you will find there's a real resistance to outside influences and to any changes. It's a pretty enough village, of course, and if you are seeking a peaceful, rural existence then I am sure you will find it to your liking. I, for one, would quite welcome the hectic, city life.'

'I'm sure I will be very happy here,' Elisabeth replied, with a small smile.

'Of course,' continued the vicar's wife, 'although it might not be as quiet and uneventful as you imagine. You will be well aware that the school is in something of a crisis.' Elisabeth had not known things were quite that bad, but decided to remain quiet. 'As you will know, it had a dire report from the school inspectors,' continued Mrs Atticus, 'and parents are taking their children away and sending them to the school at Urebank. It will be a real challenge for you.'

Elisabeth felt it had been rather underhand of the governors that the report had only been mentioned by the vicar at her interview the day before, but she maintained her composure and smiled. 'I like a challenge,' she said.

Yes, thought the vicar's wife, I bet you do. This woman was intriguing. She was certainly very different from the people she usually came across in the village, who talked about nothing more interesting than the recipes for chutney or the price of sheep.

'Here we are with the coffee.' The vicar arrived carrying a tray. 'I am afraid it's only of the instant variety.'

'I was telling Mrs Devine, Charles,' said his wife, 'that she will have her work cut out taking on the village school. It will be a real challenge turning it around.'

'I am sure Mrs Devine is most capable of doing that, my dear,' said the vicar.

'I hope so,' replied Elisabeth.

'And tell me, Mrs Devine, have you met the redoubtable Miss Sowerbutts yet?' asked Marcia Atticus.

'Very briefly,' replied Elisabeth, 'but, as your husband knows, I mentioned to the Chairman of Governors after the interview that I would like to call in to the school on Wednesday to meet the staff and the children. I am sure Miss Sowerbutts will fill me in on what I need to know when I visit.'

Mrs Atticus gave a hollow laugh. 'Oh, I am sure she will do that. She is very adept at filling people in.'

The vicar ignored such an uncharitable

observation, even though he knew there was more than a ring of truth about it. He had crossed swords with the head teacher on a number of occasions, and found Miss Sowerbutts to be intransigent and difficult to deal with. He remained shiftily silent.

'Wouldn't you say so, Charles?' asked Mrs Atticus, with a mischievous glint in her eyes.

Her husband smiled the tolerant, patient smile of the sort a teacher might employ when explaining things to a small child, and decided to disregard the question.

'Milk and sugar, Mrs Devine?' he asked.

'Just milk, please,' she replied.

'Of course,' continued Mrs Atticus, quite enjoying her husband's discomfiture. 'Miss Sowerbutts is something of a sad figure. She's taught in the school all her career. They made her head teacher, I reckon, as some sort of long-service award. I guess there has been little passion in her uneventful life, and numerous disappointments. Why else should she be so ill-tempered with people, and so crotchety?'

The vicar raised an eyebrow in wordless contradiction.

Marcia Atticus reached for her coffee and took a small sip from the china cup. 'She has lived in the same cottage in the village where she grew up, a place where nothing ever happens, ruling the roost in the school like some Victorian school ma-am and—'

'My dear,' interrupted the vicar, shuffling on his chair with obvious embarrassment, 'I feel sure Mrs Devine does not wish to hear this.'

There was a distinct coldness in his wife's reply. 'I am merely telling Mrs Devine what everyone in

56

the village thinks and preparing her for meeting Miss Sowerbutts. If she is expecting the red carpet treatment and a warm welcome then she is in for a rude awakening.'

There was an awkward silence. Elisabeth glanced in the direction of the vicar's wife. There was something dark and troubling in those green eyes.

'What a delightful picture,' Elisabeth commented, placing her coffee cup down on the small table next to her and rising to look more closely at the watercolour above the mantelpiece.

'You think so?' asked the vicar's wife pointedly.

'Oh yes,' replied her visitor, 'it's superbly painted. The artist has captured so well the atmosphere of autumn. The mist and colours of the leaves are quite superb and the detail on the church is remarkable.'

'You know something about art then, do you, Mrs Devine?' asked the vicar's wife.

'Not a great deal,' Elisabeth replied, 'but I can recognise a good painting when I see it, and this is exceptionally well painted.'

'I did it,' announced Marcia Atticus, deciding that she quite liked the new head teacher at Barton-in-the-Dale.

*   *   *

Mrs Sloughthwaite's menacing bosom and large hips carried as much weight in the village as she did structurally. She knew everything there was to know in Barton-in-the-Dale and was a most efficient conduit of gossip and information. She saw the letters that were posted, the parcels received and the telegrams sent. She knew who was on benefits, how much savings were in a person's post office book and who hadn't bought a television licence. She wanted to know every last detail of a piece of gossip or about a person's life; she was the eyes and ears of Barton-in-the-Dale.

Villagers wishing to know the news only had to call in at the shop to receive a detailed and colourful account of the latest happening or hear a fascinating fact about someone's personal life. She knew that the major had an eye for the ladies, that the vicar's wife was not a happy woman and that her poor henpecked husband had to put up with her moods and sharp tongue. She knew that Dr Stirling had not been the same since the death of his wife in a riding accident two years before and that his son, a strange, serious little boy who seldom spoke and never laughed, was a real worry to his father. She knew that Mrs Pocock's husband was a bit too fond of his drink and that Mrs Stubbin's son, that disagreeable, badly-behaved Malcolm, had to be watched, for she had discovered sweets had gone missing when he had been in the shop. She knew Mr Massey made quite a living on the side by poaching on the Limestone estate and that the landlord of the Blacksmith's Arms had received a visit from the VAT inspector. She knew that Councillor Smout's relationship with his brassy secretary was not as platonic as he imagined people thought, and she could have predicted that the sad, timorous little Miss Brakespeare would never get the post of the new head teacher in a month of Sundays.

The shopkeeper rested a dimpled elbow on the counter and placed her fleshy chin on a hand.

'She came in here puffed up like a Christmas

turkey and gave me this look that would turn you to stone,' she told her customer, a lugubrious-looking woman with a thick brown headscarf wrapped around her head and tied in an enormous knot under the chin. 'Turned her nose up at my custard creams and my Venetian section she did, and then had the brass neck to ask me if my scones were fresh and tell me the ones she'd bought before were stale. Told me I should tell my supplier. She knows full well I bake them scones myself. I didn't rise to it. I mean you don't with her, do you. 'Course, I knew why she was annoyed. She's had that nose of hers put out of joint and no mistake. According to Mrs Pocock, who's on the governing body up at the school, Miss Sowerbutts was not involved in the appointment of the new head teacher and they never even asked her opinion. You can imagine how that went down. Bypassed her they did, not that I blame them. She'd have taken over, given half the chance. She clung on to that job like a Whitby limpet, had to be prised out, even though the inspectors said she wasn't up to the job. I imagine she thought she could pick her successor.'

There was an air of obvious pleasure in the shopkeeper's contemplation of Miss Sowerbutts' misfortune. 'And, of course,' she continued, leaning forward over the counter and lowering her voice as if someone was eavesdropping, 'Miss Brakespeare hadn't a cat in hell's chance of getting the job. I mean, don't get me wrong, she's a nice enough woman and has a lot to endure, what with being at the beck and call of that disabled mother of hers. The few times Mrs Brakespeare used to come in the shop, she spent a good ten minutes listing her ailments and complaining about her daughter.

She wants to get down on her knees and thank the good Lord she's still standing up. Been on her deathbed, she has, more times than I've had hot dinners. I do feel sorry for that daughter of hers, but, let's be right, Miss Brakespeare couldn't run a whelk stall, never mind a school. She's been under Miss Sowerbutts' thumb all her life.' She patted her crisp, newly permed hair. 'Anyway, from what I gather from Mrs Pocock, this new head teacher will get things moving.'

The door of the shop opened and an elegant woman entered.

'Good morning,' she said pleasantly.

'Morning, love,' replied the shopkeeper, rising to her full height and then stretching further over the counter to get a glimpse of the woman's shoes. They were not the expected red with silver heels but of copper brown leather. Mrs Sloughthwaite turned to her other customer and dismissed her with the words, 'Well, if there's nothing else, Mrs Appleyard.' She wanted no other person privy to the conversation she was going to have with the new head teacher of Barton-in-the-Dale school. If there was any information to glean she was the one to get it first.

When Mrs Appleyard had departed, the shopkeeper gave Elisabeth her undivided attention. 'Now then, love, what can I get you?'

'I would just like the local paper, please.'

'You're the new head teacher up at the school, aren't you?' said Mrs Sloughthwaite, reaching under the counter for the newspaper. The question was academic, for she knew who this elegant woman was. She had received a blow-by-blow description of the woman, red shoes, black stockings and all, from Mrs Pocock the day before.

'That's right,' replied Elisabeth.

'I thought so,' said the shopkeeper, nodding. She peered at her customer with more than a little interest. 'We don't get many unfamiliar faces in the shop, other than the day-trippers, and you don't look like a day-tripper.'

'Do I look like a head teacher?' asked Elisabeth, an amused expression on her face.

Mrs Sloughthwaite laughed. 'No, love, you don't,' she said, thinking of Miss Sowerbutts' dowdy ensemble. 'You don't look like the present one and that's for sure. One of the governors popped in yesterday and mentioned in passing what you looked like.'

Elisabeth laughed. 'I see.'

'Well, I hope you are going to be happy at the school.'

'I am sure I will.'

'So, are you intending to live in the village?' asked the shopkeeper bluntly.

'Yes, in fact that's why I want the local paper,' Elisabeth told her. 'I thought I'd spend the afternoon looking at some properties.'

'You'll not find a deal in the *Saturday Gazette*. There's not much on the market in the village, I'm afraid. People tend to stay here and they don't like new developments. There's a new block of flats at Ribbledyke, a couple of miles away, and some houses the size of egg-boxes on the estate at Urebank, but if you have a family I don't think one of those would be suitable.'

Elisabeth smiled to herself. Like the vicar's wife, here was another person determined to find out as much about her personal life as she could. She

61

sidestepped the invitation of the shopkeeper to supply the information.

'I was thinking of something rather older with a bit of character, perhaps a stone cottage,' she said.

Mrs Sloughthwaite thought for moment. 'The only place like that around here what I know of is Wisteria Cottage, old Mrs Pickles' place up Stripe Lane, but it's been empty for a couple of months and will need a lot doing to it. Nice position though, overlooking fields and in walking distance of the school, and it has a good bit of garden and a paddock at the side.'

'That sounds promising,' said Elisabeth.

'I'll point you in the right direction before you go,' said Mrs Sloughthwaite, feeling pleased that she had at least extracted some information about the new head teacher that she could impart to those who called in at the shop. 'Will you still be wanting the paper?' she asked.

'Yes please,' Elisabeth replied, reaching into her handbag.

'We had the present head teacher in the shop only this morning,' said the shopkeeper. She hoped this would prompt a response but it fell on stony ground.

'Really?'

'Yes, she's been at the school for as long as I can remember. Some would say too long. Her family has been part of the village for centuries and used to be quite important in their day. They owned a mill down by the beck. It made shoddy. 'Course, that's all gone now. They say her grandfather lost everything over a game of cards. She's quite a character is Miss Sowerbutts.'

Elisabeth resisted the temptation to enquire

more about the woman she would be meeting the following Wednesday, when she had arranged to visit the school. It would, she guessed, be a strained encounter. The woman was clearly a difficult customer by all accounts, and at the interviews she had lacked the common courtesy to welcome the candidates, speak to them or show them around the school.

'I don't think she was too keen on taking early retirement,' continued Mrs Sloughthwaite, 'but after the report . . .' Her voice tailed off. She awaited a response.

Elisabeth smiled. 'I am sure she will enjoy it.'

'Enjoy it?' repeated the shopkeeper.

'Her retirement.'

'Have you met her?' she was asked bluntly. Mrs Sloughthwaite knew that Elisabeth had only met her briefly and then not to speak to. Mrs Pocock had informed her of Miss Sowerbutts' angry departure from the school before the interviews.

'Not really, no,' replied Elisabeth, 'but I'll look forward to meeting her when I call in at the school.'

I bet you will, thought Mrs Sloughthwaite, dropping the coins that had been passed over the counter into the till. She folded her arms under her expansive bosom. I wish I could be a fly on the wall, she thought to herself.

CHAPTER FOUR

Barton-in-the-Dale Parochial Primary School was a small, solid, stone-built Victorian structure with high mullioned windows, a blue-patterned slate roof and a large oak-panelled door with a tarnished brass knocker in the shape of a ram's head. Set back from the main street, which ran the length of the village, it was tucked away behind the Norman church of St Christopher and partially hidden by a towering oak tree with branches reaching skywards like huge arms. It was an imposing if rather neglected building. The small garden to the front was tidy enough but, apart from a few sad-looking flowers and a couple of overgrown bushes, it was bereft of plants. The paint on the window frames was beginning to flake and the path leading up to the entrance had several cracked and uneven flagstones.

It was later the same afternoon and Elisabeth was sitting on the bench by the oak tree, considering whether she had done the right thing in applying for the post of head teacher here. It had been a spur-of-the-moment decision, something completely out of character, for she was by nature a practical and prudent person and always thought long and hard before she made important decisions. Perhaps applying for this post had been too hasty and ill-considered. She should have found out more about the school before applying and then she might have learnt of the problems she would have to face. Of course there was a good reason for her wanting to come to this particular school, but she certainly had had second thoughts when she had first seen the building, which was in need of redecoration, and had got such a cold reception from the present head teacher. Then there was Miss Brakespeare, the dowdy, serious and dull deputy head teacher, who, despite her friendly approach after the interview, would no doubt be resentful that she had not been offered the post and would not take kindly to any changes Elisabeth would wish to implement. She sighed. It was not too late to give back word now. She chased the thought from her mind.

No, she would start at the school and was determined to make a success of it. She closed her eyes and let the sun, breaking through the overhanging branches of the ancient oak, warm her face. She thought for a moment, considering how she might start to make the necessary changes. The state of the building was the first priority. The school was in need of a coat of paint, the flagstones on the path wanted replacing, the hedge trimming, the garden to the front tending and the fence around the perimeter repairing. It needed to look cheerful and welcoming. She would put some large tubs of bright geraniums by the door, have vivid flowers in window-boxes and a bird table on the small lawn. This was cosmetic and would be the easy part. Her main challenge, she knew, was to raise the standards, gain the confidence of the teachers, the governors and the parents and stem the haemorrhaging of children to other schools. It would not be easy.

Helen, her deputy at the inner-city school where Elisabeth worked at present, was the sort of colleague every head teacher would wish for— enthusiastic, committed, creative and hard-working. When things had become difficult and times demanding, Helen had always been there to listen and support. She was a good friend. Elisabeth had tried to persuade her to apply for the post she was vacating. She deserved to be promoted and was sure to be appointed, but Helen had told Elisabeth that headship wasn't for her. Elisabeth thought again of the deputy head teacher at Barton-in-the-Dale. Miss Brakespeare was a very different character by all accounts. The dumpy little woman with the round face and staring eyes, dressed in ill-fitting cotton suit, dark stockings and sandals, could hardly be described as enthusiastic and creative. Elisabeth tried again to put such thoughts out of her mind.

She opened her eyes. The trees had a lustre to them that bright afternoon and the air was clear and fresh. Beyond the small school was a vast and silent panorama of fields and hills, dotted with lazy-looking sheep and flecked in sunlight. No, she told herself, it was the right decision she had made.

She stood, breathed in and smoothed the creases in her coat. She would now go in search of this little stone cottage that she had heard about from the shopkeeper.

It took quite a while for Elisabeth to discover Wisteria Cottage. It stood alone at the end of a track of beaten mud overgrown with nettles, a small pale stone building with a sagging roof, peeling paint and a neglected garden. Rough, spiky grass sprouted like clumps of green hair from the guttering, and dandelion, daisies and ragwort, left to blow to seed in a sudden wind, sprouted between the broken paving slabs leading to the porch. Great plumes of wisteria hung from the wall. The front door, partially covered by dense holly and laurel bushes, was colourless, the paint having peeled away many months ago. To the side was a heavy horse-chestnut tree, its leaves fanning out like fingers and one huge branch split and charred by lightning.

Elisabeth knew that she had to have this cottage. She stood on the tussocky lawn with its bare patches and molehills, bordered by waist-high weeds, rank thistles, tangled brambles and rampant rose bushes, and gazed through the trees at a vista of green undulating fields criss-crossed with silvered limestone walls which rose to the craggy fellside, and she marvelled at the view. The sky was delicate and clear as an eggshell. Sparrows squabbled and chattered in the dust and swallows darted and swooped. There was the smell of hay and scented flowers in the air. Somewhere in a distant field a tractor chugged. She knew she could transform this old cottage into her dream home.

Beyond the five-barred gate at the end of the track was a small boy of about ten or eleven, lifting a dry cowpat with a stick and disturbing a buzzing cloud of yellow horseflies. He stopped when he caught sight of Elisabeth and, having watched her for a moment, came over.

''Ello,' he said cheerfully, climbing up on to the gate, sitting on the top and letting his spindly legs dangle down. He was a small boy with large low-set ears, a mop of dusty blond hair and the bright brown eyes of a fox, and was dressed in a faded T-shirt, baggy khaki shorts and wellington boots that looked sizes too big for him. The child's face and knees were innocent of soap and water.

'Hello,' replied Elisabeth.

'Grand day, in't it?' said the child, grinning broadly.

'It is.'

'I likes this time o' year,' he said, scratching a muddied knee.

'So do I,' said Elisabeth. 'I hope this nice weather

67

continues.'

'Oh, it will that,' said the boy. He waved his stick like a conductor with a baton. '"If t'rooks build low, it's bound to blow, if t'rooks build 'igh, t'weather's dry."' That's what mi granddad says, and 'e's never wrong.'

'He sounds a clever man, your granddad,' said Elisabeth.

''E is,' the boy agreed. 'I've seen a nuthatch in that 'orse-chestnut tree,' he told her, pointing with the stick. 'We gets all sooarts o' birds in this garden—blue-tits, jays, redstarts, hawfinches, linnets, magpies and t'odd pheasant from t'big estate—and when that buddleia's out you should see t'butterflies—red admirals, peacocks, tortoiseshells, cabbage whites and some reight rare species an' all.'

'You're fond of this garden, aren't you?' asked Elisabeth, charmed by the boy's cheerful good humour.

'Aye, I love comin' 'ere,' he said. 'Mrs Pickles who used to own it, she used to let me come 'ere. She's deead, tha knows.'

'Yes, I heard.'

'She were nice, Mrs Pickles,' said the boy. 'She used to give me a drink of 'er 'omemade ginger beer an' a biscuit when I called.'

'I'm afraid I don't have any ginger beer or biscuits,' Elisabeth told him.

'Oh, I weren't 'intin'. I were just sayin'.'

'It's a beautiful view.'

'Aye, 'tis that,' agreed the boy. ''Course it changes wi' every season but it allus looks grand. I collect sloes from them bushes for mi granddad to make 'is sloe gin,' continued the boy, 'and rose 'ips

68

and wild blackberries an' mushrooms. There's lots of stuff you can find in t'country if you 'ave a mind.' He pointed with his stick to an oak tree with long horizontal branches and a gnarled bracket of fungi clinging to the craggy bark. 'But I don't touch that, it's poisonous.' The boy cocked his head to one side, 'You thinkin' o' buying this place then?'

'Yes, I'm thinking about it,' replied Elisabeth.

He sucked in a breath. 'Lots to do.'

'Yes, I can see that.'

'You've got moles underneath your lawn, rabbits in your borders, rooks in your chimney, swallow nests under your gutterin', bees beneath your eaves and frogs in your cellar. It'll tek some fettlin', I can tell you.'

'I think you're trying to put me off,' said Elisabeth smiling.

'Nay, missis,' said the child with a smirk, 'just purrin you reight. It'll be champion when it's done up. Best view in t'village. And well off of t'beaten track an' all. There's a little paddock come wi' it, an' all. Thas'll probably ger it at a good price. Mi granddad'd buy it 'issen if 'e 'ad t'brass.'

'It's a lovely aspect, right enough,' said Elisabeth, looking at the view before her.

'That's where I live, ovver yonder in t'caravan.' The boy pointed with his stick. 'Mester Massey lets us purr it on 'is field. We 'ave to pay 'im rent, mind. Mi granddad says 'e's a tight-fisted old so-and-so and allus on t'make. I live wi' mi granddad.'

Elisabeth wondered why the child was not with his mother and father, but decided not to pry.

''Course if ya do buy it,' the child continued, winking, 'you'd be wanting somebody to give you an 'and, to get rid o' all them pesky creatures, wouldn't you?'

'Yes, I suppose I would,' said Elisabeth.

'Aye, well tha knows where to come. I can do that fer ya.'

What a little character he is, thought Elisabeth, looking at the child. He met her gaze steadily. 'I'm a dab 'and at gerrin rid o' vermin and such.'

'I'll remember that.'

'Best leave your bees and your swallows. They don't do no 'arm. Mi granddad can sweep your chimney, if you've a mind, an' I can set mole traps, sort out your rabbit problem and get rid of t'rats.'

'There's rats?' Elisabeth shuddered.

'Oh aye, plenty o' rats. Tha's never far away from a rat, tha knows. They can grow to t'size o' small rabbit and they eat owt. Your average rat grows to about a foot long and weighs about a pound, but you can gerrem much bigger.'

'Really?' Elisabeth gave another small shudder.

'There's more rats than human beings on this planet,' the boy told her. 'Did tha know that?'

'I didn't,' admitted Elisabeth.

'Rats 'ave sex twenty times a day and can give birth every four weeks,' he said in a matter-of-fact tone of voice. 'You think there aren't so many because you don't see 'em. That's because they keep out o' sight, but they're theer all reight. You see, your rat is very clever.' The boy tapped his nose. 'They 'ave teeth harder than steel and they can gnaw through owt.'

'You certainly know a lot about rats,' said Elisabeth.

'I do. I've got a cross-breed terrier and a barmy cat what catches 'em.'

'What's your name?' she asked.

70

'Danny.'

'I'm Mrs Devine, Danny, and I'm pleased to meet you.'

'Bloody 'ell,' the boy said under his breath. 'Are you t'new 'ead teacher up at t'school?'

'I am,' said Elisabeth, stifling a laugh.

'We were telled last week in assembly that we were gunna gerra new 'ead teacher. Mi granddad were talkin' to his pals in t'pub last neet and they said you were picked yesterday and that you had a fancy name. He said it means 'eavenly an' 'e says they said you were a bit of all right.'

'Did he?'

'And that you wore these fancy red shoes.' The boy glanced down at Elisabeth's feet as if to confirm his grandfather's observation.

'Is that so?' She bit her lip to hide a smile.

'Aye, but 'e telled me I'd berrer be watching me p's and q's because you'd likely be reight strict.'

'Things seem to get around the village pretty quickly,' said Elisabeth, amused by the revelations.

'Oh, tha can't keep owt secret round 'ere. And if tha wants owt broadcastin' fast just tell Mrs S. who runs t'post office an' t'village shop.' The boy suddenly sat up on the gate and threw the stick away. 'Hey up, miss, I 'opes you dunt think I was bein' cheeky or owt and I din't mean to swear like. I was only tellin' you what folk were sayin'.'

'No, Danny,' said Elisabeth, 'I don't think you were being cheeky. The information is very interesting.'

'Beg pardon, miss?'

'Thank you for all the information. I've learnt a lot about rats and about what people are saying about me and what I need to do if I buy the cottage.'

The boy looked embarrassed. 'If I'd 'ave known you were t'head teacher, miss, I'd 'ave kept mi gob shut.'

'I'm glad you didn't.'

'Mi granddad sez I open mi gob too much sometimes bur I can't seem to 'elp it. He says a closed gob catches no flies. That's what gets me into trouble at school, talkin' too much.'

'And how is school, Danny?' she asked.

The boy blew out noisily. 'I'm not gerrin on reight well at t'moment, to tell ya t'truth. All this learnin' dunt suit me. I'm berrer off out in t'fields than stuck behind a desk in t'classroom. I look out on t'view from classroom winder and mi mind starts to wander. I want to be out theer. Mi readin's not up to much and t'teacher says mi number work's abaat same. I'm not much good at owt really when it comes to school work, and I allus seem to gerron wrong side of Miss Sowerbutts. I spends more time outside 'er room than in t'classroom for doin' summat or saying summat or other.'

He was not alone, thought Elisabeth, in getting on the wrong side of Miss Sowerbutts, and she felt she would join the many when she met the woman the following week.

'Any road, miss, I'd best get back. Mi granddad's cooking rabbit for us dinner. There's no shortage of rabbits around here. They breed like . . . like—'

'Rabbits?' suggested Elisabeth.

The boy threw his head back and laughed. 'Aye, like rabbits.' The boy jumped down from the gate. ''Bye, miss,' he said and started to run off across the field, leaping over the cowpats, but he stopped to call back. 'And I don't think that tha strict or stuck-up either.'

'Goodbye, Danny,' said Elisabeth under her breath, thinking about the first impression she had made on the residents of Barton-in-the-Dale.

* * *

The following Wednesday found Elisabeth outside the entrance of the village school. It was another bright, clear June day and the air was full of birdsong and the smell of blossom. She had telephoned the head teacher on the Monday to confirm the visit she had agreed with the governors following the interview, but Miss Sowerbutts had instructed the school secretary to deal with it rather than talk to Elisabeth herself. She was far too busy. Mrs Scrimshaw mused to herself that the head teacher was blessed with the ability to appear very busy while actually avoiding work of any kind. This was something the inspectors had discovered and detailed in their report, much to the school secretary's satisfaction.

'Mrs Devine.'

Elisabeth looked around to see a head, with a beak of a nose and large glassy eyes, appear over a bush.

'Yes,' she replied, startled.

'I'm Mr Gribbon.'

'Mr Gribbon?'

'School caretaker. I just thought I'd make my presence felt.' He emerged from behind the bush, clutching a spade. He had heard from Mrs Scrimshaw that the new head teacher was to visit that day, and had positioned himself at a vantage point so he could catch her prior to her

73

entering the building. 'Just giving the garden a bit of a tidy up,' he said, holding up the spade. She noticed that he glanced down at her shoes.

'Good morning, Mr Gribbon,' said Elisabeth, going over to him and shaking his hand. She appeared much brighter than she actually felt.

'It's a lovely little school,' he told her. 'You'll be very happy here, I'm sure.'

'I'm certain I will,' replied Elisabeth.

'Needs a bit doing to it, of course,' he said.

'Yes, I can see,' said Elisabeth, looking at the building, 'but I am sure that together we can make it look pristine.'

'Make it what?' he asked.

'Spick and span, Mr Gribbon. Nice and bright and welcoming. It just needs a coat of paint on the window-sills and a couple of new flagstones on the path. Nothing very drastic.'

'Yes,' he said deflated. 'I suppose it does. I do try my best, Mrs Devine, but there's only so many hours in the day and Miss Sowerbutts is always telling me we don't have the money for improvements and there's quite—'

Elisabeth held up her hand as if stopping traffic. 'Please, Mr Gribbon, I did not mean to sound critical. I am sure you try your best.' She saw disappointment written across his face. 'I could tell when I came for the interview that you keep the interior of the school clean and well looked after. The floor in the hall is quite splendid.'

The caretaker was clearly mollified. 'I do take pride in my floor,' he said, relieved to see that the new head teacher was wearing flat-soled shoes and wouldn't be leaving marks on it.

'I can tell,' said Elisabeth. 'And now, if you

74

will excuse me, I have an appointment with Miss Sowerbutts.'

Elisabeth was kept waiting for ten minutes in the drab entrance hall before being shown into the head teacher's office. Miss Sowerbutts sat stiffly behind the large desk, her thin white hands crossed tightly before her. Her eyes were dramatically narrowed. She wore a prim white blouse buttoned up high on her neck and a hard, stern expression on her face. So this was her successor, she thought, examining the woman who sat with legs crossed opposite her, dressed up to the nines and wearing enough make-up to shame a cosmetic counter. So this was the person the governors deemed appropriate to replace her, someone who would, no doubt, overturn everything she had established over the years, who would introduce all these modern approaches and trendy initiatives and undo all she had achieved. Her stomach tightened. It was just too much to bear. Well, she need not expect her to be warm and welcoming.

'I have to say from the outset, Mrs Devine,' said the head teacher, removing her glasses slowly and placing them carefully on the desk, 'that I was extremely disappointed, nay angry, that the governors saw fit to exclude me from the interview process. I have been in this school as teacher and head teacher all my professional life, for thirty-five years to be precise, and I should have thought, at the very least, that I would have been consulted in the appointment of my successor.'

'That was not my decision, Miss Sowerbutts,' Elisabeth told her, looking directly into eyes as cold and as grey as an autumn sky. 'Of course, I had no say in the decisions of the appointment panel or indeed which applicants would be called for interview.'

Miss Sowerbutts' gaze was one of barely suppressed animosity. 'Miss Brakespeare has been in the school for nearly as long as I have and, of course, she was extremely disappointed, as indeed I was, with the outcome. I imagined that she would be rewarded for her loyalty and dedication and offered the position.'

'Again, it was not my decision,' Elisabeth repeated, becoming irritated by the woman's undisguised hostility.

'And it seemed to me very discourteous of the governors to agree to you coming into the school this morning without consulting me first.'

'I did telephone the school on Monday to check if it was convenient,' Elisabeth told her. 'The school secretary said it would be all right. I believe you were busy at the time and unable to speak to me.'

Miss Sowerbutts pursed her thin lips. 'You will, no doubt, have heard that the school received a most unfair and inaccurate report from the school inspectors,' she said, maintaining the haughty façade.

'I had heard so,' Elisabeth replied.

Miss Sowerbutts snorted. 'The inspectors were a group of disorganised, disparaging and disagreeable people and had no understanding of the problems we face here.'

'What are the problems?' asked Elisabeth, making an effort to hide her irritation.

'I beg your pardon?'

'You mentioned the problems you have to face.'

Miss Sowerbutts retained her chilly and disapproving composure and gazed back balefully, folding her cold and bloodless hands before her as if in prayer. 'People might imagine that in a small country primary school like this one we are free of problems, that all the children are hard-working, well-behaved and value education and that their parents are supportive and appreciative of one's efforts.' This observation was clearly aimed for Elisabeth's benefit. 'Well, if they think that, then they are sadly misguided. For a start the children are a disparate group, and, what might one say, they are not top table material. Most of them come from farming families and their parents want nothing better for them than to work on the farm when they leave school. The children have limited prospects and little ambition. In consequence, they are at best lethargic and at worst uncooperative and truculent. You will discover that there are several pupils in the school—angry, violent, disobedient little boys— who are in no way susceptible to any of the fancy modern rehabilitation procedures suggested by the inspectors. They clearly did not appreciate this, and advised that I should be more proactive in raising the standards and supportive of the children who were difficult and disruptive, that I should pay more attention to pupils with special educational needs. As I told them, I have always been of the opinion that one has to have the raw material before one can achieve anything of note and that one cannot make a straight beam out of a crooked timber.'

Elisabeth was filled with an intense but unexpressed anger. She felt like giving this woman a good shake or striking her. She had no business teaching children.

Miss Sowerbutts took a small embroidered handkerchief from her sleeve and dabbed the corners of her thin mouth. A red rash had appeared on her neck and her face was flushed with displeasure.

'Then there's the offspring of the incomers to the village,' she continued, deprecatingly and now well into her stride. 'Most send their children to St Paul's, the preparatory school at Ruston, but we have a number of affluent parents who commute to the city each day and are so busy making money that they spend little time with their children or exert the appropriate discipline in the home. They think taking them abroad and letting them have televisions in their bedrooms is all they have to do. These children have too much at home, are indulged by their parents, who have more money than sense, and have far too much to say for themselves. You will find their parents pushy and demanding.'

'I see,' said Elisabeth. She considered for a moment tackling this virago and telling her that in her opinion, the keys to educational achievement were self-esteem and expectation, and that all children mattered and deserved the best a teacher could give. Clearly this woman spent little time building up the children's confidence in their own worth and expected little of them. It was no wonder that the inspectors had been so damning and that parents were taking their children away.

'Why do you think so many parents have decided to send their children to other schools?' she asked.

Miss Sowerbutts smiled a wintry smile and regarded her successor through half-closed eyes. 'Mrs Devine,' she replied, 'I am not privy to the motivations of parents. I run a well-disciplined and orderly school, employing traditional, tried-and-

78

tested teaching methods. I make no apology for doing so. It does not go down well with some of the parents, any more than it did with the inspectors, and if they decide to send their children elsewhere then that is their concern. Indeed, I have suggested to some that they do just that.'

Elisabeth sighed inwardly but refrained from saying anything. To challenge this severe and censorious woman would be fruitless, she thought, entrenched as she was in her views. Miss Sowerbutts was sad and embittered, angry at what the inspectors had said about her and resentful that she had been disregarded by the governors.

'I would like to look around the school, that is if you have no objection,' said Elisabeth, keen to get out of the office.

'Look around,' repeated Miss Sowerbutts.

'Yes, to meet the members of staff and the children,' said Elisabeth, looking her boldly in the eye.

The head teacher stared at her blankly for a moment. 'I didn't imagine that you would want to go into the classrooms,' she said dryly.

'I think it would be good to learn a little about the school before I start next term,' Elisabeth told her, 'and to meet the teachers.' She paused and continued to look the woman straight in the eye. 'Don't you?'

'I suppose it is all right,' the head teacher responded, as stiff and unyielding as the oak tree which cast its long shadow over the school. 'I did mention to the teachers that you would be visiting this morning. Miss Brakespeare teaches the older juniors and has been a stalwart in this school for as long as I. Miss Wilson is in her first year of teaching and takes the infants. She's young and inexperienced and has a great deal to learn. She tends to be a little too indulgent with the children and needs to be firmer and more rigorous in her teaching. Mrs Robertshaw takes the lower juniors and, I have to say, can be very trying and not a little difficult at times. We do not see eye-to-eye on a number of matters. This, of course, will be of no interest or importance to you as Miss Wilson and Mrs Robertshaw are both on temporary contracts and will be leaving at the end of the term.'

'I wasn't aware of that,' said Elisabeth. She was soon to learn that there were several other things of which she was unaware.

Miss Sowerbutts gave a small smile. 'Oh, didn't the governors mention that?' she said. There was an air of triumph in her voice. 'Well, I am sure you are keen to look around, so I won't delay you.' She replaced her glasses and looked down at the papers in her desk. 'You will forgive me if I do not accompany you. I have quite a lot of paperwork to deal with.'

Elisabeth gave an inward sigh of relief that Miss Sowerbutts would not be coming with her. She stood, smoothed the creases out of her skirt and said in a pleasant voice, 'Thank you for your hospitality.' The sarcasm was not missed by the head teacher, who continued, tight-lipped, to stare at the papers on her desk.

*   *   *

Miss Brakespeare's face was etched in an expression of anguish and apprehension, as if she

80

were expecting to be struck a blow at any moment. She had been informed on Monday afternoon by Miss Sowerbutts that the new head teacher would be visiting the school on the Wednesday, and the feeling of relief and contentment that she had felt over the weekend following the interviews had quickly been dissipated when the head teacher had given her considered views. Following the ordeal of the interviews, Miss Brakespeare had enjoyed a pleasant weekend, thinking she could maybe get on with the new head teacher, who had appeared very pleasant and talkative when she had met her. Indeed, on her way home that afternoon she had been quite light-headed. She did not want the responsibility; she really did not want the job and would not have put in an application form had it not been for Miss Sowerbutts' and her mother's insistence. The head teacher had been so persistent and Miss Brakespeare, ever one for a quiet life, had acquiesced.

There had been the predictable response, of course, from her mother when she had been informed of the outcome of the interviews, but this did not dampen Miss Brakespeare's high sprits.

'It doesn't surprise me that you didn't get the job, Miriam,' her mother had remarked unsympathetically. 'You've never been one to push yourself forwards. You like it in the background. You take after your father in that. He was never assertive or ambitious. The times I tried to get him to go for promotion. He could have been a manager if he had had a bit more gumption. People put on his good nature. They took advantage of him—as they do of you.'

Yes, her daughter had thought, I know that, and

you are at the very front of the queue.

'I am quite happy as I am, Mother,' she had said cheerfully. 'It is a big responsibility being a head teacher and I do have you to look after.'

Her mother had sat up in her chair and huffed. 'I can't help being invalided, hardly able to walk and in constant pain what with my arthritis. It's no bed of roses stuck at home by myself all day, I can tell you. Don't blame me for you not getting the job,' she had said sharply.

'I am not blaming you, Mother,' her daughter had replied with a sigh. 'I'm just saying that you need looking after and that had I been appointed as the new head teacher, I would have had a much bigger work load and not enough time to take care of you.'

'That is a feeble excuse, Miriam,' her mother had told her, huffing. 'You'd have had more time on your hands. Don't you go telling me that Miss Sowerbutts has a massive workload. She doesn't teach a class, sits in her room all day and is out of that school at three-thirty like a cat with its tail on fire. You've told me so yourself.'

'Yes, well,' her daughter had said. 'Things might change. The new head teacher seems very keen and is pleasant enough.'

'She might seem pleasant enough,' her mother had said, 'but she's likely to be the sort of person who will stab you in the back while smiling in your face. You want to put your foot down from the start. Behave as you mean to go on and don't be so amenable and ready to be at other people's beck and call. Now what's for tea?'

Miss Brakespeare had still been quite cheerful on the Monday morning after the interviews until

Miss Sowerbutts had asked her to join her for coffee in her room at morning break. Then, the sour seeds of doubt had been sown.

'Of course, she will alter everything,' Miss Sowerbutts had told her deputy head. Her lips had drooped in distaste. 'I've seen her sort before, full of all the educational jargon and keen on all the fashionable fads and fancy initiatives. Says all the right things to keep in with the inspectors and the education officers and out of the school most of the week on courses and conferences, leaving you to do all the work and hold the fort. She'll bring in a whole raft of modern teaching methods and change everything we have established over so many years. And, of course, you won't fit in with her plans. She'll make life difficult for you from the start. You mark my words, Miriam, you will find it intolerable having to work with her. She will be watching you, judging you, criticising you and finding every opportunity of finding fault. You will be driven out just as I have been. If I were you, I'd put in for early retirement as soon as you can.'

Miss Brakespeare had not said anything. She had blinked and nodded and smiled and kept her own counsel. Perhaps I might welcome the change, she had thought, but at the back of her mind there was that nagging worry that Miss Sowerbutts' predictions would prove to be only too correct.

CHAPTER FIVE

Before calling in at the classrooms, Elisabeth looked around the building for which she would

83

soon have charge. It came as no surprise to her that the school had come in for such heavy criticism. The small entrance, with its shiny green wall tiles and off-white paint, was cold and unwelcoming. It was bare of furniture save for a hard-backed chair and a small occasional table in the centre, on which was an ugly vase containing some dusty plastic flowers. Pinned to a noticeboard on a plain wall were various warning notices about head lice and scabies. From it the corridor, lined with old cupboards and with a floor of pitted linoleum the colour of mud, led to the four classrooms, three of which were used for teaching. The fourth, a cluttered general-purpose room, full of boxes and books, some old desks and damaged chairs, was where equipment and materials were stored. All four rooms were small and square, with high beams, large windows and hard wooden floors.

Elisabeth knocked and entered the first classroom, the windows of which gave an uninterrupted view of the dale which swept upwards to a belt of dark green woodland, the distant purple peaks and an empty blue sky. The scene seemed to shimmer in the bright light. A narrow road curled endlessly between the fields, which were criss-crossed by silvered limestone walls. Far off an invisible bird called plaintively.

Ranks of dark wooden desks of the old-fashioned lidded variety, heavy and battle-scarred and with holes for inkwells, faced the blackboard. They were entirely unsuitable for growing ten- and eleven-year-olds, and Elisabeth noticed that several of the larger boys had their legs sticking out. This would be something she would change. The highly polished floor was of patterned wooden blocks and was clearly well maintained. Here was one thing the caretaker did take pride in, she thought. At the front of the room, on a dais, was a sturdy teacher's desk made of pine, with a high-backed chair, while at the side was a bookcase containing a tidy stack of hardbacked books and folders, a set of dictionaries and some reference texts. There were no bright, glossy-backed novels, poetry anthologies or reference books in evidence. A colourful if rather unimaginative display decorated the walls, and a few pieces of children's writing were pinned alongside lists of key words, the rules of grammar and various arithmetical tables.

All eyes looked in Elisabeth's direction as she entered the room. Miss Brakespeare, a stick of chalk poised between finger and thumb, swallowed nervously, blinked rapidly and gave a small, uneasy smile when she saw the visitor.

'Oh, Mrs Devine,' she said, startled.

'May I come in?' asked Elisabeth, standing by the door.

'Yes, of course,' replied the deputy head teacher hurriedly. 'I was telling the children you would be calling into school this morning.'

Elisabeth moved to the front of the class and surveyed the faces before her. They were indeed a mixed group: large gangly boys, fresh-faced boys, lean bespectacled boys, girls with long plaits, girls with frizzy bunches of ginger hair, girls thin and tall, dumpy and small. They filled the room, which was hot and stuffy. 'Good morning, children,' she said pleasantly.

'Good morning, Mrs Devine,' chorused the pupils in subdued tones, staring at her as if she were some rare specimen displayed in a museum case.

'Now, you must be the oldest children in the school,' she said.

'That's right,' Miss Brakespeare told her. She gave a small and almost apologetic smile. 'These are the nine- to eleven-year-olds. There are three classes in the school: infants, lower juniors and upper juniors. Miss Wilson, she's just qualified, has the infants and Mrs Robertshaw, who joined us last year, has the lower juniors.'

So the head teacher doesn't teach a class, thought Elisabeth. The more she learnt about this woman, the more she decided that retirement was the very best course of action for her.

'It's a large class,' observed Elisabeth.

'Thirty-eight,' Miss Brakespeare informed her. 'It is rather a crush in here but we manage.'

'Well, it is really good to meet you all,' Elisabeth told the children in a cheerful voice, 'and I am so looking forward to coming to your school next term.' She noticed Danny sitting at the back looking warily at her. I guess he's worried that I might say something to him, she thought, and embarrass him in front of the other children. Elisabeth met his eyes steadily, smiled but said nothing.

The children continued to stare with blank expressions.

'I don't wish to disturb your lesson, Miss Brakespeare,' said Elisabeth, breaking the silence. 'I just wanted to introduce myself. Please carry on. Perhaps I might just stay for a moment.'

Miss Brakespeare looked flustered. 'Yes, yes, of course,' she said. Miss Sowerbutts may have been right after all, she thought. The new head teacher would, no doubt, be watching her, judging her, criticising her, like the inspector with the black clipboard and the smile like a crocodile had done. She had not expected that the new head would be sitting in on her lesson, particularly on her first visit. Was this a sign of things to come, she wondered. Miss Sowerbutts had never watched her teach. Of course, she had called into the classroom to ask something, impart some information, or take out a child who had misbehaved to stand outside her room, but she had never stayed to watch or to look at the children's work.

'Perhaps one of the children could tell me what you are doing this morning?' asked Elisabeth.

A red-faced girl with curly ginger hair and formidable silver braces on her teeth raised a hand and waved it like a daffodil in a strong wind.

'Miss, we're doing a worksheet on verbs,' she said.

'That sounds interesting,' said Elisabeth, thinking the very opposite.

Miss Brakespeare recalled the inspector's comment that her teaching was on the dull side and lacked vitality and that she should endeavour to make her lessons more interesting. She knew in her heart that she was just about competent as a teacher, not an outstanding practitioner, one who could hold the children's interest and excite and inspire them, but she did try her best. Since the inspection she had thought hard about the report and had made a serious effort to make her lessons more interesting, planning them more carefully and picking topics that the inspector had suggested might appeal to the children, but on this occasion, with a visitor in school, she'd thought she would play safe. Worksheets tended to keep the children quiet and fully occupied and there was less chance of any disruptions.

'Perhaps this is not the most interesting of topics,' admitted Miss Brakespeare, 'but we try to do some very interesting things in this class, Mrs Devine. Don't we, children?'

There were a few murmurs of assent.

'I must have been away that day,' mumbled a large-boned individual with tightly curled hair, short, sandy eyelashes and very prominent front teeth.

'That's not a very nice thing to say, Malcolm Stubbins,' said Miss Brakespeare, colouring a little. 'We do some very interesting things.'

'Most of the stuff we do is boring,' he said peevishly.

'That will be quite enough,' said Miss Brakespeare. 'I don't think Mrs Devine will be very impressed with that sort of comment, Malcolm.'

Elisabeth noted the boy. He stared back at her defiantly, almost inviting her to say something, but she remained silent. He would prove to be a bit of a handful, this young man, she thought, but she could handle him. She had dealt with boys much more difficult in her time.

Elisabeth had to admit that the work in which the children were engaged was dull. The class had been asked to identify the verbs in a rather tedious passage on canal-building and then use the words in an account of their own.

'And what is your name?' Elisabeth asked the girl with the bright ginger hair and braces when the children had settled back down to work.

'Chardonnay,' replied the child. 'I'm named after a drink.'

Elisabeth smiled. 'May I look at your work?' she

88

asked.

The exercise book was slid across the desk. The work it contained was untidy and inaccurate and the spellings were bizarre but the girl's stories were quite imaginative and well expressed.

'I don't like doing worksheets,' whispered Chardonnay. 'I like writing poems and stories best and using my own words.'

'You're a good story writer,' said Elisabeth.

'I know,' said the girl. 'Miss Brakespeare says I have a talent for story writing. She says I have a wild imagination, a bit too wild sometimes. I like writing about vampires. It's just that I need to be more careful with my spelling, but I just can't get my head round words. They're right tricky, aren't they, miss?'

'They certainly can be,' agreed Elisabeth, trying to decipher some of the words the girl had written. 'What is this word, "yrnetin"?' she asked.

'Wire netting,' replied the girl. 'We've had to put it around the hen coop to keep the fox out. Thing about foxes is that they kill all the hens if they get in. Bite all the heads off. It wouldn't be so bad if they just took one but they don't, they kill them all.'

Elisabeth nodded. 'I see.'

'Miss Brakespeare does do some interesting things,' continued Chardonnay, 'but when she does Malcolm Stubbins always spoils it. He shouts out and acts the fool. He's a real nuisance and he stops people getting on with their work. A lot of the time he's sent out and has to stand outside Miss Sowerbutts' room until he behaves. Once he had to stand there the whole morning when he put some orange peel in the hamster cage last year and the hamster ate it and died.'

'And he spits and swears,' divulged the child sitting next to Chardonnay, a large girl with huge bunches of mousy brown hair that stuck out like giant earmuffs.

'Really,' said Elisabeth.

'Her name's Chantelle,' Chardonnay told Elisabeth. 'She's my best friend.' The girl then lowered her voice to a whisper. 'You had better have a look at the display on the wall. Miss Brakespeare's been in at the weekend putting it up.'

'And she's had her hair done specially,' said Chantelle, 'and she's got a new dress on.'

'When we had the spectres in,' said Chardonnay, still speaking in a whisper, 'Miss Brakespeare said that if we were really good she'd give us all a bar of chocolate when they'd gone.'

'The spectres?' said Elisabeth, puzzled.

'Them men what watched the lessons.'

'Ah, the school inspectors.'

'Yeah, them. Well, when she heard they were coming in, Miss Brakespeare told Malcolm Stubbins not to bother coming into school that week,' said the other.

'I see,' said Elisabeth.

'And we practised our worksheets the week before,' said Chardonnay, 'so that we got all the right answers when the spectre looked at our books.'

'Really,' said Elisabeth, thinking how blunt and honest children could be.

Her companion nodded. 'Miss Brakespeare told us that if the spectre was in the classroom and she asked us a question, if we knew the answer we should put us right hand up.'

'And if we didn't,' added Chardonnay, 'then we

should put us left hand up and then she would pick only those with the right hand up.'

'Then the spectre would think we all knew the answer,' said Chantelle.

'That's very clever,' said Elisabeth.

'I know,' said the girls simultaneously.

Elisabeth sighed inwardly. 'I'll let you two get on,' she said, moving to the two boys at the desk behind. One boy, a moon-faced child with a shock of curly black hair and a face as freckled as a hen's egg, smiled widely.

'Hello, miss,' he said, brightly.

'Hello,' replied Elisabeth. 'And what's your name?'

'Miss, I'm called Darren,' replied the boy. 'Darren Holgate.'

'May I look at your work?' she asked. The boy reluctantly slid his book across the desk but kept his hand on the top. 'It's not right good, miss,' he explained. 'My mum thinks I've got dyslexia but Miss Sowerbutts said I've not. She says dyslexia is just a fancy word for those who can't spell. I do try with my writing but I find words really difficult.' He took his hand away.

Elisabeth looked at the boy's book. He watched her closely as she read his work. The child clearly had problems with his English. His letters were mixed up, his spellings very weak and his writing, the content of which was clear and imaginative, started off quite neatly but gradually deteriorated until at the end of the page it became spidery and illegible.

'I like this story about your dog, Darren,' she said.

The boy looked genuinely surprised. 'Do you,

miss?'

'It's really well written.'

'I know it's got lots of mistakes in it,' he said. 'It always has.'

'Well, you can do something about that later when you've got your story down on paper,' Elisabeth told him. 'The content of what you write is very interesting. The main thing is to write your story. It's very amusing.'

'Not really, miss,' he said.

'It is. It's very entertaining. I enjoyed reading it. It's a bit difficult to read at the end, though.'

'When I start off I take my time, miss,' he said, 'but then, when I get going, all these ideas come into my head and I rush things and then it gets more and more untidy.'

'I know all about that,' said his neighbour, a boy with ink-stained fingers. 'I sometimes think my pen's got a life of its own.'

Elisabeth laughed. 'It happens to me too,' she said.

Miss Brakespeare, at the other side of the room, raised her voice suddenly. 'I've told you twice now, Malcolm, to start writing and you've sat there and not put pen to paper yet.'

'Well, it's boring,' grunted the boy truculently. 'Anyway, I don't know what to do.'

'I've explained what you have to do,' the teacher told him.

'Well, I don't want to do it,' the boy said, folding his arms.

'In that case, I suggest you go and stand outside Miss Sowerbutts' room and think about it for a while.'

The boy got to his feet and shuffled out of the

92

room.

Chardonnay turned around. 'I told you, miss,' she said nodding. 'He's often sent out. He's a real nuisance.'

'May I look at your reading book?' Elisabeth asked a small boy with spiky hair that stood up like a lavatory brush and large pale eyes between almost colourless lashes. He was wearing glasses with thick lenses like the bottom of a milk bottle and had been exploring his nose with an index finger until Elisabeth bent down at his side. He produced an old and dog-eared reader from his desk entitled *Fisherman Fred*. 'Are there any newer or more modern books for you to read?' she asked. 'Novels, short stories, poetry anthologies?' The boy shook his head. Elisabeth asked the boy to read from the arid text, which he did: 'Fisherman Fred is getting ready to go to sea. He is wearing his big fisherman's boots. He likes the sea. He likes to sail in boats. He likes to catch fish.' The boy looked up. 'Crap, innit?' he observed.

Elisabeth moved on and arrived at Danny's desk. 'Hello,' she said.

The boy looked embarrassed. 'Hello, miss,' he replied quietly.

The boy sitting next to Danny was a small, pale-faced boy with curly blond hair, his head bent over his work.

'Hello,' Elisabeth said to him.

The child lowered his head further and closed his exercise book with a snap, before placing both his hands firmly on the top. It was clear he was not going to share his work.

'And what is your name?' she asked.

The boy looked up at her furtively with deep-set

eyes that seemed in search of something. There was an air of vulnerability about him which she guessed set him apart from the other children.

'James dunt say owt, miss,' said Danny. 'He never does.'

'Well, there are quiet people in the world,' Elisabeth said, just as Miss Brakespeare raised her voice again in reprimand.

'And if you don't get on with your work, Ernest Pocock, you can join Malcolm Stubbins outside Miss Sowerbutts' room.'

*　　*　　*

At morning break Elisabeth joined the teacher of the lower juniors, who was on playground duty. She had been invited by Miss Brakespeare to join her and Miss Sowerbutts for coffee in the head teacher's room at morning break but had declined, saying she was keen to meet the teachers and the children. She wished to see as little as possible of Miss Sowerbutts and she guessed the feeling was mutual.

Mrs Robertshaw was a broad, ruddy-complexioned woman with a wide, friendly face and steely-grey hair gathered up untidily on her head. She was dressed in a brightly coloured floral dress and a shapeless pink cardigan beneath her raincoat, and wore a rope of pearls and matching earrings.

'We are being observed,' confided the teacher, her lips almost pressed together, as she walked with Elisabeth around the playground. 'They're both watching us from the head teacher's room, no doubt wondering what we're talking about.' Elisabeth had noted herself that the head teacher

94

and her deputy were peering through a window. 'Having spoken to Miss Sowerbutts,' continued Mrs Robertshaw, 'it will come as no surprise to you that I don't get on with her.'

'Yes, I got that impression,' Elisabeth told her.

Before they turned the corner of the building Mrs Robertshaw twisted around and looked back in the direction of the head teacher's window. 'I can guess what those two are saying and you can bet it's not about the weather.' She stared defiantly at the figures peering at her. 'Miss Brakespeare's pleasant enough, well-intentioned and harmless, but she's well and truly under the thumb of Miss Sowerbutts and can't sneeze without asking her permission. I've been too long in the profession to be browbeaten by that sort of head teacher. I suppose I'm speaking out of turn, but I'm the kind of person to speak my mind.' Elisabeth could tell that but didn't reply. 'Anyway, things were made even worse for me after the inspection,' she continued, 'particularly when Miss Sowerbutts came in for most of the criticism and Miss Wilson and myself received some very positive comments from the inspectors. Miss Sowerbutts was not best pleased. The inspectors said that there needed to be a lot of changes here, but I guess you already know that. You will be like a much-needed breath of fresh air.'

'I believe you are thinking of leaving?' said Elisabeth.

'I am leaving, yes,' Mrs Robertshaw replied. 'My contract terminates at the end of term, so I am looking for another position. I shall miss the children but little else.'

'Would you consider staying if there were a permanent job?'

Mrs Robertshaw stopped and faced Elisabeth. 'Are you serious?' she asked.

'Yes, of course I am.'

'Well, it's not something I have given a lot of thought to.' Mrs Robertshaw fingered the pearls at her throat. 'I had assumed that at the end of the term I would be leaving. Miss Sowerbutts made it quite clear that you would probably be keen to bring in some new teachers—"a clean sweep", as she termed it.'

'Then Miss Sowerbutts is mistaken,' Elisabeth replied. 'There needs to be a period of stability, and appointing new teachers at this stage would be very disruptive, to say the least. I should like to ask you to delay applying for any posts until after I start here. I can't promise that I will be able to make your post permanent, but there is every likelihood that I can. Give me a chance to settle in and see how we like working together. Will you do that?'

'Well,' said Mrs Robertshaw smiling, 'that's come as a bit of a shock. I was thinking of applying for a post at Urebank, the neighbouring school, but after I had a look around I decided not to. It would be out of the frying pan and into the fire. I can't say that I was overly impressed with the head teacher when I visited the school. Mr Richardson's not a friend of yours, is he?' she asked guardedly.

'No. I've never met him,' Elisabeth replied.

'Blew his own trumpet all the time I was there. "Me, me, me" all the way around, and he kept on referring to the school as "*my* school" as if it was his own personal property. You are aware that he's been poaching children from this school?'

'No, I wasn't.'

'He even put an advert in the local paper singing

Urebank's praises and saying there were plenty of spare places at his school. Cheek of the man.'

Elisabeth decided this was neither the time nor the place to enquire into this with a woman she had only just met. 'So you will think again about applying for other jobs?' she asked.

'Thank you, Mrs Devine,' Mrs Robertshaw replied. 'I will.'

Elisabeth suddenly became aware of a small boy standing next to her. He was a bright-eyed, rosy-cheeked child of about eight or nine, with a thatch of straw-coloured hair and dressed in an old-fashioned outfit. His hands were clasped behind his back. He looked like a little old man.

'I'm sorry to interrupt your conversation, Mrs Robertshaw,' he said, 'but I thought I would come and introduce myself to the new head teacher.'

The teacher shook her head, smiled and placed a hand on the boy's shoulder. 'This is Oscar, Mrs Devine,' she said, 'and he's one of my star pupils. Aren't you, Oscar?'

'I should like to think so,' said the child, seriously. 'I have been identified as one of the G & T pupils after we did the verbal reasoning tests, haven't I, Mrs Robertshaw? G & T means gifted and talented, you know.'

'Hello, Oscar,' said Elisabeth, trying to restrain herself from laughing.

'Good morning, Mrs Devine,' he replied seriously.

'And how are you today?' she asked.

'Well, to tell you the truth, I'm not a hundred per cent,' he said. 'I woke up with quite a nasty headache this morning. My mother thinks there's a bug going around and suggested that I stay at home, but I knew you were coming into school this morning and didn't want to miss you.'

'Oscar likes to know what's going on,' explained the teacher, giving Elisabeth a significant look.

'I do like to keep up to speed with things,' said the boy. He looked up at Elisabeth. 'I painted a poster over the weekend welcoming you, but Miss Sowerbutts wasn't too keen on the idea when I asked her if I could put it up in the entrance. If you are coming into our class later this morning I'll give it to you.'

'That was very nice of you, Oscar,' said Elisabeth, amused by his curiously adult way of speaking.

'And I've also written a short poem,' he told her. 'I'm good at rhythms and rhymes, aren't I, Mrs Robertshaw?'

'You are good at most things, Oscar,' replied the teacher.

'Well, I'll let you continue your conversation,' said the boy. 'Maybe I will see you later, Mrs Devine.'

'He keeps me on my toes, does Oscar,' Mrs Robertshaw confided. 'Quite a little character, isn't he?'

*   *   *

Elisabeth left Mrs Robertshaw and went in search of Miss Wilson. The infant classroom was neat and tidy, and children's paintings, collages and poems had been carefully mounted and displayed. A large, bright alphabet poster and a list of key words for children to learn decorated one wall, and an attractive reading-corner contained a range of colourful picture and reading books and simple dictionaries. She learnt later that the young teacher had purchased most of the books herself.

Elisabeth thought how very youthful-looking Miss Wilson was. A slender woman with short raven-black hair, a pale, delicately boned face and great blue eyes, she looked decidedly nervous as she stood at the classroom door.

'Your classroom is delightful,' said Elisabeth. 'I always think the environment in the early years should be particularly bright and cheerful.'

The great blue eyes surveyed her for a moment. 'Thank you. Do come in.'

'And this is your first year of teaching?' asked Elisabeth.

'Yes, it is.'

'I wasn't aware that you and Mrs Robertshaw were both on temporary contracts,' said Elisabeth. 'I mentioned to Mrs Robertshaw that she might like to stay on. Perhaps you might consider that too. I can't promise anything until I've discussed it with the governors and been in touch with the Education Office, but it may be possible to make your contract a permanent one. Would you like to stay if I can arrange it?'

'I should love to,' replied the teacher quickly. 'It's just that I imagined that you would want to appoint some new staff.'

'Why should I want to do that?' asked Elisabeth.

'Mrs Sowerbutts said—'

'Ah yes,' interrupted Elisabeth, 'I think I know what Miss Sowerbutts has said.'

Noise in the corridor indicated that the children were returning from morning break. The little ones lined up outside the classroom chattering excitedly.

'Come along in, children, quickly and quietly,'

Miss Wilson told them.

When the infants were settled at their tables, the teacher turned to Elisabeth.

'This is Mrs Devine,' she said, 'our new head teacher.'

*   *   *

Elisabeth decided to call into the school office before departing but paused for a moment in the drab entrance hall to consider what she had seen that morning. Through the door the magnificent oak tree seemed to embrace the building with its spreading branches. The ancient Norman church, illuminated by a bright sun and beneath a cloudless azure sky, looked like the backdrop for a medieval drama. A lone sheep grazed by the village green and from some distant field there came a curlew's fitful cry. Barton-in-the-Dale, she thought, had much to offer.

There was a great deal to be done, of course, but she felt confident she could turn this school around and would welcome the challenge. She was much happier having met the staff. The success of a school, she knew, depended on the calibre of the teachers as much as on the strong and purposeful leadership of the head teacher. Elisabeth felt in her heart that she could provide that firm direction and that she could work with Mrs Robertshaw and Miss Wilson, who seemed personable, committed and enthusiastic teachers. Their lessons, which she had observed that morning, were interesting and well taught and the children responded well to instructions and to questions. Miss Brakespeare, however, was a different matter. She seemed a pleasant enough woman, rather like a frightened little mouse to be honest, and so staid and stolid. How she had managed to become a deputy head teacher was a mystery. She appeared amenable and good-natured, unlike the head teacher, but the lesson Elisabeth had observed that morning was one the inspectors would undoubtedly have described as less than satisfactory.

'Pensive.'

Elisabeth's thoughts were interrupted by a small voice.

'That's what my mother says,' said Oscar, 'when I look out of the window day-dreaming.'

'Well,' said Elisabeth, smiling down at the bright face which looked up at her, 'I was lost in thought. I was just thinking how beautiful it is—the trees and the sky and the church.'

'Yes, it's very picturesque, isn't it,' agreed the child, cocking his head and following her gaze. He turned and looked up. 'I hope you have had a pleasant morning, Mrs Devine.'

'Very pleasant, thank you, Oscar.'

'You forgot your poster and the poem I wrote for you,' he said, holding out a rolled up piece of paper with a pale blue ribbon around it. 'I did it especially.'

'That's very kind of you. I shall treasure it.'

'Miss Robertshaw said I might come out of class to give it to you,' he said.

'Thank you,' she said, reaching out for the paper in the boy's hand.

'Would you like me to read my poem to you?' he asked.

'Yes,' said Elisabeth. 'I should really like to hear it.'

Oscar unrolled the paper, looked at the writing for a moment, gave a small theatrical cough and read in a clear and confident voice.

'The birds are twittering in the trees,
And leaves are rustling in the breeze,
The sun is shining in the sky
And fluffy clouds are floating by.
This is a very special day,
So clap your hands and shout, "Hooray!"
Put out the flags and give a cheer
For a new head teacher's coming here.
I hope that she will not be cruel
And like it at our village school.'

'I had a bit of a problem with the last two lines,' Oscar admitted. 'I couldn't think of a good rhyme for "school". I thought I might write "cool"—"I hope the new head teacher's cool"—but that's slang, isn't it? My father says you should avoid using slang.'

'You are a very good little poet,' Elisabeth told the boy, taking the paper from his hands. 'It was a lovely thought, and when I start next September it will be first thing I shall put up on the wall. It will make me feel very much at home.'

Oscar smiled widely. 'You know, Mrs Devine,' he said, nodding sagely like a professor in front of his students, 'I think that you and I are going to get along famously.'

'I'm sure we are, Oscar,' Elisabeth replied.

*   *   *

'I hope you've had a pleasant morning,' said the

102

secretary cheerfully when Elisabeth entered the school office.

'Very pleasant, thank you, Mrs Scrimshaw,' she replied, laughing.

'Something's amused you, anyway,' said the secretary.

'I've just been having a conversation with Oscar and he asked me exactly the same thing.'

'Oh, you've met our Oscar, have you? Old beyond his years is that young man. Some would say too clever by half. His mother's a psychologist and his father's a barrister, so you might guess where he gets it from.'

'Well, if all the children at the school are so well-mannered and interesting, I think I shall be more than happy here,' Elisabeth told her.

'They are not all like Oscar,' said the secretary. 'We have our share of difficult ones.'

'I thought I might just say goodbye to Miss Sowerbutts before I leave,' said Elisabeth, changing the subject.

'Oh, she's gone out,' said the secretary. She smiled, in an attempt to cover her embarrassment. She had thought to herself how blatantly rude it had been of Miss Sowerbutts to leave the premises before the newly appointed head teacher had left, but of course that was just like her. She was making a point. 'She often pops out at lunchtime,' she lied.

'I see,' said Elisabeth. 'Well, perhaps you would thank her for the generous reception I have received.' The sarcasm was not lost on the school secretary.

'Yes, of course.'

'I wonder if I might have a copy of the school report?' asked Elisabeth. 'I would like to see what the inspectors said.'

The secretary looked decidedly uncomfortable. She smiled awkwardly. 'Miss Sowerbutts keeps the report in her room,' she replied. 'She doesn't like me going in when she's not there. I think I would need to ask her before I let you see it.'

Elisabeth looked at her calmly. 'I am sure she won't mind me borrowing it,' she said in a determined tone of voice. 'Of course, had Miss Sowerbutts been here I would have asked for it, but she isn't. You will understand, I am sure, that I need to get a view of what needs to change before I start.' She stared at the secretary with penetrating blue eyes. 'So if you wouldn't mind . . .' She left the end of the sentence unspoken.

The secretary swallowed nervously. The last thing she wanted was to get on the wrong side of the new head teacher. 'Yes, of course, Mrs Devine,' she replied, rising from her chair and imagining what Miss Sowerbutts would say when she returned. It was just as well she was out of the school, she thought. 'I'll get it.'

'Thank you.'

'Miss Brakespeare said she would like a quick word before you go, Mrs Devine,' said the school secretary, 'if you could spare her a few minutes.'

Elisabeth found the deputy head teacher in her classroom, tidying up after her class.

'Oh, there you are, Mrs Devine,' said Miss Brakespeare, as Elisabeth entered the room. 'I'm glad I caught you before you left. I . . . I just wanted to apologise for Miss Sowerbutts' behaviour this morning. She's not been herself of late and has been feeling very hurt and depressed what with the school inspection and then not being involved in the

104

interviews for her successor. She's spent her whole life at the school and feels very aggrieved. I . . . I . . . want you to know that I harbour no resentment whatsoever about you getting the position of head teacher here.' Her tone was genuine. 'To be frank, I didn't want the job and I was very pleased when you were appointed. I would be the first to say that I would not be up to it. It was just that people said I ought to put in an application and I was swayed into doing so. I want you to know, Mrs Devine, that I will be supportive of all your efforts and I look forward to working with you.' She breathed out heavily. 'There, I needed to say that before you left.'

'Thank you, Miss Brakespeare,' said Elisabeth, rather touched by the woman's simple and unpretentious comments. 'I appreciate your honesty and I too look forward to working with you.' She held out her hand and smiled reassuringly. 'I think that if we all pull together, we can make Barton-in-the-Dale Primary School the best in the county.'

Miss Brakespeare shook her hand lightly and returned the smile. 'I hope so,' she replied.

CHAPTER SIX

On arriving home after her visit to Barton-in-the-Dale, Elisabeth read the school inspectors' report. It was indeed damning of the leadership and management of the school, critical of Miss Brakespeare's lessons, which were described as 'poorly planned and uninspiring', but had many positive things to say about the other two teachers. Elisabeth, referring frequently to the findings in the report, penned a long letter to the Chairman of Governors outlining in some detail what changes she wished to implement when she took over the following September. A copy was sent to the Director of Education and to the inspector who had written the critical report of the school. She asked for the Chairman of Governors to convene an extraordinary meeting of the governing body for late July, at the beginning of the school's summer holidays, so she could outline her plans. Her second letter was to the teaching and non-teaching staff, saying how much she was looking forward to joining them in September and asking them to attend a short meeting a week prior to the start of the new term to discuss her proposals. Elisabeth then turned her attention to other pressing matters.

When she received confirmation of her appointment at Barton-in-the-Dale, she resigned from her position at the school at which she was head teacher, put her house on the market, sold it within a fortnight, and started making plans for her new life.

One Saturday she returned to the village to view the cottage she was determined to buy. It was quite an ordeal getting to the rear of the building. Accompanied by the estate agent, a rather dapper young man in a smart grey suit and designer sunglasses, she found the path to the side of the cottage blocked by a herd of heavy-uddered cows, jostling and pushing at each other, lowing in complaint at the narrowness of the track. A black and white sheepdog ran at their heels, snapping to keep the bumbling beasts moving forward, and

106

behind it ambled a red-faced, narrow-eyed farmer with a bearded chin, his greasy cap set on top of a mane of thick ill-cut hair. He touched his cap as he passed them and growled, 'Nice day.'

'It appears that some of the farmers have started using this as a means of access to their fields,' the estate agent explained, 'but the path belongs to the property, and should you buy it you will need to make this clear. Some of these village folk take advantage of what they call the "off-comed-uns". I noticed too that the paddock, which also belongs to the cottage, has sheep grazing on it. You will need to find out whose they are if you become the owner of the cottage.' He looked down at his highly polished shoes, now caked in mud and manure, and made a clicking noise with his tongue. 'Bloody cows,' he mumbled.

Inside, the cottage looked damp and cheerless with its thick and faded curtains, threadbare carpet, window-panes which had been broken and replaced by cheap glass and a naked light bulb dangling from a yellowing electric flex, but Elisabeth immediately saw its potential.

'It's in a bit of a run-down state,' the estate agent admitted, looking around unimpressed, 'and needs a fair bit doing to it. I should have thought that someone in your position, Mrs Devine, would be more interested in one of the new state-of-the-art apartments we are selling at Ribbledyke. Modern, spacious, low-maintenance and wonderfully well equipped—they're selling like hot cakes.'

Elisabeth gave the young man a disarming smile. 'Then you would be mistaken,' she told him. 'This is exactly the sort of place I want.'

To the estate agent's surprise, she made an offer

there and then and was informed the following day that it had been accepted.

At the beginning of the summer holidays she moved in. Now she stood in the small front room of the cottage, a bucket, sweeping brush, mops and dusters before her, looking around and wondering where to start. 'What have you done, Elisabeth Devine?' she murmured to herself. 'What have you let yourself in for?'

'Quite a bit, by t'looks on it.'

Elisabeth jumped as if ice-cold water had been flicked in her face and she swung around. In the doorway stood an old man. The visitor had a friendly, weathered face the colour of bruised parchment, grizzled, smoky-grey hair and an untidy beard, and his smiling eyes rested in a net of wrinkles. He was dressed in a clean, long-sleeved, collarless shirt, open at the neck, baggy corduroy trousers and heavy boots.

'Gosh, you startled me,' she said, placing a hand on her heart.

'Beg pardon, missis,' said the speaker. 'I din't mean to frit you. I'm Danny's granddad. He told me he'd met you. We live in t'caravan on t'yonder field. I 'eard that thy 'ad bought t'cottage and thowt tha might welcome a bit of an 'and. Tha's a fair bit to do, knocking this place into some shape.'

'That's very kind of you, Mr—' began Elisabeth.

'Just Les, Mrs Devine,' he told her. 'Everyone 'ereabouts calls me Les. Never Leslie. Just Les. I 'ates the name Leslie. Can't understand for the life o' me why my old ma called me such a name. Leslie! Sounds like summat out of one o' them romantic novels, dunt it?'

'Well, I'm very pleased to meet you, Les,' said

108

Elisabeth, extending her hand, which he shook vigorously.

'Our Danny telled me abaat thee. He said tha were reight tekken wi' this owld place when 'e fust met thee and that 'e 'ad an idea that tha'd buy it. 'E also said 'e reckoned tha could do wi' a bit of an 'and. Builders in t'village will be queuing up to get crackin' on t'place soon as they 'ear it's been sold, but between thee and me and t'gatepost, there's some of 'em who 'ud tek thee for a ride. Charge t'earth for doin' nowt. Single woman like thee. Now, I do charge for mi services but I can promise thee that I'm reasonable, fair, hard-working, tidy and punctual. Thas'll not be regrettin' it if tha tek me on. Ask anyone in t'village and they'll tell thee that Les Stainthorpe is an 'ard worker and won't let thee down.'

Elisabeth smiled. She warmed to the man straight away. 'Well, Mr Stainthorpe . . . Les,' she said, 'if you are as good a worker as you are a salesman, I think I've found a builder in a million. So, where do we start?'

Any doubts Elisabeth had about buying the cottage were soon dispelled by Danny's granddad.

'This place'll look gradely when we've fettled it,' he told her. 'Solid as a rock, been 'ere for a fair few centuries and wi' best view in t'village. I'd 'ave bought it missen 'ad I 'ad t'brass. It just needs a few repairs an' a bit o' paint, then it'll look champion when it's done.' He stared at a bulging wall and winked. 'An' mebbe a bit o' plasterin' and a few other things.'

The next month and a half saw a transformation in the cottage. Danny's granddad was true to his word and worked tirelessly and painstakingly.

109

He re-plastered the bulging wall, re-pointed the stonework, exposed the beams and stained them a lustrous brown, replaced the broken guttering, sanded down and varnished the old pine doors, repaired the rotten window frames and fitted some shelves. When Elisabeth had looked doubtful at the times when he had scratched his beard and come up with suggestions for improvement, he had smiled, winked and told her, 'Trust me.' And she had trusted him and it had paid off.

'You see, Mrs Devine,' the old man told her one bright sunny August afternoon, towards the end of the school holidays, as they sat at the table in the newly decorated kitchen, 'I've 'ad all these ideas in mi 'ead for years. I've been in this cottage many a time when old Mrs Pickles were alive and thowt to missen that if I owned it, I knew just what I'd change.'

'You've done a splendid job,' she told him. 'I'm so pleased with it.'

Elisabeth had the oak floors polished, new carpets laid, put up some bright curtains and hung some colourful prints and pictures on the walls, arranged the chairs and sofa and the old oak dresser in the sitting room and put the long-case clock in the hall. The place looked like home— warm and cosy. She invited Les around for a drink to celebrate the completion of the work.

As she stood with the old man at the door of the cottage she suddenly began to cry.

'Hey, hey, Mrs Devine,' said Les Stainthorpe, 'I din't reckon I'd done that bad a job.'

'It's wonderful, Les,' she told him, wiping her eyes. 'It's just what I imagined.'

*   *   *

During the time of the cottage's restoration, Danny had kept his distance. He seemed embarrassed to be in Elisabeth's company and spent most of the time in the garden, hacking away at the overgrown bushes, pruning the trees, mowing the lawn and digging in the borders. He also laid traps for the rats.

'He's quite a little worker, is Danny,' Elisabeth told his grandfather as they watched him through the kitchen window.

'Aye, 'e's a good lad,' said the old man, nodding.

'He's been keeping out of my way these past few weeks,' she said. 'Have I said something to upset him?'

'Gracious me, no, Mrs Devine,' spluttered the man. 'It's just that t'lad dunt want to be ovver familiar like, what with you being t'new 'ead teacher at 'is school an' all. He reckons tha not like the last 'un, owld Miss Sowerpuss. Nivver liked 'er an' I can't say as 'ow I blames 'im. Always at 'im she was about 'is work. Our Danny might not be t'brightest apple in t'orchard when it comes to readin' and writin' and arithmetic an' such but 'e's good-natured an' 'e can turn 'is 'and to owt if it's practical.'

'Yes, he's a nice young man,' Elisabeth told the boy's grandfather. 'He's a credit to you.'

The old man coloured up. 'I tries me best, Mrs Devine. It's not been easy, I can tell you. Danny's mi daughter's lad. She were a bit of a tearaway was my Tricia. Stubborn she was, and wayward. I reckon I was a bit soft with 'er after 'er mother up and left and I was left to bring 'er up. She 'ad Danny at

111

seventeen. No father in sight, of course. Any road, one neet police called and said she'd been knocked down on t'way 'ome. Driver never stopped. 'It an' run, it were. She were walking down some dark lane she were, pushing 'er babby in 'is pram. I mean, you expect that you'll outlive yer children, don't you, but it 'appens they sometimes go afore you. You think you'll allus go ahead of 'em but sometimes it's not t'case.' The old man rubbed his beard. 'Social worker passed little Danny to me and 'e's been wi' me ever since. There's just 'im and me now. We're like two peas in a pod.'

'So Danny doesn't see anything of his grandmother?' asked Elisabeth.

'Tricia's mum? No, no, Maisie's not been in touch. She came to t'funeral, of course, but I've not seen 'ide nor 'air of 'er since. Danny sometimes asks about 'er but what can I say?'

The boy looked up from digging as if he knew they were talking about him. He waved. 'Just 'im and me,' his grandfather repeated under his breath, waving back.

*   *   *

Mrs Sloughthwaite stopped mid-sentence as Elisabeth walked though the door. She had been in animated conversation with a customer, leaning over and resting her substantial bosom and her chubby arms on the counter, but she stopped talking suddenly at the sight of the new head teacher.

'Good morning, Mrs Devine,' she said, standing upright and straightening her overall. She turned to her customer, an extremely old, wrinkled individual with a long gloomy face. 'This is the new head

112

teacher of the school,' she told her, speaking slowly, like a nurse to a senile patient.

'Pleased to meet you, I'm sure,' said the woman glumly, looking Elisabeth up and down like a teacher inspecting a child's school uniform. Elisabeth smiled. The woman's eyes lingered on the shoes.

'Well, Mrs Widowson,' said the shopkeeper, keen to get rid of the customer and have Elisabeth all to herself, 'I should imagine you've got a deal to do. I'll not be keeping you.'

'I'm not in any hurry,' said the woman, making no effort to move.

'Yes, well, I want a quiet word with Mrs Devine, if you don't mind.'

'Oh,' said the customer, looking peeved. 'I'll be on my way then.'

When the old lady had departed, shaking her head and mumbling something to herself, Mrs Sloughthwaite turned her attention to Elisabeth.

'I don't want all and sundry listening in to our conversation,' she said in a confidential tone of voice. 'Least of all Edith Widowson. She's a terrible gossip that woman. Tell her anything and it goes round the village like a dose of salts.' Elisabeth smiled. Three words came to her mind—'pan', 'kettle' and 'black'. 'Husband hasn't done a day's work in his life,' continued the shopkeeper, 'and spends most nights in the Blacksmith's Arms or at the betting shop. She's a sad case. Now, Mrs Devine, what can I get you?'

'I have a list here,' said Elisabeth. 'Quite a lot, I'm afraid.'

'I'm not complaining,' said the shopkeeper. 'Keeps me in business. Them who come to live here

113

in the village usually shop at the new supermarket at Gartside.'

'Well, I won't be,' said Elisabeth. 'I think it's important to support the local businesses. I shall be placing an order each week.'

Mrs Sloughthwaite glowed. The more she saw of the new head teacher the more she liked her. She glanced down the list. 'As regards the biscuits, Mrs Devine, could I interest you in a box of my special Venetian selection?'

'Why not,' said Elisabeth.

'I hear you're doing up old Mrs Pickles' cottage?' said the shopkeeper as she placed the various items on the counter.

'Yes,' replied Elisabeth. 'That's one of the reasons for calling in, to thank you for drawing my attention to it. It's exactly what I wanted.'

'I'm very pleased. I always try to be of help. That's what my husband used to say, God rest his soul. Always there to give a helping hand and listen to people's problems. "You're too good-hearted for your own good, Doris," he used to say. I also heard you've got old Les Stainthorpe doing the place up for you.' Elisabeth opened her mouth to answer but the shopkeeper rattled on. 'He's a rum one is Les, and no mistake, but he's a good worker and he'll not take you for a ride.'

'He is. I've been delighted with the work he has done. He's really transformed the place.'

''Course, he's had a rough time of it what with his wife running off and then his daughter getting killed.'

'Yes, I heard,' said Elisabeth. 'Very sad.'

'He married late in life, you know.'

'Really?'

114

'Oh, yes, he was a confirmed bachelor was Les Stainthorpe until Maisie Proctor appeared on the scene and set her cap out for him. Worked behind the bar at the Royal Oak at Gartside she did—big brassy blonde in her thirties. I mean, he must have been getting on for fifty when he married her. Everyone in the village could see she was a gold-digger but not Les. Too trusting and good-natured by half, that's his trouble. After his money, that was her little game, and when she got her hands on it, my goodness, she knew how to spend it. Cleaned him out before she ran off with a brush salesman from Rotherham and left him with the kiddy.'

Elisabeth made a mental note not to tell this woman anything or it would be around the village in a flash.

'Rumour was,' continued Mrs Sloughthwaite, leaning over the counter and lowering her voice, 'that the child wasn't his, but I'm not one for gossip. You wouldn't like another box of Venetian biscuits, would you? They're on special offer.'

'No thank you,' replied Elisabeth. 'I need to watch my figure.'

'She was a tearaway was young Tricia. You would never believe the clothes she used to wear. Nothing left to the imagination. Like a firecracker waiting to go off, she was. Then she goes and gets pregnant. People said she had had a bit too much to drink when she was knocked down and shouldn't have been pushing a pram with a kiddie down a darkened road anyway, but I don't believe a word of it. I don't think she was that bad a mother. Mind you, he's done a good job has the lad's grandfather, bringing up young Danny. It'll be an upheaval for him having to move his caravan.'

'I didn't know that,' said Elisabeth.

'Oh, I should have thought that you would have heard. Fred Massey, who owns the field the caravan is on, has told Les Stainthorpe to shift it before the week's out. They had a right set-to in the Blacksmith's Arms. Nearly came to blows, so I heard.'

'Mr Stainthorpe never mentioned it,' Elisabeth told her.

'Well, that does surprise me. I mean the argument was about your cottage, in a manner of speaking.'

'My cottage?' Elisabeth asked.

'Evidently Les Stainthorpe told old Massey that he shouldn't be grazing his sheep on your paddock without your permission or using your track as a thoroughfare for his cattle. Fred Massey told him to mind his own business and they were at it hammer and tongs. They had a right old ding-dong, by all accounts. I'm not one for gossip myself, but Mrs Pocock, whose husband's on the darts team, told me all about it. It ended up with Les Stainthorpe being told to move his caravan.'

'Oh dear,' sighed Elisabeth, 'I've hardly moved into the village and I'm causing trouble.'

'It's not you, Mrs Devine,' said the shopkeeper, 'it's that Fred Massey taking liberties. He's a nasty piece of work and no mistake, and is so fond of hard work he lies down beside it. You couldn't nail a smile on that face of his. Miserable old so-and-so, and as mean as they come. You want to tell him to shift his sheep.'

The following week Les Stainthorpe moved his caravan into the paddock next to Elisabeth's

116

cottage.

*   *   *

On the afternoon when Les and two of his pals were moving the caravan into the paddock, Elisabeth looked out of the kitchen window to see Danny with the small, pale-faced boy with curly blond hair she had met when she had visited Miss Brakespeare's lesson the previous month. She went into the garden to see them.

'Hello, you two,' she said, brightly. Danny smiled and waved, while the other child lowered his head shyly.

'Hello, miss,' said Danny nervously. The other child looked up at her blankly.

'You're not helping your grandfather with the move then?' she asked.

'No, miss,' replied the boy, ''e said I'd only get under 'is feet. 'E told me to pack all my things in some boxes and 'e said to mek missen scarce. I'm showin' Jamie my mole-traps, if that's all right, then we're goin' rabbitin'.'

'Yes, of course it is,' Elisabeth told him, surveying the lawn. 'I see the little gentleman in black has made an appearance again.'

'Who?' asked Danny.

'Mr Mole.'

Danny had flattened the molehills the previous day, but during the night the sleek, elusive little creature had been hard at work, digging and tunnelling, and a rash of new mounds of soil had suddenly appeared.

'Aye,' he said sagely, 'and t'rabbits 'ave been at your plants an' all.'

117

'So, you two are after sorting out my mole and rabbit problems for me, are you?' asked Elisabeth.

'That's what we plan, miss,' he replied. 'You see yer mole is extremely difficult to get rid of. Did tha know that?'

Elisabeth smiled. 'No, I didn't.'

The boy placed his hands on his hips and nodded sagaciously. 'Some folk think that slices of onions in t'runs will make 'em go away, or pouring bleach down, but it dunt work. Neither does flooding their tunnels, 'cos they can swim for it. In t'past they used to put earthworms full o' poison under t'ground but tha can't do that these days. It's illegal, see. My granddad says yer mole is a persistent beggar. They don't mind frost and snow and t'only creature what eats 'em is a barn owl because they taste summat rotten. Mi granddad told me that up at t'big house, Limestone Hall, in t'past, owner had a full-time mole-catcher. I wunt mind a job like that.'

'And how are you going to catch this persistent little mole of mine, Danny?' asked Elisabeth.

'Catch him!' cried the boy, throwing his head back. 'Catch him! I'm gunna kill him.' He reached down, dug into a sack at his feet and produced a vicious-looking scissor-like contraption with springs. 'I'm purrin this down 'is run. That'll stop 'is little game.'

'Oh no, Danny!' exclaimed Elisabeth, 'don't kill him.'

'Look, Mrs Devine, if you don't get rid of 'im, you'll never 'ave a flat lawn.'

'I don't like the idea of killing him,' she said. She turned to his pale, solemn-faced friend, who was listening. 'What do you think, James? Do you think we should let Danny put his trap down?'

The boy looked up and shook his head. What a sad child, Elisabeth thought, wrapped in his protective shell, never speaking, never smiling. He was like a small timid creature, deep in a world in which it seldom showed its face.

'It's t'only way. I'm tellin' thee, miss,' said Danny, returning the trap to the sack and putting it down.

'Pardon?'

'I was just sayin', miss,' said Danny, placing his hands back on his hips, 'that t'only way of sortin' out your mole problem is to kill 'em.'

'Well, I think your friend and me have outvoted you, Master Stainthorpe,' said Elisabeth. 'Haven't we, James?' The boy gave a slight smile and nodded. 'Now you take that dreadful piece of equipment away, Danny Stainthorpe, and I'll get you two some lemonade and one of the special chocolate biscuits I bought at the village store.'

'Not that Venusian selection?' asked Danny, shaking his head and laughing. 'She's been trying to get rid of them for weeks.'

'Is there something wrong, James?' asked Elisabeth, seeing the boy wriggling as if he had chronic worms.

'It's me ferret, miss,' laughed Danny. 'He gets a bit lonely if 'e's left in t'dark for too long. Ger 'im out, Jamie.'

James reached into his pocket and produced a little sandy-coloured, pointed-faced creature with small bright black eyes. He held the animal under its front chest, his thumb under one leg towards the ferret's spine, and using the other hand he gently stroked the creature down the full length of its body.

'I've shown Jamie 'ow to 'old 'im, miss,'

119

explained Danny. 'They have to be held special like so as they feel relaxed and comfortable. 'E's champion, i'n't 'e?'

'I'm not so sure I agree with you about that,' replied Elisabeth, looking at the creature suspiciously. 'Isn't he vicious?'

The boy laughed. 'Nay, miss. Yer ferret meks a gradely pet. 'E don't bark, 'e's clean as a whistle and is a reight mischievous little beggar.'

'But they smell,' added Elisabeth.

'Only when they're frightened or when they come into t'breeding season. Yer hob—'e's t'male—gives off a smell to attract t'jill—she's t'female. It's a bit like men purrin on aftershave.'

'Rather a different smell, I should imagine,' remarked Elisabeth.

'Well t'jill likes it, miss, and that's all as matters, i'n't it?'

'Does he bite?' she asked.

'Only a bit,' replied Danny, nonchalantly. 'Do you want to 'old 'im, miss?'

'Not on your life!' exclaimed Elisabeth. She turned to Danny's friend. 'And what about you, James? Do you like ferrets?' The boy looked up shyly and nodded but didn't speak.

'I've 'ad this ferret since he were a kit. That's a babby,' Danny explained. ''E gets really tame if thy 'andles 'im a lot and are really patient wi' 'im. Mind you, thy 'as to look after ferrets, clipping their nails regularly, cleaning their ears, bathing 'em and givin' 'em plenty of exercise.'

Listening to this boy, Elisabeth appreciated just how knowledgeable the country child could be and how ignorant she was in country matters.

'So you're giving your ferret some exercise this

morning?' she said, smiling at him warmly.

'I am that,' replied Danny. ''E's a workin' ferret as well as a pet and 'e's goin' down t'rabbit 'oles today. 'E'll stop them rabbits, I can tell thee, won't 'e, Jamie?'

Danny's friend nodded and continued to stroke the ferret gently.

'Poor rabbits,' said Elisabeth. She decided not to enquire what the ferret would be doing but she had a good idea. 'Well, when you two have finished come and have some lemonade,' she said.

As she walked towards the house, Elisabeth heard Danny whisper to his friend, 'I telled thee she were all reight, Jamie. She's really nice is Mrs Devine.'

Elisabeth smiled, but thought to herself what a sad and nervous little boy Danny's friend was, and so quiet; she felt certain, though, that with time and patience she could bring him out of his shell.

*   *   *

At the governors' extraordinary meeting, held at the beginning of the school's summer holidays, Major Neville-Gravitas apologised for the absence of so many of his colleagues.

'Mr Nettles, the education officer, and Councillor Smout are both on holiday,' he explained. 'Mrs Bullock, the foundation governor, is not well and Mrs Pocock is also indisposed, so that just leaves myself, Dr Stirling and the vicar and, of course, your good self, Mrs Devine.'

'I quite understand,' Elisabeth replied, rather disappointed with the turnout. At her last school the governors had been keen and supportive and attended meetings religiously. 'It is a busy time of year. I do appreciate you giving up your time.'

'I hope we are not going to be too long,' said the major, glancing at his watch. 'I have an important appointment scheduled later today.' He had arranged to play a round of golf that afternoon.

'No,' replied Elisabeth, 'I shouldn't think this will take too long.'

'Well now, Mrs Devine,' said the major, 'perhaps you would like to tell us why we are here.'

'As I outlined in my letter to you, Mr Chairman,' Elisabeth told him, 'I felt it would be prudent to let the governors know early on my intentions and seek their approval for the changes I wish to make. I intend to keep you all fully informed about the life of the school and will not make any major decisions until I have consulted you.' She looked in the direction of a serious-faced Dr Stirling, who sat impassively but listening intently. 'I have already outlined to Major Neville-Gravitas in my letter what I would like to do, and here is a copy of my proposals.' She passed around a folder containing a sheaf of papers. 'First, I intend to convert the head teacher's room into a staff-room. I think you will agree that the teachers should have somewhere to take a break and have a little privacy. This room will house all the confidential material, documents, guidelines and files, which will be moved from the school office to give the secretary more space. It is very cramped in there at the moment.'

'Where will you go?' enquired the vicar.

'This brings me on to the next change I wish to make. I intend to teach, and shall use the spare classroom. The top juniors, which will number over forty at the start of the next term, is too large a class in my opinion. I would like to split this with Miss Brakespeare.'

'You're going to teach?' asked the major.

'Yes, Mr Chairman, that is my intention. I shall ask Miss Brakespeare to take the nine-year-olds and I shall teach the ten- and eleven-year-olds.'

'That's all very well,' said the major, 'but when will you do all the administration and deal with the letters and such?'

'At home, before and after school,' Elisabeth told him. 'I shall be the first to arrive at the school and the last to leave. Parents, should they wish to see me, can make an appointment for when I am not teaching.'

'I see,' he murmured.

'I think that is a splendid idea, Mrs Devine,' said the vicar, rubbing his long hands. 'I have always been of the opinion that the junior classes are far too large, and indeed this was observed by the inspectors.'

The major sighed audibly. 'Can we not go over yet again what the inspectors said?' protested the Chairman of Governors. 'I am heartily tired of hearing about the report at every meeting we have.'

'I am merely pointing out, major,' the vicar told him, 'that this was a real concern, and indeed the large class size is a significant reason for so many parents choosing to send their children to Urebank school. Is that not so, Dr Stirling?'

'Yes, I believe it is,' the doctor replied without elaborating.

'I do hope, however, that Mrs Devine is not taking too much on,' continued the vicar.

'Thank you for your concern, Reverend Atticus,' she said, 'but I am used to working hard and putting in the time.'

'I noted,' said the major, flicking through the folder, 'that in your letter to me there are some resource implications. I guess the Local Education Authority will baulk at expending any money, if you follow my drift.'

'That is why I am hopeful, Mr Chairman, that the governors will lobby the Local Education Authority for such resources. The old desks must go, as they are entirely unsuitable. Some of the big boys can't get their legs under them.'

'Miss Sowerbutts liked the desks,' the major told her.

'Well, I don't, major,' she replied. 'We need tables, and the dreadful linoleum in the corridor needs replacing. A carpet would be good. There are also damp patches on the ceiling and I wish to refurbish the entrance hall. All this is outlined in my report. Finally I come to the most important request, and that is to make the two teachers, Miss Wilson and Mrs Robertshaw, permanent members of staff. As you will be aware, they are at present on temporary contracts.'

'I didn't know that,' said the vicar. 'Were you aware of that, Dr Stirling?'

'No, I wasn't,' the doctor replied. His expression remained blankly impersonal.

'Yes, yes,' said the major quickly. 'Miss Sowerbutts felt they should be offered temporary contracts to see how well they got on and if they were suitable. Indeed, Mr Nettles was very much for not making the teachers permanent and said there was really no need to bother with an appointment panel.'

'I feel we might have been consulted,' said the

vicar, sounding annoyed.

'As I said, there was really no need,' said the major, brushing the comment aside. 'Mr Nettles, the education officer, was in full agreement.'

'Nevertheless—' began the Reverend Atticus.

'It's water under the bridge now, vicar,' said the major irritably.

'As to the question of the teachers' suitability,' said Elisabeth, 'both Miss Wilson and Mrs Robertshaw seem very suitable and I should be sorry to lose them. They are looking for jobs at the moment, and I think it would have an adverse effect on the school if there was a change of staff at this time. They have proved themselves and I think they should be offered permanent positions.'

'At the risk of raising your blood pressure again, major,' said the vicar, 'the school inspectors spoke most favourably of their teaching.'

'I shall have to talk this over with Mr Nettles at the Education Office before making any decision on this,' said the major. 'And now I have this important meeting to attend, so I will close the meeting.'

'Before you do, Mr Chairman,' said Elisabeth, 'I take it then that you and the governing body are supportive of the proposals and you will inform the Education Department at County Hall?'

'Yes, yes,' said the major, in a less than enthusiastic tone of voice, which indicated that this woman might be a little too forceful for his liking.

CHAPTER SEVEN

Dr Stirling was waiting for Elisabeth as she made her way out of the school. He was a tall, not unattractive man, aged about forty, with a firm jawline and a full head of dark hair greying at the temples and parted untidily. What was most striking about him was his pale blue eyes. Elisabeth noticed that he stooped a little, that his suit was unfashionable and had seen better days, that his shirt was frayed around the collar and that his shoes could do with a good polish. He spoke in a quiet, sometimes almost inaudible voice, not that he had said much that morning. He had been less than friendly at the interview and it was clear to Elisabeth that he found something about her that he did not like.

He shifted nervously in the small entrance area of the school, like a schoolboy sent to the head teacher for misbehaving. 'Might I have a word with you, Mrs Devine?' he said.

'Yes, of course, Dr Stirling,' she replied.

'I felt it only fair to let you know that my son will not be returning to Barton-in-the-Dale school after the summer holidays and that I shall be resigning as a parent governor.'

'I see,' said Elisabeth.

'I can assure you that it's nothing personal. I have been thinking about it for some time but I didn't want to move James mid-term.' When Elisabeth didn't reply he swallowed, his gullet rising and falling like a frog's. 'My son is a quiet, rather sensitive boy and I feel that St Paul's Preparatory

School in Ruston will suit him better. The classes are smaller, there are more specialist teachers and it has better facilities.'

So the small, pale-faced boy with curly blond hair who never spoke was the doctor's son. 'Well, Dr Stirling,' said Elisabeth, 'I am obviously disappointed with your decision but you are entitled to do what you feel is best for your son. I might have hoped that you would have kept him here and given me a chance to make the changes necessary. Maybe I could have brought James out of his shell.'

The doctor bristled. 'Bring him out of his shell?' he retorted. 'There are people in the world, Mrs Devine, who are quiet. James is one of them. He is a thoughtful child, a little withdrawn at times, but he is intelligent and interested in things around him. He reads avidly, and his artwork I think is extremely good. He is indeed a quiet boy but that is understandable. He still misses his mother a great deal. You probably are not aware that he lost his mother a couple of years ago. My wife had a riding accident and, of course, her death distressed him greatly.'

'I am very sorry to hear about your wife, Dr Stirling,' Elisabeth told him. 'You must both have been devastated.'

'We were,' he said sadly, 'but time is a great healer, and James will I am sure eventually come to terms with it.'

'I think there is more to it than that, Dr Stirling,' Elisabeth told him. Her voice was level and cautious.

His blue eyes flashed. 'In what way, more to it?' His tone was sharp and defensive.

'I think that James has a condition which needs to be addressed,' she said.

'A condition?' he repeated. 'And what condition would this be?'

'James, I gather from Miss Brakespeare, is fully capable of speech and understanding language but is completely silent in lessons. Despite her efforts he just doesn't speak. This, of course, is of concern, and perhaps—'

'He speaks quite happily and indeed expressively at home,' interrupted Dr Stirling. 'He can communicate normally in a situation in which he feels comfortable, and to be frank I don't think he feels comfortable in this school—hence my decision to send him to St Paul's.'

'Dr Stirling, it is not quite as simple as that. James may indeed converse freely at home but, as I have said, he is completely silent in class. He never asks or answers a question and, from what I gather, only speaks to one other pupil.'

'And how would you know all this, Mrs Devine?' asked the doctor.

'From what I have been told by his teacher and by observing it myself,' she replied.

'And when have you met my son?' he asked.

'I met James when I visited the school and later when he came into my garden.'

'Came into your garden?'

'Yes, he came with his friend, Danny.'

'The boy who lives with his grandfather in the old caravan? Yes, I knew he was a friend of James's.'

'Although the boys were at my cottage for some time, your son never spoke one word, not even to say hello. It must be clear to you, a doctor, that your son has a communication disorder, and his consistent unwillingness to speak at school will inevitably interfere with his emotional development and his educational achievement. Early intervention is crucial to deal with the condition in the first few years of a child's life. At my last school there was a boy with a similar problem and—'

'Mrs Devine,' interrupted Dr Stirling again, 'James has no condition, disorder or problem. He is just a quiet, under-confident little boy who is still grieving for his mother. I weary of hearing and reading about all these so-called children's disorders and syndromes. James is growing up. He will soon grow out of it. I did discuss his unwillingness to talk in school with the previous head teacher here and she was of the same opinion. Miss Sowerbutts felt it was a stage many children go through, something to draw attention to themselves.'

'Well, I don't agree, Dr Stirling,' said Elisabeth. 'Most children do not go through this stage, and the very last thing James wants to do is draw attention to himself. Quite the opposite, in fact. I believe James has a condition which is called selective mutism.'

Dr Stirling sighed noisily. 'I might have guessed there would be some fancy educational label to describe it,' he said, without looking at her.

'And if his condition continues,' Elisabeth told him, 'and if it is ignored, then it tends to be self-reinforcing and those around such a person may eventually expect him or her not to speak so they don't bother talking to them. This makes the prospect of his speaking seem even more unlikely. Sometimes in this situation a change of environment, such as a change of school, may make a difference, but the upheaval could also be distressing and harmful. Providing love, support and patience, offering emotional encouragement, which James clearly gets at home, is all important but—'

'Mrs Devine, I am grateful for your concern over my son but it is academic, since he will be moving to St Paul's next term. He will not be any responsibility of yours. I must admit to some surprise that, having met my son just a couple of times, you have come to such firm conclusions about him.'

'If I could get you to talk to an educational psychologist—' Elisabeth started.

'No, Mrs Devine, that will not be necessary,' said Dr Stirling abruptly. 'I really do not feel we have anything further to discuss. I am certain that in a fresh environment with new friends, James will feel more confident to speak.'

'I was sorry to hear about your wife, Dr Stirling,' said Elisabeth. 'I am sure it has affected James greatly and I do hope that in time, as you say, he will feel more able to speak.' She looked into the blue eyes. Here was a man, she thought, with a sense of unswerving purpose, a man used to asking questions and telling people what to do, a stubborn man who clearly was not prepared to listen, who had closed his eyes to his son's obvious disability. There was little chance of convincing such a man as he. 'And I sincerely hope you are right and that your son will be very happy at St Paul's,' Elisabeth told him.

*   *   *

Elisabeth found the meeting of teachers and

non-teaching staff that took place the week before the start of the school term an altogether more reassuring affair than the meeting with the governors had been. In the newly designated staff-room she outlined to those present—Miss Brakespeare, Miss Wilson, Mrs Robertshaw, Mrs Scrimshaw and Mr Gribbon—what she intended. The staff had arrived at the school amazed at the changes that had already taken place, and sat in silence too stunned to speak. When Elisabeth explained that she would be teaching the upper juniors, Miss Brakespeare broke her silence.

'Split the class?' she said in disbelief. 'You intend to teach the top half of the juniors?'

'That's right,' Elisabeth confirmed. 'I think it is unreasonable for you to have to teach so many children. The classroom is small and cramped for so many pupils and the marking of the children's work must be very time-consuming for you. Quite apart from that, it must be difficult for you to differentiate the work for so wide an age and ability range.'

'It is,' acquiesced the deputy head teacher, looking astonished. She recalled how dismissive Miss Sowerbutts had been when she had hesitantly raised the possibility of dividing the class.

'Does this meet with your approval, then?' asked Elisabeth.

'Well, it has come as a bit of a shock, Mrs Devine,' said Miss Brakespeare, 'but I must say a very welcome one.'

'That's settled, then,' Elisabeth told her. She turned to the two other teachers. 'I hope to hear from the Education Office early next term about your contracts. The governing body, which met with me at the beginning of the summer holidays, was unanimous in supporting my request for you to become permanent members of staff if you wish to stay and we are happy working together.'

'That's wonderful,' said Mrs Robertshaw.

'Thank you,' said Miss Wilson, looking well pleased.

'Now, as you can see,' continued Elisabeth, 'the former head teacher's room has now become our staff-room, which gives you, Mrs Scrimshaw, more space in the school office.' The school secretary was too dumbstruck to say anything and stared open-mouthed. 'Mr Gribbon has done an excellent job,' continued Elisabeth.

Following the meeting with the governors, Elisabeth had talked through with the caretaker the changes she wanted to make. Inwardly Mr Gribbon's heart had sunk into his boots at the thought of all the work it would entail, but he had smiled weakly and said he would start immediately. The following week he had opened up the fourth classroom and moved half the desks from Miss Brakespeare's room, to be used until the new tables arrived.

'Thank you for all your hard work, Mr Gribbon,' said Elisabeth now.

The caretaker smiled and nodded and rubbed his chin, pleased with the recognition of his efforts.

'I noted on my visit, Mrs Scrimshaw,' continued Elisabeth, 'that you said you remained in the office after school, sometimes for more than half an hour, in case there was an urgent telephone call from a parent or from the Education Office.'

'Yes, that's right,' replied the secretary, at last finding her voice. She was about to mention that she felt it unreasonable, since she was only paid until four o'clock, but Elisabeth forestalled her.

'Well, that will not be necessary from now on. As I told the governors, I shall be the first into the school in the morning and the last to leave in the afternoon.'

The school secretary looked startled. 'You will?'

'I will,' said Elisabeth. 'Now I am sure that there must be quite a few issues some of you wish to raise and suggestions you want to make, and I am very willing to listen to them.'

The five colleagues stared back at the new head teacher but remained silent. None of them had anything to suggest, for any requests they might have had in their minds had been answered. Then Miss Brakespeare spoke. 'Welcome to Barton-in-the-Dale, Mrs Devine,' she said. Her tone was genuine. 'I hope you will be very happy here.'

*　　　*　　　*

It was a bright early September morning when Elisabeth arrived for her first day as the new head teacher of the village school. The caretaker had made a real effort to make the building attractive and welcoming. Elisabeth noticed that the window-frames had been cleaned, the broken flagstones on the path replaced, the hedge trimmed and the fence around the perimeter repaired.

Mr Gribbon, wanting to make a good impression, was there early, dressed in a new pair of bright electric blue overalls and busy at work digging in the border surrounding the tussocky lawn at the front of the school. He had thought to himself that since he would be working with the woman in the

133

red shoes, it seemed sensible to get on the right side of her from the very start.

'My goodness, Mr Gribbon,' Elisabeth exclaimed, standing at the gate, 'you've transformed the place. What a difference.'

'I try my best, Mrs Devine,' he replied, clearly pleased with the praise. He had seldom received any commendations from the previous head teacher, so had made little effort apart from with his floors, which he prized. It was nice, he thought, to receive some recognition for all his labours. 'I just need to give the window-frames a lick of paint and sort the lawn out now.'

'Well, I am very grateful for all your hard work,' Elisabeth told him.

'I've given the classrooms another good going over,' he told her, 'and buffed up the floors.'

'Thank you,' Elisabeth said. 'It is much appreciated.'

It wasn't long before the school secretary and the teachers arrived. The many doubts Elisabeth had harboured about taking on this post, and her nervousness at starting as the new head teacher, seemed suddenly dispelled when she saw the people she would be working with. There was a cheerfulness and buoyancy in the air, a lively, genial chatter and a real sense of optimism. Elisabeth took a deep breath. She shared their hopefulness and confidence about the future. These people, I can tell, she thought, are going to work with me and not against me. Together it would not just be the transformation of the building. Attitudes and aspirations would change; there would be a spirit of cooperation and a workmanlike atmosphere characterised by good-humour, respect and

134

affection.

Before the start of school Elisabeth called a meeting in the new staff-room, at which she provided coffee and biscuits. She welcomed everyone and said she looked forward to what she knew would be a successful term. She noticed there was a visible difference from the Miss Brakespeare she had met previously. Like the caretaker, the dowdy, serious and conventional deputy head teacher she had encountered on her visits to the school had made a real effort and now looked and sounded quite a different person.

Miss Brakespeare indeed felt quite a different person and was in a particularly jaunty mood that morning. With hair newly permed and tinted, dressed in a bright floral dress and with a rope of large amber beads draped around her neck, she chatted away amiably. She had been into the school following the staff meeting that had taken place before the start of term to mount displays in her classroom and found, after Mr Gribbon's efforts, that her room was bright and clean. Now, with half the desks gone, it was veritably spacious. During this visit there had been the opportunity to spend some time with the new head teacher and to talk through the changes envisaged, and Miss Brakespeare had found her affable and easy to talk to. Mrs Devine was not, as Miss Sowerbutts had predicted, full of educational jargon and keen on fashionable fads and fancy initiatives, nor was she intending to bring in a whole raft of modern teaching methods and change everything. Furthermore, she was keen to involve all the staff in decisions and had sought out Miss Brakespeare's opinions, something the former head teacher

135

had never done. Rather than finding the situation 'intolerable', as Miss Sowerbutts had foretold, Miss Brakespeare had a feeling that she was going to be very content with her new situation. When she looked down the list of pupils she would have in her now depleted class, she found, to her delight, that the new head teacher, as she had said, was to teach the oldest children, who included the two most difficult and disruptive pupils. She would no longer have to contend with the likes of Malcolm Stubbins and Ernest Pocock, or with the local GP's son, that strange, hypersensitive, disturbed little boy who never said a word. She was well pleased with the changes.

Miss Brakespeare, on that first morning of the new term, smiled wryly when she saw Elisabeth arranging some chocolate biscuits on a plate.

'Join the club, Mrs Devine,' she said, amiably.

'I beg your pardon?' asked Elisabeth.

'I see Mrs Sloughthwaite has managed to sell another packet of her Viennese biscuits or, as she likes to tell people, her Venetian selection box,' she said. 'I think everyone in the village must have a box somewhere. Rumour has it that she ordered ten boxes thinking she was only going to get ten, but there were ten to a box and she was lumbered with a hundred.' She didn't wish to sound ungrateful so added quickly, 'They're very nice, actually.'

Later that morning, when she saw the parents arriving with their children, Elisabeth straightened the creases in her skirt discreetly, buttoned her jacket, took a deep breath and walked slowly down the school path to meet them. It was an unusually large turnout of mothers and fathers standing at the gate that morning, no doubt there to see the new head teacher about whom they had heard so much. Elisabeth had deliberately dressed for the part, in a stylish red turtleneck sweater, navy blue jacket and skirt and the famous red shoes with the silver heels she had worn at the interview. Small earrings glittered in her ears. She smiled and greeted each parent with a friendly 'Good morning'. Most nodded and smiled but stood shyly at the gate.

'Do come through,' Elisabeth told them. 'You can see your children into school if you wish.'

'Miss Sowerbutts made us wait at the gate,' mumbled a mousy-looking woman.

'Well, I like parents to come into the school,' Elisabeth told her. 'You are all very welcome.'

One mother, accompanied by a bright-eyed, rosy-cheeked child of about nine, approached her. She was an extremely thin and intense-looking woman dressed in a charcoal grey suit with narrow chalk stripes. Her large eyes had dark shadows under them and her greying hair was caught back untidily in a black ribbon.

'This is my mother, Mrs Devine,' said Oscar brightly. He gestured with a small hand. 'Mumsie, this is Mrs Devine, the new head teacher. I've told you all about her.'

'Good morning, Mrs Devine,' the woman said, and smoothed away a strand of hair that had escaped and fallen over her face. 'I hope you will be very happy here. I must call in some time when it's convenient to have a word about Oscar.' She lowered her voice. 'He's somewhat wise beyond his years, is my son, and I guess he can be quite a handful at times,' she confided.

'I'll look forward to that,' replied Elisabeth.

'You can go now, Mumsie,' the boy told her

dismissively, proffering a rosy cheek which she kissed. 'You won't be late this afternoon, will you? Remember I have piano practice at four fifteen and you know how Miss Platt likes me to be prompt.'

'No, Oscar,' said his mother wearily. 'I won't be late.' She gave Elisabeth a weak smile. 'I don't know where he gets it from,' she confided quietly.

'I see Mr Gribbon has replaced the broken paving slabs,' observed the child when his mother had departed. He inspected the path. 'I did mention it to him.'

'Thank you for your lovely poster, Oscar, and your poem,' said Elisabeth. 'It was a very nice thought.'

'My pleasure,' he replied, heading for the school, his small briefcase tucked under his arm.

In assembly that morning the children, silent and wary, sat cross-legged on the highly polished floor in the school hall as Elisabeth introduced herself and said how much she looked forward to getting to know everyone. She then described the changes that would be taking place. Later, as her class lined up outside the classroom door, she explained that she had placed name cards on the desks to show where children would sit and so that she could learn their names. The placing of each pupil was strategic: boy next to girl and the two potentially disruptive children—Malcolm Stubbins and Ernest Pocock—seated at the very front but well away from each other.

Malcolm Stubbins was, as Elisabeth expected, the first to raise an objection.

He slouched in his chair. 'Can't we sit with our pals?' he asked tetchily.

'Do call me "miss" when you speak to me,

138

Malcolm,' replied Elisabeth pleasantly. 'And sit up.'

The boy grimaced, shuffled forward and repeated the question.

'I asked if we could sit with our pals?' he asked, and then added loudly, 'Miss.'

'No, you can't,' replied Elisabeth. 'You can see your friends at break and lunchtimes, that is, of course, if you behave yourself and are not kept in. In the classroom you are here to work and I want no distractions.'

The boy muttered something.

'What did you say?' snapped Elisabeth.

'Nothing,' he said.

'I have asked you to call me "miss",' said Elisabeth, standing over him and looking him straight in the eyes. 'Please do so in future or you and I will fall out. Do I make myself clear, Malcolm?'

'Yes, miss,' he grumbled.

This was going to be a battle of wills, thought Elisabeth, but it was a battle she was determined to win.

*   *   *

'So, how have you liked your first day at Barton-in-the-Dale, Mrs Devine?' asked the school secretary. She had called into Elisabeth's classroom at the end of school.

'I've had a most pleasant day, thank you, Mrs Scrimshaw,' she replied. 'I think I am going to be very happy here.'

'I'm very pleased to hear it,' said the secretary. 'I have to say, I do like my office now that all the cabinets and drawers have been moved into the new staff-room. There wasn't the space to swing a cat before.'

'While I was teaching, was there a phone call from the Education Office?' Elisabeth asked. 'A Mr Nettles?'

'No, there's been no one,' replied the secretary.

'I was expecting a call. I rang him at lunchtime but there was no reply, and I left a message on his answering machine asking him to give me a ring. It said he was tied up.'

'They want to tie them up permanently at the Education Office, if you ask me,' observed Mrs Scrimshaw, pursing her lips. 'And he's one of the worst. He's about as much use as a chocolate fireguard is that Mr Nettles. He used to be in charge of school transport and made a pig's ear of that. Buses arriving late or not at all, and a right mix-up with the timetables. And you could never get hold of him. He was always in a meeting or tied up.'

'Well, I'll try again later,' said Elisabeth. 'You get off home, Mrs Scrimshaw.'

At the school office Elisabeth dialled the number of the Education Office.

'Hello.' It was a young woman's matter-of-fact voice.

'I'd like to speak to Mr Nettles, please.'

'He's tied up at the moment,' came the reply.

'When might he be free?'

'I've no idea. He's in a meeting.'

'I did leave a message asking him to give me a ring,' Elisabeth told the speaker. 'This is Mrs Devine, head teacher at Barton-in-the-Dale Primary School. I shall be here for the next hour, so if he could ring me, I should be very grateful. It is important.'

'I'll tell him,' said the young woman curtly and put down the receiver.

'Hello, miss.' Danny stood at the office door.

'Hello, Danny,' she replied. 'You should be getting off home.'

'I wanted to see you, miss.'

'Come in.' She sat on the end of the desk. 'Now what is it about?'

'Is it reight that Jamie's not comin' to this school no more, miss?'

'It is,' replied Elisabeth. 'His father thinks St Paul's will suit him better.'

'It won't.'

'Well, I am pleased you think he would be happier here,' said Elisabeth. 'I would like him to have stayed, but it's his father's decision to send him to another school and there's not really much I can do about that.'

'He dunt want to go,' said the boy.

'Did he tell you that?'

'Yeah, I saw 'im yesterday. We were at t'duckpond fishin' for sticklebacks and he said 'e weren't comin' back 'ere. 'E were really upset, miss.'

Elisabeth thought for a moment. 'James talks to you a lot, doesn't he, Danny?'

'Yea, I suppose 'e does,' replied the boy.

'Why doesn't he talk to anyone else, do you think?' she asked.

Danny shrugged. 'I dunt know, 'e just dunt. Jamie stopped talkin' to other people after 'is mum 'ad t'accident. 'E talks to his dad sometimes, but it's mainly me 'e talks to.'

'He must feel really comfortable with you,

141

Danny,' said Elisabeth. 'I guess he thinks of you as a very special friend.' The boy nodded and looked embarrassed. 'And James told you he doesn't want to go to another school, did he?'

'Yeah, 'e did, miss.'

'And has he told his father this?'

'No, miss, 'e dunt want to upset 'im. 'E thinks if 'e tells 'is dad it'll make 'im unhappy. 'E says 'is dad gets real sad these days. Sometimes 'e telled me 'is dad looks out o' t'window for ages and ages, starin' at nowt.'

'I see.'

'Will you speak to his dad then, miss?' asked the boy.

'It's difficult, Danny,' she replied.

'Why?'

'Well, you see, his father and I have had a bit of a disagreement. I don't think he will take any notice of what I say. He is determined that James will start at his new school when term starts there.'

''Asn't he started there yet then, miss?' asked Danny.

'I don't think so. St Paul's starts later than we do.'

'Then 'appen you could change his dad's mind before it's too late.'

'I doubt it,' Elisabeth told him. 'James's father's mind seems made up.'

'You could try, though. Will you try, miss?' The boy twiddled his hair nervously. 'Please.'

'All right, Danny,' she said, 'I'll try.'

*   *   *

Elisabeth called at the surgery on the way home.

142

She sat in the waiting room with a sneezing hay fever sufferer, a pale-looking woman with a tragic expression, an elderly man with a bent back, a whinging toddler and his harassed mother and Mrs Sloughthwaite.

'Hello, Mrs Devine,' said the shopkeeper, shuffling up the bench so Elisabeth could sit next to her. 'Not badly on your first day at school, I hope?'

'No,' Elisabeth replied. 'I'm fine.'

'There's a lot going around. Bugs and such like. Vicar's wife's took to her bed with it, I hear. Mind you, Mrs Atticus is of a weak constitution at the best of times. You're not coming down with something then?'

'No.'

Since she was getting nowhere extracting information about Elisabeth's health, Mrs Sloughthwaite changed the topic, never missing a chance to glean more news to channel around the village.

'And how's the cottage coming along?' she asked.

'Nearly finished,' Elisabeth told her. 'Mr Stainthorpe's done an excellent job. I'm very pleased with it.'

'And what's your first day at school been like?'

'It's been very good,' replied Elisabeth. 'I think I shall be very happy there.'

'A lot to do, I suppose?'

'Indeed.'

'I see Mr Gribbon has been hard at work sprucing up the place. I can't say as how I've ever seen him so industrial. Let's hope it lasts.'

'He's made a great difference,' Elisabeth told her.

'And I gather you've changed quite a bit around in the school already?'

'Yes, there have been one or two changes.'

'Mrs Pocock was in the shop telling me this afternoon. Her lad told her it's not like the old school. You'll have to keep your eye on him, by the way. Regular little tearaway is Ernest Pocock. And that Malcolm Stubbins is another. Nothing's safe on the counter when he's in my shop. Unfortunate-looking lad and no mistake, isn't he though? He could eat a tomato through a tennis racket with those teeth. He's the spit-and-image of his father. Buck teeth run in his family like that lad's nose. His father was a ne'er-do-well and left his mother for a mousy little woman who ran a boarding-house in Clayton. 'Course, the boy's mother can't cope and lets him get away with murder. I hope he's behaving himself for you. I know Miss Brakespeare had problems with him. Speaking of Miss Brakespeare, how does she like the changes?'

'She seems very happy with them,' said Elisabeth, wearying of the interrogation. 'You'll have to ask her when she comes into the shop.'

Mrs Sloughthwaite was quiet for a while, but it wasn't in her nature to keep silent for long. 'I'm sorry to hear that Dr Stirling's taking his son away.'

My goodness, thought Elisabeth, news travels fast in the village.

'Yes, so am I,' she replied, determined not to elaborate on events.

'Mrs Pocock was saying that at this rate there won't be any kiddies left to teach.'

'I don't think it's quite got to that stage yet, Mrs Sloughthwaite.'

'Let's hope not. It will be a sorry day if the village

144

school closes.'

'I don't think you need to worry on that score.' Elisabeth changed the subject. 'I hope you are not unwell.'

'I've been in bed with my kidneys,' the shopkeeper confided under her breath. 'They come and go. And then there's my swollen joints, amongst other things. Never been right since I fell off the ladder. I've been proper poorly in my time but you struggle on, don't you?' She winced. 'I'm a martyr to my joints. All that bending and stretching.' She lowered her voice to a stage whisper and pointed a finger downwards. 'And I've got downstairs problems.' She pointed discreetly. 'Dr Stirling reckons I'm a walking pathological marvel, way I carry on what with all my ailments.' She sniffed noisily before returning the conversation to the school. 'So, are you here to see Dr Stirling about—'

'Mrs Sloughthwaite,' the receptionist called. 'Doctor will see you now.'

'Oh, I'd better go,' said the shopkeeper, easing herself to her feet. 'I'll be seeing you again, no doubt, Mrs Devine.' With that, she waddled off in the direction of the consulting room.

Elisabeth had explained to the receptionist that she would wait until Dr Stirling had seen all his patients, as this was a personal matter of some importance.

Eventually the waiting room emptied and Elisabeth was told by the receptionist that the doctor was now free to see her.

'Ah, Mrs Devine,' said Dr Stirling, managing a small smile. He rose from his desk. 'Do come in.'

Elisabeth noticed again how neglectful he was of

145

his appearance. His hair had been combed untidily and it was clear he hadn't shaved that day. His linen jacket was creased and had a button missing and his shirt had not been ironed properly.

'Now,' he said, 'what seems to be the problem?'

'I'm here about James,' Elisabeth told him. The mention of his son's name resulted in a change to the doctor's countenance. He inhaled noisily, scratched his tousled hair and tapped his fingers impatiently on the top of his desk. 'Look, Mrs Devine, I have made my decision. If you are here to ask me to let James stay at the school, you are wasting your time. I appreciate that you are losing another pupil, which is distressing for you, and that you want to keep as many as possible at Barton, but as I thought I had explained to you, I feel St Paul's will offer my son a better education and one more suited to his—' he struggled to find the word, 'to his situation.'

'Have you asked your son if he wants to go to St Paul's, Dr Stirling?' asked Elisabeth.

He sighed and continued to tap his fingers on the desk. 'James and I have discussed it,' he replied, 'and he sees the sense in what I have decided, that the move is in his best interests.'

'I don't think he does,' said Elisabeth.

Dr Stirling bridled. 'Excuse me?'

'I said I don't think James wants to move school.'

'And how would you know that?' he asked.

'Because his friend, his only friend and the one he speaks to the most, told me so.'

'This would be the young man who lives in the caravan with his grandfather?'

'That's right,' she replied. 'Danny seems to be the only one in the school James speaks to, and he

146

confides in him.'

'Look, Mrs Devine, I appreciate your interest—' began the doctor.

'No, Dr Stirling, I don't think you appreciate my interest at all,' she interrupted. 'You are assuming, quite wrongly, that I am here to persuade you to let James stay at the school for my own selfish reasons, that I don't wish to lose yet another pupil, particularly the son of the local GP who is influential in the village and a member of the governing body.'

'As I told you, Mrs Devine,' said the doctor, his jaw set firm, 'it is my intention to resign from the governing body at the next meeting. I sympathise with your situation, but I repeat that I must do what I feel is right for my son.' A small muscle jumped in his cheek.

'If I thought James would be happier at another school,' Elisabeth told him, 'I would be the first to suggest it, because, believe it or not, I do have the child's best interests at heart, as I have for all the children in my care. In my opinion, a move to another school, one to which he doesn't wish to go, could set him back. Dr Stirling, your son has a problem that you seem unable to accept. I ask you—'

'Mrs Devine,' the doctor said, a slight tremble in his voice, 'we have had this conversation before. As I see it, I am doing the best for my son. James is to start at St Paul's in a couple of weeks and that is the end of the matter. Now please, please, let it rest.'

Elisabeth sat there for a moment looking at the sad, distressed figure who refused to meet her eyes and suddenly felt desperately sorry for the man. He had lost a wife he dearly loved and had a son with emotional problems; he was living a cheerless, empty life. If anyone was in need of a doctor's help, it was the man sitting before her.

'Very well, Dr Stirling,' said Elisabeth softly. 'Thank you for seeing me. As I said to you before, I genuinely hope that James will be happy in his new school.'

CHAPTER EIGHT

It was early Friday morning when Elisabeth, sitting opposite Mrs Scrimshaw in the school office, managed at long last to speak to Mr Nettles. When she mentioned that she had left several messages for him requesting that he call her back, he sounded dismissive.

'Yes, yes, Mrs Devine, I do appreciate that you wished to speak to me but the first week of a new school term is always a very busy time and I have had many pressing matters to deal with.'

'This is something of a pressing matter, Mr Nettles,' she reminded him.

'Well, what can I do for you?' he asked.

'There are quite a few things I would like to discuss,' Elisabeth told him.

'Well, we in the Education Office are here to help in any way we can,' he replied in a patronising voice.

'I am pleased to hear it,' said Elisabeth, 'because there are, as I am sure you are aware, a number of things in the school which need to change. I have had the opportunity of studying the inspectors' report and it does not make very positive reading.'

'No, it came as quite a shock to us at the Education Office,' he replied.

'One wonders,' said Elisabeth, 'why the problems were not picked up earlier.'

Mr Nettles was rather annoyed by the comment and the implied criticism.

'You will understand, Mrs Devine,' he said, defensively, 'that there are a great number of schools in the county to deal with and we are a small staff here at the Education Office. Furthermore, the former head teacher was not the easiest person to get on with. She never attended any meetings and made it difficult to gain entry to the school.'

Elisabeth could have reminded him that education officers cannot be barred from visiting any school, that they have right of entry by law, but she said nothing. 'I can assure you that this will not be the case with me. I welcome and indeed I would appreciate any help, support and advice you may wish to give.'

'I am pleased to hear it, Mrs Devine,' he said, somewhat mollified. 'Now, how may I be of help?'

'Has the Chairman of Governors been in touch with you?' asked Elisabeth.

'I did speak to Major Neville-Gravitas after the Education Sub-committee meeting earlier in the week,' he told her.

'So you are aware of the requirements that I set out in my letter to him. I sent a copy to the Education Office for your information. I hope you received it.'

'Yes, yes, I did receive your letter.' He remembered that he had put it at the bottom of the pile.

'Then you will be aware of the refurbishments required and the equipment which I need, in particular new tables and chairs.'

'I have considered your request regarding the tables, and the thing is, Mrs Devine, it might prove difficult, in the present economic climate, to meet it at present.'

'Why is that?' Elisabeth asked.

'As you will no doubt be aware, we have to make savings, and expenditure of this nature needs to be budgeted for. Indeed, the Education Sub-committee meeting this week was to discuss the proposed savings. It will be lean times for us all, I am afraid.'

'So other schools in the authority have to make do with desks which are old and unsuitable like the ones at this school, is that what you are saying, Mr Nettles?' Elisabeth asked.

'Miss Sowerbutts liked the old-fashioned desks,' Mr Nettles told her.

'So the major told me, and I told him I do not,' said Elisabeth, 'and neither did the school inspectors and the sooner they are replaced the better. Growing children should not be expected to sit at small, old, lidded desks. I am sure I don't need to remind you that the inspectors also made comments about the need for some renovations in the school—to sort out the damp and replace the linoleum in the corridor—and the need for more up-to-date reading material.'

'I have read the report, Mrs Devine,' said Mr Nettles, 'and these things take time and money.'

'And while you are on the line,' said Elisabeth, 'perhaps you can explain to me why the teachers at this school are on temporary contracts?'

150

'Ah, well, Miss Sowerbutts requested that, so she could be entirely sure they were suitable.'

'Mr Nettles,' said Elisabeth, getting increasingly irritated by the evasive answers, 'Miss Sowerbutts is no longer the head teacher here, I am, and I would like the contracts made permanent. All the governors were unanimous at the meeting, which you were unable to attend, in supporting this.'

'That too might prove a little tricky in these stringent economic times,' the education officer told her.

Elisabeth took a deep breath. 'So, Mr Nettles, let me get this clear. You are not going to provide me with the necessary resources, you are ignoring the inspectors' recommendations and you do not intend to make the teachers' contracts permanent. Is that what you are saying? Because if it is, I do need to know this so I can inform my governors, the parents and the school inspectorate.'

'No, no,' replied Mr Nettles, clearly rattled. 'I am not saying that at all. I think this matter needs to be discussed at the next full governors' meeting.'

'Which will be when?'

'Generally the school governors meet a few weeks into the new term,' he told her. 'I guess it will be some time in mid-October.'

'Can't we meet before then?' asked Elisabeth. 'It seems to me that things need to be sorted out as soon as possible. Perhaps I could call a meeting myself?'

'No, no, Mrs Devine, please don't do that,' he said quickly. 'Extraordinary meetings are only held in exceptional circumstances. I'm sure I do not need to remind you that governors are very busy people. I suggest you leave it to the Education

Department to convene meetings. I am sure you can wait a few weeks.'

'I see,' said Elisabeth, getting the feeling that the man was being deliberately evasive.

'And you will be attending the meeting this time, Mr Nettles?' she enquired.

'I shall endeavour to do so,' he replied.

'And in the interim you will seriously consider these requests?'

'Indeed. Now, I do have a number of urgent matters to deal with.'

'Until the next governors' meeting, then,' said Elisabeth, putting down the receiver.

'I did say that you would get nowhere with that man,' observed Mrs Scrimshaw. 'He's a waste of space. You know, Mrs Devine, I think there is more to this than meets the eye. A few tables wouldn't cost anything, and I bet none of the teachers in the other schools are on temporary contracts.'

'Yes, that had occurred to me,' replied Elisabeth. 'I have my suspicions that there is another agenda here.'

She was soon to discover that her suspicions were warranted.

*   *   *

'I will not tolerate fighting in this school!' Elisabeth leaned over her desk, her nose a few inches from the boys' faces. It was the following Monday morning and the two miscreants stood before her desk. 'Is that clear?'

'Yes, miss,' said Danny.

'Malcolm?' the head teacher asked sharply, looking at the large, brown-faced boy with the

152

tightly curled hair and the sour expression.

'Yes, miss,' he muttered. 'It was him what started it. I didn't do nothing.'

'Be quiet!' snapped Elisabeth. 'Just keep your mouth closed. I will find out soon enough what the cause of this argument was. Not only could you have hurt yourselves, but Miss Brakespeare could have been seriously injured.'

The deputy head teacher was at that moment in the staff-room, sipping a cup of sweet tea with a trembling hand. It had been a frightening ordeal for her, as she explained to Miss Wilson. The young teacher had found it difficult to keep a straight face, for Miss Brakespeare, hair stringy and wet, looked as if she had emerged from a pond and was making the little spat sound like a scene of carnage. On playground duty that morning break, the deputy head teacher had attempted to separate the two boys pushing and punching each other and could have very well ended up in the middle of the mêlée had not Mr Gribbon come to her assistance. However, his intervention with a bucket of soapy water, which he had been using to clean the toilets, had not been entirely successful. Not only had Miss Brakespeare suffered a blow to her arm from one of the boys, and the loss of her mother's amber beads, which had been scattered far and wide in the playground, but she too, along with the combatants, had received a thorough soaking with dirty water reeking of disinfectant. In a fraught state, she had been taken to the staff-room on Miss Wilson's arm to calm down.

'The silly man made it worse,' she was telling Miss Wilson, 'throwing a bucket of dirty water all over me as well as the boys. I'm soaked to the skin and smelling like a lavatory.'

Something of an exaggeration, thought Miss Wilson, observing the damp dress her colleague was wearing, but she nodded sympathetically and stifled a smile.

Back in Elisabeth's classroom the cross-examination continued.

'We will start with you, Malcolm,' said Elisabeth. 'What have you got to say for yourself?'

'It was him what started it,' grumbled the boy. 'I didn't do nothing. He told me to put my hand in his bag and when I did, it bit me.' He held up his index finger.

'What bit you?'

'His ferret.'

'You brought your ferret to school, Danny?' asked the head teacher.

'Yes, miss,' he said quietly.

'Why did you bring your ferret to school?'

''E were a bit under t'weather, miss.'

'And it bit my finger,' huffed the other boy, 'and hung on. It bloody hurt.'

'I beg your pardon?' exclaimed Elisabeth.

'It were right painful,' complained the boy, in a voice hardly audible.

''E had no need to hurt him, miss,' said Danny. ''E was strangling 'im. If 'e 'ad kept still, Ferdie would 'ave let go.'

'Just a moment,' said Elisabeth. 'You told Malcolm to put his hand in your bag, did you, Danny?'

'No miss,' replied the boy. 'I didn't. Malcolm thought there were some sweets in there and grabbed mi bag and run off wi' it. Then when 'e put 'is 'and inside, 'e frightened Ferdie and 'e bit 'im.

'E were really rough trying to pull 'im off and that's when I 'thumped 'im and 'e thumped mi back, so I thumped 'im again. Then Miss Brakespeare comes runnin' up and tries to stop us and Mr Gribbon chucks a bucket o' watter ovver us.'

'That's not what happened,' mumbled the other boy, staring down mulishly at his feet.

'It appears to me that you are both as bad as each other,' said Elisabeth. 'Firstly, Danny, you should not have brought your ferret to school. Secondly, you had no business hitting Malcolm and he had no business retaliating. Thirdly, you, Malcolm, should not have gone into somebody else's bag, and fourthly, neither of you should have come to blows. I want you to listen to me carefully: there will be no more fighting. Is that clear?'

'Yes, miss,' said Danny.

'Yes, miss,' the other boy mumbled.

'Now you will both go to Miss Brakespeare's room and apologise to her. Go on, off you go and I will see you both again at the end of school.'

It was later that day that Elisabeth learnt the truth. Chardonnay had seen the whole incident and collaborated Danny's story.

'It were Malcolm Stubbins what started it, miss,' she told Elisabeth. 'He's always nicking people's sweets. He grabbed Danny's bag and ran off with it.' She scratched her scalp and gave a self-satisfied smile. 'I'm glad the ferret bit him. It'll teach him not to nick other people's sweets.'

As the other children made their way home at the end of the day, Elisabeth saw the two boys again.

'I do not like children who don't tell the truth,' she told a glowering Malcolm Stubbins. 'Danny did not tell you to put your hand into his bag as you claimed, did he?'

'Yeah, he did,' replied the boy, stubbornly.

'Please don't make it worse by telling lies, Malcolm,' said Elisabeth. 'I have asked the other children who saw it happen and they all confirm what Danny has said. You ran off with his bag, and perhaps you have learnt a hard lesson not to go into other people's things. I believe you like to take other children's sweets, which will stop. Danny is not blameless in all this either, because he hit you, which he should not have done. Now I am telling you both that should anything like this happen again you will be in deep trouble, and I shall be having words with your mother, Malcolm, and your grandfather, Danny. As a punishment you will both spend the breaks and lunchtimes next week picking up litter and doing various jobs around the school under the direction of Mr Gribbon. Is that clear?'

'Yes, miss,' replied Danny.

'Yes miss,' muttered the other boy.

*   *   *

It wasn't long, of course, before news of the fight circulated in the village.

'There were no fights in the school when I was head teacher,' announced Miss Sowerbutts in the village store the following afternoon. She was sharing her observations with another customer. 'I prided myself on keeping very good discipline in the school. Children did as they were told and I set clear parameters when I was in charge. Of course, all these modern methods, where children are given free rein and allowed to say and do what they want,

156

undermine the teacher's authority. It was a sad day when they got rid of the strap. Give some children an inch and they take a mile.'

'Well, I suppose boys will be boys,' observed Mrs Widowson, 'although I have to say some of the carryings-on of young people these days leave a lot to be desired.'

'Spare the rod and spoil the child—and there is a whole lot of truth in that,' said Miss Sowerbutts. 'I would certainly not have tolerated such behaviour.' She was clearly revelling in the news that there were problems at the school.

Mrs Sloughthwaite, listening to the diatribe from behind her counter, didn't like Miss Sowerbutts with her preening self-satisfaction and she didn't take to being lectured at either. What a narrow-minded, self-righteous woman she was. With her thin beaky face and protuberant eyes she reminded the shopkeeper of the stone faces projecting from the gutter of the church. The woman rarely called into the shop and when she did she complained about the produce and bought few items. She was one customer the shopkeeper would not miss if she took her custom elsewhere. Mrs Devine, on the other hand, was friendly and good-humoured and did all her shopping at the village store. She had made a real effort to be part of the community.

'Oh, you know what they say, Miss Sowerbutts,' she said, deliberately being provocative, 'a bit of rough and tumble is to be expected in growing lads. My Nigel was always getting into scraps when he was a boy. It's part of growing up, and you know yourself what Malcolm Stubbins is like. From what I've heard, when you were head teacher he was always outside your room for misbehaving, wasn't he?'

Miss Sowerbutts listened with cold mechanical interest and didn't deign to answer. 'And all these changes,' she grumbled to no one in particular. 'I'm told the school is not the same. Everything's been changed. I feel sorry for poor Miss Brakespeare, having to endure it.' She purred with satisfaction.

'She seems very happy,' remarked Mrs Sloughthwaite, smiling indulgently. 'She called in the shop last week and she looks years younger. The changes the new head teacher is making seem to have gone down very well with her by all accounts.'

'I very much doubt it,' scoffed Miss Sowerbutts. She wore the expression a stranger might mistake for a smile. 'And I hear the doctor has taken his son away,' she remarked, clearly rejoicing in the bad news. Mrs Sloughthwaite saw something like triumph flash across her customer's face. It was strange, she often thought, how the misfortunes of others brought solace to sad and gloomy people like Miss Sowerbutts. 'Well, of course, that doesn't surprise me in the least,' the former head teacher added.

Mrs Sloughthwaite folded her dimpled arms under her substantial bosom and pictured the silent, pasty little boy who sometimes came into the shop with his father. 'I suppose Dr Stirling reckons the lad needs more specialist help, what with his communication problem, which the school can't— and didn't—provide.' There was a heavy emphasis on the word 'didn't'.

'The boy was perfectly happy when I was head teacher,' retorted Miss Sowerbutts, with casual disparagement.

'Well, I don't suppose you knew, Miss Sowerbutts,' said the shopkeeper, with the fixed smile she had perfected over the years, 'him never speaking a word.' She chuckled inwardly at the evident consternation that her words had caused.

'I'll just have the tea-bags,' announced the former head teacher, looking sharply at the shopkeeper and placing the exact amount of money on the counter.

'And are you sure I can't interest you in a Venetian selection box?' asked the shopkeeper, smiling and knowing full well, as she had been told, that the woman did not have a sweet tooth.

*   *   *

Miss Sowerbutts decided to call in on Miss Brakespeare later that day. She was keen to learn first hand about all the changes that had taken place at the school. She found her former colleague in the small garden to the front of her cottage, sitting in the late afternoon sunshine marking exercise books. She was dressed in a bright summer frock and pink cardigan, in contrast to her visitor, who wore an outfit better suited to midwinter. Miss Sowerbutts noted grudgingly that her former deputy looked remarkably relaxed considering the ordeal she had been through. She rather imagined that the woman would be in a nervous state.

'I just thought I'd call, Miriam,' she said, 'and see how you are.'

'Oh hello,' said Miss Brakespeare.

Miss Sowerbutts dusted the garden chair with her hand and sat down. She noticed that there was something of a change in her former colleague. She seemed somehow brighter and more self-assured, and there was something different in her expression.

Miss Brakespeare closed the exercise book she had been marking and looked at the former head teacher. Even on such a mild September evening, she thought, Miss Sowerbutts was still dressed in her usual drab pleated tweed skirt and that awful coat the colour of gravy and was wearing that silly knitted hat like a tea-cosy.

'So how are you getting on?' asked Miss Sowerbutts in an overly solicitous and kindly manner. She didn't wait for an answer, but then, thought Miss Brakespeare, she rarely did. 'I have heard some very distressing news. I believe you were attacked.'

'Attacked!' exclaimed Miss Brakespeare. 'Stuff and nonsense. I tried to stop a fight, that was all, and got a bit wet in the process. It was the silly caretaker throwing water all over us that made it worse. I have to own I was a bit upset at the time, but when I look back it was rather amusing.'

'Amusing!' exclaimed Miss Sowerbutts. 'Hardly amusing, to be assaulted and nearly drowned. What was this fight about?'

'Young Danny Stainthorpe had brought his ferret to school and it bit Malcolm Stubbins. It couldn't have chosen a better victim. He lies easier than he breathes, that boy, and was such a pain when he was in my class.' She paused. 'As you well know.'

'What do you mean *was* in your class?' asked Miss Sowerbutts, staring at her former colleague uncomprehendingly. 'He still is, is he not?'

'Oh no, Mrs Devine teaches the oldest children now and he's in her form.'

'She teaches?' Miss Sowerbutts exclaimed, incomprehension creeping across her face.

'It works very well,' explained Miss Brakespeare, nonchalantly. 'We've split up the older children. I have a smaller class and far less preparation and marking to do, and my classroom is much more spacious now. I also don't have Malcolm Stubbins and Ernest Pocock to contend with. Yes, it's worked out really well.'

Miss Sowerbutts gave a sniff of disapproval. 'It would not have happened in my day,' she announced stiffly. There was more than a hint of irritation in her voice.

'What wouldn't?' asked Miss Brakespeare. Her face was impassive.

'A head teacher teaching.' She sniffed again self-righteously.

'No, I don't suppose it would,' replied Miss Brakespeare. She gave a quiet little smile. 'Of course, you never taught, did you?' There was something rather pointed in that remark, thought Miss Sowerbutts, and completely out of character for this diffident little woman with whom she used to work. Miss Brakespeare would never have spoken to her in that tone of voice when she was her deputy head teacher. However, she let it pass.

'In my opinion,' stated Miss Sowerbutts, pompously, 'a head teacher's role is not to teach, it is to lead and to manage and deal with problems which may arise.'

Miss Brakespeare was about to reply but hesitated. It seemed to her to be the moment to speak and then she thought it was not. She decided

161

it would be cruel to remind her former colleague of the inspectors' report, in which the head teacher's management and leadership skills had been judged to be poor. She wanted to tell this self-important and cynical woman, frosty and buttoned-up as she was on a warm afternoon, and whom she had put up with for more years than she cared to recall, that she found the changes in the school liberating and had never felt happier, but she refrained from doing so and merely remarked: 'Mrs Devine manages to do that as well.' The traces of the smile remained at the corners of her mouth.

'Do what?'

'Teach and manage the school.'

'I see,' said Miss Sowerbutts, annoyed by the inference. She smiled grimly. 'Well, I am pleased you find the new arrangements are to your liking, Miriam. Let us hope that you remain as content.' She could not resist a final observation. 'Of course, things might very well alter if many more children leave. Dr Stirling's decision to move his son will, no doubt, have further repercussions. I imagine that, unlike you, he is far from happy with the new arrangements and, of course, I guess other parents will feel the same as he.' A triumphant smile was insinuated on her face.

'I think it's time I was getting Mother's tea,' said Miss Brakespeare.

*   *   *

Wednesday after school found Mrs Stubbins in Elisabeth's classroom. Malcolm's mother smoothed an eyebrow with a little finger and shuffled uncomfortably in her seat. She was sitting wedged sideways on in one of the small desks used by the children and looked a comical character, this round, shapeless woman with bright frizzy dyed ginger hair, an impressive set of double chins and immense hips. Her mouth was turned downwards as if in perpetual hostility.

'Well, he says you're picking on him,' she told Elisabeth angrily.

'He would say that, wouldn't he, Mrs Stubbins?' replied Elisabeth calmly.

'How do you mean?'

'Malcolm never sees himself in the wrong. It is always someone else's fault.'

'He told me—'

Elisabeth held up a hand and stopped the woman in her tracks. 'One moment please, Mrs Stubbins. Now that you are here, and I have to say I am very pleased to see you, there are one or two things I have to say about your son. Malcolm can be a disruptive and a difficult boy, and what is more, he is lazy.'

The woman looked dumbfounded. She opened her mouth to speak but fell silent.

'He doesn't like to work and will not apply himself,' continued Elisabeth, 'or do as he is told, and he disturbs the other children. His behaviour is unacceptable.'

'Well, that's not what he says,' blustered the woman. 'He says as how you're always picking on him and you called him a liar.'

'Mrs Stubbins, do you believe everything your son tells you?' asked Elisabeth.

The woman shifted in the desk, which creaked beneath her weight. 'Not always, no, but I believe him when he says you pick on him and that he was

163

attacked by a savage rodent. He could have got rabies or anything.'

'It was a ferret,' Elisabeth told her, 'and if Malcolm had kept his hands out of another pupil's bag he would not have been bitten.'

'Well, that's not what my Malcolm says,' protested the woman in a sudden flush of anger.

'Do you want your son to be a success in life, Mrs Stubbins?' asked Elisabeth. 'Do you hope he will get good results in his school examinations, secure a good job which he will enjoy doing, grow up into a polite, well-adjusted and caring young man and to be a credit to you?'

''Course I do, but he says you're picking on him. Soon as you started here he says you've had it in for him.'

'Yes, you have told me several times,' said Elisabeth. 'Well, I am telling you I am not in the habit of picking on children. I expect them to work hard and enjoy school but I also expect them to do as they are told and behave themselves. If they do not then they must face the consequences, like your son.'

'He's not happy here,' said the boy's mother, 'not since you started. He says you won't let him sit with his friends and you're always picking on him. He liked it better in Miss Brakespeare's class.'

Elisabeth could have told the woman that he liked it better in Miss Brakespeare's class because he was allowed to do as he pleased. She remained calm and motionless. 'Well, as long as your son is in this school,' she said, 'he will behave himself.'

'If that's your attitude,' replied Mrs Stubbins, 'I don't think he will be staying in the school for much longer.' She smoothed the eyebrow again and creaked in the desk. 'I thought I'd speak to you first and see what you have to say, but I can't say as how I'm pleased with what I've just heard. You've done nothing but criticise my Malcolm since I sat down. So, I've decided to move him. Tomorrow I shall go and see Mr Richardson, the headmaster at Urebank, and get a place for my Malcolm at his school. Quite a lot of parents have sent their kids there, as you well know, and I don't doubt there'll be others following. I've heard that Dr Stirling for one has taken his son away, so he can't be happy with the way things are going here no more than I can. I thought I'd wait and see how things went on with a new head teacher because I never particularly liked the last one, but I've not been happy with the way you've treated my Malcolm, picking on him and all.'

Over the years Elisabeth had learnt, when dealing with antagonistic parents, the simple technique of staring until he or she became silent. It was a powerful method of overcoming opposition.

If the woman expected her to be placatory and ask her to reconsider, to plead with her to keep her son at the school, she was very much mistaken.

'Then there is nothing more to say, Mrs Stubbins,' she said, rising from her chair. 'I hope that Malcolm settles at his new school and that no one picks on him there.' The hint of sarcasm in the tone of her reply was not lost on Mrs Stubbins, who, with a stony expression on her round red face, eased herself out of the desk and left the classroom, brushing past Mrs Scrimshaw on her way out.

'That woman,' said the school secretary. 'You can see where her Malcolm gets his bad manners from. Talk about rude.'

165

'What is it, Mrs Scrimshaw?' asked Elisabeth, sighing. 'Not another problem, I hope.'

'Chardonnay's mother's just phoned,' said the school secretary, 'Her daughter's got nits.'

*   *   *

Elisabeth sat in the school office on Friday afternoon when all the children had gone home, catching up on paperwork. The last week had been a long and dispiriting one. On the positive side, the children in her class had been attentive and interested and had produced some very good work, and she was getting on with her colleagues, but such positives were overshadowed by other thoughts that continued to prey on her mind. There had been the fight, of course, and the difficult interview with the angry parent, and there was the niggling feeling that there was far more to the prevarications from Mr Nettles about the new equipment and the teachers' contracts. Mrs Scrimshaw's observation that there was more to this than met the eye kept recurring in her mind.

Malcolm Stubbins had been particularly well-behaved that day and had said very little, but Mrs Robertshaw had overheard him in the playground at morning break, announcing gleefully to anyone who would listen that he wouldn't be picking up any litter or doing any other jobs for the head teacher the following week because he was moving to another school on Monday. He had been somewhat deflated when his revelation had been greeted with cheers from the other pupils. The information that the boy would be leaving had delighted Miss Brakespeare, of course, but not Elisabeth. She was saddened that a parent should wish to send her child to another school, for she knew that with a little more time and a firm hand the boy's behaviour would improve. She had come across Malcolms before; children who had no strong father figure to guide them, who got their own way at home and were indulged by their mothers, boys poor at their schoolwork and disliked by the other children. Elisabeth guessed that beneath Malcolm's bluster and impudence there was a boy who needed help.

CHAPTER NINE

The telephone rang.

'Hello.'

'Mrs Devine?'

'Yes.'

'This is Robin Richardson here,' came a cheerful voice down the line. 'I'm the headmaster at Urebank Primary School in the next village. I thought I might catch you before you departed for the weekend.'

'Good afternoon, Mr Richardson,' replied Elisabeth.

'I just thought I'd give you a call to see how you are settling in.'

'That's very thoughtful of you,' said Elisabeth. 'I'm settling in really well, thank you.'

'Good, good. I know it must be a little daunting taking the helm at a new school, so please don't hesitate to call upon me if I can give any help or advice. I've been headmaster here now for three years and, even if I say so myself, I run a pretty tight ship and have a lot of useful contacts in the Education Department. I should be only too happy to give you a few tips on how to handle difficult governors and demanding parents and those visiting school inspectors who bedevil our lives. Speaking of inspectors, I guess after their critical report at Barton there is much to do.'

'Yes, there is,' replied Elisabeth. She didn't like the sound of this condescending man.

'Of course, you will discover that being a head teacher is very different from being deputy head. It is a lonely, demanding and often frustrating job that we do and the buck always stops with us. I always say that if a school is attacked, it's the head teacher who bleeds.' He chuckled at his own witticism. 'Where were you deputy head teacher then?'

'I wasn't a deputy head teacher,' Elisabeth told him. 'I was head teacher at a large inner city school prior to moving here.'

'Really? I didn't know that,' he replied, rather taken aback. 'You were a head teacher then?'

'Yes, I was the head teacher there for four years,' Elisabeth told him.

'This will be something of a change for you, then.'

'Yes, it will be something of a change,' Elisabeth replied, 'but I am enjoying it so far.'

'I'm pleased to hear it,' said Mr Richardson.

'So, I have a pretty good idea how to handle governors and parents and those at the Education Office,' she told him amiably. 'But thank you all the same for the offer.'

'No problem,' he said. The arrogance had disappeared from his voice. 'I did read the report,'

168

he said, 'and I must say that the leadership and management at the school came in for heavy criticism. Your predecessor, I gather, was extremely angry.'

'Yes, I believe so.'

'Of course, Miss Sowerbutts was of a different age,' he continued. 'I don't wish to speak out of turn, but she harked back to a golden age when bobbies walked the beat, people stood up for the national anthem and children did as they were told. Of course, she could be very difficult at times, rather remote and unapproachable and not the most accommodating of people. She never attended head teacher meetings or went on courses. I have to admit our relationship was rather strained. Some would say she was a rather autistic character, cool and distant and subject to quite angry outbursts.'

'Mr Richardson,' said Elisabeth, her hand tightening on the receiver, 'in my experience autism does not mean cool and distant, and not all autistic people are subject to angry outbursts. It is a condition with a wide spectrum. No two autistic people are alike. In my experience they can be warm and affectionate and most accommodating.'

'Yes, yes, of course they can,' he said quickly. Mr Richardson was not a man who liked to be put in his place, and his voice betrayed his irritation. 'I was using the term in a generic sense.' There was a silence. 'Actually, while I'm on the phone, Mrs Devine, I would like to have a word with you about another matter.'

I guessed as much, thought Elisabeth. 'Is it about Malcolm Stubbins?' she asked, knowing full well that it was.

'As a matter of fact it is,' he replied. 'I have had

a request from his mother. She wants her son to come to my school here at Urebank. Mrs Stubbins came to see me yesterday and wishes young Malcolm to start on Monday.'

'Yes,' said Elisabeth, 'she mentioned that she was hoping to send him to your school.'

'I gather she had something of a difference with you. I didn't go into all the ins and outs of why she wants to move the boy,' said Mr Richardson, 'but it appears that she feels her son will be better suited at my school.'

'I think she may be right,' replied Elisabeth.

'Really?' He was clearly startled by that response.

'I think you might possibly be able to cater for Malcolm's needs better than we can,' she told him. 'Maybe a fresh start will be good for him.'

'I see,' said Mr Richardson. 'We will, of course, do the very best for him.' There was another moment's silence. 'I have to admit, Mrs Devine, that I find the situation of these departures of children from your school somewhat embarrassing. I want to assure you that in no way do I encourage it. This is the tenth pupil who has come to my school from Barton over the last year. I am sure it must be quite distressing for you and your teachers losing so many children.' She could visualise the smug face at the other end of the line. 'Yes indeed, it must be quite upsetting.'

'I'm disappointed, of course, Mr Richardson,' replied Elisabeth with forced cheerfulness in her voice, 'but once I've established myself and got things moving in the right direction here, I hope to stem the flow. One has to accept that parents have the right to send their children to another school if they so wish.'

'Yes, indeed,' said the headmaster. 'I have to admit that I don't particularly like it myself, but that is the situation we are in. It's the world of parent-power. I try to dissuade them when they come to me wanting to move their children to my school, but if they are insistent what can I do?'

You can start by not putting advertisements in the local paper advertising your school, Elisabeth thought to herself, recalling her conversation with Mrs Robertshaw.

'Are you still there?' he asked.

'Yes, I'm still here.'

'I was just saying that if a parent wishes to move a child from one school to another there is little one can do about it.'

'No, there isn't,' agreed Elisabeth.

'Exactly so,' he replied. 'I just thought as a courtesy I would let you know.'

'That was very thoughtful of you, Mr Richardson,' Elisabeth told him.

He appeared oblivious of the sarcasm in her voice and cleared his throat. 'I suppose if your numbers decrease any more the Education Committee will have to consider whether or not it is viable to keep the school open. I do so hope that they don't decide to close Barton.' When Elisabeth didn't reply, he continued. 'I don't suppose you have heard anything?'

'No, I haven't,' replied Elisabeth.

'That's good to hear,' the headmaster remarked unconvincingly. 'It's just that I have heard rumours. Probably nothing to get too concerned about. Well, it's been good talking to you, Mrs Devine. Do come and have a look around my school if you have the

171

time. We've got quite a few exciting things going on here at the moment. By the way, Mrs Stubbins tells me young Malcolm is a very good footballer.'

'Amongst other things,' said Elisabeth.

She thumped down the receiver. Odious man, she thought, with his 'my school this' and 'my school that'. Mrs Robertshaw was quite right about him. Elisabeth stared out of the office window for a moment. So that was that why the Chairman of Governors and the education officer had been so evasive about expending money on the equipment, and the reason for the temporary contracts. That was why Mr Nettles was eager not to have a governors' meeting early in the term. They were intent on closing the school. They'd probably known that when they had appointed her. She could feel the blood rising to her face. Well, if that was their intention they had another think coming. She would fight them all the way.

Walking back to her classroom Elisabeth was surprised to see the deputy head teacher still at her desk.

'Friday afternoon and you're still here?' she said.

'I just wanted to finish off a bit of work,' replied Miss Brakespeare. 'The material you gave me on the Vikings to try with the children went down a treat and I've got some lovely writing. Oh, and those new books for the classroom library are very welcome.'

'You seem very happy in your work.'

'I am,' replied Miss Brakespeare. 'It's been so much easier with the smaller class and the children are better behaved without a certain unruly element to distract them. I wish Malcolm Stubbins' mother had moved her son to another school before now.

He was such a thorn in my side was that boy, always answering back and refusing to do his work. I didn't tell you, but when the inspectors were in school he was determined to be difficult.'

'I thought he was away during the week of inspection,' said Elisabeth innocently, recalling what Chardonnay had told her.

'No, no, he came in,' said Miss Brakespeare. 'I prayed he wouldn't but he showed up as cheeky and disruptive as ever. When he was asked by one of the inspectors, a very frightening-looking man in a black suit called Mr Steel, what he was doing he told him to "Bugger off!"'

'Oh dear,' said Elisabeth shaking her head.

'He was outside Miss Sowerbutts' room for the rest of the day. So good riddance to the boy, I say. The school will be a lot better off without him.'

'I reckon with a bit more time we could have sorted that young man out and got him to behave himself,' said Elisabeth.

'I will be interested to learn how the teachers at Urebank cope with him,' said Miss Brakespeare, a smug smile on her lips. 'I freely admit I found him very difficult. I dreaded coming into school some days. And I can't say that Miss Sowerbutts was that much help in that direction.'

It was the first time Elisabeth had heard her colleague speak critically of the former head teacher and it had quite a cheering effect. When she had started at the school she had prepared herself for Miss Brakespeare and the staff to constantly remind her that the former head teacher used to do things in a certain way and that they would be resistant to change. She had assumed wrongly, for her predecessor was rarely mentioned, and if she was it was never in a particularly favourable light. Furthermore, the staff had embraced the changes willingly.

'Miss Sowerbutts often used to make the Stubbins boy stand outside her door when he misbehaved,' continued Miss Brakespeare, 'which he was quite happy doing because he got out of doing any work. He could also be very insolent when he spoke to her. Once he wrote something extremely rude in spray paint on the back wall of the school which took Mr Gribbon a full morning to remove. Of course the boy denied it and it couldn't be proved, but I knew it was him because the other boys in the class could spell "bitch".'

Elisabeth gave a small smile. 'Well, let us hope no more parents decide to take their children away.'

'They won't,' said Miss Brakespeare. She touched Elisabeth's arm. 'You know, Mrs Devine, you've made a great difference to the school in the short time you've been here. It's a happier place. The children are happier now and the staff are too. You've been a tonic.'

'Thank you,' Elisabeth said. She could feel tears pricking her eyes. 'After a long dispiriting day I can really do with that encouragement.' She thought for a moment. 'I think they want to close the school.'

'Close the school,' Miss Brakespeare repeated. 'Stuff and nonsense! They've been talking about closing the school for as long as I can remember.'

'I have an idea that they are serious about it this time,' Elisabeth told her. 'I've just had Mr Richardson from Urebank on the phone and he certainly gave me the impression that the Education Committee is keen on the idea. I think

174

he knows more than he was letting on.'

'That man is devious,' cried Miss Brakespeare. 'He's been poaching children from here for over a year, advertising his school in the local papers, saying how wonderful it is at Urebank and all the facilities they have, and he's been lobbying parents. Of course, after the poor inspection here, he was in his element and there was an exodus. I shouldn't wonder if he isn't still stirring things up. He's got contacts at the Education Office, you know. As thick as thieves with that bumptious Councillor Smout.' She saw Elisabeth's gloomy expression. 'Anyway,' she said reassuringly, 'I shouldn't worry. I can't believe that they would close Barton-in-the-Dale.' But at the back of Miss Brakespeare's mind she began to share the same doubts with the new head teacher.

*   *   *

'It's very good to see you, Mrs Devine,' said Mr Williams, resting his elbows on the desk and steepling his fingers. He was a small, dark-complexioned, silver-haired Welshman with shining eyes.

It was the following morning, and Elisabeth sat with the head teacher at Forest View Residential Special School in his study. 'John's an easy-going young man and copes as well as he can. He's a grand lad, no problem at all, and is already very popular with the staff.'

'I see,' replied Elisabeth. 'He seemed happy enough last Saturday when I saw him, but of course with his condition it's so difficult to tell.'

'Oh, I think I can safely say your son is a happy

175

enough boy and has settled in here remarkably well.'

'I cannot tell you, Mr Williams,' said Elisabeth, 'how relieved I was when he was offered a place here. His teachers at his last school did their best, but I wanted the specialist care for him that you provide here. Even in the short time John has been at Forest View, he seems to have made some progress.'

'Indeed he has, but like many autistic children progress can be slow, and John still seems to be content in his own world. He eats healthy, balanced meals, sometimes takes part in the activities when he feels inclined, but like many of the other children in the school he tends to be independent and likes his own company. You know, there is no disorder as confusing to comprehend or as complex to diagnose as autism and I have no idea how much John understands. The main thing is that we assume that he has some comprehension and we try to give him the best possible care and education and the richest of experiences that we can.'

'Do you think he really knows who I am?' Elisabeth asked. 'Sometimes he looks at me and I think I see some recognition in his eyes.'

'That I cannot answer for certain,' replied the head teacher, 'but I think it is very likely that he does. He just doesn't feel inclined to display any recognition, that's all.' He rested his hands on the desktop. 'I should like to think that the visits from parents and visitors are beneficial and I should be delighted to see you at any time, not just on the Saturday visits. You really don't have to make an appointment, just call in.' He smiled and coloured a little.

'I shall take you up on that,' said Elisabeth. 'I intend to visit John as much as I can.'

'Then you will be one of the very few parents who do frequently visit their children. I find it sad that most don't come very often or even at all, but it's understandable I suppose. At the start they visit regularly, sometimes coming long distances to do so, but it tails off over time. They have other children to deal with and they have to work, of course. When they come to understand that there is no cure for this condition, and that they can't ever foresee a time when their autistic child will lead a truly independent life, they wonder what the point is, and of course it can be upsetting for them as well, so they don't come as often as before. Most telephone to see how their child is getting on but rarely spend much time with them.'

Unlike Mr Williams, Elisabeth found it hard to understand why a parent should take such little interest in their child, not to visit regularly, watch them grow, see what progress they were making. 'They know, I suppose,' she said, 'that in this residential school their child will be well looked after, that they get the best attention and care. I think you do an amazing job here.'

'Thank you,' said the head teacher. 'That's what the school inspectors said, although they used the word "outstanding" rather than "amazing". They visited last week, and you, as a parent, will be very pleased, as indeed we on the staff were, with the findings in the report. Actually, one poor inspector felt quite awful during the visit. He was in quite a state. When he was observing a lesson one of the children managed to get hold of a metal paperclip that was on his clipboard. Little Rebecca put it in

177

her mouth and spent the whole of the morning poking out her tongue with the paperclip on it. He, of course, was distraught, but she smiled and continued to tease him. She thought it was some sort of funny game. We had the devil's own job trying to get the paperclip off her. Every time we made a move, she would clamp her lips together and smile. Of course, it could have been very nasty had she decided to swallow it. Anyway, Dr Stirling, who was in school, came to the rescue. He managed to retrieve it. I think Rebecca has a bit of a soft spot for the good doctor, as indeed do many of the children.'

'Dr Stirling visits here, does he?' asked Elisabeth.

'Yes, he's the local doctor on whose services we frequently call. Nice man. Do you know him?'

'Yes,' she said, 'I know him. He's on my governing body—well, for the time being anyway. I can't say that I have found him very nice. He's quite a cold fish.'

'He's not actually,' Mr Williams told her. 'Until you get to know him, that reserve almost amounts to aloofness, but he is far from cold and unfriendly. The death of his wife had a real effect upon him. He was a very gregarious man until her death. Then he became much quieter and more thoughtful. His wife was such a lively and outgoing woman, a doctor like himself. It was such a tragic accident. Outwardly Michael Stirling might appear a bit distant, but I reckon his demeanour is a kind of deceptive covering to protect the sensitive man beneath. My goodness, I'm sounding like the educational psychologist.'

'I'm afraid that Dr Stirling and I are not seeing eye to eye at the moment,' Elisabeth told him.

'Really?'

She was tempted to tell the head teacher about James and the fact that his father was blind to the boy's problem, but she felt it would be unprofessional to do so. 'He intends to resign from the governing body,' she said.

'That is a great pity. He is the sort of person you need on your side. By the way, I hope you have settled in at Barton-in-the-Dale. From what I gather there is a lot to do there but I am sure you will "fettle it", as they say in this part of the world.'

'Well, I've at least made a start,' Elisabeth told him.

'It's a very pleasant little school and set in some of the most magnificent countryside in the county. The former head teacher, as you have probably heard, had a fearsome reputation. Not a woman to argue with, I gather. I believe she ordered one of the inspectors out of the school when he had the temerity to criticise her.'

'Yes, she is quite a character,' Elisabeth replied, noncommittally.

'So you are just down the road from us now,' said Mr Williams, 'and you won't have a long journey every time you wish to visit us.'

'That was the main reason for moving,' she told him, 'so I could see more of John. As soon as he got a place here I started looking for jobs in the area, and Barton was the first school that came up. Sometimes I think I was a bit impetuous and should have waited rather longer.'

'You sound as if you have some regrets,' said Mr Williams. 'Is it not what you expected?'

Elisabeth thought for a moment and looked out of the window, as if reminded of something.

'I have mixed feelings at the moment,' she said. 'The children and staff are fine, but some of the governors and the parents I reckon will be hard work, and I think I am going to cross swords with those at the Education Office. I have a sneaking suspicion they want to close the school.'

'I very much doubt it,' replied Mr Williams. 'Why would they appoint a new head teacher and then close the school?'

'It's just that certain things have been said,' Elisabeth told him, 'and my Chairman of Governors and the education officer have been very evasive. I have this sneaking suspicion that there is more to it than they are telling me.'

'I have to say that I've had battle royals with the education people over resources,' the head teacher told her. 'They always want to cut costs. You want to try and hang on to Dr Stirling. He was massively supportive when we put in a bid for more equipment and extra staffing.'

'I don't think I can rely on Dr Stirling's support,' Elisabeth told him. 'I am afraid, as I have said, we don't see eye to eye on a number of matters. He's taken his son away from the school and is sending him to St Paul's, the preparatory school in Ruston. He thinks it will offer him a more appropriate education.'

'Well, he's mistaken. The boy would be much better off at Barton,' Mr Williams told her. 'Knowing St Paul's, I very much doubt whether he will enjoy it there. The school is a hothouse. I should know, my brother's boy attends.'

'That's as may be,' agreed Elisabeth, 'but there's little I can do. Dr Stirling is adamant that his son will be better off and he's determined to move him.'

180

'I'm sorry about that,' said Mr Williams. 'Well, I'll take you along to see John.'

Elisabeth, like most mothers with their newborn baby in their arms, had thought her son was the most beautiful child in the world. Baby John had great blue eyes and a dazzling smile, tiny fingers like sticks and nails as pink and shiny as seashells. Simon, his father, had held him high in the air and told him he would be a son in a million, go to Cambridge as he had done, make everyone so proud of him. At the hospital, her bed surrounded by flowers and cards, Elisabeth had held her smiling, healthy baby in her arms and had felt happier than she had ever been.

The baby had smiled early and fed easily, but when he had made no effort to walk like other children of his age or to speak and began increasingly to reject physical contact, Elisabeth had known something was wrong. The doctor and health visitor had reassured her that the child was fine. She had seen in their expressions that they thought her a fussy, over-protective mother. Children develop at different rates, she had been told; the little boy was healthy and happy and would soon start making progress.

'Oh, he's just a bit slower than other children,' Simon had said dismissively, when she had tried to talk to him about her worries. 'Stop fussing.' She had seen in his eyes that he refused to believe that there was anything wrong with his son.

But Elisabeth had known that things were not right. At three and still not speaking, John had stiffened when touched, avoided eye contact and was happiest when left alone sorting out shapes. He had been meticulous in arranging things, and would

181

spend hours organising his bricks and making sure everything was exactly in order. He had become quite obsessive about neatness and routine.

The meeting with the specialist, which Elisabeth had insisted upon, had confirmed her misgivings. The parents had learnt that their son was a child with a disorder called autism, which meant he would likely never speak, interact with others, embrace her, kiss her, never understand humour or irony and could be subject to seizures and maybe violent outbursts. He would never lead a 'normal' life, if this meant going to the local school, passing examinations, finding a job, getting married and having children. Her husband had been devastated and, on hearing this diagnosis, had stared out of the window as if in a trance. She had reached out to hold his hand. It had felt cold and dead. That night Elisabeth had held the child in her arms and wept.

Her marriage began to teeter on the rocks. Her husband spent less and less time at home. There was always an excuse why he had to be away on business, always some reason why he couldn't go with her to see the specialist or spend time with his son. Whereas she wanted to find out more about her son's condition, desperate to know about education and diet and therapy, Simon was reluctant even to talk about it. He wouldn't move from the expectation that the boy would grow out of it, that there was a kind of cloak that shrouded his true self and which one day would finally fall away to reveal the clever and articulate child he had always hoped for. Then the illusion that nothing really was wrong gradually disappeared, and her husband knew that for the rest of his life his son would have to cope with this disability and be totally dependent on adults. He felt guilty and hopeless, unable to cope with this silent little boy who lived in his own closed world. Although he denied it furiously, Elisabeth knew Simon found the child an embarrassment. His colleagues at the prestigious accountancy firm where he was a senior partner would talk about their offspring, how clever and articulate they were, how well they were doing at school, the instruments they could play and the sports they enjoyed. Simon kept a miserable silence, thinking of his own son. No one ever asked him about John.

There were arguments and simmering silences, and one day when John was five, Simon packed his things and left. Following the divorce, Elisabeth heard that Simon had remarried. She had telephoned him up just the once to tell him how John was getting on, and had been told it would be for the best if she didn't get in contact again. It distressed Simon's new wife. Since then Elisabeth had heard nothing from him. She had felt depressed and isolated.

Determined to give her son the best possible education, she enrolled John at a local special school with an excellent reputation. Here the teachers were committed and hard-working and seemed able to handle autistic children who struggled to communicate and interact. Elisabeth, by now a deputy head teacher, would drop him off in the mornings and a carer would collect him in the afternoons and stay until she arrived home. It worked well for a time, but when her son reached eleven, the age when children transfer to secondary education, the head teacher took her aside. John, he felt, could make greater progress and receive more help at a school that could offer more specialist care for young people with his condition. Forest View, a residential special school for young people with autism, was suggested. Elisabeth managed to secure her son a place. Here the teaching was simple, coherent and structured to meet the individual needs of the pupils. It was a calm and secure environment with soft lighting and no strident bells sounding every hour, and there was plenty of space. The school was surrounded by beautiful countryside and the air was fresh and clean. The problem was that it was fifty miles away in the heart of the Yorkshire Dales.

Elisabeth, by now a head teacher, realised that the long journey each weekend to Forest View to see John would inevitably begin to take its toll. Her job had become increasingly demanding and time-consuming. She knew she would feel guilty when a conference or training course came up which she had to attend and which meant she couldn't make the journey to see her son. So she scoured the educational papers looking for a head teacher's position in a school near Forest View, and when the post came up at Barton-in-the-Dale, a small rural primary school only a few miles away, she applied for the post, got it and started her new life.

Elisabeth now found John sitting at a table carefully arranging small coloured beads in straight lines. His forehead was furrowed with concentration. She sat next to him and watched for a moment. He was such a good-looking eleven-year-old, with his large dark eyes, long lashes and curly blond hair.

'Hello,' Elisabeth said cheerfully. 'What are you up to?'

Her son continued to arrange the beads. He seemed oblivious of her.

'You used to love playing with my beads when you were younger. I remember once when I broke a rope of pearls and they scattered all over the floor and you managed to find every one and arrange them in the exact order. Quite a feat.'

John stopped what he was doing for a moment, as if recalling a distant memory, and then returned to the beads.

'The cottage is just about finished,' she said, placing her hand next to his. 'Carpets are down, curtains are up, walls painted and the garden is taking shape. I did have moles in the garden but they have mysteriously disappeared. I have an idea Danny, who I told you about last week, has been putting down traps.' Her son never looked around but edged his fingers towards her until they touched her own. Elisabeth talked for some time, telling her son about the teachers at her school, the changes she was making and her niggling worry about a possible closure. He continued to arrange the beads, never looking up. His face was expressionless.

'Oh, John,' Elisabeth sighed. She remained silent for a moment. 'I love you so much, you know,' she told him. 'I hope that you know that, and that I'm so proud of you.' How she wished that she could hold him and smooth his hair and kiss his cheek, but she knew she couldn't. To do so would distress him greatly. He couldn't be touched. If was as if he lived in a glass case, silent, cut off, unreachable. It broke her heart that he would probably never know how much she loved him and that he was incapable of loving her back. But in spite of all that, she would

185

not have him any other way.

As a teacher she had taught many children, bright, articulate and healthy youngsters. She would sometimes watch the boys of John's age as they ran and chased each other around the playground and think of her son locked away in his own distant world. But she never felt bitter or angry that he was not like these boys, or envious of the children's parents. John was her quiet, gentle son and she loved him just as he was. He never argued, offered advice, sympathised or criticised; he merely listened and reminded her that much of life was not so very important. Bright spots of tears appeared in the corners of her eyes. She quickly brushed them away with the back of her hand.

'Mrs Devine.' Elisabeth jolted up in her chair as if she had been bitten. She swung around to find Dr Stirling at the door. He was wearing the same crumpled linen jacket he had worn at their last meeting, and his hair looked unbrushed and curled around his ears and at the back of his neck.

'Oh, Dr Stirling.' She sniffed and reached quickly into her bag for a handkerchief.

'Mr Williams told me you were here,' he said, glancing at her nervously. 'I'm sorry if you were startled.'

Elisabeth continued to rummage in her bag. 'I think I must be coming down with a cold,' she said.

'Perhaps you should call in at the surgery?'

'Pardon?'

'I could give you something for your cold. We don't want you off school in your first few weeks.'

'I'll be fine,' she said, finding a handkerchief and blowing her nose.

'I hope I'm not disturbing you.'

'No, no. I'm just having a few quiet moments.' She sniffed. 'I find it very therapeutic to get away from everything, school and parents and governors' meetings and all the paperwork.'

'Yes, I know what you mean. Life can be very hectic at times.' He gave a reassuring smile.

He sat down next to the boy and watched him. John, head down, face fierce with concentration, continued to meticulously arrange the beads.

'Hello,' said the doctor, resting his hand gently on the boy's. John quickly pulled his hand away.

'Sometimes he doesn't like to be touched,' Elisabeth told him, 'particularly when he's engaged in some activity.'

'I'll remember that,' said the doctor and smacked the back of his own hand playfully.

Perhaps the man was human after all, thought Elisabeth, smiling. He certainly seemed to be a great deal calmer and pleasanter than when she had last seen him.

'I didn't know you had a son at Forest View?' the doctor said. 'Mr Williams has just told me.'

'Yes, this is John,' she said. 'He's just started here.'

'It's an excellent school,' he told her. She noticed that a small bead of sweat had rolled from beneath the curls at the back of his neck. He turned to look at her son, seemingly fascinated by what the boy was doing. 'You're making a great job of that,' he said.

Elisabeth studied the man's profile. Seeing him from this angle with his untidy hair and his lopsided smile, he had something of the small child about him, careless of his appearance, innocent, vulnerable. She had a powerful urge to reach out and touch his cheek.

'Of course,' Elisabeth said quickly, trying to cover her embarrassment, 'now I have moved closer to him I can visit John whenever I like. He loves to arrange things. I think he finds the repetition comforting and reassuring. I come on Saturdays to see him and during the week if I can manage it.' She looked down at her hands and for some unaccountable reason her heart began to gallop. What was it about this man, she thought, which put her in such a state?

'How is he doing?' asked Dr Stirling, turning to look at her. His eyes were as bright as blue glass.

'Pardon?'

'How is he getting on here?'

'Oh, fine,' she replied. 'There's not been any great change really.' She looked down, almost afraid of meeting his eyes. 'I think there's been some limited progress. Some children with autism have seizures and outbursts and they can punch and bite, as you probably know. Thankfully, John is a quiet and even-tempered boy and seems happy in his own private world. He loves music and can be affectionate at times. I have no idea how much he understands, of course, or whether he really knows who I am, but I like coming here and I hope he enjoys my visits.'

'I am sure he looks forward to seeing you,' said the doctor. 'You know, the more I see of this condition, the less I seem to understand.' He looked back at John, engrossed in arranging the beads. 'He's a fine-looking young man.'

'Yes, he is,' said Elisabeth, looking up.

'John's about James's age, isn't he?' Dr Stirling asked.

'He is,' she replied, thinking what a pity it was that the man sitting next to her didn't understand that his own son was in need of help. She pictured the fragile, silent little boy, like her own son hiding deep within himself, but she said nothing.

'I hear you are quite the dab hand with retrieving paperclips,' she said.

Dr Stirling smiled. 'Ah, you have heard about little Becky. She's quite a character.'

'However did you manage to get it out of her mouth?'

'I put a paperclip on my tongue,' he explained, 'and copied what she was doing. Perhaps not the best way of going about things, but the teachers had tried unsuccessfully all morning to get the clip back and were increasingly concerned that she might eventually swallow it. Anyway, Becky became fascinated when I copied her, sticking out my tongue, and when she was distracted I plucked the clip from her mouth and at the same time closed mine. Actually I very nearly swallowed the wretched thing myself, which would have been rather embarrassing.'

'And how is James settling in at St Paul's?' asked Elisabeth.

'Oh, he's not started yet,' Dr Stirling told her. 'The independent schools tend to begin the term a couple of weeks later than the state ones. But, you probably know that. He starts on Monday.'

'As I said,' Elisabeth told him, 'I hope James gets on well there.'

There was an embarrassing silence.

'Yes, yes, I hope so too,' he said, getting to his feet. 'Well, I had better be making tracks. I have quite a list of patients to visit today.' He held out his hand. 'Well, goodbye then, Mrs Devine.'

'Goodbye, Dr Stirling,' she replied, placing a small cold hand in his.

Why was it, he thought, that this woman made him feel so uneasy and awkward? Why was it that she seemed to be in his thoughts so much of the time? He stopped at the door and thought for a moment, pinching the bridge of his nose. Then he turned to look at Elisabeth with searching, worried eyes. 'I was a little short with you when you called in at the surgery,' he said. 'I said things which I now regret. I'm sorry if I appeared rude and dismissive. I'm sure that your comments were well-intentioned and I spoke out of turn.' Elisabeth looked into his face, which suddenly seemed to wear a dejected expression, and felt a great surge of sympathy for him. Her lips moved slightly, as if she was about to say something, but the words would not come.

'It was good to see you again, Mrs Devine,' said Dr Stirling, and with that he was gone.

CHAPTER TEN

The Reverend Atticus, rector of Barton, surveyed his usual Saturday breakfast. He sometimes said a silent prayer that he would be given a lightly fried egg, a rasher of crispy bacon, a slice of black pudding and some wild mushrooms, but his wife was innocent in the use of the frying pan. In the centre of the plate was an insipid-looking, undercooked poached egg on a square of burnt toast.

'Is there something the matter with your breakfast, Charles?' asked the vicar's wife.

190

'No, no, my dear,' he replied, smiling wanly, 'I was just thinking about what I might say in my sermon tomorrow.' He cut a corner from the toast. 'I thought I could focus on the Good Samaritan.'

'Well, don't make it too long,' she told him.

'I shall endeavour not to,' replied her long-suffering husband. The vicar chewed thoughtfully and nodded. 'I was prompted to think of this theme when I was told that the new head teacher has let old Mr Stainthorpe, the odd-job man, site his caravan on the field adjoining her property. That was very good of her, was it not?'

'Yes, I'd heard,' replied his wife. 'It was indeed very good of her. I certainly wouldn't want that unsightly caravan near my house.'

'The caravan's not that unsightly, my dear,' said the vicar. 'It's just a trifle the worse for wear. I guess the poor man has little money to maintain it.'

His wife sighed inwardly, resisting the temptation to remind her husband yet again of his irritating habit of always putting a positive gloss on things of which she spoke critically. 'The garrulous woman in the village store, who is forever trying to foist those stale Viennese chocolate biscuits on me, was informing all and sundry. Evidently that unpleasant Mr Massey threw him off his land after some argument in the public house.'

'It has to be said that Mr Massey is not the easiest of characters,' observed the vicar.

'Not the easiest!' snapped his wife. 'He's a lazy, mean-minded, grasping old man who thinks he owns the village, and please do not start to list his excellent qualities, Charles. He is a most objectionable individual.'

The vicar refrained from comment and stared at

the corner of dry toast.

'And I really cannot see why you still employ him to cut the grass in the churchyard. He leaves it for so long that the weeds have grown waist high by the time he gets around to it and dandelion seeds have blown over into our garden. You need to have another word with him or find somebody else.'

'It's difficult to get people to do that sort of thing,' the vicar replied, 'but I shall, however, speak to him.'

The vicar contemplated what to do with the remainder of his deeply unappetising breakfast, by now cold on his plate. He had once secreted a particularly inedible concoction of his wife's in his handkerchief and deposited it later down the toilet bowl but decided against this, as he was sure he would be observed. He posted the piece of toast in his mouth and crunched.

'I met Mrs Devine in the village,' remarked his wife. 'She has asked me to go into the school.'

'Really?' The vicar looked up, suddenly taking an interest.

'Yes,' continued his wife. 'We had a pleasant conversation actually. I have quite taken to Mrs Devine. She has a lot about her and has made a great many changes for the better since she arrived. Of course some of the changes have not been welcomed by the Luddites in the village, but then any changes are likely to be met with opposition in Barton. It's so insular and claustrophobic. It's a wonder that they allowed gas to be replaced with electricity.'

'Omnia mutantur, nos et mutamur in illis,' said the vicar.

Mrs Atticus sighed. 'I wish you wouldn't do that,'

said his wife. 'Not all of us have a knowledge of Latin.'

'Times change, and we change with them,' the vicar translated.

'Whatever,' said his wife. 'Anyhow, Mrs Devine is trying to encourage people with some expertise to go into the school and wondered if I might give a helping hand with the artwork there. Evidently the children have had little experience of any sort of painting and Mrs Devine would like some advice. As you know, she was quite taken with my work. I have to say I was somewhat reticent at first, but she persuaded me and you know I think I might enjoy it. It's a while since I picked up a paintbrush.'

'I think that is an excellent idea,' said her husband, deciding not to tackle the egg. 'It will take you out of yourself.'

'Charles,' sighed his wife. 'I do not wish to be taken out of myself. I am quite content as I am, to some extent anyway, although I still would like to have moved to the city. It is merely one afternoon of my time. I am not taking on a permanent teaching position there.'

'Of course,' he said.

'Mrs Devine did mention that she would welcome a visit from you, to take an assembly and speak to the children.'

'Did she?'

'More than the last head teacher ever did. Why, when she was there you were never asked to go into school to talk to the children and to become more involved. How you put up with her for so long, I shall never know. And when you once suggested having the children take part in the Harvest Festival and having a Nativity play in the church, she nearly had a seizure.'

'Speaking of the Harvest Festival, my dear,' said the vicar, 'the bishop has intimated that he would like to attend our celebrations this year.' Mrs Atticus rolled her eyes. 'I thought I might ask his lordship to call into the school while he is here. I am sure Mrs Devine would not be averse to a visit.'

'I think it's very good idea,' agreed his wife, 'if that means that he will be spending less time with us. You know how I dislike his irritating good humour.'

The Reverend Atticus decided to ignore his wife's uncharitable observation. He chuckled. 'He was telling me that at one school he visited he was showing the children his mitre and his crozier and was explaining to the children the significance of his pointed headdress and his hooked staff. Some time later he received a letter from one pupil thanking him for coming in and saying that he now knew what a crook looked like.'

'Yes,' said Mrs Atticus, pointedly not amused, 'children can be very honest.'

The Reverend Atticus felt it prudent not to continue with this conversation. 'Mrs Devine seems to have settled in very well by all accounts,' he said. 'The school looks so much brighter from the outside and I am hearing very good things from some of the parents. Mrs Pocock—'

'Oh, that dreadful woman with the shouty voice,' interrupted his wife, 'and that disagreeable child of hers.'

'Mrs Pocock,' continued the vicar, deciding, against his better judgement, not to spring to the woman's defence, 'tells me her son is making much better progress and speaks very highly of

Mrs Devine. I did see her in church last Sunday, sitting at the back.'

'Mrs Pocock? I don't recall ever having seen her in church.'

'No, no, Mrs Devine. She slipped away at the conclusion of the service and before I could have a word. I thought I might prevail upon her to join us on the fund-raising committee. What do you think, my dear?'

'I think it's a very good idea,' replied his wife, agreeing with her husband on this rare occasion. 'That committee needs some fresh blood. They sit there like the living dead. Yes, I think you should ask her.'

*   *   *

Miss Brakespeare dabbed perfume on her wrists and behind her ears and stared at herself in the mirror. Beneath, in pride of place on the mantelshelf, was a photograph of her father in a silver frame. He looked trim and happy in his army uniform, eternally young, his hair recently cropped short and neatly parted and his moustache a dark shadow on his upper lip. She often looked at the photograph and vaguely remembered the quiet, gentle-natured man who had died when she was a girl.

'Are those new shoes?' asked her mother. Her voice was doleful and plodding.

'They are, yes,' replied her daughter.

'They're not the sort you usually wear. They're a bit fancy for you, aren't they?'

'I thought I'd go for something a bit different this time.'

'And I've not seen that dress before, either.'

'No, Mother, that is because it is new as well.'

'It's too bright for your colouring, Miriam,' the old woman grumbled, shaking her head. 'You don't suit emerald green with your colouring. It's too loud.'

'I like it,' replied her daughter.

'You're splashing out a bit, aren't you?' observed her mother.

'As you know, I spend little enough on myself,' replied Miss Brakespeare. There was an edge to her voice.

Her mother gave her a quizzical look. Was there something pointed in that remark, she wondered. But she decided not to pursue the matter. 'And where are you going?' she asked.

'Into town.'

'Into town,' Mrs Brakespeare repeated. 'It'll be chock-a-block on a Saturday. It's so crowded at the weekends these days that people don't go there any more. Why are you going into town?'

'I'm having my hair done and then I have things to do,' replied her daughter.

'Having your hair done?' exclaimed her mother.

'That's right. Then I have things to do.'

'What things?' her mother asked scornfully.

'Just things, Mother.' Miss Brakespeare's voice betrayed a trace of irritation.

'So what about my lunch?'

'There's a salad in the fridge.'

'You know I'm not that partial to salads.' Her mother's face was set in a hard thin line. 'I can't eat tomatoes and cucumber gives me wind. I thought you might have done me some steamed fish with parsley sauce.' Miss Brakespeare didn't reply.

196

'What time will you be back?'

'I'm not sure.'

The old lady shuffled irritably in her chair. 'I really don't know what has got into you these days, Miriam,' she said. 'You've been acting very strangely of late, ever since that new head teacher took over. You go earlier to school and come home later and have been quite sharp with me, and now you're spending money like there's no tomorrow on new clothes and all this gallivanting.'

Miss Brakespeare turned to face her mother. 'I hardly think buying a few new clothes is extravagant and that going into town is gallivanting. And if I have been behaving differently, it is because I feel different. Since Mrs Devine took over I don't feel quite the same as I used to do. Actually, Mother, for once in my life, I feel valued and listened to. I like going to school, which I can't say I ever did in the past. I was always at the beck and call of Miss Sowerbutts and nothing anyone did suited her. She was like a black cloud hovering over everything. Mrs Devine has been like a breath of fresh air. She teaches half of the class I used to have, has introduced some very welcome changes and has given me responsibility I have never had before. It suits me very well.'

'I can't say that I like the change, Miriam,' complained her mother.

'Well, I am afraid you are going to have to put up with it, and I have to say now that you have raised the matter that you, like Miss Sowerbutts, have rather taken me for granted and put upon my good nature.' Her mother opened her mouth to speak but paused, as if searching for the right words. Her daughter continued blithely, 'I know

197

you have various ailments and it can't be all that pleasant spending all day by yourself, and that there are things you can't manage and I am sorry for that, but you must understand that I do have a life outside this house. Now, the salad is in the fridge, and an egg custard. I shall be back some time this afternoon. Is there anything you want from town?'

'No,' said her mother, at last finding her voice. 'Nothing.'

*   *   *

'What's up wi' you, our Danny?' asked his grandfather.

'Nowt,' replied the boy, resting his head in his hands.

'Now come on, lad, there's summat up. Tha's not spoken a word all mornin', which isn't like you. You should be out and about on a champion Sat'day like this and not mopin' about t'caravan wi' a gob like last month's rhubarb.'

'There's nowt up wi' me, granddad,' replied the boy.

'I thowt we allus agreed to talk about things,' said the old man, 'get things off of us chests. I can allus tell when summat's up. Now, come on, what's mitherin' thee?'

'Well, it's Jamie,' the boy told him. ''Is dad's takin' him away from our school and sendin' 'im to some posh place in Ruston. Jamie's mi best friend and I don't want 'im to go and 'e dunt want to go eether.'

The old man scratched his chin. 'Did 'e tell you this?'

'Aye, 'e did.'

198

'And 'as 'e telled 'is dad 'e dunt want to go?'

'No, 'e says 'is dad's enough to worry abaat and 'e dunt want to upset 'im.'

The old man sighed.

'You see 'e can't talk to 'is dad like I talk to you, granddad. If I'm worried about summat I allus tell yer.'

'It's allus best to get it out in t'open and not bottle it up. What about you tellin' t'head teacher?' suggested the old man. 'Let Mrs Devine 'ave a word wi' 'is dad.'

'I telled 'er,' said the boy, 'an' she said she'd see Jamie's dad but I reckon she 'asn't. You see thing is, granddad, I'm t'only one Jamie talks to apart from 'is dad and I don't reckon 'e says much to 'im. I don't know 'ow 'e'll get on at t'other school not knowing anybody and wi' nobody to stick up for 'im.'

'Why dunt the lad speak to other people then?' asked the old man.

'I don't rightly know,' Danny told him. ''E just dunt say owt.'

'There are quiet folks in t'world, tha knows, Danny. 'Appen 'e's one of these. Not everyone's got a gob on 'em like thee and me. We can talk for Britain.'

The boy gave a small smile. 'It's funny 'im not talkin' to other kids an' t'teachers though. 'E used to speak but then 'e just stopped. 'E just says he dunt feel like it.'

'Lad's lost 'is mother,' said the boy's grandfather. ''Appen that's mebbe summat to do wi' it. Perhaps 'e's still grievin'.' The old man thought of the daughter he had lost and how quiet and reclusive he had become for a while after her death. 'Give it time and 'e'll be talkin' like t'best of 'em.'

'Mebbe,' muttered the boy, sounding unconvinced.

'You should ask Mrs Devine if she's 'ad a word wi' t'lad's dad,' said the old man.

'I'm keepin' out of 'er way,' replied Danny, scratching his scalp. 'I'm not in 'er good books at t'moment.'

'How come?'

'I got in a bit o' trouble at school. I took mi ferret in and it bit Malcolm Stubbins. 'E ran off wi' mi bag and pur his hand in it and Ferdie bit 'im an' 'ung on.'

'Tha shouldn't be takin' tha ferret to school, Danny,' said the boy's grandfather.

''E were off colour, granddad.'

'Still, school's not a place for ferrets.'

'So Mrs Devine's not best pleased wi' me at t'moment. Malcolm Stubbins grabbed 'old of Ferdie and were 'urtin' 'im so I clocked 'im one and 'e 'it me back and we gor in a scrap. Mrs Devine were right mad wi' us for feightin'.'

'Well, it's not the end o' the world, is it?' said his grandfather. 'And if that lad 'ad kept 'is 'ands out of your bag 'e wouldn't 'ave got bitten. Now, come on, our Danny, you can help me go and pick some blackberries from down by t'old railway line.'

*   *   *

Elisabeth had barely returned from Forest View that Saturday when there was a sharp rap on the door. Outside in the porch was a ruddy-complexioned man in a greasy cap and dressed in soiled blue overalls.

'May I help you?' she asked.

'Aye, could you move your car, missis? I need to get my beasts back to yonder field.'

'It's Mr Massey, isn't it?'

'Aye, that's me.'

'I was hoping I might meet you,' said Elisabeth, 'to have a word about the use of my track.'

'Oh aye.' His narrow eyes narrowed further and his forehead furrowed. 'What about it?'

'I would prefer that in future, Mr Massey,' said Elisabeth, 'you do not bring your cows down there. As you can see, I park my car on the track and your cows do make a mess.'

'Not bring my cows down there,' he repeated, loudly. 'I've allus brought my beasts down there.'

'Well, I am asking you not to,' said Elisabeth calmly.

'Look here, missis,' said the man, 'I've brought my cows down that track as long as I can remember. It's a right of way.'

'No, Mr Massey, it is not a right of way,' Elisabeth told him. 'It belongs to me. It is private property, something I think you are well aware of.'

'Well, I'm telling you, missis, that it's a right of way,' the man said belligerently, 'and I've lived in this village a damn sight longer than you have. It always has been a right of way and I have the right to bring my beasts down it. I don't know what you've been told by old Stainthorpe, but I'm telling you that track is for anyone's use.'

'Would you care to see the deeds of this cottage, Mr Massey, in which it states quite clearly that the track is part and parcel of this property?'

'Mrs Pickles had no problem with me bringing my cows down there,' he said peevishly.

'Mrs Pickles didn't have a car,' Elisabeth told him.

'You can park your car on the road.'

'Where I park my car is up to me, Mr Massey, and I wish to park it on the track next to my cottage. So please in future take your cows by another route.'

'I don't believe what I'm hearing,' growled the man.

'And while you are here it gives me the opportunity of asking you to remove your sheep from my paddock.'

'Move my sheep!' The man's face became flushed with anger. 'Move my sheep?'

'Had you asked my permission to graze your sheep there and not been so mean-minded as to evict Mr Stainthorpe from your field, I might have been more inclined to let your sheep stay in the paddock, but as it is I would like them removed.'

The man stared at her for a moment and then moved closer. 'I've heard about you,' he said.

'And I you, Mr Massey,' Elisabeth replied, not at all daunted and looking him straight in the eye.

'If you think you can come here into our village and start laying down the law then you've another think coming. You may try and rule the roost in that school and tell kids what to do, but you're not getting away with it with me. I shall carry on using that track and grazing my sheep as I've done before and nobody will stop me.'

'I think they will, Mr Massey,' Elisabeth informed him. 'If you continue to trespass on my property I shall have to resort to taking legal action to prevent you. Good day.'

He turned and stomped off, stopping at the gate

to deliver a threat.

'You've not heard the last of this!' he shouted, stabbing the air with a bony finger. 'Not by a long chalk.'

*   *   *

Elisabeth, sitting in the sunshine the following morning, looked up. A small hairy head was poking through the bushes to the rear of the cottage garden. The dog observed her for a moment with small bright eyes, cocked its head, and then, sensing she was not a threat, eased its body through the shrubs and scampered towards her, wagging its tail frantically.

'Hello,' said Elisabeth, lowering the book she had been reading and reaching down to pat the bristly body. 'And who are you?'

'His name's Gordon,' came a strident voice from the gate.

The speaker was a large woman who, despite her appearance—old tweed skirt, shapeless waxed jacket and heavy green rubber boots—was of a statuesque bearing. She spoke with the sort of voice which had echoes of the elegance and comfort brought by wealth and breeding, of cut-glass chandeliers and silver salvers, nursemaids and governesses.

'He's called Gordon,' she informed Elisabeth, 'because when I got him he reminded me so much of my dear grandfather, who sported sandy whiskers and had the same bright eyes.'

'He's delightful,' said Elisabeth, scratching the hairy little head.

'He's a little rascal,' said the woman. 'Always

going where he shouldn't. Come here, Gordon.' The dog dutifully scurried to its owner.

'He's a fine dog,' said Elisabeth.

'He is, isn't he?' agreed the woman. 'Border terrier. Good at ratting. I often take my Sunday constitutional by this cottage. Mrs Pickles, who used to live here, gave him scraps. I think he was hopeful you might have something for him. He has a remarkable memory when it comes to food.'

Elisabeth went over to the gate. 'I'm afraid he's out of luck this morning.'

The woman put the dog on a lead. 'You are Mrs Devine, I take it?' she said. 'The new head teacher at the village school?'

'That's right.'

'I'm Helen Wadsworth,' said the woman, holding out a hand which Elisabeth shook. 'I live up at Limebeck House. On a fine day like this you can see it from here. This was originally a tied cottage, you know. Mr Pickles was my father's gamekeeper for many years and when he retired it was given to him.'

'I didn't know,' said Elisabeth.

'We don't have a gamekeeper now, more's the pity, and as a consequence we are bedevilled with rabbits and moles and foxes and I don't know what, not to mention the poachers.'

'Well, I think I can help you there,' Elisabeth told her. 'Not with the poachers, that is, but with the pests. I have a young man who is an expert at catching moles and rabbits, although I really don't approve of his methods. He puts down traps and has a ferret.'

The woman laughed. 'Mrs Devine,' she said, 'you really cannot be sentimental about moles and rabbits. Moles are particularly annoying little creatures and spoil a lawn overnight. Rabbits can clear a vegetable patch in a day. As a child I always felt rather sorry for poor Mr McGregor and had little sympathy for Peter Rabbit and his family of greedy, burrowing pests. I guess Miss Beatrix Potter never had a vegetable patch of her own, for if she had she would not have been quite so approving of the creatures. You must direct this young man my way. I could make good use of his talents.' The woman made no effort to move, but closed her eyes and breathed in noisily. 'It's such a pleasant day, is it not? On my walk I often used to call in and see how Mr Pickles' widow was getting along. She was a delightful woman. Made splendid raspberry jelly and very acceptable sloe gin. I was greatly saddened to hear of her death, but I was very pleased that someone had bought the cottage at long last. As you probably know, it had been empty for some time and needed a deal doing to it. It is looking so much better now.'

'Would you care to come in and have a look at what I've done on the inside?' asked Elisabeth. 'You are very welcome.'

'Well, you know I might just do that,' said the woman. 'By nature, I am a terribly nosey person.' She tied the dog up to the gate. 'I won't be long, Gordon,' she said.

'I hope you approve of the changes,' Elisabeth told her, as she led the way to the cottage.

The interior, with its polished oak floors, thick red curtains, pale cream sofa and chairs and exposed beams, came as a surprise to Elisabeth's visitor.

'My goodness!' she exclaimed. 'You've

transformed the place. Not a humble gamekeeper's cottage any more, is it?'

Elisabeth, listening to the observation, couldn't tell whether the woman approved of the changes or not.

The visitor looked around the room, taking everything in. 'And I see that you have smartened up the exterior to the school as well,' she said. 'You may not be aware, but it was my grandfather who endowed the building. It was originally intended for the children of the estate workers. The school was given over to the Local Education Authority in the 1920s. Sadly, I have had nothing to do with the school for a number of years. I am afraid that I did not get along with the former head teacher and we had words over the plaque.'

'The plaque?' repeated Elisabeth.

'Yes, there was an ornamental tablet fixed to the wall in the entrance commemorating the school's opening, which my grandfather unveiled. I was most upset when Miss Sowerbutts removed it. She had the entrance repainted like a hospital, a ghastly white, and declined to restore the plaque to its former position. I went in to see her and she refused my request to reinstate it. I took the plaque home with me. I have it up at the house. I am afraid that after that I have had nothing to do with the school and have never spoken to the woman since. There is really no phrase capable of describing just the right mixture of complacency, smugness and ill-humour that makes up Miss Sowerbutts' personality.'

'Perhaps you might like to visit the school now,' Elisabeth said.

'I should like that very much,' replied the

woman.

'And show me where the plaque should go?'

The woman's face broke into a great smile. 'I should be delighted,' she said.

*   *   *

Later that morning Danny appeared. Elisabeth saw him from the window, mooching around by the bushes with his hands pushed deep into the pockets of his jeans. She went out to see him.

'Hello, Danny,' she called.

'Hello, miss,' he called back. He looked ill at ease and made no effort to approach her.

'The moles haven't returned, thank goodness,' she said, walking towards him.

'No, I reckon you'll not 'ave any more trouble wi' them.' He looked at the ground, nervous of meeting her eyes.

'I am not going to ask you how you got rid of them,' Elisabeth said.

'Best not, miss,' he replied.

'I was speaking to the lady who lives at Limebeck House this morning,' said Elisabeth cheerfully. 'She has a bit of a mole problem. I said I knew a certain young man who might be able to help out.'

'Yeah, I reckon I could, miss,' he mumbled.

'And what are you up to today?' asked Elisabeth.

'Oh, nowt much,' replied the boy. 'I were supposed to be meetin' Jamie down by t'mill pond this mornin', but 'e never turned up. We've med a den in t'woods and we sometimes go there.'

'I think he'll probably be a bit busy today,' Elisabeth told him. 'He'll be getting ready to start at his new school tomorrow.'

207

'Miss, did you 'ave a word with his dad about 'im not wanting to go to that new school?' asked Danny. 'You said you would.'

'I did, yes.'

'Did you tell 'im that Jamie dunt want to go?'

'I did. I told him what you told me.'

'What did 'e say?'

'I'm afraid I wasn't able to change his mind, Danny,' she told him. 'I did try my best.'

The boy looked deflated. ''E won't like it there, miss. I know 'e won't. There'll be all these strange teachers and new kids and Jamie won't know anybody and they won't understand about 'im not speaking and that.'

'I should imagine his father has told them all about that, Danny,' said Elisabeth trying to reassure the boy. 'They will all be aware of how quiet James can be. I am sure he will be fine and soon make friends and settle there.' I wish I could be certain of that, she thought to herself, but she shared his friend's unease. She could foresee the difficulties the boy would face. The image of a rabbit came into her mind, a small huddled frightened creature shivering in the road, unable to move, caught in the headlight's glare.

'Thanks for tryin' anyway, miss,' he said. He looked up and shuffled his feet. 'Miss, I'm sorry about bringin' mi ferret to school. Mi granddad said it were daft of me and it caused a lot of bother. I won't do it again, even if Ferdie's off-colour.'

'That's water under the bridge,' said Elisabeth, 'and I don't think you'll be getting into any more fights now that Malcolm is at another school.'

'He's not going to t'one Jamie's goin' to, is 'e?' asked Danny suddenly.

'No, no, Jamie's off to St Paul's and Malcolm will be at Urebank.'

'Malcolm used to pick on Jamie,' Danny told Elisabeth.

'Did he?'

'He din't do it when I was around though,' said Danny. ''E knew I'd smack him one.'

Elisabeth shook her head. 'Well, now Malcolm's left, I hope there will be no more fighting, young man.'

'No, miss. I'm glad 'e's not at t'same school.' Danny scratched his head. 'I 'ope Jamie still wants to be mi friend,' he said. 'Do you think 'e will, miss?'

'I'm sure he will,' Elisabeth told him, thinking to herself that James needed friends like Danny.

CHAPTER ELEVEN

Barton-in-the-Dale had two public houses: the Mucky Duck and the Blacksmith's Arms. The former, once called the Dog and Duck, was a bright, brash and noisy place with loud music, games machines, karaoke nights, happy hours and pub quizzes. It was avoided by the locals and frequented by some of the 'off-comed-uns' and the young. In contrast, the Blacksmith's Arms hadn't changed in years. The outside looked dark and run-down, with its dull red brick walls, sagging roof of odd-shaped tiles and brown-painted window-frames. A faded wooden board, depicting a heavily muscled blacksmith hammering on an anvil, hung from a gallows-like structure to the front of the inn. It was at the latter hostelry that some of the farmers, shopkeepers and businessmen of the village gathered in the evening and at Sunday lunchtimes to argue about sport and politics and put the world to rights.

The interior of the pub was dim and smoky, reeking of beer and wood smoke. Despite the mildness of the weather a blazing fire crackled in the inglenook fireplace. It was the landlord's boast that the fire had been kept burning in the grate for over a century. The walls were bare save for a few coloured hunting prints, some cracked blue willow-pattern plates, a pair of old bellows and a couple of antique shotguns. A few dark wood, sticky-topped tables were arranged on the grey flagstone floor with an odd assortment of chairs and stools. When the landlord had once foolishly suggested that the place could do with some refurbishment, the regulars had protested strongly. They liked it the way it was. The place, they told him, had character and they were opposed to any changes.

At the public bar Fred Massey, dressed in his ill-fitting Sunday best suit, a bargain from a charity shop, finished his pint of bitter in one great gulp.

'I'll tell you what, Albert,' he told his companion, a ruddy-faced individual of immense girth and with several impressive chins, 'if that there woman thinks she can start laying down the law to me, she's in for a bloody shock.'

Albert nodded but said nothing. Like most in the village, he didn't like the constantly complaining, tight-fisted, bad-tempered Fred Massey but he felt it prudent not to cross swords with the man, since, as he supplied him with animal feeds, it was in his best interest not to fall out with one of his customers. Massey was a greedy man who saved money not for what it could buy, which was precious little in his case, but as a pure possession. He liked nothing better than to see the figures on his bank statements increase monthly, and if there was a bargain to be had, he was at the front of the queue.

'She's not been in the village more than a few weeks,' he grumbled, 'and already she's causing havoc.' He stabbed his finger on the bar. 'I've took my beasts down that there track since I was a young-un and she's not stopping me doing it now.' He shook his head and glowered. 'Can I have another pint here?' he shouted down the bar.

Albert drained his glass in the hope that he might be offered a similar drink, but none was forthcoming. 'And another thing,' continued the disgruntled farmer, 'now she's told me to take my sheep off her paddock. Can you believe that?' Albert could indeed believe that and could have pointed out that it was, in fact, the woman's paddock and she had every right to ask him to remove his animals, but he said nothing and fingered the empty glass. When the pint arrived, his companion produced a small leather pouch from his pocket and counted out the exact money. Albert realised that there would be no pint for him in the offing. Tight-fisted old bugger, he thought to himself.

'And another for you, Mr Spearman?' asked the landlord.

'Nay,' replied Albert, glancing at his watch. 'Dinner will be on the table in a minute.'

'I was telling Albert here,' grumbled Fred, 'that

211

that there woman who's bought the Pickles' cottage has told me I can't use the track what runs past her cottage. She had a go at my nephew Clarence only yesterday when he took two of my beasts past her cottage. Put the fear of God into the lad, she did. Well, I'll tell you this, Albert—'

'Don't start all that again, Fred,' interrupted the landlord, leaning over the bar and pointing. 'I've heard quite enough from you about that. I told you that if you and Les Stainthorpe have another set-to in this pub, you'll both be barred and you'll have to drink down the road at the Mucky Duck. You drive customers away with that sort of carry-on and I'm not having it.'

'I was only saying—' started Fred.

'Well, don't,' said the landlord, walking away to serve another customer at the other end of the bar.

Fred was quiet for a while. 'I reckon it were Les Stainthorpe what put the idea in her head, telling her it were her track. I had a right argument with him in here about it.'

'Aye, so I heard,' said Albert, shuffling off the bar stool ready to depart. He had come into the pub for a quiet Sunday lunchtime drink and interesting conversation and had heard quite enough from this unremittingly miserable man.

'She comes into this village all la-di-dah as if she owned the place,' continued Fred, 'and I'll tell you this, it's not only me she's upsetting. She's getting up everyone else's noses as well. I was told that Mrs Stubbins and Dr Stirling have taken their kids away from the school and Miss Sowerbutts is outraged at all the changes this new woman's making.'

'Well, I'm off,' said Albert, weary with listening

and thinking of the Sunday roast that awaited him, and he left Fred Massey scowling into his pint.

'You know Fred, you have a real talent,' said the landlord.

'Oh, aye, what's that then?'

'Of driving customers out of my pub, that's what. Has it ever occurred to you that anyone listening to you at the bar for more than five minutes seems to make himself scarce?'

'Gerron with you,' replied Fred. 'And get us another pint.'

Fred's diatribe had been overheard by two customers at the other end of the bar. Major C. J. Neville-Gravitas smoothed his moustache with an index finger before finishing his single malt.

'Interesting,' he remarked to his companion.

'Aye, so I 'eard,' replied Councillor Smout. 'Bit of a rum do this, i'n't it?'

'She seems to have made a few enemies since starting at the school, our Mrs Devine,' observed the major.

'Well, I felt she were a bit on t'forceful side when we interviewed 'er, and as you well know, major, I did have my reservations.'

The major could not recall anything of the sort, for all the governors, with the exception of Dr Stirling, had been strongly in favour of the appointment of Mrs Devine, but he remained silent on the matter. 'By the sound of it, it appears more children are leaving the school,' he said, 'including the son of one of our governors. I was not aware that Dr Stirling was taking his son away. It does not bode well.'

The councillor gave a small smile. 'Well, in a way it does,' he said. 'I mean, if we are to close t'school,

213

as was proposed at t'last Education Sub-committee meeting, it sort of plays into our hands.'

'In what way?' enquired his companion.

'Well, if t'school is continuing to lose children and t'community as a whole don't 'ave no confidence in t'head teacher and, as we've just 'eard, she's ruffling a few feathers, well, it does make it rather easier to go ahead wi' closure, dunt it?'

'Ah, yes, I see,' said the major. 'I follow your drift.'

The councillor tapped his fleshy nose with his forefinger. 'Any road, we shall have to play it a bit on t'careful side at t'next governors' meeting.'

'Softly, softly, catchee monkey, eh?' said the major.

'What?'

'Exactly, councillor, play it carefully,' agreed the major.

'Another whisky?' asked Councillor Smout.

'That would be very acceptable,' his companion replied, before draining his glass.

*   *   *

There was a sharp and urgent rapping on the cottage door. It was early Sunday evening and Elisabeth was in the kitchen preparing her supper.

If that's who I think it is, she thought, walking through from the kitchen into the hall, I shall not be quite as polite as I was when he last called and threatened me. There is no way that objectionable man is driving his cows down my track.

She opened the door to find Dr Stirling on the threshold, looking dishevelled and clearly

214

distressed.

'Mrs Devine,' he said breathlessly. 'I'm sorry to trouble you at this hour, but I wonder if you've seen James?'

'Come in,' said Elisabeth.

He walked into the hall wringing his hands. 'Is he here?' he asked, looking around.

'No,' Elisabeth replied, 'he's not.'

'Oh dear,' he sighed. 'I thought perhaps he might have come over here. You did mention that he had been to your cottage before and I thought he might have come here and forgotten about the time.'

'I'm afraid I haven't seen him.'

'I had an afternoon call, an emergency out at Littlebeck, and left James at home around five,' the doctor told her. 'Mrs O'Connor, my housekeeper who lives close by, usually calls round to keep an eye on James when I go out but she was at church. She goes to six thirty mass at Urebank every Sunday and then over to see her sister. James said he would be all right by himself, this once. When I arrived home he wasn't there. I can't imagine where he's got to. Do you think he's with the boy he's friendly with? Danny, isn't it?'

'I don't think so,' said Elisabeth. 'James was to meet Danny by the mill pond earlier today, but he never showed up.'

'The mill pond!' exclaimed the doctor. 'Oh God, I hope—'

'Dr Stirling,' said Elisabeth calmly, 'I am certain there is nothing to worry about. James has probably just forgotten about the time.' She glanced at the long-case clock in the hall. 'It's only a little after seven and still light. He's probably at home this very minute. Maybe he went for a walk. It is a lovely

215

evening and—'

'No, no,' he said impatiently. 'He wouldn't do that, not without telling me.'

'I really wouldn't worry—' began Elisabeth.

'Anything could have happened to him,' interrupted the doctor, hardly listening. 'I mean if he's lost he won't be able to tell strangers where he lives and you hear such stories of missing children and abductions.'

'If he's lost,' said Elisabeth, trying to allay the man's fears, 'he can write down where he lives. James is a sensible boy and abductions are extremely rare. I am sure you are worrying unnecessarily.'

'But he's never done anything like this before,' the doctor told her. 'He always tells me or Mrs O'Connor where he's going and he's always back home at the time I tell him. Could we have a word with this friend of his?'

'Of course we can,' said Elisabeth. 'The caravan is next door, in the paddock.'

Dr Stirling followed Elisabeth down the path and across the paddock to the caravan. Elisabeth knocked lightly on the door.

Les Stainthorpe poked his head out of a window. 'Oh, hello, Mrs Devine. Come on in.'

Elisabeth entered the caravan. She had not been inside before and was surprised to see how clean and tidy everything was. The beds had been made up neatly, and pots and pans had been tidied. There wasn't a thing out of place. Danny, sitting writing at the table, looked up anxiously.

'You'll be pleased t'lad's doin' 'is 'omework, Mrs Devine,' said the old man. He caught sight of Dr Stirling waiting outside, a worried expression in

216

his face. 'Hello, doctor,' he said. 'There's nowt up, is there?'

'I wonder if Danny has seen anything of James?' asked Elisabeth.

'No, miss,' said the boy getting up from the table. 'I telled you I was supposed to meet 'im this mornin' down by t'mill pond but 'e never turned up.'

'The thing is, Danny,' explained Dr Stirling, coming into the caravan, 'James is missing.'

'Missing!' the boy exclaimed.

'He's not at home,' said the doctor, 'and I don't know where he is. You haven't seen him at all today?'

'No.'

'Have you any idea where he might be?' asked Elisabeth.

'No, I don't,' said Danny, 'but I know why he's run off.'

'Run off!' repeated the doctor. 'What do you mean, he's run off?'

'It's because of that bloody school you were sending him to!'

'Hey, hey, Danny Stainthorpe,' said his grandfather sharply. 'Less of that sort of language and don't be so rude to t'doctor.'

'Well, it is, granddad,' said the boy angrily. 'Jamie didn't want to go to that school, 'e wanted to stay where 'e was and 'e was real upset that 'is dad was makin' 'im go. I telled you that, granddad. Jamie tried to tell Dr Stirling but 'e wouldn't listen and then Mrs Devine tried to tell 'im and 'e wouldn't listen to 'er either.' He breathed out heavily. 'I don't know why adults don't listen.'

Dr Stirling looked at Elisabeth. 'I never knew

217

that James was so set against going to St Paul's. I really didn't. If I'd known . . .' His voice tailed off.

'He din't go on about it because 'e said it made you unhappy,' Danny told him. 'You should 'ave listened to 'im, Dr Stirling, and seen 'ow unhappy 'e was.' The boy began to rub his eyes.

'Now don't get upset, Danny,' said Elisabeth calmly. 'I'm sure James is all right. Perhaps he just wanted to get away somewhere to think things through, to have a bit of time by himself. Maybe he's gone down to that den you mentioned. Do you think he might be there?'

'He could be,' said the boy, sniffing.

'Well, shall we go and have a look and call in at some of the other places you and James like to go to and see if we can find him, that's if it's all right with you, Mr Stainthorpe?'

''Course it is,' said the old man. 'I'll put mi coat on and give you an 'and.'

Elisabeth turned to Dr Stirling. 'It might be a good idea if you were to go back to your house in case James returns. I think you'll probably find him there waiting for you and wondering where you've got to. Leave your number and if he turns up, I'll give you a ring.'

'Aye, you gerron back to Clumber Lodge,' said Les, resting a hand on the doctor's shoulder. 'Like as not t'lad's theer waitin' for thee.'

'Yes, I'll do that,' said Dr Stirling, rubbing his forehead. 'And thank you.'

'If we can't find him,' said Elisabeth, 'then I think you should call the police.'

* * *

218

It was getting dark now. There was a drizzle of rain and a cold white moon in a gunmetal grey sky and there was still no sign of the missing boy. They sat on heavy hard-backed chairs around the large oak table in the gloomy dining room at Clumber Lodge: Dr Stirling, Elisabeth and the two young police officers. It was a cold, empty room, devoid of pictures and dominated by a white marble fireplace. Before them on the table were photographs of James.

The young policeman with the red nose, colourful acne and greasy black hair flicked his notebook shut and leaned back in the chair.

'I wouldn't worry too much, Dr Stirling,' he said casually, 'Children run off all the time.'

Elisabeth found his patronising tone irritating. She might have mentioned to him that some children go missing and are never found and that he should get off his backside and start looking, and she might have added that of course the boy's father was very worried.

'I've known a number of cases when kids have had a bit of a tiff with their mums and dads and run off,' continued the young policeman. 'We soon find them.'

Elisabeth knew that this was not the case, but she remained silent.

'I have not had a tiff with my son, officer,' said Dr Stirling. His face was drawn and troubled. 'There was no argument.'

The young policeman looked at his colleague, a pale-faced woman with her hair scraped back on her scalp into a small bun, and rolled his eyes. 'What I mean,' he said, 'is that children leave home for a number of reasons. There was a girl who

219

couldn't face sitting her school exams and took herself off to her grandma's in Halifax, and a lad who went looking for his dog and got lost. There was the girl who popped to the corner shop, met a friend and went to her house and forgot about the time. We had a teenager missing for two days last month but he turned up no worse for wear. Been at a pop concert. It's not unusual for kids to run away or go missing. We soon find them. Now you say you have looked in all the places he might have gone?'

'Yes,' said Elisabeth, resisting the temptation to ask him if he was taking the situation seriously.

She and Danny and the boy's grandfather had searched for a good hour, looking in the den, down by the mill pond, in the small copses and hedgerows, the deserted barns and around the village, getting increasingly worried as the evening grew darker and there was no sign of the missing boy.

'Well, I've got a picture of your son,' said the young policeman, rising from the chair. 'I'll alert all my colleagues to keep an eye out for him and if he's not turned up by tomorrow we'll organise a proper search.'

Dr Stirling stared into the distance as if looking for something.

'The boy is only just eleven,' said Elisabeth, 'and he should not be out all night at that age. I suggest you start a search immediately.'

'We will keep our eyes open,' said the young policeman. 'As I've said, youngsters do sometimes run away but they usually return when they are hungry and it starts getting dark.'

'It is out of character for this particular young man to leave home without saying where he was going,' Elisabeth told the policeman, 'and, as you can see, it is now dark. You will appreciate how very worrying this is. The other thing you should know is that James is a very shy and reticent boy.'

'He does speak,' explained the doctor, 'but only to certain people.'

'Why is that?' asked the young policewoman, suddenly taking an interest. She had recently been on a course relating to child abuse, and the lecturer had mentioned that one of the tell-tale signs of cruelty and maltreatment was a child not speaking.

'It's . . . it's difficult to explain,' he replied.

'Was he unhappy?' the young policewoman asked. 'Has something upset him? Has something happened to trigger his running away?'

'Well, my son was to start at his new school tomorrow. I suppose he was nervous about that,' Dr Stirling told her. 'He's quite a sensitive boy, you see. He takes things perhaps a little seriously. I thought—'

'James is a pupil at my school,' said Elisabeth, coming to his aid. 'He is a very well-adjusted, happy and well-cared-for boy. He has probably just wandered off and forgotten about the time, but I do think you should be out looking for him.'

The young policewoman looked unconvinced.

'Perhaps you and your colleague might start looking now,' said Elisabeth.

'As I said, we will certainly keep an eye out for the boy,' the officer replied. 'Let's not get too over-anxious at this stage.'

'And we will need to speak to him,' added his colleague, 'when he returns.'

'Thank you for that,' said Dr Stirling to Elisabeth after the police officers had gone. 'It sounded to them as though James had run away because I was maltreating him. They made me feel like a criminal.' He wrung his hands. 'I just cannot understand why he didn't tell me he hated the idea of going to another school and why he should have run off like that.'

Elisabeth could have told him but she remained quiet. The poor man had enough on his mind.

'You had better go,' he told her. 'There's nothing more you can do. I'll stay here and hope James comes home.' He was close to tears. 'I don't know what I'll do if anything has happened to him.'

Elisabeth rested a hand on his arm. 'Are you going to be all right?' she asked.

'Not really,' he replied.

'Mr Stainthorpe and some of the men in the village are out looking. If you like, you could join them and I'll stay here in case James returns.'

'Yes,' replied Dr Stirling, 'I'd like to do that. Thank you.'

The search party returned after a couple of hours. Elisabeth saw from the dejected expressions on the men's faces that they had not found the boy.

'Well, we've looked everywhere for t'lad,' Les told Elisabeth in a lowered voice, 'but there's no sign. 'Appen he's fallen asleep somewhere. I pray to God 'e 'as and that nowt's 'appened to 'im.'

Elisabeth left Dr Stirling sitting staring out of the window. The clock in the hall struck ten. She had tried again to reassure him but she was now as worried as he was about his son. She walked slowly though the village in the fading light. Despite the mildness of the night, she felt cold. There was a light on in the Methodist chapel and she could hear the organist practising. Noisy voices could be heard in the Blacksmith's Arms. When she arrived at the cottage she didn't feel like going inside. She negotiated the fresh cowpats that spattered the track, came to the gate and looked down the shadowy garden that she had brought to life again; it was now a place of order and fruitfulness and beauty. She breathed in deeply, aware of the stillness of the night. Above her bats, like scraps of black cloth, fluttered in the air, which smelled of damp earth and holly berries. A fresh molehill had appeared on the lawn and she saw the white bob of a rabbit's tail among her shrubs. The wind had dropped and the clouds moved away, leaving bright stars and a crescent moon curved silver and as bright as a sabre in the sky. Soft rain sifted through the treetops and the wet grass glittered in the moonlight.

'Dear God,' she prayed aloud, 'let the boy be all right.'

As her eyes became more accustomed to the darkness she saw a small hunched figure on the bench at the corner of the lawn. Her heart jumped. She ran through the gate and bent before the child and rested her hand on his.

'James?' she said quietly.

The boy looked up. His hair was wet with rain and his cheeks were smeared where he had been crying and his small lip trembled.

'James,' she said again. 'We've all be looking for you. Danny and me and your father.'

Suddenly the tears came welling up, spilling over. The boy began to sob, great heaving sobs, and he fell into Elisabeth's arms and hugged her.

'It's all right,' she said. 'You're safe. It's all right.' She stroked his hair and held his shuddering shoulders and thought of her own son, unreachable, shut away in his own private world. How she longed to hold *him* in her arms, stroke *his* hair and comfort *him* as she was now doing with this frightened little boy. She snuffled. 'My goodness, you've got me crying now,' she said.

They sat there in the darkness holding each other. The wet slates on the cottage roof glistened, the cold crescent moon shone in a coal-black sky and the stars winked. In the distance she heard the howl of a fox.

'Shall I take you home?' asked Elisabeth.

There was a small imperceptible whisper. 'Yes.'

*   *   *

Dr Stirling stood by the fireplace in the sitting room. Elisabeth sat opposite him on the large padded sofa, a glass of brandy cupped in her hands. It was a cold, unwelcoming room, dim and neglected with its heavy fawn-coloured curtains, earth-brown rug, dark cushions and dusty furniture. James had been tucked up in bed and the evening's drama, so they both thought, was over.

'I've been a bloody fool,' he said, taking a gulp from his glass.

Elisabeth didn't answer.

'A bloody fool,' he repeated. 'I never realised how much James disliked the idea of moving school. Young Danny was right, I should have listened, talked to him about it more.' He thought for moment. 'And I should have listened to you.'

'Well, I'm as guilty as anyone for listening but not hearing—if that makes any sense.' She took a sip of her drink and spluttered. 'I'm not used to spirits.'

'Really?'

'Oh yes. I always get the hiccoughs.'

'No, I meant about you not hearing.'

'I am afraid I am one of those people at education conferences whose mind wanders when I am listening to some speaker chuntering on about things that hold little interest for me, and I am not great at receiving other people's advice.'

He finished the brandy and placed the glass on the mantelpiece. 'Since my wife died I've thrown myself into my work,' Dr Stirling told her. 'I should have paid more attention to James. I've neglected the boy.'

'Hardly neglected,' said Elisabeth.

'Yes, I have. I've been too wrapped up in my own world.'

'Well, perhaps this has been a salutary lesson,' Elisabeth said, 'that we should listen more to what children try and tell us.'

Dr Stirling looked at her for a moment before speaking. He had been wrong about her, judged her unfairly. That evening she had been there for the boy and for him too.

'You know I was against you being appointed at the school,' he told her.

'I guessed as much,' said Elisabeth. 'You scowled all the way through the interview.'

'Scowled?' he cried. 'I never scowl.'

'You looked like a bulldog with toothache.'

He laughed. 'Really?'

'I could tell you were not impressed.'

'Actually I was very impressed with your answers,' he told her. 'It's just that I couldn't understand why someone who was a head teacher

225

of a large and successful school and on a good salary and with this wonderful inspectors' report and excellent references should want to come to a small school in a pretty remote village. I had the idea you were coming here for a quiet life. If you had explained about your son and the reason—'

'Why should I?' Elisabeth interrupted. 'It's not anyone else's business and I can't be doing with those overly sympathetic comments, the "Oh, you poor dear, it must be so hard for you." Anyway, there were other reasons for wanting to move. I needed a fresh start, a challenge, a break from the past.'

'I see.'

'My husband left me,' Elisabeth said suddenly. She had not told anyone about her past since moving to the village but for some inexplicable reason she wanted to tell him. When she thought about it later she couldn't explain to herself why she had felt the impulse at that moment to speak about it. 'Simon, he was my husband, wanted a "normal" son, whatever that means. He couldn't cope with his son's disability and left when John was five.'

'I'm sorry,' he said.

'Well, that's all water under the bridge.'

They were silent for a while.

'Does he see John at all?'

'No,' she said. 'He married again and started a new life. I don't feel any bitterness or anger; in fact I hope he's happy.' She looked into the quiet watchful eyes, blue as china marbles, which stared into her own. 'As happy as I am.'

Dr Stirling smiled. 'I'm glad,' he said. 'I can't tell you how grateful I am for what you have done tonight.' He continued to look into her eyes. 'I hope we can be friends, good friends, and that you'll have James back at Barton.'

'Do you need to ask?'

'No, I don't suppose I do,' he said. 'And your suggestion that James should see the psychologist.'

'Yes?'

'Perhaps you could arrange that.'

'Of course,' she replied.

They looked at each other for a moment and both realised they had changed from being combative strangers to becoming friends.

CHAPTER TWELVE

On the Monday morning Elisabeth looked at her pupils as they filed quietly into the school hall. She felt a certain satisfaction at what she had achieved. Things had certainly changed since she had taken over as head teacher two weeks ago, and not just in the appearance of the building and with the morale of the staff. Her insistence during the first week on silence as the children entered and left the hall at assembly time (with a few practice runs until they got it right), that they should make less noise at dinnertime and move around the school in a more orderly fashion, had been accepted by the children, who had responded surprisingly well. The only pupil who had taken exception to the firmer approach had been Malcolm Stubbins, but he was no longer with them and would be starting at his new school at Urebank that morning.

Miss Brakespeare attributed the improvement of the children's behaviour to the fact that the head teacher, when she was not teaching, spent most of her time around the school, unlike her predecessor, who had tended to keep herself closeted in her room. At morning and afternoon breaks and at lunchtime Elisabeth could usually be found in the hall supervising the lunches or in the playground getting to know the children. Her commitment and enthusiasm began rubbing off on her staff, who, like her, started arriving at school early, leaving later and spending little time in the staff-room.

'If you had a magic wand,' Elisabeth would ask a child, as she walked around the playground or sat with him or her at dinnertime, 'what changes would you make in the school?'

The answers were predictable. Many of the children bemoaned the fact that there was little happening out of lessons, no sports teams or after-school clubs, lunchtime activities and trips out of school, needs that Elisabeth had identified herself and which she was determined to meet.

The better behaviour of the children had been greatly welcomed by the teachers, not least Miss Brakespeare, who now, with a much reduced class, younger children and minus the troublemakers, found herself happier than she ever remembered being since she had started at the school.

When the children had assembled that morning, sung the hymn and said a prayer, Elisabeth addressed them.

'Now I have some quite exciting news,' she said. 'I have been having a word with different people in and around the village and I have asked some of them to come into school and offer a number of activities during the lunch-hour and after school, for those who are interested. Mrs Atticus, who is a very fine artist and who lives at the vicarage, will be coming in on Tuesday lunchtimes to take an art class. Mr Tomlinson, who plays the organ in the chapel, has agreed to help Mrs Robertshaw start a choir, and they will see those who are interested on Wednesdays. I have also persuaded Mr Parkinson, who is a scout leader, to take those boys and girls who are keen for football practice for an hour on Thursdays after school, and, if he feels we have the talent, which I am sure we have, he will start a couple of teams so that we can compete in the county competitions. Miss Wilson is eager to start a rounders team and the practices will take place, for boys and girls, at Friday lunchtimes. On some days you will see around school the vicar, the Reverend Atticus, who has agreed to take assembly now and again. There will also be a reading group, which I shall take every Monday and Friday lunchtime, and later I am hoping we can start a drama club too. I also have in mind organising some school trips and for the older children perhaps a visit to France next year.' There was a hubbub of excited chatter. 'Quietly, please.' The noise subsided. 'Now, all these things will be put in a letter which each of you will take home to your parents or guardians. I know you will make all our visitors very welcome when they come into our school and be on your best behaviour.' She paused. 'Won't you?'

'Yes, Mrs Devine,' the children chorused loudly.

On the way out of the hall, Elisabeth was approached by the large girl with the ginger hair and shiny braces on her teeth. 'Miss,' she said loudly, 'my mam's got rid of the nits.'

'I'm pleased to hear it, Chardonnay,' replied Elisabeth, smiling.

'She said they weren't mine.'

'Not yours?'

'No, miss,' said the girl. 'I've got ginger hair and my mam said they weren't ginger nits. I got them from somebody else.'

'I don't think nits come in different colours,' said Elisabeth, trying to stop herself laughing. 'Anyway, I'm glad you've got rid of them.'

'Miss, I thought James Stirling was leaving,' said the girl, changing the subject.

'Whatever gave you that idea, Chardonnay?' asked Elisabeth.

'Everybody said he was going to another school.'

'Well, you shouldn't believe what everyone says,' said Elisabeth. 'James has just been off school for a couple of weeks, but now he is back and we are very pleased to see him.'

'Miss,' said Chardonnay, pulling a face, 'is Malcolm Stubbins coming back as well?'

'No, I don't think so,' replied Elisabeth.

'Thank God for that,' said the girl, striding off.

On her way to the classroom Elisabeth was waylaid by Oscar. She noticed that he was wearing a pair of large glasses with very colourful frames.

'May I have a word, Mrs Devine?' he said.

'I like the glasses, Oscar,' Elisabeth told him.

He took a deep breath. 'Yes, unfortunately I have to wear them now, which is a bit of a devil. *I* picked the frames. My mother wanted me to have some others but I told her that since I was going to have to wear them, I should have the choice. I think they look quite stylish. They're designer. Anyway, I wanted to have a quick word with you about my mother. Now, I think it is a jolly good idea of yours to have all these activities going on in the school,

230

Mrs Devine.'

'I'm pleased you approve, Oscar,' said Elisabeth.

'And it occurred to me,' continued the boy, 'that my mother could teach everyone about ikebana. It's Japanese flower-arranging, you know. She is very good at it. She wins prizes. She could also run a yoga class. She only works three days a week now, so she has time on her hands. Shall I ask her?'

'That's really good of you to suggest that, Oscar,' Elisabeth said, trying to suppress a smile, 'but I don't really think there would be a lot of interest in the school for Japanese flower-arranging and yoga. However, I will certainly bear it in mind.'

'Very well,' the boy said cheerfully as he walked away. 'Just a thought.'

*   *   *

During the weeks that followed, the school became a hive of activity at lunchtime and after school. The clubs and extra classes, the sports activities and the music took off to such an extent that Elisabeth started to receive many positive comments from parents at the school gates about how pleased they were with these initiatives.

Mrs Robertshaw had recruited a good number of pupils for the choir, and the children, who delighted the minister and the congregation at the Methodist chapel at their first performance, became regular features at the services. The finest singer had been Chardonnay, who had a clear and powerful voice and had sung a solo. Mr Parkinson had formed a football team in which Chantelle had turned out to be the star player, and Miss Wilson's rounders team had very nearly won its first match against St Paul's. The Reverend Atticus had started to visit the school each week and had agreed to teach some religious education lessons in addition to taking assemblies. Elisabeth was delighted with the response and had been surprised at how much talent and enthusiasm there was among the children. The greatest revelation had come in the form of Ernest Pocock.

'He has a natural aptitude,' Marcia Atticus informed Elisabeth over a cup of coffee in the staff-room one Tuesday lunchtime. 'The boy has an excellent eye for detail and colour and a great sense of perspective. He's a miserable child at the best of times and tends to grunt rather than talk, but when he has a brush in his hand it is quite remarkable what he produces. It's a sort of primitive latent talent. I think he has a real chance of getting an award in the County Art Competition.'

Miss Brakespeare took a sip of her coffee, then smiled and shook her head. 'Ernest Pocock an artist. We shall have to start calling him Picasso,' she said.

*　　　*　　　*

On the morning following the dramatic events of the Sunday night, when James had run away and been discovered in Elisabeth's garden, Dr Stirling had brought his son into school early, before the other children had arrived. James sat with his father in Elisabeth's classroom as quiet and subdued as ever, but she had noticed, as she spoke, that on a number of occasions the boy had lifted his dark eyes shyly and looked at her. She would smile at him and he would give a small smile back before averting

232

his eyes. He was like some mollusc retreating into its shell when touched, a child locked, like her own son, into his own tight little world.

'It was quite a drama,' Dr Stirling said. He put an arm around his son's shoulders. 'We were really worried about you, young man,' he said, speaking to his son. 'Anyway, it's sorted out now and there will be no more running away. All right?'

The boy nodded.

'And you'll be a good boy for Mrs Devine.'

'He will be,' Elisabeth said. 'From what Miss Brakespeare has told me, he's never been anything other than a good boy and I am looking forward to teaching him.'

She walked with James's father to the entrance hall.

'I am very grateful for all you did last night, Elisabeth,' the doctor told her. 'It was quite a shock to the system, my son running away like that. One imagines the most dreadful things that might have happened. I had a talk with James this morning and, although he didn't say a great deal, I can tell he is happy to be staying here.'

'I'm very pleased to have him back,' Elisabeth said.

Dr Stirling stopped outside the school office. 'As I said last night, I've been a bit pig-headed and not been a very good listener,' he told Elisabeth. 'I don't wish to make excuses, but it has not been easy for me or for James since my wife died. It's affected him deeply. Perhaps, as you suggested, I could come in and talk about James's condition and see if we can work together to get him to open up a little more. Maybe see that psychologist you mentioned.'

'Of course,' Elisabeth replied, 'I'll arrange it.

Before you go, there are a couple of favours I would ask of you though, Dr Stirling.' There was a twinkle in her eye.

'Oh dear, this sounds ominous.' His face broke into a smile. 'Come along then, what are they?'

Elisabeth rested a hand on his arm. 'Nothing too onerous, I can assure you. Firstly, I want you to remain as a governor at the school.'

'Done,' he replied.

'Now that wasn't too bad, was it?' Elisabeth told him, smiling with the sort of tolerant patient smile a teacher might employ when comforting a small child.

'No, not too bad,' he agreed. 'What next?'

'Sex.'

'Sex!' he spluttered.

'The older pupils need a few sex education lessons,' Elisabeth told him.

The doctor laughed. 'And you want me to do them? I think there are people much better qualified to talk to children about sex than I.'

'Oh, I think I can manage talking to the girls on this topic, but I think the boys might be less embarrassed and better informed and be prepared to ask questions if their lessons were from a man. And who better than a doctor, and you have such a wonderful way with words.'

'You are teasing me, Mrs Devine,' he said good-naturedly.

'So?' she asked.

'I'll have to think about it,' Dr Stirling told her.

'No, Dr Stirling,' said Elisabeth, resting a hand in his arm. 'I want an answer here and now and if you refuse—'

'OK, OK,' he interrupted. 'I'll do it. But if I do,

234

you must start calling me Michael. I think we can dispense with the Dr Stirling bit, don't you? After all, we are friends now, aren't we?'

'Very well, Michael,' she said and felt a small rush of blood to her face.

When James's father had gone Elisabeth returned to the classroom. The boy looked a sad little figure, sitting at his desk staring out of the window.

'Come along, James,' she said cheerfully, 'you can have a walk around the school with me. I often do this before everyone arrives, to make sure it's clean and there's no litter.' As they toured the school, Elisabeth outlined the plans she had for all the extracurricular activities and how she was going to tell everyone in assembly that morning. James listened but said nothing. They stopped and looked across the school field to the vast, white expanse of sky, the undulating green pastures dotted with sheep, the tall pine woods and distant sombre peaks. They stood there in silence. 'And you know, James,' Elisabeth said after a while and resting a hand gently on the boy's shoulder, 'if there's anything that troubles you again, you must tell your father. He loves you very much and wants the best for you.' The boy reached out and touched her hand, and then he rested his head gently on her arm for a moment.

*   *   *

Dr Stirling arrived at his surgery that morning in a buoyant mood. He could not recall when he had been quite as happy as he felt that day. His secretary, used to his familiar serious expression, looked up startled when she heard him whistling as he breezed through the door.

'Good morning, Dr Stirling,' she said.

'And a very good morning to you too, Margaret,' he said smiling.

He sat at his desk, leaned back in the chair and thought for a moment. It was as if a great pressing burden had been lifted from his shoulders. He had felt desperate and fearful when his son had gone missing, imagining the most terrible things. It had been almost more than he could bear. And the more he thought about it the more Elisabeth Devine came into his mind. It was she who had helped him through it all. She was, without doubt, a forceful, opinionated, strong-minded woman, but there was more to her than that, another side to her which he had witnessed when he saw her at Forest View sitting next to her son, with tears in her eyes. She hadn't appeared so forceful then. And all the time James was missing she had been there with him, supportive and tender. He had misjudged the woman. He liked her company, he liked it very much.

The first patient of the morning was Mr Gribbon. He walked into the consulting room with the gait of a zombie and a face etched in pain.

'Ah, Mr Gribbon,' said the doctor cheerfully. 'How good to see you.'

'You're in a good mood,' observed his patient glumly, as he eased himself into a chair.

'Indeed I am, Mr Gribbon, and who wouldn't be on such a lovely bright sunny day?'

'Me for a start,' said the caretaker morosely.

'What seems to be the matter this time?' asked Dr Stirling, knowing full well that it would be

236

the troublesome back. He knew that there was nothing much wrong with his patient's back and that the caretaker was here for a doctor's note to give him a few days off work. Over the years Mr Gribbon had been referred to numerous specialists, physiotherapists, osteopaths, hydrotherapists, acupuncturists and chiropractors, all of whom could detect nothing.

'Same old problem,' said the caretaker, wincing.

'The back?'

'Aye, the back. It's giving me more gyp.'

'I'm sorry to hear that.'

'That new head teacher's got me lifting boxes, lugging desks about, laying paving slabs, climbing up ladders, fitting shelves, and it's taking its toll. She's a real Tartar and no mistake is Mrs Devine. I've never worked so hard since she started.'

'Perhaps you are in the wrong line of work,' suggested Dr Stirling.

'Eh?'

'Perhaps you should consider a more sedentary occupation.'

'Eh?'

'Perhaps you are not up to the job any more.'

'Not up to the job? I never said that, doctor.'

'Perhaps a younger and fitter person might be better suited to the work at the school. I could have a word with Mrs Devine if you wish.'

'No, no, I like the job, but a few days' rest and I'll soon be right as rain.'

'I think we need something more drastic this time, Mr Gribbon,' said the doctor, in a mock-serious tone of voice.

'More drastic?' the caretaker repeated, looking shocked. 'How do you mean, more drastic?'

'I think we will have to operate,' the doctor told him.

'Operate?'

'It will be a long and painful experience and, of course, not guaranteed to work, but I feel it is for the best. I am going to refer to you a specialist in Urebank and he will arrange for your hospitalisation and the operation.'

'I don't want no operation,' said the caretaker, getting up from the chair in a surprisingly agile movement.

'Well, in that case, it's a matter of taking painkillers and grinning and bearing it,' Dr Stirling told him.

'Well, I'll bear it, doctor, as I always have, but as to the grinning I'll give that a miss.'

With that the caretaker headed for the door rather faster than he had entered.

*   *   *

At school lunchtime, Mrs Scrimshaw came scurrying into the playground to find Elisabeth.

'Oh, Mrs Devine,' she said, resting a hand on her chest as if she had a pain, 'she's in the entrance. She wants to see you. I'm all of a fluster. I said that you were not available at the moment but she said she'd wait and then I said you teach in the mornings and afternoons and could she make an appointment to come back at another time when you would be free but she insisted. She wants to see you now. Talk about forceful. I couldn't say no to her, being who she is and all, so I put her in the staff-room. I hope I did right.'

'Who is it who wishes to see me?' asked

238

Elisabeth, intrigued and not a little anxious. Is it Miss Sowerbutts, she wondered, making a dramatic reappearance like some pantomime villain to complain about the changes, or a return visit from Mrs Stubbins? Or maybe it's another angry parent come to complain.

'It's Lady Wadsworth,' said Mrs Scrimshaw. 'She lives at Limebeck House. She's titled and owns all the land around the village. She makes the Queen sound common.'

'Oh,' said Elisabeth.

'And she's brought it with her.'

'It?'

'The plaque. Miss Sowerbutts and her had a terrible falling out over the plaque. It was removed from the entrance when they did the redecoration and Miss Sowerbutts refused to put it back up. She thought it looked ugly and out of place. Lady Helen's here with it. I suppose she wants you to stick it back up on the wall.'

'Which I intend doing, Mrs Scrimshaw,' said Elisabeth. 'Lady Wadsworth has already had a word with me.'

'She has?'

'And I think it is an excellent idea.'

'You do?'

'I do. It's part of the school's history. Now, would you get Lady Wadsworth a cup of tea and tell her I shall be along presently.'

'I'll get out the best china cups,' said the secretary, scurrying off.

Elisabeth found her visitor sitting in the staff-room with a cup on her lap. She wore a ridiculously colourful checked tweed suit as shapeless as a sack of potatoes, and a

239

wide-brimmed green felt hat sporting two long pheasant feathers and held in place by a silver brooch in the shape of a fox's head. The outfit was complemented by thick brown stockings and shoes of the heavy, sensible brogue variety with little leather acorns attached to the front. She looked magnificently outlandish.

'Mrs Devine,' she said heartily, rising to her feet as Elisabeth entered the room. 'I do hope I have not come at an inconvenient time.' Before Elisabeth could answer she gestured to the uneaten chocolate biscuits on the plate beside her. 'The tea was most acceptable but I shall forgo the confection,' she said. 'Mrs Sloughthwaite's Venetian selection box, as she insists on calling it, gets everywhere. I see she has managed to foist some on to you. They are the sickliest, stalest and altogether most unappetising concoctions I have ever tasted. I swear she has had them in her shop since before the war.'

'Yes, I can't say that I am over-keen on them,' said Elisabeth. 'It's good to see you, Lady Wadsworth.'

'Helen, please,' she said. 'I feel I know you already, and now we are neighbours, so to speak, we will no doubt see a deal of each other.' She gulped the remainder of her tea. 'I've brought it.' She placed the cup down and pointed to a large brass plaque leaning against a wall. 'After our very pleasant conversation on Sunday, I thought I would drop it off before you change your mind. It is admittedly a little on the large side, rather like my grandfather really, who was larger than life, but it is quite tasteful, don't you think, and of good workmanship? Watson, my general factotum at the

240

house, has given it a good buffing up. I can show you where it used to go.'

The plaque was indeed rather large—at least three feet square. 'I'll get Mr Gribbon to fix it to the wall,' said Elisabeth, wondering if she had done the right thing in agreeing to have it reinstated.

'Splendid,' said Lady Wadsworth.

'Perhaps, while you're here, you might like to look around,' suggested Elisabeth.

'I told you I was a rather inquisitive person,' Lady Wadsworth replied, 'and I should like that very much. I have to say I didn't recognise the place when I walked through the door. You have certainly made some changes, as you have at the cottage.' Again, Elisabeth wondered if her visitor altogether approved. It was her rather sharp tone of voice and the way she scrutinised everything.

It was clear after her tour of the school that Lady Wadsworth did indeed approve and was suitably impressed with the changes that had been made.

'I have an idea,' Elisabeth told her as they viewed a dark corner near the toilets, 'that if I can squeeze some funding out of the Education Office we could have a small library here, with a carpet and cushions, a small table and chairs and a good selection of books.'

'It's a splendid idea,' agreed Lady Wadsworth. 'I am all in favour of children reading. "Books are the architecture of a civilised society," as my grandfather used to say, "and reading is the very protein of growth in learning." He was a very erudite man, the second Viscount, and wrote books himself, you know.' She smiled before adding, 'Although Miss Beatrix Potter's books about fluffy, cotton-tailed bunny rabbits would not be on my

241

reading list.'

*   *   *

That afternoon Elisabeth's class, having heard a story she read to them about a man who lost the winning lottery ticket, was asked to write an account of something valuable or precious which had been lost.

'I'm writing about the time my mum lost her ring,' said Chardonnay, when Elisabeth went to look at her work. 'It was her engagement ring and she took it off last Christmas to try on a ring my gran had given her and it got thrown out with all the wrapping paper.'

'Oh dear,' said Elisabeth.

'My dad went barmy,' the girl said, folding her arms before her and launching into a quick-fire description of the events. 'My dad said she should have been more careful, and she said he shouldn't have thrown out all the paper. We spent ages looking though the dustbin. Then they had a right ding-dong. I think my dad had had a bit too much to drink. Then my gran got this turkey bone stuck in her throat and nearly choked and my sister had an argument with Duane, her boyfriend, because he bought her this cheap perfume and she was expecting some jewellery and he went home and she ended up crying in the toilet all day and then the dog was sick on the carpet and my little cousin Oliver pushed a nut up his nose and had to go to the hospital to have it taken out and they used this big silver needle with a little hook on the end.' The girl took a breath. 'He's always doing daft things like that. He pushed some popcorn up his nose once and when my Auntie Carol got it down he ate it and she went—'

'It sounds a very eventful Christmas,' interrupted Elisabeth, stemming the flow.

'We had a rotten Christmas as well,' said Chantelle, who had been listening. 'My dad bought my mum this red silk underwear and she stuffed it back in the box and told him that only tarts wear red underwear and she'd not be seen dead in it and she wanted a deep fat fryer. My nan looked at this red underwear and said that my mum's dad had gone through that stage.'

'And did your mother find her ring, Chardonnay?' Elisabeth asked, eager to change the subject from the red silk underwear.

'No, she never did,' replied the girl. 'Anyway she's got another now and it's a bigger one.'

'So it all worked out for the best,' said Elisabeth.

'Yes, miss,' said Chardonnay. 'My mum's new partner bought it for her after my dad left.'

That evening Elisabeth sat down to mark the children's exercise books. Her pupils had really made an effort to write interesting accounts on the topic she had set for them and they had taken care with their writing. There was an authenticity about much of the work. Chardonnay's long, rambling description of the misplaced ring and Chantelle's account of the time her mother had lost her contact lens in the cinema made her laugh out loud. Danny's detailed and informative account, predictably about his ferret, described the time Ferdie had disappeared down a rabbit hole and had been missing for three days. Darren Holgate wrote of the occasion at his cousin's wedding when his father had ended up in a fight in which he had lost

243

two teeth. Then Elisabeth got to James's piece of work.

'The most precious thing I have lost is my mum,' he wrote. Elisabeth's heart missed a beat. 'Sometimes when I'm in bed at night I try and think of her face but I can't see it and it makes me upset. The next morning I have to look at the picture on the shelf in the kitchen and the one in the sitting room to remind me. In the photographs she's dressed in her riding outfit, sitting on Spangle, the horse she was riding when she died. I remember the smell of her though, really clearly. It's a smell of hay and stables and freshly mown grass and summertime. Sometimes a piece of music she liked reminds me of her and I begin to cry. I remember too the way she laughed. It used to make my dad laugh. He doesn't laugh much any more. He spends a lot of time staring out of the window. It makes me feel very sad. The most precious thing that I've lost is my mum and I shall never forget her.'

He had written underneath, 'Please don't read this out to the class.'

Elisabeth closed the exercise book. 'Oh, James,' she said aloud.

*   *   *

The following Monday, Elisabeth arranged for Dr Stirling to see Mrs Goldstein, the educational psychologist. He listened intently as the condition of selective mutism was explained to him.

'James has a relatively rare condition,' Mrs Goldstein told him, 'but I have every reason to believe that he can be helped and that things will improve. From what you have told me he is

244

perfectly capable of speech and understanding language and can read well, but in certain social situations he is silent. At school I gather he doesn't say anything except to his best friend.'

'Yes, that's right,' said Dr Stirling, 'although I believe he has said a few words to the head teacher on occasions.'

'Is there anyone else he speaks to?'

'He sometimes speaks to Mrs O'Connor, my housekeeper.'

'But he speaks quite freely at home to you?' she asked.

'Yes, he's still a little quiet, but then, as I've said, he's always been rather reticent since my wife died. After his mother's death, which he still has not really come to terms with, he's seemed to go into a shell when he's with other people.'

'It's not uncommon for a child to withdraw into himself like this after some trauma which gives a sense of incredible loss. It is a fact, and I am sure I don't need to tell a doctor this, but time is a great healer.'

'So what do we do?' asked the doctor.

'Well, there's no magic cure for a start, but lots of love and support and patience from family and friends can have a real impact on any success in treating this condition. Providing James with emotional encouragement can be very beneficial. He should never be prompted to speak, but attention should be taken to making him feel comfortable and relaxed and confident in social settings. From what I saw in the school this morning, I think your son is in very good hands here and is well placed to make real progress. Mrs Devine strikes me as a very competent and capable head teacher.'

And she's much more than that, thought Dr Stirling.

* * *

Mrs Atticus's Tuesday lunchtime art class proved very popular and successful and the school corridors and classrooms soon became richly colourful, with vibrant paintings and sketches, delicate watercolours and line drawings. The vicar's wife turned out to be a natural teacher. Elisabeth called in at the art class and found Mrs Atticus well organised, enthusiastic and with a firm, no-nonsense approach with the children.

'I can see you have really taken to this,' Elisabeth told her one lunchtime.

'Do you know,' replied Mrs Atticus, 'I have to say I had some misgivings about coming in to teach the children, but I am really enjoying working with them and I have discovered some real talent. I shall be entering some of their work for the County Art Competition.'

'You know, perhaps you ought to think of training as a teacher,' suggested Elisabeth. 'I've mentioned it to you before. You should think about it. I've checked—there is a course at St John's College and you could do your teaching practice here. We should be delighted to have you.'

'Thank you, Elisabeth,' replied Mrs Atticus. 'I might just do that. I shall speak to my husband on the matter. Do you know, I have to admit that I've felt quite liberated since coming here. I've been stuck in that dark and depressing vicarage for so long with very little to do, it really got me down.'

246

Her eyes glinted with pleasure. 'It's been like a breath of fresh air coming here.'

Dr Stirling arrived at the school the following Tuesday to take the lesson on sex education as he had promised. He entered the classroom with Elisabeth, who introduced him and explained to the children what the lesson that day would be about. She imagined that James would be embarrassed by seeing his father at the front of the classroom talking about such a delicate subject, but he seemed unconcerned. Elisabeth appreciated that the subject of sex required very sensitive and careful handling, and seeing several of the boys smirking and nudging one another she felt it appropriate that she should stand eagle-eyed at the front of the classroom. She noticed that a cheeky smile had appeared on the face of Ernest Pocock. She would watch that particular young man, she thought to herself.

The children listened attentively as Dr Stirling explained, simply and clearly, the human reproductive system and the changes that would be taking place in the children's bodies as they grew older. Elisabeth took over to talk about the moral implications of sexual relationships. At the end she asked if there were any questions.

She was met with silence.

'There must be some questions you would like to ask Dr Stirling,' she prompted.

Ernest Pocock raised a hand. He had a cheeky smile right across his face.

I might have guessed it would be him, thought Elisabeth. What deeply embarrassing question had he thought up?

'Yes, Ernest, what would you like to ask?' she

247

said, bracing herself.

'Will there be the art class this lunchtime, miss?' he asked.

CHAPTER THIRTEEN

Mrs Scrimshaw was putting on her coat ready to go home when Mr Gribbon appeared at the door of the office with a gloomy expression in his long face.

'You're off, then,' he said.

'I am,' replied the secretary. 'I've got a WI meeting tonight. Mr Smith, from the undertakers in Clayton, is talking on "The Lighter Side of Funerals".'

'Sounds a barrel of laughs,' observed the caretaker. 'I'm glad the weekend's here, I can tell you. It's been a week and a half.'

'Really?'

He jangled the heavy bunch of keys in his pocket. 'You know, I miss our little chats at the end of the day. I used to like coming in here after school.'

'Yes, well,' replied Mrs Scrimshaw, 'I'm just pleased I can get off home at a reasonable hour instead of hanging about here as I used to do, twiddling my thumbs and waiting for some non-existent phone call from the Education Office or a parent, while Miss Sowerbutts shot out of the school at the sound of the bell.'

'Mrs Devine's on at me to put that plaque back on the wall,' the caretaker complained. 'I thought if I left it for a bit she'd forget about it, but she hasn't, so I suppose I shall have to stick it back up. I could tell her where I'd like to stick it, if it was up to me—'

'Yes, I know about the plaque,' interrupted Mrs Scrimshaw. 'Lady Helen brought it in herself before half-term. Mrs Devine was wondering when you'd get around to putting it back up.'

'It's bloody heavy, I can tell you. Pardon my French. It took a right job getting it off the wall and now it's to go back up. I wish they'd make up their minds.'

'It should never have been removed in the first place,' said the secretary. 'I said at the time that Lady Helen would not be best pleased.'

'There's been some changes since Mrs Devine's took over,' sighed the caretaker. 'Every day there's something new. If it isn't one thing, it's another. Now all these people coming in and out, it's like King's Cross station at rush hour.'

'The changes have been all for the better as far as I am concerned, Mr Gribbon,' replied the secretary curtly. 'The children are better behaved, the staff are happier, my office has more space, I can have my lunch in the staff-room instead of at my desk and I can get off home at a reasonable time. I think it's a very good idea to have all these things going on. And it can't have escaped your notice either that parents aren't taking their children away as they used to do. In fact I've had enquiries from some who are thinking of sending their children here, and from what I've heard from Mrs Sloughthwaite, some of those parents who took their children away and sent them to Urebank are now having second thoughts.'

'I know that things have changed for the better,' said the caretaker. 'I'm not denying that, Mrs Scrimshaw, it's just that it's meant a lot more work

249

for me and what with my bad back—'

'Oh, for goodness sake, Mr Gribbon!' she snapped. 'Do stop complaining. Give the woman some credit for what she's done.' Of course, thought the school secretary, the caretaker would find some of the changes not entirely to his liking. He had had to work a whole lot harder since the new head teacher had taken over. Mrs Devine was in the habit of patrolling the building before and after school to make certain everything was clean and orderly. It certainly kept Mr Gribbon on his toes.

'You've changed your tune,' said the caretaker.

'I beg your pardon?' asked the secretary.

'As I recall, you were not all that happy when she was appointed.'

'Excuse me, Mr Gribbon,' Mrs Scrimshaw said sharply, 'I don't remember saying anything adverse when Mrs Devine was appointed. If my memory serves me right, I said she was very pleasant and chatty. I merely made a comment about her appearance when she came for the interview. And as to that, I think she looks very smart and eye-catching. As far as I am concerned, I think Mrs Devine is doing an excellent job and I agree with all the changes she's made.'

'I'm not saying things haven't improved,' said the caretaker quickly, 'it's just that—'

'Just what?' snapped the secretary.

'Well, just that there's been so many changes.'

'Change can be a good thing,' said Mrs Scrimshaw.

'Well, I don't know why she wants to go inviting all these people into school,' moaned the caretaker, jangling the bunch of keys in his pocket.

'It's to give the children the opportunity of hearing from different people,' the secretary told him. She was wearying of the caretaker's continual carping.

'I thought it was teachers what taught kids, not every Tom, Dick and Harry.'

'It's all about extending the children's education, Mr Gribbon,' she told him. 'I'm all for it.'

'Yes, well, you don't have to clear up after the vicar's wife's been in. It's the devil's own job getting that paint off of the desks after she's been in there with that art class of hers, and I'm sick to death of telling old man Tomlinson not to keep wheeling that piano backwards and forwards on my parquet floor when he's been in the hall with the choir. There's been scuffs. Then there's the clearing up after the rounders team and looking after the football pitch. I never had all this to do when we had Miss Sowerbutts in charge.'

'You do get paid overtime,' observed the secretary.

'That's not the point,' grumbled the caretaker.

'I'll mention your complaints to Mrs Devine,' replied the school secretary, knowing full well what reaction this observation would receive.

'No, no, don't do that,' said Mr Gribbon quickly. 'I'm just saying.'

Mrs Scrimshaw stopped what she was doing and looked at the caretaker. 'So you think it was better when Miss Sowerbutts was in charge, do you, Mr Gribbon?' asked the secretary.

'I didn't say that,' he replied defensively.

'Because if you are, then you're the only person who does.'

'I'm just saying—' he began.

251

'Well, I think it's an excellent idea having these visitors in school. And I'll say this, that if the rumours about the school closing are true, you won't have all this extra work you're complaining about, will you?' The caretaker was silent and grimaced. 'Now I shall leave you to stick the plaque back on the wall,' said Mrs Scrimshaw, edging past him.

*   *   *

'So how are you liking it at your new school then, Malcolm?' asked Mrs Sloughthwaite. She kept a wary eye on the items displayed on the counter as she asked the question. The boy might not be very good at much but at sleight of hand he was the master.

'It's all right,' mumbled the boy.

It was the following afternoon, and Mrs Stubbins had called in at the village store to do her weekly shopping. She smoothed an eyebrow with a little finger. 'Oh, he's settled in really well,' she told the shopkeeper. 'Best thing I ever did was move him. He was never happy at Barton, were you, Malcolm?'

'No,' the boy muttered. He glanced surreptitiously at the counter where the sweets were displayed.

'Teachers were always picking on him,' continued Mrs Stubbins. 'That Miss Brakespeare did nothing but find fault, and Miss Sowerbutts hadn't a good word to say about him. He spent more time standing outside her door than in the classroom. I thought I'd give this new head teacher a chance, but she's like the rest and she had it in for

252

him as soon as he started. Didn't she, Malcolm?'

The boy nodded.

'I went in to see her, you know,' Mrs Stubbins told the shopkeeper.

'Really?' said Mrs Sloughthwaite.

'She was all hoity-toity with me and looked down her nose as if I was something she'd found on the soles of those fancy red shoes of hers.'

'You don't say.'

'Only got savaged by a ferret!'

'You didn't.'

'Not me,' said Mrs Stubbins, prodding her son. 'Him. That's why I went into school. That Stainthorpe lad brought in this ferret, smelly, vicious thing it was, and he let it loose and when it attacked my Malcolm and nearly took half his finger off and he tried to pull it off, he hit him. He come home with a lump on his forehead the size of a pullet's egg, didn't you, Malcolm?'

'Yeah, I did,' the boy muttered.

'That Mrs Devine tried to blame it on my Malcolm. I told her in no uncertain terms that I wasn't having it.'

'You didn't.'

'I did. So I've took him away and sent him to Urebank. He's better off there, aren't you, Malcolm?'

The boy didn't reply.

If truth be told, Malcolm had not settled in at Urebank and he felt he was not better off at all. The first week at his new school he had kept his head down and behaved himself, watching and listening, but he found the work hard and tedious and he didn't like his teacher, a tall thin man with lank hair and a dull reddish face, a man

253

devoid of humour who spoke through his nose in a monotonous drawl. The new boy was made to sit at the front by himself; he soon found that the teacher was less than impressed with the work he produced and covered his exercise book with red ink as if he had bled over it.

Then there was reading around the class. On Friday morning, each child in turn was required to read a page of the class reader, a very boring and difficult book. Most of Malcolm's fellow pupils were very good readers and read quickly and accurately. When it came to his turn the boy's stomach did kangaroo jumps and he mumbled and stumbled over the words, much to the amusement of the other children and the displeasure of the teacher. He hated it.

Any attempts on Malcolm's part to make friends with some of the other boys in his year proved unsuccessful. Whenever he approached a group in the playground at breaktime the boys observed him like some alien creature and wandered off laughing. They were in their last year at primary school and these boys had grown up together, forming close friendship groups, and were not inclined to let this outsider who lived in the next village into their midst. One thing he knew he was good at was football, but the team was well established and successful and his offer to play in a match fell on deaf ears. When, after a week of miserable silence in class, Malcolm started to make his presence felt in a misguided attempt to impress his peers, by shouting out and making clever comments, he was sent to stand outside the head teacher's room. He stood there wretchedly unhappy and lonely and wished he had never moved from Barton.

'You might have got away with such behaviour at Barton,' Mr Richardson had told him, the veins in his temple standing out and throbbing angrily, 'but you will not get away with it here!'

Malcolm had pouted and looked at the floor, shifting uncomfortably from foot to foot and wishing he was back at Barton.

'Yes,' his mother told the shopkeeper now, 'he's much better off there, aren't you, Malcolm?'

Her son didn't answer.

Mrs Sloughthwaite was adept at gleaning information and gossip from those who patronised her shop. She was also very skilled at teasing those customers she did not like, and she did so in such an apparently innocent way, with a sympathetic expression on her round and friendly face, that they failed to see that she was deliberately provoking them. She disliked this loud woman with the sullen, light-fingered son but, being a shrewd shopkeeper, did not wish to lose her custom.

'Oh, I'm sure he is better off where he is,' said Mrs Sloughthwaite. 'It's surprising, though, that Malcolm didn't get on at the village school. All the parents who come into the shop since Mrs Devine took over seem very content with the way things are and very happy with the changes that the new head teacher is making. And from what I hear, some of those parents who sent their kiddies to Urebank are regretting it now they've heard about the improvements. I reckon some of them will be sending them back here before too long.' She chuckled inwardly at the evident consternation her comments were creating.

'What, some children are coming back here?' piped up Malcolm. 'Can I—'

His mother ignored him. 'Be quiet!' she snapped.

'Yes, the village school is getting quite a reputation,' said the shopkeeper.

'Well, I wouldn't know about that,' said Mrs Stubbins. 'Anyway, not everybody's that happy. Dr Stirling has taken his son away.'

'That was just a silly rumour,' the shopkeeper told her. 'Mrs O'Connor, the doctor's housekeeper, was telling me that only yesterday and she should know. The boy's still at Barton, so she said.'

'Oh,' was all her customer could say.

'They've got a choir there now,' Mrs Sloughthwaite continued. 'The children sang in the Bethesda chapel on Sunday and Mrs Widowson said they sounded lovely, and she's not one to give out compliments easily.'

'I've never been one for hymns and such myself,' disclosed Mrs Stubbins, rather scornfully.

'And I hear they've got a rounders team,' continued the shopkeeper, amused by the woman's sour-looking expression.

'You don't say,' said Mrs Stubbins, trying to sound indifferent.

'And a football team,' announced the shopkeeper.

'A football team!' cried Malcolm, his body becoming suddenly animated like a puppet with its strings pulled.

'So I hear,' said the shopkeeper.

'They never had a football team when I was there,' he said petulantly.

'Well, they have now,' Mrs Sloughthwaite informed him. 'And they've started a chess club and an art group. Mrs Pocock was telling me her Ernest is quite a dab hand with a paintbrush and has taken

256

to painting like a duck to water. Had a picture entered for a competition. She says he's coming along a treat at school these days.'

'I didn't know they had a football team,' said Malcolm sourly. 'It's probably rubbish.'

Mrs Sloughthwaite leaned over and rested her Amazonian bosom and her dimpled arms on the counter. She looked down at the sulky boy. 'And are you in the football team at Urebank, then, Malcolm?' she asked.

'No,' he muttered, scowling.

* * *

'The thing is,' said Mr Richardson over the telephone, 'it's not quite working out.'

'Oh, I'm sorry to hear that,' said Elisabeth, trying not to sound too pleased.

She had received the call on the day when the governors' meeting was to be held, and was busy preparing the papers in the office with Mrs Scrimshaw.

'Yes,' said the head teacher of Urebank school. 'I wasn't aware when I agreed to accept this boy of his track record.'

'Track record? What track record would that be?' Elisabeth asked, feigning ignorance.

'What he was like,' said Mr Richardson. 'I am sure that the Stubbins boy was as big a nuisance when he was with you as he is with us. You gave me no indication that he was a particularly difficult and disruptive individual.'

'You never asked,' replied Elisabeth.

'I beg your pardon?'

'Mr Richardson, you never asked about Malcolm

Stubbins or why his mother wished to move him. You merely told me that Mrs Stubbins had been to see you and that you were intending to admit her son to your school. You pointed out, as I recall, that his mother didn't go into all the ins and outs of the situation as to why she wanted to move the boy, just that she felt her son would be better suited at your school.'

'Indeed,' he said, trying to keep control of his obvious anger, 'but had I known how rude and uncooperative and unruly he is, I should not have considered letting him come here. He has had a dire effect on my school and I have teachers and parents complaining about his behaviour. Why, only yesterday he got into a fight with another boy and last week he was insolent to his form teacher. I also have an idea it was this boy who stole some dinner money from the school office when the secretary was at lunch, and wrote some particularly obscene words on the wall in the boys' toilets. I had the devil's own job calming one of my dinner ladies down when he appeared in the dining room wearing a condom on his head. Yes, indeed, a condom! The boy is completely unmanageable and I do not intend to have him here any longer.'

'You also said, Mr Richardson,' said Elisabeth, 'that if a parent comes to you wanting to move his or her child and is insistent, then there is nothing you nor I can do about it.'

Mr Richardson decided not to respond to that comment. 'Mrs Devine, I am asking you to take this boy back. I should like to send for his mother and inform her that I feel he is better suited to return to Barton.' He waited for a response but Elisabeth intentionally remained silent. 'After all,' the

258

speaker continued, 'he is in your catchment area and should by rights attend your school.'

'Like the other children who live in the village but who attend Urebank,' replied Elisabeth. She felt like telling him that already several parents were intending to move their children back to Barton, but she thought it judicious not to do so. He would soon find out.

There was a silence. 'So I take it you will not have the boy back?' he asked.

'If Malcolm's mother wants him to attend your school rather than mine, Mr Richardson, then there is really nothing I can do.'

'You could have a word with his mother and tell her it would be for the best if her son returns to you.'

'No, I don't think that is a very good idea, Mr Richardson,' said Elisabeth. 'I think it is up to you to speak to her.'

'I see,' he said sharply. 'Well, I shall not be letting this matter rest and shall be contacting the Education Office.' He thumped down the phone.

Mrs Scrimshaw, who had been listening intently to this exchange, put down the papers she had been stapling together and pulled a face. 'My goodness, Mrs Devine, you certainly told him where to go.'

'Have you ever come across the word Schadenfreude, Mrs Scrimshaw?' Elisabeth asked the school secretary.

*　　　*　　　*

Elisabeth was feeling in particularly high spirits that day. Prior to Mr Richardson's telephone call she had shown two sets of parents around the school

259

and been assured by them that their children would be starting there the following week. The reputation of Barton-in-the-Dale had increased so greatly over the relatively short time since she had taken on the headship that a growing number of parents of children from outside the catchment area were enquiring about sending their sons and daughters to the school. Elisabeth had not informed Mr Richardson, but only that morning she had received two letters from parents who had sent their children to Urebank and now requested that they return. For Elisabeth it was a clear vindication of all the things she had done, and she felt a great sense of pride and achievement.

One very weepy and garrulous mother had made an appointment to see her and begged Elisabeth to take her son back, sniffing and tweaking at her ring anxiously as she sat in the school entrance.

'Mrs Devine,' she said plaintively, 'do please let him return. Jason has never settled at the other school. I wish I'd never taken him away. He didn't like it here when the former head teacher, Miss Sowerbutts, was in charge. Frightened to death of her he was. I put his bed-wetting and his nail-biting and his nervous rash down to his unhappiness.'

'Mrs Moss—' Elisabeth began, intending to tell the mother that she would be delighted to have the boy back, but the woman continued to gabble on regardless.

'I thought Jason would be happier at Urebank and when other parents started moving their kiddies, I did the same. I regret it now. Everyone you speak to says the school is really good now.'

'Mrs Moss—' Elisabeth tried again but to no avail.

260

'But Jason doesn't like Urebank any more than he did when he was here. Cries himself to sleep he does and then his rash has erupted and his bed-wetting got out of control. I'm at my wits' end. I did go into the school but got nowhere with the head teacher, who was very offhand and didn't want to know and then when Jason came home with a cut lip—'

'Of course he can come back,' interrupted Elisabeth. 'I should be delighted to see Jason next Monday. You just need to inform Urebank of your intentions.' As she said it Elisabeth tried to picture the face of Mr Richardson when he was informed.

'Oh, Mrs Devine,' sighed the parent, beginning to sniffle, 'thank you.'

As she toured the bright, orderly building now and went into classes where the children were working purposefully and looked clearly happy, she felt a genuine pride. The school was flourishing, numbers were increasing and the haemorrhaging of children to Urebank had been staunched. All this was ammunition that she needed for the governors' meeting that evening, when she would raise the question of the school's future.

*　　　*　　　*

The three conspirators met in conclave in the corner of the Blacksmith's Arms, prior to the meeting of the governing body.

'I think it might be best, major,' said Mr Nettles, 'if you let me take the lead when we come to the first item on the agenda, about the school closure. I am fully conversant with the various procedures and processes for closing a school, and the meeting, in my experience, could be a little controversial.'

'Oh, I think not, Mr Nettles,' remarked Councillor Smout, draining his pint glass. 'As I was sayin' to you t'last time we were in 'ere, I don't think there'll be that much opposition. 'Owever, we need to tread carefully.'

'I wish I could be as confident, councillor,' observed the education officer smugly before taking a sip of his slimline tonic. 'In my experience these meetings can be quite heated.' Mr Nettles, in fact, had no experience in the closure of a school but his two companions were not to know that. The education officer, who had only recently moved from school transport, where he had been less than successful, was a man, despite his lack of experience in educational matters and his limited ability, supremely confident in his own talents. The fact that he had few abilities and little talent, save the ones of pushing himself forward and ingratiating himself with those who mattered, did not deter him from telling all who would listen that he was well versed in every aspect of the educational system. He was a self-satisfied and ambitious man and looked with greedy eyes to the time when he would be the Director of Education and occupy the large mahogany desk at County Hall.

'Look, Mr Nettles,' said Councillor Smout, 'let's be clear about this. T'school is small by any standards, it's losing pupils 'and-over-fist, includin' Dr Stirling's lad, and 'im a governor as well, and this new 'ead teacher 'as, from what I can gather, caused a lot of waves in t'village, upsetting t'locals. And, I might add, she's also got on t'wrong side of other 'ead teachers. I've 'ad a call only today from Mr Richardson at Urebank about some spat 'e's

262

'ad with 'er. I can't see that there'll be that much of a problem when we tell 'em what we 'ave in mind. Mebbe there'll be some resistance from t'vicar but 'e's such a weak and watery individual, 'is opinion won't count for much. Mrs Pocock's complained about t'teaching of 'er son more times than I've 'ad 'ot dinners, so she won't kick up a fuss, and as for Mrs Bullock, well, she hardly 'ears owt what's said and will agree wi' owt we say. I don't expect Dr Stirling will show 'is face now that 'is lad's at t'other school, so I can't see as 'ow there'll be all that much controversy.'

'And then there's the critical school report,' added the major. 'We shouldn't forget that.'

'I mean,' said Councillor Smout, 'everyone comes out of this smelling of roses as far as I can see. Miss Brakespeare gets early retirement, a lump sum and a pension, t'school can be sold off and t'field at t'back used for a much-needed 'ousing development and bringin' in a tidy sum to t'authority to boot, and we can easily deploy Mrs Devine to another school, p'rhaps not as an 'ead teacher but on a protected salary. I can't see as 'ow she'll be all that bothered.'

'I'm not so sure about that,' ventured the major. 'I think you underestimate Mrs Devine. She is quite a formidable character and might not take too kindly to having the school close, particularly when she's only just been appointed. She is a strong-minded woman and may put up quite a fight. It did seem to me to be a little unethical to appoint her when we had every intention of closing the school.'

'Major,' said the education officer, smiling like a wide-mouthed frog, 'it was not finally decided until the Education Sub-committee met, so I don't think we need to worry on that score.'

'Nevertheless,' said the major, 'I don't think she will take kindly to the idea.'

'I have dealt with strong-minded head teachers before,' said Mr Nettles, a confident smile on his face. 'I think I can manage Mrs Devine.'

* * *

Elisabeth was waiting to greet the governors on their arrival for the meeting. When the members of the board had gathered in the entrance hall, she invited them to join her on a tour of the school to see what changes she had effected.

'I see that you have reinstated the plaque,' observed the major, staring at the large brass tablet in a prominent position in the entrance.

'Lady Wadsworth was very keen to have it restored to its former place,' Elisabeth told him, 'and I was only too happy to oblige.'

'You are acquainted with Lady Wadsworth then?' remarked the major, raising an eyebrow.

'She is a neighbour of mine,' Elisabeth told him. 'She called in to the school to have a look around. Do you have any problem with the plaque being displayed again? Perhaps I should have informed you.'

'No, no,' said the major quickly, 'not at all. In fact, I was somewhat upset when Miss Sowerbutts refused to put it back.' He wondered just how Lady Wadsworth would react when the plaque was removed again with the closure of the school. She had complained vociferously to him when Miss Sowerbutts had removed it but he had failed in

264

persuading the head teacher to restore it.

Dr Stirling arrived. 'I'm sorry I am late,' he apologised to Elisabeth, 'I had a call-out.'

'Dr Stirling,' said Councillor Smout, looking startled. 'I'm surprised to see you 'ere.'

'And why is that, councillor?' he was asked.

'Well, I understood that you 'ave taken your son away from t'school and under those circumstances, I thought that—'

'Whatever gave you that idea?' enquired the doctor. 'James is still here and very happy.'

'I see,' said the councillor, giving the major and Mr Nettles a knowing look.

'Shall we proceed?' asked Elisabeth.

One could not fail to be impressed by the changes that had taken place in the school. The building was immaculate: clean, bright walls, highly polished floors and displays of work well mounted. Children's paintings and poems, posters, pictures and book jackets covered every available space. Shelves held attractive books, tables were covered in shells, models, photographs and little artefacts, and there were coloured drapes at the windows.

'Very impressive,' said the major, in a somewhat subdued tone of voice. He could see that there would be problems ahead.

'Yes indeed,' murmured Councillor Smout, thinking to himself that he had been perhaps rather premature in assuming that the matter of the school closure would be plain sailing.

'And what about you, Mr Nettles?' asked Elisabeth. The education officer had remained silent, but, having seen the remarkable changes, shared his colleagues' opinions that closing the school would not be such an easy task as he had imagined.

'I beg your pardon?'

'I hope it meets with your approval,' said Elisabeth.

'Yes, yes,' he replied unenthusiastically. 'Very nice.'

'Nice!' repeated Dr Stirling. 'That's something of an understatement, isn't it? The change in the school is quite extraordinary.'

'It's fantastic,' said Mrs Pocock. 'I've never seen the place look so lovely.' She pointed to a large painting of a rural scene displayed to good effect on the wall at the end of the corridor. 'That's my Ernest's,' she said proudly to Mrs Bullock. 'He's very artificated you know.'

'He's what?'

'He's very good at painting.'

'What needs painting?'

'Doesn't matter,' sighed Mrs Pocock, rolling her eyes.

'You are to be congratulated, Mrs Devine,' enthused the vicar, rubbing together his long hands. 'Quite a remarkable transformation. The school looks wonderful.'

'What is needed now, major,' Elisabeth explained, directing her attention to the Chairman of Governors, 'is a new set of tables for each classroom to replace these ancient desks and maybe a carpet down the corridor to reduce the noise and make it more homely. This linoleum has just about had its day.' She pointed upwards. 'These damp patches need seeing to as well. I would also like to have a small library in the dark corner by the toilets, with better lighting so that the children can read books there, and perhaps a wild garden and a

266

pond at the rear of the school.'

The major glanced at Mr Nettles. The education officer gave a weak smile but said nothing.

The first topic for consideration on the agenda and one sent from the Education Department was of course the proposed closure of the school. The item was couched in the rather ambiguous phrase of 'The future of the school'. Elisabeth had a shrewd idea what this meant and was determined to pre-empt any discussion about proposed closure. She therefore deliberately misinterpreted it.

'I'm delighted to see this as the first item on the agenda,' she said in an ingenuous voice. 'In preparation I have put together for the governors my first report on the changes I have made and a detailed outline of my short- and long-term development plans. I think the future of the school is looking very bright.'

The major stroked his moustache. 'I . . . er . . . thank you for that, Mrs Devine,' he said. He looked towards the education officer. 'I believe Mr Nettles has something to say on this matter.'

There was no complacent look on the education officer's face now. He gave a small cough. 'The thing is, Mrs Devine, the Local Education Authority, of which I am merely the mouthpiece, is of the opinion that we should consider the future of the school.'

'Well, I agree with Mrs Devine,' piped up Mrs Pocock. 'That lino in the corridor is disgusting and them damp patches on the ceiling have been there for as long as I can remember. Them old desks need replacing as well. My Ernest can't get his legs under. He's a big lad and comes home with splinters in his knees.'

'It's not a question of replacing desks,' said Mr Nettles. 'It is a much wider scenario.'

'Excuse me,' said Mrs Pocock mulishly, 'but you don't have to sit under them. I bet your desk at the Education Office isn't something what came out of the Ark and you can get your legs under.'

Mr Nettles exhaled loudly. He appealed to the major, 'Mr Chairman, if I might be allowed to proceed. As I have just said, this is not a question of refurbishment and the replacement of furniture. The future of the school is of a much broader nature.'

'In what way?' asked the vicar.

'The Education Sub-committee is of the opinion that we need to consider the viability of the school.'

'Viability? May I ask exactly what that means?' asked Dr Stirling.

'As you are well aware, doctor, the school is losing pupils,' began Mr Nettles, 'and—'

'If I might come in here,' said Elisabeth, 'the school is no longer losing pupils. In fact it is quite the reverse. The parents of two children who live in Gartside, which is out of this catchment area, have decided to send their two daughters here and a new family has moved into the village and the three children will start next week. In addition a former pupil of the school, who moved to Urebank, will be joining them. I should tell you also that I have had a number of enquiries from interested parents wishing to look around the school, so I think the numbers are looking very healthy and will increase.'

'Really,' said the vicar rubbing his long hands. 'That is excellent news.'

'That's as may be, Mrs Devine,' said the education officer, getting rather hot under his collar, 'but it is a fact that the school has been losing pupils and—'

'But as I have just explained, Mr Nettles,' said Elisabeth, 'not any more.'

The education officer looked to the major. 'Mr Chairman,' he said, irritated by the interruptions, 'if I might be allowed to finish. Barton-in-the-Dale is just one of the many small schools in the county which possibly might close.'

'Close!' exclaimed the vicar.

'Nonsense!' added Mrs Pocock.

'Perhaps I might ask Councillor Smout to come in here,' said Mr Nettles. 'He is a member of the Education Sub-committee and can acquaint you with the situation better than I.'

Councillor Smout, leaning back expansively on his chair and sucking in his teeth, announced, 'The thing is, this is a small school and expensive to maintain and t'Local Education Authority 'as to make financial savings.'

'Are you saying you want to close the school?' demanded Mrs Pocock.

'We are considering it,' replied the councillor.

'You close this school, Cyril Smout, over my dead body!' she cried.

'It's outrageous!' said the vicar.

'What's outrageous?' asked Mrs Bullock, leaning forward.

'They want to close the school,' Mrs Pocock shouted.

'They can't do that,' replied Mrs Bullock. 'We have our Countrywomen's meetings here.'

'Might I ask, Mr Chairman,' enquired Dr Stirling, 'if Mrs Devine has been consulted on this matter or indeed given any indication that the school might close? As far as I remember there was no mention of this at her interview, and we governors have certainly heard nothing before this afternoon.'

'No, this is the first occasion it has been raised,' the major told him.

'And were you aware of the proposal?'

The major was becoming increasingly uncomfortable. The Chairman of Governors, true to his time in the army, had no intention of standing in the firing line. 'Councillor Smout might have mentioned it.'

'Look,' said the councillor, 'I don't like the idea of closing t'school any more than anyone 'ere, but we 'ave to face the 'ard facts. We need to cut t'education budget and t'savings must come from somewhere. Now I know that some people will be upset—'

'Upset!' huffed Mr Atticus. 'I think "upset" is something of an underestimation, councillor. The people in the village, if they think their school is to close, will not be merely upset, they will be up in arms. I tell you now, it will not be countenanced.'

'If I could finish, vicar,' said Councillor Smout. 'I appreciate, I really do, that there will be some strong feelings, but small schools like this are very expensive to maintain and, as I 'ave said, we need to make savings.'

'Well, make the savings somewhere else,' said Mrs Pocock, 'because you are not closing this school. My Ernest is really coming on here now. He's working harder, likes coming here, got in the football team and sings in the choir and what is more he's a gifted artist. I am not sending him on a bus to Urebank or any other a school out of the village. I've never heard the like.'

'May I ask what the chairman has to say on the matter?' asked the vicar. He brought his long fingers together, flexed them and rested them on his lap.

'Well, I . . . er . . . quite understand the . . . er . . . governors' reaction, and indeed I share them, but er . . . it does seem to me that, we need to . . . er . . . consider what the Education Department is suggesting.'

'It sounds, major,' said Dr Stirling, 'as if you are in favour of considering this proposal, and if you are, it seems to me that your position as the chairman of the governing body at this school is untenable.'

'I never said I was in favour of the proposal,' replied the major weakly.

'If I might come in here, Mr Chairman,' said Mr Nettles loftily, 'the governing body is obliged to consider this proposal.'

'Nonsense!' exclaimed Mrs Pocock, 'I for one don't intend considering anything. This school has improved no end since the beginning of term and it's madness to think of closing it.'

'Indeed,' said the vicar raising his voice, 'Mrs Devine has made a tremendous difference since her arrival. I think you will find a great deal of opposition to any attempt to close the school.'

'Hear, hear,' echoed Mrs Bullock.

'And what is more,' added the vicar, 'to appoint a head teacher and then announce that the school might close as soon as she is in post is tantamount to gross dishonesty.'

'Hear, hear,' echoed Mrs Bullock in an even louder voice.

The major looked appealingly at Mr Nettles, who sat stony-faced.

'I would hope,' said Dr Stirling, 'that we are unanimous on this governing body in resisting all attempts to close the school. I suggest we put it to the vote with the motion that we, the governors of Barton-in-the-Dale Primary School, strongly oppose any effort on the part of the Education Authority to close the school.'

'I think we are a little premature in this,' observed Mr Nettles. 'I would urge you to consider what the Education Department is suggesting before taking any such premature and impulsive action. After all, we haven't discussed the proposal yet.'

'And we are not going to,' announced Mrs Pocock.

'Mr Nettles,' said Dr Stirling, 'as I understand it, your function in attending the governors' meetings is to advise. You are an officer of the authority and not a governor, and, as such, you do not have a vote.' He glanced at the major, who looked bewildered. 'I propose we vote on the matter.'

And so it was that, with one abstention from the chairman and one against from the councillor, the motion was carried.

CHAPTER FOURTEEN

The following week Elisabeth received two unwelcome letters in the post. The first was from Mr Richardson, expressing his anger with regard to Elisabeth's refusal to take Malcolm Stubbins back, accusing her of unprofessional conduct and informing her that he was seeking legal advice from his union. Elisabeth dropped it in the waste paper basket. The second was from Mr Nettles, informing her curtly that a public meeting was to be called at which a representative of the Local Education Authority would address 'governors, parents and teachers and any others who might have an interest in the school'. At the meeting the suggested plans and the possible timetable for closure would be outlined and the representative would answer any questions that might be raised. He regretted that the governors had not seen fit to at least discuss the proposals and pointed out that the motion proposed by Dr Stirling carried little weight, as the authority had the power to institute proceedings. He went on to assure her that, should the school close, she would be offered 'a suitable position' within the authority.

Elisabeth threw this letter down on the desk. 'There is no way that I am going to be intimidated by that odious man,' she told the school secretary. 'If he thinks he can ride rough-shod over everyone he is making a big mistake.'

'What does the letter say?' enquired Mrs Scrimshaw.

'You can read it for yourself,' said Elisabeth, red with anger. 'He will have his public meeting all right but he will not be prepared for the reaction.'

'What are we going to do?' asked the school secretary, scanning the letter.

'We will make a plan of action,' Elisabeth told her. 'We will rally support, display posters throughout the village, write letters and get items in the local papers. We shall fight this tooth and nail.'

'I have an idea what's in this other letter,' said Mrs Scrimshaw, holding up an official-looking brown envelope with an elaborate crest on the rear. 'It's them. They're coming back. I knew they would. They said they would be calling again after the holidays and they couldn't be coming back at a worse time.'

Elisabeth too knew only too well what the second brown envelope contained when she examined it herself. It would be a letter informing her of an impending visit straight after half-term by one or two of Her Majesty's Inspectors of Schools. 'Not necessarily,' she said. 'This could very well work to our advantage.'

'In what way?' asked Mrs Scrimshaw.

'If we come out of this visit with a good report, which I don't doubt we will, we will have some powerful ammunition.'

'But why are they coming back so soon?' asked the secretary. 'That's what I want to know.'

'There's really nothing to worry about, Mrs Scrimshaw,' she told her. 'It is common practice for one or two of the inspectors to return to a school some weeks after an inspection to see how things are going and whether the issues which were identified in the report have been addressed. I have been through it before at my last school and it's not that onerous. There will probably only be a couple of inspectors at the most and they will be here just for the day. We have to carry on as normal and make everything available for them to look at. I have an idea we will come out of it all right.'

'That's as may be, Mrs Devine,' said the secretary, looking ill at ease, 'but it's still very stressful and I could well do without it.'

'When the inspectors visited before,' Elisabeth reminded her, 'they found a lot wrong, hence the poor report, but since then, and I think you will agree, things have changed for the better. We have all pulled together and worked hard to turn this school around, and I think the inspectors will see this and we will receive a good report.'

'I hope so,' said the secretary. 'And I do hope we don't get that inspector with the face like one of those gargoyles on the church and with the dandruff and the bad breath. He looked as if he'd been dug up. I don't think he knew how to smile. As I said to Mr Gribbon when he showed his face on the first morning of the inspection, if he died with a face like that nobody would want to wash the corpse.'

'Can you recall the name of that inspector?' asked Elisabeth, tearing open the envelope and scanning the contents.

'Mr Steel,' Mrs Scrimshaw told her.

'Oh dear,' said Elisabeth.

'What is it?'

'The letter's from Mr Steel,' Elisabeth told her. 'He will be coming in on the thirty-first of October.'

'Hallowe'en,' remarked Mrs Scrimshaw. 'That figures.'

They both burst out laughing.

*   *   *

The half-term holiday came. Danny appeared in Elisabeth's garden for the first two days to help his grandfather clear away the dead flowers, dig over the soil, weed the borders and prune the bushes, but then wasn't seen again for the rest of the week.

'He's gone off with 'is pal and 'is dad,' explained Les to Elisabeth when she asked where Danny was. 'Doc Stirling's arranged some trips out for 'is lad an' asked if our Danny wanted to go along. 'E were as chirpy as a songbird this morning. They're goin' swimmin' and being tekken to t'cinema in Clayton.'

On one such outing—a trip on a riverboat down the canal at Skipton—who should the doctor and the boys see pedalling merrily down the towpath but Mr Gribbon. Dr Stirling shouted to him from the boat and nearly caused the startled cyclist to fall headlong into the water.

'Ahoy there, Mr Gribbon!' called the doctor. 'It's good to see your back is on the mend.'

'Oh yes, doctor,' the caretaker shouted back, still pedalling furiously, 'it's in remission.' And he shot off down the path.

It was inevitable that the meeting would eventually take place. On the Wednesday Elisabeth entered the village store to collect her weekly shopping to find Miss Sowerbutts at the post office counter. She took a deep breath.

'Good morning,' she said cheerfully.

'Morning, Mrs Devine,' said the shopkeeper. It was clear from the expression that came on to her round face that Mrs Sloughthwaite was going to relish this confrontation.

The former head teacher swivelled around. Her face was hard and set. She fixed Elisabeth with a piercing stare but managed a cool acknowledgement before turning back to the counter.

'I was just telling Miss Sowerbutts here,' said the shopkeeper, 'about all the changes at the school. She wouldn't recognise the place now, would she,

Mrs Devine?'

Elisabeth gave a weak smile but felt it politic to say nothing.

'No, I don't suppose I would recognise it,' said Miss Sowerbutts in the penitent tone of the aggrieved, 'and to be quite frank, I am not that interested.'

'Oh, there's all sorts of things going on now,' continued the shopkeeper, deliberately trying to provoke her customer. 'They've got an art class, chess club, football and rounders teams, a choir, a drama club—'

'Yes, well, that's all very well,' said the former head teacher, with a downturn of her mouth, 'but I never allowed my professional priorities to be distracted by frills and furbelows when I was in charge.' Her features were alien and hostile.

Elisabeth felt her throat tightening. She did not wish to get into a heated argument with her predecessor but could not remain quiet in the face of such antagonism.

'I must take issue with you there, Miss Sowerbutts,' she retorted, her voice calm and measured. 'Such activities are not frills and furbelows as you call them, they are an essential part of a broad and balanced curriculum and are very important in a school. Indeed, they add immeasurably to the richness of a child's experience.'

Miss Sowerbutts turned and faced Elisabeth. She gave a small cynical smile. 'Please don't lecture me, Mrs Devine,' she said. 'I have heard all this before and I am not oblivious to the deleterious changes you have made in the school. No doubt such changes go down well with some, but I have been in education long enough to believe that such things—art and drama and choirs and such like—decorate the margins of the more serious business of teaching children how to read and write and add up.'

It was pointless arguing with this woman, thought Elisabeth. 'Well, let us agree to differ,' she said.

But Miss Sowerbutts had not finished, and played her trump card with great satisfaction. 'And of course, should the school close, and I have it on good authority that it may very well do so, all these changes will have been for nothing. I'll just have the two second class stamps,' she told the shopkeeper.

*   *   *

Mr Steel, HMI, arrived at the school the following week on an overcast drizzly morning. Mrs Scrimshaw's description was apt, for Mr Steel was a tall, cadaverous man with sunken cheeks, greyish skin and a mournful countenance. He was dressed in a black suit, wore shiny black shoes that creaked when he walked, and carried a black briefcase with a gold crown embossed on the front.

Mr Gribbon, who was on lookout the morning of the visit, saw the black car pull up in the car park at morning break and hurried down to Elisabeth's classroom.

'The Gestapo have arrived,' he informed her.

Mr Steel spent the first part of the morning looking through the various documents: guidelines, lesson outlines, teaching strategies, development plans, pupil profiles, attainment details and test results, which had all been carefully presented in a series of folders. Elisabeth had spent every

278

evening that week making sure everything was in place. The previous report had mentioned that the documentation in the school was 'demonstrably inadequate', so as soon as she had taken up her post she had worked hard to produce the necessary documentary evidence, which Mr Steel now scrutinised.

The school inspector's first port of call was the infants at morning break. He found the children, unable to go out into the playground on such a rainy day, involved in various activities in their classroom. Some were playing in the sand tray, others were measuring water in jugs and beakers, some were sitting looking at the picture books in a corner and others were creating buildings with wooden blocks. A small group was in the home corner, dressing up and acting out parts.

One small boy, hidden inside a huge cardboard box, was brumming and screeching.

The inspector peered over the top.

'Are you in your racing car?' he asked the infant.

The child looked up with a quizzical expression on his small, round face. 'No,' he replied, 'I'm in a cardboard box.'

Miss Wilson smiled. The inspector didn't.

Following the morning break, Mr Steel made notes in a small black book while Miss Wilson read the children a story. She found it quite unnerving seeing him sitting in the corner of the classroom scribbling away, and wondered what he could possibly find to write about, but she carried on with the story and the class listened attentively and behaved impeccably. When she had set the children writing, the inspector looked through her lesson plan, questioned the children and selected several

279

to read to him.

One small, pale-faced, crop-headed boy sat by himself by the window. He had cheeks like a gerbil, round and bulging and clearly full of something.

'Have you something in your mouth?' asked the inspector.

The boy nodded.

'Now you shouldn't be eating in class,' he was told.

The boy shook his head.

'I think you should take out whatever it is in your mouth,' Mr Steel told him. 'Come along now, spit it out.'

The boy did as he was told and covered the inspector's shoes with vomit.

'I'm not feeling very well,' moaned the child.

The inspector made no further notes and left without a smile or a word.

Having cleaned his shoes as best he could, the inspector headed for Miss Brakespeare's classroom. He was particularly interested in the work the lower junior children were undertaking, since it was their teacher of whom the inspectors had been most critical on their last visit. With a smaller, younger and better-behaved group of children and minus the one difficult pupil, Miss Brakespeare felt she had taught a very good lesson. She had discussed the topic with Elisabeth and planned it carefully, and this time when she was observed by the inspector did not resort to the artifice which had been suggested by the former head teacher and which Chardonnay had described to Elisabeth.

In Mrs Robertshaw's class, the lower juniors had settled down quietly to write their description of a Viking settlement. The inspector decided to examine the children's work and question them. The first child he quizzed was a bright-eyed, rosy-cheeked child of nine with a thatch of straw-coloured hair and very colourful glasses. Oscar was staring out of the window, his elbow on the desk and his chin cupped in his hand.

'Have you finished your work?' asked the inspector.

'No,' replied Oscar seriously. 'Actually, I've not started yet. I'm contemplating.' He scrutinised the man in the dark suit. 'There's rather a strange smell,' he said. The school inspector's face reddened. 'Can you smell something?'

'No, I can't,' replied Mr Steel. 'Perhaps you would like to tell me what you are doing.'

'I'm about to start my account about the Vikings,' Oscar told him. 'Do you know anything about Vikings?'

'A little,' replied the inspector. He was unused to children asking him questions. It was his job to ask *them* questions.

'Some people think they wore helmets with horns on,' said the boy. 'Well, they didn't.'

'No, so I understand,' said the inspector. 'What do you—'

'And they were not as bad as they were painted.'

'So I believe. What do you—'

'They were extremely good sailors and navigators and travelled long distances. Some people think they discovered America. Do you know what they came in when they went to other countries?' asked the boy.

'Longboats?' suggested the inspector wearily. He gave up trying to ask a question.

'What else?'

'Helmets, minus the horns?'

'What else?'

'I don't know,' the inspector admitted.

'They came in hordes,' the boy told him. 'The word is spelt differently from hoards.' He wrote two words on his jotter and pointed with a pencil. 'Hordes are large groups of people like invaders, hoards are stores of money. Did you know that?'

'Yes, I did,' replied the inspector, intrigued by this strange, articulate, old-fashioned boy who observed him over the top of his coloured frames, as if he had come across some exotic flower in the middle of a dark jungle.

Oscar slid his exercise book across the desk. 'I imagine you wish to see my book,' he said. 'One of the inspectors looked the last time. He told me that I had a lot to say for myself.'

Mr Steel sympathised with his colleague. 'What is your name?' he asked.

'Oscar,' the boy replied. 'And you are called Mr Steel.'

'And how would you know that?'

'You are wearing a badge,' said the boy.

Mr Steel turned the pages in the boy's exercise book. 'You are a very good speller,' he remarked.

'Yes, I know,' replied Oscar. 'Spelling is one of my strong points.'

The inspector raised an eyebrow. 'Really.' In his travels around schools he had rarely come across a child so amazingly self-possessed and confident.

'You can test me if you like.'

'That won't be necessary,' replied Mr Steel.

'I find the way words are spelt very interesting,' Oscar told him. 'Like hordes and hoards. They sound the same but have different spellings. They are called homophones, words with the same sound but different meaning. There are lots of words in English like that.' He then launched into a long and serious description on the quirks of the English spelling system, leaving the school inspector rather lost for words.

Mr Steel, not wishing to be lectured at or interrogated any further, decided to move on and rose to his feet.

'We have had an interesting conversation, haven't we, Mr Steel?' Oscar remarked.

'Yes, we have,' replied the inspector.

'We can continue it at lunchtime if you like,' said the boy.

'I shall look forward to that,' said Mr Steel, making a mental note to avoid this particular pupil.

'I can still smell something,' said Oscar, sniffing as the inspector made for the door.

Mr Steel reported back to Elisabeth at the end of the day.

'There has been a remarkable improvement in all aspects of the school,' he said, 'and you are to be congratulated. The teaching is good or better and the quality of the children's work has greatly improved. Particularly impressive is the range of extra-curricular activities on offer and which the children were at pains to describe to me. The leadership and management are more than satisfactory, the documentation is thorough and appropriate and the environment for learning is very good. I do not envisage that I will be calling again in the foreseeable future.'

Elisabeth glowed inside. 'That is good to hear,' she said. 'I am very relieved you are happy with what you have seen.'

'More than happy. I shall be writing a report for your governors, a copy of which will be sent to the Education Office in due course,' said the inspector, getting to his feet.

'And were you aware, Mr Steel, that the Local Education Authority has it in mind to close the school?' asked Elisabeth.

'No, I wasn't,' replied the inspector.

'Well, it has. A public meeting is to be called in the next few weeks. I should be most grateful if you were able to send your report before then.'

Mr Steel smiled for the first time that day. It was a small, tight-lipped smile. 'I don't envisage any problem with that,' he said.

*   *   *

The Reverend Atticus, rector of Barton, surveyed his dinner.

'What is this, my dear?' he asked his wife.

'Cobblers,' she replied.

The vicar raised an eyebrow. 'I beg your pardon?'

'Beef cobblers. I got the recipe from the secretary at the school.'

'It's a very substantial meal,' the vicar said, staring at the mound before him.

'Well, you could do with building up, Charles. You've looked decidedly pale and peaky of late.'

The vicar posted a mouthful of fatty meat and chewed slowly.

'It occurred to me,' said Mrs Atticus, 'that in your efforts to prevent the school from closing you might enlist the support of the bishop. Knowing him, he will have cultivated some important and

284

influential people and it's just the sort of campaign he would like.'

'That sounds an excellent idea,' replied her husband, having managed to swallow a gobbet of fat. 'I shall most certainly drop him a line. We need all the support we can get.'

'It's outrageous that they should consider closing the school,' said Mrs Atticus. 'Of course that Chairman of Governors, that be-whiskered buffoon, has dragged his heels, and before you spring to his defence, which you are wont to do, if he had exercised more leadership and displayed more gumption, instead of sitting on the fence, they might very well have abandoned the whole idea.'

'Actually, my dear,' said the vicar, placing down his knife and fork and becoming animated, 'I was not going to spring to his defence at all. You are perfectly right, he could have done a whole lot more, and appointing a head teacher knowing the school was in imminent threat of closure was entirely unprincipled, not to say deceitful.'

Mrs Atticus smiled. 'Well, thank you, Charles,' she said.

The vicar picked up the cutlery and tackled a particularly stubborn piece of thick crust, but abandoned the effort and thought to himself. Since his wife had started the art class at the village school she had been altogether more good-humoured, and he welcomed this change in her temperament. Now occupied with more things than her garden, she had become far less tetchy and complained about him a good deal less. The art class had given her a new interest and one she clearly found interesting and challenging.

'You appear to be enjoying your time at the

school, my dear,' observed the vicar.

'Yes, Charles, I am,' she replied. 'I have to say that when it was first mooted by Mrs Devine I was chary about trying to teach a group of children, but the class has proved very popular and I have uncovered some real talent. I have also found Mrs Devine very accommodating. Actually, she recommended that I might consider training as a teacher.'

Reverend Atticus did not wish to be shown as overly enthusiastic, but the thought of his wife occupied all day, and out of the vicarage, filled him with delight.

'That sounds an excellent idea,' he said. 'I think you would make a splendid teacher, Marcia.'

'Why, thank you, Charles,' she replied, smiling.

The vicar spiked an undercooked potato and said a silent prayer of thanks.

'Do hurry up with your dinner,' said Mrs Atticus. 'There's Spotted Dick for pudding.'

*   *   *

Over the next two weeks leading up to the public meeting, everyone opposed to the closure of the village school worked hard to draw the community's attention to the situation. Elisabeth mobilised support, writing to all parents, enclosing a copy of Mr Nettles' letter and urging the recipients to write in protest to the Education Office and members of the Education Sub-committee and other influential people. Miss Brakespeare was industrious in making sure the shops, pubs and houses in the village displayed the large and colourful posters painted by the children, with 'SOS: Save Our

286

School' emblazoned at the top. The vicar and the local Methodist minister raised the matter at their services and Mrs Pocock organised a petition. Local newspaper feature writers, always on the lookout for newsworthy items, were only too pleased to report the story. Elisabeth was both surprised and delighted with the response.

Mr Preston, the Director of Education, sat behind the large mahogany desk in his office, drumming his fingers and contemplating what to do about the large pile of strongly worded letters he had received and the several critical newspaper articles concerned with the closure of Barton-in-the-Dale school which lay before him. A particular and precise man in all that he did, he was a stickler for things being done quickly and efficiently. He stared out of the window, which gave an uninterrupted view over the busy and bustling high street, and considered how best to deal with this tricky and troublesome business.

There was a tap at the door.

'Enter!' shouted the Director of Education.

Mr Nettles appeared, smiling inanely. Mr Preston disliked the man, with his obsequious manner, round smiling face and irritatingly nasal voice.

'I think you could have handled this matter rather better, Mr Nettles,' he said.

The smile disappeared from the education officer's face. 'Well—' he began.

'I have been inundated with letters and petitions from vicars and ministers, doctors and shopkeepers, governors and parents and every Tom, Dick and Harry in that wretched village. Members of the Education Sub-committee and even the chief

287

executive have been on to me this morning. They have been bombarded with the same. I've even had the local MP on the phone. Now,' he stabbed his desk, 'we have the local newspapers up in arms too. Whatever happened at the governors' meeting? A situation like this requires very sensitive handling. Do you know the meaning of the word tact?'

'The thing is, Mr Preston,' the education officer whined, 'the governors were not at all receptive to the idea.'

'Well, I don't imagine that they would be delighted when they were told we are thinking about closing the school, but I understood, from the memoranda you sent to me and the latest briefing, that there was likely to be very little opposition.'

'You see, Mr Preston,' the education officer explained, 'following the critical school inspection of Barton-in-the-Dale and the fact that more and more parents were taking their children away and sending them to the neighbouring school, and that the head teacher, Miss Sowerbutts, was nearing retirement age—'

'Yes, yes, I know all this,' said the Director of Education irritably.

'It was thought,' continued Mr Nettles, a nervous rash appearing on his neck, 'it was thought that the governors and parents would appreciate that it was no longer practicable for the school to remain open and hence there would be little opposition. That is why the Education Sub-committee earmarked Barton-in-the-Dale as the first school for closure.'

'On your advice.'

'Yes, I did recommend it.'

'So?'

'Things have rather changed at the school since it

was first mooted that it should close.'

'In what way?' asked the Director of Education.

'The school has improved quite dramatically with the arrival of Mrs Devine.'

'Who?'

'The new head teacher,' the education officer told him. 'She's turned the school around, and some of the governors and a great many parents are now very keen to keep the school open. When Mrs Devine was appointed it was always assumed it would be temporary. She would hold the post, so to speak, until the school closed. We never expected her to be so . . . so . . .' he struggled for the right word, 'well, successful.'

'I assume that she was aware it was an interim contract when she accepted the position?' asked the Director of Education.

'Well, no, she wasn't. We felt—that is, Councillor Smout and the Chairman of Governors—felt that if we advertised it as a temporary post there would be few applicants. As you know, Mr Preston, it takes over a year for a school to close. We have to go through a thorough consultation process and liaise with the Ministry of Education before anything can be done.'

'Mr Nettles,' said the Director of Education, crossly, 'you do not need to remind me of the processes for closing a school. I am fully aware of the procedures. Why did you not ask the present deputy head to take over in the interim?'

'We did consider that, but she was thought unsuitable. The inspectors' report was quite critical of her. Indeed, it singled her out for criticism. So we made no mention to the candidates for the headship of the possibility that the school might close when we advertised the position.'

'Something of an oversight, that, wasn't it, not to say rather unethical?'

'I guess with hindsight, it might be construed—'

'So this Mrs—what was her name?' The Director of Education cut him short.

'Devine.'

'So this Mrs Devine,' observed the Director of Education, 'came to the school with no idea that it might close?'

'Yes.'

'And the governors agreed not to mention it to her?'

'Well, it was in its embryonic stage, so to speak, and had only just been broached at the Education Sub-committee, and actually only Councillor Smout and the Chairman of Governors were privy to this.'

'And you.'

'Yes, and myself. Councillor Smout was very insistent that we should not mention anything about a possible closure to any of the applicants and indeed to the other governors, apart that is, from the chairman.'

The Director of Education thought for a moment and stared out of the window. Here was a pretty kettle of fish, he thought. It sounded to him that it was too far down the road to turn back now. The school had been identified by the Education Sub-committee as the first to close, and as far as he was concerned it should go ahead. There would be other schools in line for closure in due course, and the local authority couldn't be seen to fall at the very first hurdle. If it changed its mind on this and was seen to surrender to the pressure placed upon it by the residents of this village, it would set a precedent. No, Barton-in-the-Dale school should close. Mr Preston was an astute man, clever with words and with that plausible, good-humoured persona able to win people over to his way of thinking. He subscribed to the view that it is not so much what you say, it is the way that you say it, and often thought to himself that he should have taken up politics, such was his skill at persuading people to believe something. He also was not a man to bow to pressure groups. He would have to take charge.

'I've arranged a public meeting at the school for me to explain the situation and answer any questions,' explained Mr Nettles.

'When?' asked the Director of Education.

'Next Thursday,' he replied.

'I shall go myself,' said the Director of Education. 'I do not want this to escalate. We will have the national media getting in on the act if we are not careful.'

'Very well,' said the education officer.

'And in future, Mr Nettles, perhaps you might consult me on such matters as this and also exercise a little more tact in your dealings with governors and head teachers.'

*   *   *

The school hall was packed for the public meeting. It seemed that everyone in the village and many from without were there.

'Playing havoc with my parquet floor is this,' Mr Gribbon told Mrs Scrimshaw as he surveyed the assembly. 'Look at all those shoes with heels. I'll have the devil's own job removing all the scuff marks and scratches and getting it back to what it was.'

'Well, Mr Gribbon,' the secretary replied tartly, 'as I've told you, you won't have to worry about your floor if the school closes and you are out of a job, will you?'

Earlier Elisabeth had stood at the entrance of the school, smiling and welcoming everyone as they arrived and thanking them for coming. The major, hovering behind her, had looked decidedly uncomfortable and received many a cold look. The substance of the contentious governors' meeting had been relayed in great detail by Mrs Pocock to Mrs Sloughthwaite in the village store, and the major's refusal to vote against the proposal to close the school came in for particular comment. Mrs Sloughthwaite had nodded sagely and agreed that the man was a 'spineless individual' and 'in the pocket of the education people'.

'He's nailed his colours firmly to the fence,' she had said to her friend. 'He's as much use that man as a grave robber in a crematorium.'

Councillor Smout had sent his apologies for his absence from the meeting. A pressing engagement had arisen which necessitated his attendance. He had, of course, heard on the grapevine that the meeting was likely to be highly contentious and he, being the only one to vote for the closure of the school, knew he would be the most unpopular person there.

Elisabeth glanced at her watch and noticed that the time had very nearly arrived for the start of the meeting. She was disappointed to see that Dr Stirling had decided not to attend. She had thought, at the very least, that he would have come and lent his support, particularly since he had

292

been so impassioned at the governors' meeting against the proposed closure. It seemed to her that his contribution at the meeting would have held a great deal of sway. She also wondered why Les Stainthorpe had decided to stay away. He had spoken so warmly about all the things she was doing at the school. He could have added his weight to the protest too.

Mr Nettles and his superior were the last to arrive, one minute before the five o'clock start. Elisabeth had never met the Director of Education, but knew who he was immediately when she saw this suave-looking man in a dark suit and wearing a crisp white shirt and expensive silk tie walk through the door.

'This is Mrs Devine,' said Mr Nettles, ushering the Director of Education in the direction of the head teacher.

Mr Preston gave a most disarming smile and pressed Elisabeth's hand warmly. 'I am delighted to meet you, Mrs Devine,' he said. 'It is a great pity that we have to meet under these circumstances.' He then turned his attention to the major. 'I felt, Mr Chairman, that it would be appropriate if I came to the meeting myself.'

'Yes, yes, of course,' replied the major.

'I am very pleased to see you, Mr Preston,' Elisabeth told the Director of Education. 'Perhaps after the meeting you might care to look around the school?'

'Maybe another time, Mrs Devine,' he said. He smiled like a hungry vampire ready to sink his teeth into a neck. 'I have another meeting later which demands my attendance and I must be away.' He glanced at his expensive wristwatch. 'I think we are about ready to start, are we not?'

The Chairman of Governors mumbled a few words of introduction to a stony-faced hall of people and then retreated to the side, relieved to be out of the firing line.

'Good evening,' said the Director of Education. He stared down at the sea of grim faces before him. It did not deter him, so confident was he in his powers of persuasion. 'I am so pleased to see that so many of you have been able to make it this afternoon.'

There were a few mumbles and mutters in response.

'I should like to say at the outset,' he continued, 'that it is important for me to hear what you have to say. This is a consultative meeting in which you will have the opportunity of asking questions and giving your views. But first of all I need to explain what the Education Department's overall plan is for the future of the service. I wish to stress that nothing has been decided about the future of this school or any other in the authority. It is being considered, no more. It is a hard fact that the authority has to tighten its belt and make drastic savings, and one of the ways is to close some of the smaller and least viable establishments. It is very regrettable that we have to do this, but we do have to reduce our spending. The Education Sub-committee has identified a number of small schools, Barton-in-the-Dale being one, which we might consider closing.'

There were grumbles and inaudible comments from the assembly.

'Let me be perfectly clear about this and repeat that nothing has been decided yet and that we are still looking at all options.'

There followed a series of testimonials. Mr Atticus stressed the positive changes that had taken place since the beginning of term, and pointed out how all in the village were massively supportive of the head teacher. Mrs Pocock and a number of other parents spoke of their satisfaction with the education provided. Then a small voice came from amongst the gathering.

'Could I say a few words?' asked Oscar. He stood up and with all the confidence of a seasoned orator delivered his opinion.

'A great many people have said a lot of things,' he began. 'Well, I am a pupil here and I want to say it's a first-rate school with good teachers and an excellent head teacher. I can't say that I particularly enjoyed my time here very much before but I really do now and hope that it will remain open. That really is all I wished to say.' He sat down to loud applause.

'He should be at home doing his homework,' remarked Mrs Sloughthwaite to her neighbour. 'He could audition for the part of Little Lord Fauntleroy could that one.'

Mrs Pocock pulled a face. 'Too much to say for himself that young man,' she said.

'He'll either end up in prison or running the country,' observed the shopkeeper.

The meeting proved to be less heated and noisy than Elisabeth had expected. This was as a result of the adept handling of his audience by the Director of Education. He had reached this elevated position in the education hierarchy with reason. He was a clever and articulate man who could read his audiences like a book. He had reiterated that no decision had been made yet, that he would consider all representations carefully, and that he would look at other options. He was a man practised at pouring oil on troubled waters.

The Director of Education thanked Elisabeth as she walked with him to the door and apologised for not being able to stay any longer. She placed a red folder in his hand. 'You might wish to read my plans for the development of the school,' she said, 'and the most recent report from Her Majesty's Inspector, who recently made a return visit.'

Mr Preston looked Elisabeth full in the face, not with a smile but with an intense gaze. 'Thank you, Mrs Devine,' he said. 'I shall read it with great interest.'

CHAPTER FIFTEEN

It was eight o'clock when Dr Stirling knocked on the cottage door later that evening.

'Oh, hello,' said Elisabeth.

'I thought I had better come and explain why I wasn't at the meeting,' he said.

'Come in.'

'You might have heard already from Mr Stainthorpe what happened.'

'No,' replied Elisabeth. 'I've just got in myself and I haven't seen him. Come through.' She led her visitor into the small sitting room and gestured to a chair for him to sit down.

'I was called out on a rather grisly emergency,' Dr Stirling explained, sitting down and taking a deep breath. His face looked deathly pale. 'I still feel quite queasy, to be honest.'

296

'Would you like a drink?'

'A brandy would be good,' he said.

Elisabeth poured him a large brandy and sat opposite him. 'So, what happened?' she asked.

Dr Stirling took a sip and began to talk.

Fred Massey, having attached the sugar-beet cutter to his ancient tractor, had proceeded to feed in the edible roots down the long funnel for them to be mashed for cattle feed. At the foot of the machine was an auger, a corkscrew-like rod that pulped the sugar-beet as a sausage grinder might chop up meat. Such being the considerable age of the machine and its unpredictability, the beet frequently got stuck and required encouragement to go down the funnel. Mr Massey, rather than using a piece of wood as any sensible person would do, had used his foot, which descended into the machine to be pulverised with the sugar-beet. Fortunately the tractor was old too and the engine immediately cut out, but the farmer had got stuck and was in agonising pain.

It was fortunate that Les Stainthorpe had been in hearing distance of the man's screams and was able to go to his assistance. The emergency services and Dr Stirling had been called and the fire crew had cut the farmer out. Dr Stirling, used to dealing with mumps and chicken-pox and the minor ailments of the villagers, had never had to deal with such a horrific accident and at the sight of the mangled foot had been promptly sick.

'And how is Mr Massey?' asked Elisabeth now.

'He's a very lucky man. If Mr Stainthorpe hadn't heard him shouting for help he could very well have bled to death. He saved his life. Unfortunately I think that Mr Massey might lose part of his foot,

297

but it could have been a whole lot worse. One sometimes wonders at the stupidity of people. Fancy pushing your foot into a machine.'

'It must have been terrible for the man,' said Elisabeth. 'What an ordeal.'

'Had it not been for the quick thinking of Mr Stainthorpe and the way he kept calm and stayed with Mr Massey, the man could very well have died of shock. He sent young Danny to phone for an ambulance and to fetch me. He's a good lad is Danny.'

'He is,' agreed Elisabeth. 'I've come across many children in my job and he's one of those frank, good-natured and helpful children all teachers like to have in their class.' Then she added, 'And he's a good friend for James.'

'Yes, indeed,' he admitted. 'Anyway, how did the meeting go?'

When he had heard Elisabeth's account, Dr Stirling nodded. 'It sounds rather more optimistic, from what you've said. At least they are listening, and the strength of the reaction must mean they will now reconsider.'

'I think they listened,' Elisabeth told him, 'but I would be surprised if the meeting meant that they will reconsider. The battle's not won yet by any means. The Director of Education was very plausible and charming and reassuring and all that, but I pride myself on being a pretty good judge of character on first meeting someone and I think he's as slippery as an eel.'

'A good judge of character,' the doctor repeated. 'I'm a terrible judge of character—but you know that anyway.' He thought for a moment, looking at the woman whom he had come to like and respect

298

. . . and more. 'I wonder how you judged me at our first meeting?'

Elisabeth smiled. 'I sometimes get it wrong,' she replied.

'I think the fault was with me, to be honest,' he said. 'I'm not that good with words.'

'I thought you did very well when you took the sex education lesson.'

'Ah, well, I was on my own ground then,' he told her. His face suddenly became flushed. 'I didn't mean I'm an expert on sex but on medical matters relating to sex. You know what I mean.'

Elisabeth threw back her head and covered her mouth, snorting and spluttering. 'I'm sorry,' she cried, weeping with laughter.

'Was it that funny?'

She nodded, still laughing uncontrollably.

He began laughing too.

They were interrupted by a loud knocking at the cottage door.

'I've never been so popular,' Elisabeth said, getting up and wiping her eyes.

'It will probably be Mr Stainthorpe,' said the doctor, 'coming to tell you what happened.'

It was not Les Stainthorpe. It was his grandson. He stood on the step, clearly upset.

'Whatever is it, Danny?' asked Elisabeth.

'It's . . . it's mi granddad,' the boy stammered, ''e's been taken badly. 'E's really poorly, miss.' He gripped Elisabeth's arm. 'Please, Mrs Devine, will you come and look at him and will you phone the doctor?'

'Dr Stirling's here,' she told the boy. 'Come along, we'll go and see your grandfather, and don't worry, I'm sure he'll be all right.'

Later that evening, after Danny's grandfather had been taken to hospital and the boy was tucked up in bed in the spare room at the cottage, Elisabeth sat down with Dr Stirling. She rested her head on the back of the chair and sighed.

'What a day,' she said.

'You can say that again,' he replied.

'I think it's me who needs the brandy now. Will Mr Stainthorpe be all right?' she asked.

Dr Stirling thought for a moment. 'I can't really say. He was doubled up with pain in the ambulance. It could be anything, but it doesn't look all that good.'

'Oh dear. Do you think it might be serious?'

'As I said, I can't say exactly, but from what the registrar said at the hospital, Mr Stainthorpe is a very sick man. We'll know more when he's had the tests. I'll call in at the hospital tomorrow and see how he's getting on. He's as stubborn as a mule is Mr Stainthorpe, and not one to go to the doctor if he feels ill. I have a feeling he's known for some time that he's not well.'

'Poor Danny,' said Elisabeth. 'He'll be lost without him. He was in a terrible state when the ambulance took his grandfather away. He looked so desperate.'

'He'll be all right with you tonight?' asked Dr Stirling.

'He will. Tomorrow I'll contact Social Services and I guess they can arrange for him to be fostered for a time while his grandfather is in hospital. I am very sorry for the boy. He must feel so lonely and afraid. He's lived with his grandfather all his life. They've never been apart. I don't know how he'll get on if he has to go to live with a new family and start a new school, maybe miles away. He could stay here I suppose, but it's not really that appropriate— the head teacher and one of the pupils.'

'He could stay with me and James for the time being,' suggested Dr Stirling.

'Really? That would be so much better for him,' said Elisabeth.

'I'll see if it can be arranged. You have enough on your plate at the moment. The boy needs people around him. I'm sure James would like to have him stay with us. Danny needs his friends now.'

Elisabeth looked at the good-natured, unaffected man in the crumpled suit and scuffed shoes who sat before her. 'Thank you,' she said. 'That's very kind of you.'

'It's the least I can do,' he replied, and she noticed for the first time how his eyes lit up when he smiled.

*   *   *

Mrs Scrimshaw appeared at the classroom door the following morning.

'He's in the entrance,' she told Elisabeth.

'Who?'

'Major double-barrelled,' the secretary said, pulling a face. She lowered her voice so she was not overheard by the children. 'I don't know how he has the nerve to make an appearance after yesterday. As my mother would say, he's about as welcome as haemorrhoids to a jockey. I mean, you would have thought that the Chairman of Governors at the very

301

least would have said he was against the closure at the meeting, but he just stood there like a spare part. Anyway, I told him you were teaching but he said he'd like to see you. Shall I tell him to come back later?'

'No, I'll come down.' Elisabeth turned to her class. 'Now I have an important matter to deal with, children,' she said. 'I want you to get on with your work quietly while I am away. Is that clear?'

'Yes, miss,' chorused the class.

The Chairman of Governors stood waiting in the entrance, staring at the large plaque on the wall and stroking his moustache. He smiled rather sheepishly on seeing Elisabeth.

'Mrs Devine,' he said extending a hand.

'It's good to see you, major,' said Elisabeth cheerfully, shaking his hand.

'I've just heard about poor Mr Massey's accident,' he said. 'Terrible, terrible by all accounts. And then Mr Stainthorpe being rushed to hospital. What does the bard say: "Troubles come not in single spies but in battalions", or something to that effect. I'm sure you follow my drift.'

'Yes, it was quite a night,' agreed Elisabeth. 'I'm taking Mr Stainthorpe's grandson to the hospital this afternoon to see him.'

'Oh, well, do pass on my good wishes.'

'I was meaning to give you a call. It is rather inconvenient for me to speak to you at the moment because I do have a class to teach, but I am free at morning break and at lunchtime.'

'Ah, right,' he said. 'Then I'll call back.'

'No, no,' said Elisabeth. 'You are very welcome to stay and join a couple of classes. I am sure you would like to see what we do in the school, and I know the teachers would be pleased to see you.'

'Well, I wouldn't want to intrude and—'

'Nonsense! You wouldn't be intruding. Come along, you can start in the infants.'

Major Neville-Gravitas, with his red cheeks, bristly moustache and short cropped hair shooting up from his square head, was something of a talking point when he entered the small infant classroom. Elisabeth introduced him to Miss Wilson, saying he would be staying with her for a while, and asked her if he could be taken next door to Mrs Robertshaw's room next and then to join her in her classroom at morning break.

No visitor could be other than very impressed with the environment the young infant teacher had provided. The former head teacher had regarded displays of the children's work as window dressing, 'decorating the margins of serious study' as she called it, and as a consequence had placed little importance upon them. In contrast Elisabeth had actively encouraged her staff to make their classrooms bright and cheerful, and Miss Wilson had made a massive effort to do so. The walls were resplendent with the pupils' paintings, sketches, drawings, poems and stories, all of which were carefully double-mounted and clearly and neatly labelled. Shelves held glossy-backed picture books, small tables had vases of bright flowers, corners had little easy chairs and large fat cushions where children could relax and read.

'Perhaps you might like to see what the children are doing?' Miss Wilson asked the major after Elisabeth had gone. 'They are busy on a range of activities this morning. Do wander around and see what they are up to.'

'Yes,' he replied somewhat unenthusiastically, as he observed the sea of small serious faces staring at him. 'I should like that.'

Major Neville-Gravitas felt uncomfortable. He had never, in Miss Sowerbutts' time, set foot in a classroom and, having no children or grandchildren of his own and only very rarely having been in the company of small children, he was uneasy about speaking to them. In his limited experience he knew they could be very unpredictable, easily moved to tears and sometimes extremely demanding. In the army he had given an order and his command had been immediately obeyed without question. He knew this would be rather different with children. He had observed demanding children in the supermarket, and young people's behaviour in the town centre, and had frequently complained about their activities at the bar in the Blacksmith's Arms.

He approached a girl with shiny blonde hair in sausage-shaped curls and bright brown eyes. She looked up and stared at his round, red face with bristling moustache.

'Are you Miss Wilson's daddy?' she asked.

'No, my dear, I am not,' he replied.

'Are you her grandpa?'

'No.'

'Are you an infector?'

'An infector?' he repeated.

'The man who comes in to watch lessons?'

'No, no, I'm not an inspector.'

'What's that growing in your face?' she asked, stroking her top lip.

'A moustache,' he told her.

'What's it for?'

'It's not really for anything. I just like it.'

'Well, *I* don't,' said the child, wrinkling her nose before returning to her writing.

The major moved on and came to a stocky little six-year-old with red cheeks and a runny nose. The boy, surrounded by painting materials and coloured crayons, was splashing poster paint on to a large piece of paper with the confidence and enthusiasm that only very young children and very experienced artists have. His work depicted a world of bright, bold, creatures that seemed to dance across the paper. He had painted with abandon, making great swirling curves and huge blobs with his brush, spattering and daubing, smudging and smearing to produce the most vivid effect.

'Hello,' said the major, 'and what are you doing?'

'Can't tha see?' asked the boy bluntly, wiping his nose on the back of his hand. 'I'm paintin'.'

'And what's your painting about?'

'Can't tha tell?' came a similarly forthright reply. The boy observed the visitor for a moment. 'Are thy a school infector?' he asked.

'No, no, just a visitor,' replied the major, examining the painting.

'It's a jungle,' the child told him.

The major thought he might see if the child knew the names of all the animals he had depicted, so, pointing to a large grey blob, he asked, 'What's that creature?'

'Elephant.'

'And that?' he asked pointing to another.

'Rhinoceros.'

'And what's this one?'

The boy shook his head. 'Don't tha know owt abaat animals?' he asked. 'It's a cheetah. They're t'fastest animal in t'world. They can run like billy-o.

305

Did tha know that?'

'Yes, I did.'

The boy pointed to a dark brown pool in which two long-jawed creatures with teeth like tank traps stared from the picture with bright yellow eyes. 'This one 'ere's a crocodile and over 'ere is han halligator,' he said. 'Lot of people don't know t'difference, tha knaas. Do you?'

'Well, I'm not all that certain,' admitted the major.

'Tha not alone,' said the boy, 'a lot of people don't.'

'Do you know the difference?' he asked.

'Crocodile's jaws are different,' the child told him. He tapped his painting. 'See.'

'Ah, yes.' The major pointed to a round, fat, bright green creature with a wide grin and a curly tail. 'Is this a lizard?' he asked.

'It's a chameleon,' the boy told him.

'I've seen one of those. They can change colour, you know, so that they can't be seen.'

The boy gave him a sort of patient, sympathetic, tolerant look, the look of the expert in the presence of an ignoramus. 'It's called camouflage,' he said.

A girl with a feathery fringe and large eyes approached with a book, which she thrust in the major's hand. 'Will you hear me read?' she asked.

'Yes, of course, my dear,' replied the major.

'I'm a very good reader,' she told him.

'Good for you.'

'I'm on green book 7a. My book is about the gingerbread man. He gets eaten up by a greedy fox.'

'Oh dear.'

'Run, run as fast as you can,' the child chanted, 'you can't catch me, I'm the gingerbread man.'

'That'll teach 'im not to be big-'eaded, t'daft bugger,' remarked the artist with the red cheeks and runny nose, who had overheard the conversation.

It was inevitable that in Mrs Robertshaw's classroom the major would meet Oscar.

'I'm Oscar,' he said. 'Who are you?'

'I'm Major Neville-Gravitas,' replied the Chairman of Governors.

'We had a dog called Major,' said the boy. 'He was a Labradoodle. That's a cross-bred Labrador and Poodle.'

'Really, how interesting.'

'It died of distemper. That's a disease dogs can get, you know.'

'Yes, I am aware of that.'

'A major is a rank in the army, isn't it?'

'It is.'

'I know that,' said Oscar. 'It's below a colonel and a general and a field-marshal.'

'What a clever young man you are,' remarked the major, rather taken aback by this precocious individual.

'Next door to us is Major Pannett,' Oscar told him. 'He plays the tenor horn in the Salvation Army band. Do you play anything?'

'I'm not that sort of major,' he was told. 'I was in the British Army.'

'And did you see any action?' quizzed the boy.

'No, not really.'

'Have you any medals?'

'Yes, as a matter of fact I do.'

'Have you got the Victoria Cross?'

'No, I haven't.'

'The George Cross?'

'No.'

'They are given for bravery.'

'Yes, I am aware of that, young man.'

'Have you any medals for bravery?'

'Why don't you get on with your work,' said the major, trying to keep his voice steady. 'I am sure you have a lot to do.'

'No, actually I've finished what I was doing.'

'Well, I am sure there is something else you could be getting on with.' He found the questioning, particularly of one so young, disconcerting.

'You're not the major my mother was talking about who wants to close the school, are you?'

Thankfully, the Chairman of Governors was saved by the bell for morning break and made a hasty exit.

'So how did you find things this morning?' asked Elisabeth when the major joined her in her classroom.

'Very impressive,' he remarked.

'That is what Mr Steel, the inspector said.'

'Yes, I have read his report. It shows a great deal of improvement.'

'So why should they wish to close such a successful school?' she asked bluntly.

The major stroked his moustache and sighed. 'Mrs Devine,' he said, 'as was explained at the Governors' Meeting, there need to be some savage cuts and sadly some schools will have to close.'

'I rather expected, major, that you, as the chairman of the governing body, would have given your wholehearted support in opposing such a move. I have to say I was very disappointed that you chose not to.'

'I am in a very difficult position, Mrs Devine,' he

told her. 'I feel like Janus, if you follow my drift.'

'In what way?' she asked.

'He looks in both directions at the same time. I'm between the devil and the deep blue sea. I, along with Councillor Smout, who incidentally phoned me this morning to inform me that he wishes to resign from the governing body, am a nominee and a representative of the Education Authority and I have to act in its best interests. Then, as Chairman of Governors, I have to be supportive of the school. I'm in a sort of no-man's-land, if you follow my drift. That is why I abstained from the vote, which, in retrospect, was the wrong decision.'

'So what are you saying?' asked Elisabeth.

'I'm saying that, having thought over the matter, I should have supported the other governors and that now maybe I should, like Councillor Smout, resign as the chairman of the governing body. The Reverend Atticus, who is usually such a mild-mannered man, informed me angrily last night after the meeting that he is going to propose a vote of no confidence in me at the next governors' meeting. As soon as he was off the phone it rang all evening with people complaining. I received some very upsetting comments and personal attacks. The whole situation has become very distressing for me. I called in at the village store for my paper this morning and Mrs Sloughthwaite, an amiable woman at the best of times, was very sharp with me. Then as I walked through the village Mrs Pocock crossed the road to avoid speaking to me and Mrs Bullock could barely pass the time of day.'

'People in the village are very angry, major,' Elisabeth told him.

'Yes I know, and it was remiss of me not to

support Dr Stirling's motion. I very much regret that now.'

'If, from what you have said, major,' Elisabeth told him, 'you are now going to support the other governors in opposing the closure, I think you should stay on as the chairman. I know I can work with you and I hope that you can work with me.'

The major's face brightened. 'Well, if you really think so—' he began.

'And I will draft a letter to the parents, with a copy to the Education Department, informing them that the head teacher, staff and all the governors are now unanimous in wanting Barton-in-the-Dale village school to remain open.'

*   *   *

The day following the public meeting, at the very moment when Major Neville-Gravitas was being grilled by Oscar, one might have imagined that the sole topic of conversation in the village store would be the school closure, but it got barely a mention. There was another subject altogether more interesting to talk about, namely Fred Massey's accident.

'He's well and truly put his foot in it this time,' said Mrs Sloughthwaite to Mrs O'Connor, her first customer of the day. The shopkeeper nodded knowingly and folded her dimpled arms under her bosom. 'And in more ways than one,' she added. 'He wants his head examining doing such a daft thing.'

Mrs O'Connor was Dr Stirling's housekeeper. She was a dumpy, round-faced little woman with the huge liquid brown eyes of a cow and a permanent smile on her small lips. Her hair was set in a tight perm. Mrs O'Connor, like many of her nation, embroidered the English language with the most colourful and original axioms and expressions, most of which were throwbacks to her grandmother Mullarkey, who had a caustic comment, a saying or a snippet of advice for every occasion. Mrs Sloughthwaite sometimes found it hard to understand the meaning of these words of wisdom, but nodded sympathetically as if she did.

'You should never bar the door with a boiled carrot,' was one such adage. 'If life throws a clutch of lemons at you, then make lemonade,' was another. 'Never let your mother comb your hair after an argument,' was a favourite saying. Such aphorisms rattled off her tongue as melted butter off a knife, as she herself might have remarked. That morning the doctor's housekeeper was in her most figurative mood.

'It was terrible tragic by all accounts,' she told the shopkeeper, giving a small shudder. 'There was blood everywhere and Dr Stirling was physically sick at the sight and came home with a face as white as milk without a word to throw at a dog. He came into the house as quiet as a speck of soot, so he did. Evidently his foot was ripped open like something on a butcher's slab, the bone stuck out like the fin of a shark and blood spouted out of his leg like hot tea from a teapot.'

'Dr Stirling was hurt?' asked an amazed Mrs Sloughthwaite.

'No, no, am I not talking of Mr Massey, eejit that he is.'

'You would think a doctor would be used to the sight of blood,' said Mrs Sloughthwaite. 'Mind you, I recall when my mother had that terrible nosebleed he looked queasy. She used to have terrible nosebleeds did my mother. I reckon she was one of those hermaphrodysiacs. I take a bit after her, you know. I've got very thin blood and if I cut myself it takes an age to stop the bleeding. She had her nose cauterised in the end.'

'Who did?' asked the customer.

'My mother. I remember when I called Dr Stirling out after one of her do's, he went as white as a slab of lard.'

'He's a very sensitive man is Dr Stirling,' said the housekeeper, 'and, of course, he's not been the same since his poor wife died. She was a lovely woman Mrs Stirling so she was, God rest her soul, and it was such a tragic accident. The little boy can't string two words together these days and he was such a little chatterbox when she was alive.'

'It'll be the shock of it all,' said Mrs Sloughthwaite.

'Mind you, Dr Stirling's not the same either,' said Mrs O'Connor. 'When I think—'

'Mrs Pocock told me there were two fire engines and an ambulance called out,' interrupted Mrs Sloughthwaite, not wishing the conversation to deviate to something far less interesting.

'First I knew was when I heard them coming through the village,' said Mrs O'Connor, patting her hair, 'so I knew something was up. Then Dr Stirling asked me to come over and look after young James and he rushed off. They say Mr Massey was in a right old state after they'd cut him out.'

'He'll lose the leg, of course,' said Mrs Sloughthwaite in a matter-of-fact voice.

'Do you think so?' Mrs O'Connor pressed her hand hard against her bosom, so hard she could feel the beat of her heart.

'Oh yes. It'll have to come off.'

'Jasus, Mary and Joseph,' said Mrs O'Connor, shaking her head.

'Course, he might very well get gangrene. I mean, that machine was as rusty as sin, from what I've heard.'

'What an eejit to go and do such a stupid thing,' said the customer.

'Well, he's learnt a lesson he's not likely to forget.'

'I can't say that I've ever liked the man,' confided Mrs O'Connor, lowering her voice as if she was being overheard. 'I've heard him shouting the odds at that nephew of his—'

'Clarence?' interrupted Mrs Sloughthwaite. 'Nice enough lad, but he's limp under the cap as my mother would say.'

'Mr Massey was cursing and swearing he was. Air was blue,' said Mrs O'Connor. 'As my owld Grandmother Mullarkey would say, a lick of carbolic soap would not do his tongue a bit of harm.'

'No, I've never taken to him either,' agreed Mrs Sloughthwaite. 'As tight-fisted as they come is Fred Massey. I mean, look at the state of him— hand-me-down clothes, unwashed face, dirty hair and that unpleasant smell that travels with him. And his teeth—like the Ten Commandments themselves—most of them broken.'

'Oh, he's a stingy owld man,' agreed Mrs O'Connor. 'Wouldn't give me a penny when I collected last Christmas for the children's

313

charity. "Charity begins at home," he told me, and closed the door on me. He makes Scrooge sound generous. The man could peel an orange in his pocket,' she added, sharing another of Grandmother Mullarkey's words of wisdom.

'And I'll tell you this, Mrs O'Connor, from what I've heard he doesn't treat them animals of his all that well.'

Her customer nodded in agreement.

'You can tell everything you need to know about a farmer's skill,' continued the shopkeeper, 'by the way he treats his animals and looks after his fences and his walls. And you've seen Fred Massey's place. I say no more.'

But Mrs Sloughthwaite had a great deal more to say, and the two women continued to discuss the man in question.

'Of course,' continued Mrs O'Connor, 'it was lucky Mr Stainthorpe heard him otherwise the man could have easily bled to death.'

'It was,' agreed Mrs Sloughthwaite, 'and after all the trouble he's had with Fred Massey, nobody would have blamed him if he had left him where he was. Well, as I've said, it'll teach him a lesson he's not likely to forget.' Yes, she thought to herself, and he won't be driving his cows up Mrs Devine's track in a hurry. 'But you know Fred Massey, he could fall into a pile of manure and come out smelling of roses. You mark my words, Mrs O'Connor, he'll be back on his feet—or his foot—in no time.'

'Of course, if he hadn't have gone to help,' said the customer, 'Mr Stainthorpe would still be at home now instead of being in the hospital.'

'Shock of it all must have brought on a heart attack,' said the shopkeeper. 'Did the doctor say what it was?'

'Sure I wouldn't be knowing the details,' said Mrs O'Connor, 'but he was rushed to hospital. It must have been terrible for him finding Mr Massey stuck in the machine and all that blood. Poor Dr Stirling, he was never off his feet. It was a good job he was on hand when Mr Stainthorpe was taken badly.'

'How do you mean?' asked Mrs Sloughthwaite. This was interesting news.

'Well, he was round at Mrs Devine's at the time when young Danny came for help.'

'Was he indeed?' remarked Mrs Sloughthwaite, raising an eyebrow.

*   *   *

It was arranged that Danny should stay with Dr Stirling. The social worker, having spoken to the boy's grandfather and interviewed the doctor, agreed that the boy could remain where he was for the time being.

Elisabeth saw a great change in Danny over the next few days. The bright-eyed, chatty boy became a retiring, uncommunicative, sad little figure who sat staring out of the window in class and could often be found crying when out of sight of the other children.

Danny had been with Elisabeth to the hospital the afternoon after the boy's grandfather had been admitted. The old man sat propped up in bed, trying to appear cheerful. He looked pale and drawn and his eyes had lost the brightness Elisabeth had been used to seeing. It was clear to her that he was a very ill man.

315

The boy buried his head in his grandfather's arms and wept.

'Hey, hey,' Mr Stainthorpe said, patting his grandson's head gently. 'What's all this? You're supposed to be cheering me up, young Danny. Now come along and tell me what you've been up to.'

'Will you be all right, granddad?' the boy sobbed.

The old man had looked at Elisabeth knowingly. 'We'll see. I've got more doctors and nurses looking after me than rabbits in Mrs Devine's paddock and moles under 'er lawn. Speakin' of t'paddock, I reckon it'll be a while now before Fred Massey can move 'is sheep.'

'I wouldn't worry about that,' Elisabeth said.

''Ow is 'e, by the way?'

'He's on the mend,' she told him, 'thanks to you. I spoke to the doctor when I arrived this afternoon and he said Mr Massey will be up and around in a week or two. The blades were pretty blunt, I gather, and the machine stopped before it could do a lot of damage. It must have been quite a shock for you finding him as you did.'

'Aye, it was. I can't say as 'ow I've ever liked t'man, but I 'ope 'e'll be all right. It was a nasty accident for anyone to 'ave, but it was a daft thing to do.'

'When will you be coming 'ome, granddad?' the boy asked, rubbing his eyes.

Again the old man's gaze met Elisabeth's. His face looked furrowed and bleak. 'Oh, it's early days yet,' he replied breathlessly. He had changed the subject. 'I 'ear you stayed with Mrs Devine last night?'

The boy sniffed and nodded.

'I hope you behaved yourself,' the old man

said, looking at his grandson with a mock serious expression.

'He did,' Elisabeth told him. 'Did all the washing up this morning and left the room tidy.'

'That's what I likes to 'ear,' the old man said, ruffling the boy's hair.

'We are hoping—that is Dr Stirling and myself— that Danny could stay at the doctor's for the time being, if that's agreeable to you, of course.'

'It's just until you're out of hospital,' the boy said.

'Dr Stirling has been in touch with Social Services this morning,' Elisabeth told the boy's grandfather, 'and I think a social worker will be coming to see you to get your permission for Danny to stay a bit longer with Dr Stirling. I believe it's something called private fostering.'

'That's a weight off my mind,' the old man said. 'Would you like to stay wi' Dr Stirling for the time being, Danny?'

'Just until you're out of hospital,' the boy repeated.

'Well, if you do, I 'opes you'll be a good boy, Danny Stainthorpe, and not put t'doctor out.'

'He's a very good boy,' Elisabeth told the old man, her face soft with concern. 'He's never any trouble and he's a real credit to you. Don't you worry, we'll take very good care of him.'

'Thank you Mrs Devine,' Mr Stainthorpe said, his eyes filling with tears, 'I really appreciate that.'

CHAPTER SIXTEEN

It was the following week that Les Stainthorpe had an unexpected visitor. Fred Massey was wheeled in by a cheerful nurse and parked by the side of the bed.

'I'll be back for you in ten minutes, Fred,' she told him.

'Did you hear that? They ought to be more respectful, these nurses, calling their elders by their first names,' grumbled the old farmer. 'It should be Mr Massey. I'll give her Fred!'

Les smiled. ''Ow are you then?' he asked.

'How am I? Well, I've just had my foot nearly cut off so I'm not dancing for joy.'

'It could have been worse.'

'Aye, it could. Any road, I wanted to see you to thank you for what you did.'

'Anybody would have done t'same.'

'Happen they would, but I wouldn't be here now if you hadn't have helped, calling the emergency services and Doc Stirling and stopping with me until they came. I appreciate that. I thought I was a goner and no mistake. Any road, I wanted to thank you.'

'Any time.'

'It'll not bloody happen again, I can tell you that!' exclaimed Fred Massey. 'There's not likely to be another time.'

'You should 'ave been more careful.'

'Aye, I know. How are you feeling anyway? I hear you had a bit of a do of your own after I'd been sorted out. Ambulance only just got me to the hospital and it was back for you.'

'I'm not too bad considering.'

'I'm sorry to see you in here, Les Stainthorpe, and I mean it. I didn't want to give you a heart attack.'

'It weren't an 'eart attack.'

'Well, whatever it were, I'm sorry you're here. I know we've had our differences over the years, but I want bygones to be bygones and when you come out I'll take you for a pint in the Blacksmith's Arms.'

'That'll be a first, Fred Massey, you buyin' somebody a pint.' The old man lay back on his pillow. He caught his breath. 'Any road, I don't reckon I will be comin' out,' he said.

'Don't talk daft! 'Course you will. They can do all sorts of things these days. You'll be up and about in no time.'

'No, Fred, I won't. My time's nearly up.'

'Is that what they say?'

'As much as. I've 'ad these tests and they've found summat.'

'Bloody hell! I didn't know that.'

'It's got into mi bones and there's nowt much they can do.'

Fred Massey sighed noisily. 'I don't know what to say, I really don't. I never have been good with words. Hey, it's a rotten shame, that it is. Your lad will take it badly.'

'Aye, he will,' sighed the old man. 'Don't you go mentioning owt to 'im or anyone else for that matter, Fred Massey! I'm not sayin' owt for t'time being. I'm gunna pick reight moment to tell Danny and it won't be easy.'

'Nay, it won't,' agreed his visitor, nodding.

319

'That's mi biggest worry—what's gunna 'appen to Danny. 'E's only got me. Got no other family. We've never been apart. Like two peas in a pod we are. 'E's staying with Dr Stirling at t'minute and Mrs Devine brings 'im to see me most days. 'E's a champion doctor is Dr Stirling, and she's a good woman is Mrs Devine, a good woman.'

'Aye, well, maybe I misjudged her. She were a bit stiff and starchy with me.'

'That's 'cos you were trespassing.'

'Let's not start all that again,' said Fred Massey. They were quiet for while. 'Is there anything you want?' he asked at last.

'Aye, there is,' said Les. 'I want you to shift them sheep of yours from Mrs Devine's paddock and stop usin' 'er track.'

An unaccustomed smile spread across Fred Massey's face. He chuckled and shook his head. 'Aye, I reckon I could do that. Any road, I'll not be doing much herding for a bit. My nephew Clarence is in charge while I'm in here. He's about as much use as a candle in a gale. Only left hens out last week and a fox got them. All these headless bloody chickens all over the place. I'll swing for that lad, I really will. Anyway, I'll tell him not to go down her track and I'll move my sheep when I get out of here. Least I can do after what you've done.'

The young nurse arrived. 'Come along now, Fred, let's be getting you back. Doctor's on his rounds and wants to look at you.'

'I'm Mr Massey to you, nurse,' he growled. 'I'm not your favourite uncle or your brother or your boyfriend. I am Mr Massey and not Fred.'

'I'll call you Mr Grumpy in a minute,' said the nurse, undaunted and starting to manoeuvre the wheelchair at some speed around the bed.

'Hang on, hang on. I'm not bloody Ben Hur!' cried Fred. 'Push me back.'

The nurse tut-tutted but did as she was bid.

'Will you shake my hand, Les Stainthorpe?' asked Fred Massey.

'I will.'

And the two old men, who had been enemies for years, shook hands warmly.

*   *   *

'Miss, will you spell giraffe?' asked Chardonnay.

When she had started teaching the class, Elisabeth had asked the children to keep a weekly journal and write an entry in it each Monday morning. It had proved very successful. The children enjoyed describing what they had been doing over the week, and Elisabeth had learnt a great deal about her pupils, their interests and their activities out of school.

'Chardonnay,' Elisabeth said, 'you have a dictionary on your desk, why don't you try and find the word for yourself?'

'I've looked, miss, but I can't find it,' replied the girl.

Elisabeth wrote the word on the blackboard. 'And did you see one at a zoo?' she asked.

'See what, miss?'

'A giraffe.'

'I haven't seen any giraffes, miss.'

'Well, why do you want the word?' asked Elisabeth intrigued.

'For my journal, miss.'

'Read out what you have written,' said the

teacher.

The girl read out her entry: 'My mum said I could join the choir at St Christopher's. I asked her if giraffe to go to all the services.'

'I think you need three words,' said the teacher, smiling. '"Do you have to."'

'Thanks, miss,' said Chardonnay. 'I always get my knickers in a twist when it comes to spellings.'

Elisabeth reminded herself to have a quiet word with the girl later about some of the expressions she was fond of using. She looked at her class. Their work, attitude and behaviour had improved immeasurably since she had taken over, and she felt justifiably proud with what she had achieved. There were some real success stories. The educational psychologist had been called into school and confirmed that Darren Holgate, as his mother had claimed, did indeed have dyslexia, and a structured programme of support had been devised for him. He was now making excellent progress. Chantelle had proved herself to be a very skilful football player and had scored the winning goal against a rival team the week before, and Chardonnay's solo performance with the choir at the Methodist chapel had gained her much praise.

Ernest Pocock seemed a very different boy from the truculent and disinterested pupil she had first met. His coming second in the County Art Competition, and the display of his paintings down the corridor, had made him something of a celebrity in the school. When the school inspector had visited, Ernest had taken him aside to point out his work.

'Of course,' he had said, repeating Mrs Atticus' words to his mother, 'I have a latent talent in art.'

He had no idea, of course, what this meant.

Sadly, Elisabeth had had very little success with James. She had imagined that after the evening when she had found him alone in her garden and he had said that one tentative word to her, he would open up and be more forthcoming, but he had not spoken to her since then. Mrs Goldstein, the educational psychologist, had spent several sessions with James, who had listened quietly but attentively to what she had to say but had said nothing. 'Give it time,' she had told the boy's father. The morning after Danny's grandfather had been taken to hospital, Elisabeth had asked James to remain behind one morning break.

He had looked at her with large, round, bewildered eyes and a serious expression in his face.

'I want to have a word with you about Danny,' she had told him. James had seen the sudden change in his friend, how Danny had become quiet and uncommunicative and spent the morning staring sadly out of the classroom window in a world of his own, just like his father. 'I think you know that he is going through a difficult time at the moment. He's very upset about his grandfather and he really needs a friend like you. You're his best friend, James, and I want you to look out for him. Will you do that for me?'

The boy had nodded.

'And have you settled back in here?' she had asked.

James had nodded again.

'I'm really pleased to have you back, and you know where I am if you want to see me about anything. All right, James,' she had said, 'that's all I wanted to say.'

After break, before the children settled down to work, Chardonnay waved a hand in the air and asked, 'Miss, is the school going to close?'

'Not as far as I know,' replied Elisabeth.

'Miss, my mum and her new partner were at that meeting and they said they want to close the school.'

'Miss, that's what I've heard,' said Chantelle. 'Miss Sowerbutts told my mum in the post office.'

'They are thinking about it,' Elisabeth told her, 'but I don't intend to let that happen. You don't want the school to close, do you?'

The class loudly chorused, 'No, miss.'

'Miss, if they do, I don't want to go to Urebank,' said Eddie Lake. 'Malcolm Stubbins hates it there. I saw him on Saturday at the swimming baths and he says he wishes he was back here. He says they pick on him all the time and the teachers are horrible and the other kids laugh at him and call him names.'

'He should never have left,' announced Chardonnay, 'but I'm glad he did. He was a pain in the ar . . . backside.'

'Now, now,' said Elisabeth. 'That will do. I am sorry to hear that Malcolm doesn't like his new school but I think he'll soon settle down.'

'He's been excluded, miss,' Eddie told her.

'Has he?'

'Miss, they've sent him home for a week for calling the teacher a—'

'Ah, ah,' interrupted Elisabeth. 'I really don't think we need to hear this, Eddie. Let's get on with our diaries, shall we, and then it's time for spellings.'

The most poignant entry in the children's journals that week was from Danny. His account spoke of his grandfather's illness and how worried and frightened he felt.

'There is no one in the world like my granddad. He brought me up when my mum was killed and we do everything together. He's my best friend. He's different from other grown-ups. He doesn't shout at me and he's never hit me. If I do something wrong like when I took my ferret to school, he just sits me down and talks to me about it and then he tells me to go and apologise. He tells me to always tell the truth. "Tell the truth and shame the devil," he says. I can tell him anything and he can tell me anything. If my granddad gets it wrong, he says so. He says an apology costs you nothing and it's not being weak to admit you don't always get things right or that you don't know something. Now he's in the hospital and I think he's really ill and I don't know what to do. I'm lost without him.'

Elisabeth thought of the time when someone would have to tell Danny that his grandfather would never be coming out of hospital, and she had a feeling that someone might very well be her. Dr Stirling had called to see her after he had been informed by the specialist of Mr Stainthorpe's condition. The tests had revealed that the old man was terminally ill and that nothing could be done for him.

Later that morning Elisabeth found Danny sitting with James in the hall, his lunch uneaten before him.

'Now, it's not like you to leave anything on your plate, Danny,' she said, cheerfully.

'I'm not that 'ungry, miss,' he murmured.

'I'm sure your grandfather wouldn't be very happy with you if he knew you were not eating.'

The boy picked up his fork and poked at the food on his plate.

'You're very quiet these days, Danny,' said Elisabeth.

'Yes, miss.'

She rested a hand on his arm. 'It's hard for you, isn't it?' she said. He nodded. 'I'm so sorry about your grandfather.'

The boy looked up and into her eyes. Perhaps he expected her to say what most adults would say— that things would turn out all right and that his grandfather would soon be home and life would return to normal. He knew in his heart that this would not be the case. 'I'm frightened, miss,' he said.

'I know,' she replied quietly. 'It's a worrying time for you.'

'I really miss my granddad, Mrs Devine,' the boy told her, beginning to cry.

'I know you do,' she said, patting his hand. She quickly changed the subject. 'And how are you getting on with Dr Stirling?'

Danny looked at James and rubbed his eyes. 'OK. 'E's a nice man, your dad. 'E's been really kind to me and there's a housekeeper called Mrs O'Connor and she's nice too, but I don't understand sometimes what she's on about.'

'After school we'll go to the hospital and see your granddad shall we?'

'Yes, miss,' he replied. 'Thank you, miss.'

'Now, you eat your lunch.'

*　　　*　　　*

326

They found Danny's grandfather in a side ward on his own. He was ashen-faced but raised a smile when he saw them.

'Now then,' he said, trying to sound cheerful. 'I thought you might be calling in to see me.'

Danny ran to the bed and buried his head in his grandfather's arms and began to cry.

'Hey, hey, come on, Danny. What's all this? I wants cheering up and to 'ear what you've been up to.'

Elisabeth stood at the foot of the bed.

'How are you, Les?' she asked.

He evaded the question. 'All the better for seeing you two,' he replied.

'We've been very busy,' she told him, 'trying to muster more support to stop the Education Authority from closing the school.'

'It's a disgrace,' said the old man.

'It's gone very quiet since the afternoon of the public meeting. I hope this means that they've reconsidered.'

'Let's 'ope so,' said the old man. He ruffled his grandson's hair. 'Now come along, young Danny, stop all this crying. You'll have me at it in a minute.'

'Are you going to be all right, granddad?' the boy asked plaintively.

'We'll see. You run down to the shop and get me a newspaper and yourself some sweets. There's some small change in the drawer. Then I want all your news. I've been bored to tears sitting here relaxing all day.'

When the boy had gone he asked Elisabeth to come and sit beside him. His face was gaunt and he breathed with difficulty.

'How are you really, Les?' asked Elisabeth.

The old man shrugged. 'I think you've probably guessed, Mrs Devine,' he said, 'that t'future's not looking too bright for me.'

'Yes,' Elisabeth replied quietly. 'I'm so sorry.'

'I'm afraid t'prospects of any improvement are not good and t'doctor reckons I've not got all that long.'

'I see.'

'Aye well, it comes to all of us in t'end. The thing is, I'm not afeared o' dying. I've known that there's been summat up wi' me for a while. What does worry me is what'll 'appen to Danny. 'E's got no one in t'world, Mrs Devine. I reckon 'e'll end up being fostered out or in a children's 'ome and I know it'll 'appen not suit t'lad. It's a real worry for me. 'E'll be like a caged bird beating its wings agin t'bars to try and get out.' The old man's eyes began to fill with tears. ''Ee's a bit of a free spirit, is Danny, likes t'sun on 'is face, rain in 'is 'air. 'E lives for t'outdoors. 'E's a country lad.' He wiped his eyes. 'I want to ask you summat, Mrs Devine. You're t'only one I can ask.'

'You don't need to ask me, Les,' Elisabeth told him, taking his leathery farmer's hand in hers. 'I'll make sure that Danny is well cared for. I shall be looking out for him all the time. You can be certain of that.'

The old man sighed and smiled. He rested his head on the pillow. 'Thank you,' he said. 'Thank you.'

They sat there in silence for a while. 'I 'ave to tell 'im,' said the old man. 'I can't put it off. It'll be t'most difficult thing I've ever done in mi life but I 'ave to do it. We've allus been 'onest wi' each other,

328

you see. I've never kept nowt from t'lad and he's allus telled me t'truth. I think it's best if I tell 'im today. Better sooner than later.'

'Would you like me to stay in the room?' asked Elisabeth.

'No, I reckon it's between 'im and me, but I'd appreciate it if you were there for 'im after I've told 'im. 'E'll need you.'

'I'll wait outside,' she said.

When Danny returned, Elisabeth made an excuse and sat in the corridor outside thinking about what was being said by the dying man to his grandson.

Danny wept all the way back to Dr Stirling's house and then ran up to the bedroom. James was about to follow him, but Elisabeth told him that she thought Danny would want to be alone for a while and to leave him for ten minutes before going up. He looked at her with huge, bewildered eyes and nodded.

'His grandfather told him,' Elisabeth said quietly as she followed Dr Stirling into the sitting room.

He nodded. 'I guessed as much.' He moved a pile of papers from a chair. 'Do sit down,' he said.

'Poor Les,' sighed Elisabeth. 'He looked very weak today. His main worry is what will happen to Danny. I guess I need to inform Social Services so they can arrange things for when his grandfather . . .' her voice tailed off.

'Yes, they will need to know,' agreed Dr Stirling. 'Of course the boy can stay here until something is sorted out.'

'That's very good of you.'

'I spoke to the specialist this morning and she thinks it's a matter of days rather than weeks.'

'Oh dear,' sighed Elisabeth.

'In one way it's a blessing,' said Dr Stirling. 'He won't have to endure a long and very painful illness. I think that would distress young Danny more, to see his grandfather gradually decline.'

'He'll be lost without him,' said Elisabeth.

Dr Stirling looked across at her. 'You've been very good,' he said. 'I can't imagine what they would have done without you.'

'It's what anyone would have done.'

'No, it's not,' he said. He was about to say something more, but stopped himself.

'Well, I had best be going,' Elisabeth told him. 'I'll take Danny along to the hospital tomorrow and drop him off later. Goodnight.'

'Goodnight, Elisabeth,' said Dr Stirling.

*   *   *

'They say he's not long for this world,' remarked Mrs Sloughthwaite in a matter-of-fact tone of voice.

The shopkeeper was in discussion with Mrs O'Connor, who had called in to the general store for the week's provisions.

'No,' agreed the customer. 'I heard Dr Stirling on the phone to the hospital, talking to one of the specialists, and from what I can gather he won't last out the week, poor man. He's a real gentleman is Mr Stainthorpe. It's a terrible shame, so it is.'

'It is,' agreed Mrs Sloughthwaite, 'but it comes to all of us, Mrs O'Connor, there's no escaping that, and if truth be told Les Stainthorpe was getting on a bit and it can't have been very healthy him living in that damp caravan for all those years. As my sainted mother used to say, he's had a good innings.'

'I feel sorry for young Danny,' said Mrs O'Connor. 'He's such a good-hearted lad. Always leaves his room tidy and he's polite and well behaved. He's a credit to the owld man, so he is. Not much of a Christmas to look forward to, has he, poor wee child?'

'He's still living with Dr Stirling then?'

'He is, and not a spot of bother either. Whatever will become of him, poor wee lad that he is?'

'They can say what they want about Les Stainthorpe,' said the shopkeeper, 'but he's brought that boy up proper, not like some I could mention. Parents who are afraid to put their foot down, in my experience, get their toes trodden on.'

'He's been in a right old state since his granddad went into hospital,' said the housekeeper. 'Poor lad's not stopped crying.'

'It was very good of Dr Stirling to take him in like that,' said Mrs Sloughthwaite. 'Not many would do it. You don't get many good Samaritans like that these days. The boy's got no other family as I know of, so I suppose when his grandfather does pass on he'll end up in that children's home at Banktop.' The shopkeeper was nothing if not blunt.

''Tis a terrible shame, Mrs Sloughthwaite,' said Mrs O'Connor, shaking her head sadly.

'And I hear that Mrs Devine has been very good, taking the lad to the hospital.'

'To be sure, she has,' agreed the customer. 'She's been back and forth like a fiddler's elbow this last week. Every day she's been driving him there and back and she's been such a comfort for the boy. Sure she's a grand woman. It was a fine day when they appointed her to the school. I only hope they

331

don't go and close it. They say that the woman who was there before, that Mrs Sowerface as I call her, has had an accident.'

'So I hear,' said Mrs Sloughthwaite indifferently.

'Went full length, so she did, at the supermarket on a wet floor by the frozen pizzas. Broke her arm she did and went over on her ankle.'

'Serves her right for shopping in town when there's a perfectly good selection of products here in the village store,' said the shopkeeper uncharitably. 'Anyway, as I was saying—'

'My goodness, that woman could clip tin with her tongue,' continued Mrs O'Connor, as if Mrs Sloughthwaite had not spoken. 'And she could stop a clock with that face of hers. As my sainted Grandmother Mullarkey said, a smile costs you nothing and every time you laugh another nail is removed from your coffin. Hard and proud as a pie crust she is. I remember once—'

Mrs Sloughthwaite was not one to be deflected from the topic of conversation in which she was most interested, and swiftly brought the discussion back to Dr Stirling and Mrs Devine. 'And I hear she's getting on well with Dr Stirling these days,' she said cutting the speaker off mid-sentence.

'Who is?'

'Mrs Devine.'

'She is,' replied Mrs O'Connor, 'but then everyone gets on well with the doctor and I can't imagine anyone taking against Mrs Devine.'

'I mean, from what Mrs Pocock told me,' continued Mrs Sloughthwaite, 'Dr Stirling was very much against her getting the job at the school. He took against her from the start for some reason.'

'I can't believe that,' said Mrs O'Connor. 'The

good man wouldn't take against anyone.'

'As God's my judge, that's what Mrs Pocock told me. She said he was the only one at the governors' meeting who voted not to appoint her.'

'She had no business telling you that.'

'Then they had a difference of opinion about a number of things and he was going to take his son away. The next thing I hear he's changed his mind, the lad's back at the school and they're getting on like a house on fire.' Mrs Sloughthwaite allowed her customer the time to reply, but when none was forthcoming she continued to probe. 'From what I've heard, Mrs Devine spends as much time at Dr Stirling's as she does at her own cottage. They seem to be on very good terms these days.'

Mrs O'Connor was well aware of Mrs Sloughthwaite's skill at extracting information from her customers which would then be relayed in quick time around the village. She also knew what was implied in the comment. Dr Stirling's housekeeper had learnt to be very circumspect when talking to the shopkeeper on certain matters. She had already been quizzed about James running away, a piece of gossip that had been disclosed by Mrs Widowson, who, when the boy had gone missing, had seen the doctor asking around the village, but the housekeeper had dismissed this as 'a storm in a teacup'.

'You know Dr Stirling,' Mrs O'Connor replied nonchalantly. 'Sure doesn't the man get on with everybody, a real gentleman he is and so well educated he always pulls the legs of his trousers up when he sits down. I think I'll take a box of those Viennese chocolate biscuits. Dr Stirling has a sweet tooth.'

Incomprehension crept across Lady Helen Wadsworth's face.

'Close the school!' she exclaimed.

'That's their intention,' replied Elisabeth.

Her neighbour, who had been on holiday at the time of the public meeting and had only just learnt from the font of all knowledge at the village store of the plans to close the school, had hurried around to Elisabeth's cottage to hear first hand of the proposals.

'It's quite out of the question!' she cried, her face decorated with fury. 'I've just got my grandfather's plaque back on the wall and they want to go and close the school! He built and endowed the village school for the welfare and education of the children and there is not the slightest possibility of it closing.'

'I wish I had your confidence,' said Elisabeth, 'but they appear determined to go ahead. Whenever I phone the Education Office for an update they are particularly evasive.'

Lady Helen gave a dismissive grunt. 'We'll see about that. You would have thought that I would have been informed of this plan, since there would be no village school had it not been for the benevolence of my grandfather. He'll be turning in his grave.'

'I have an idea they hoped things could be done quickly and quietly,' Elisabeth told her, 'and that there would be little opposition.'

'Well, if that is their hope they will be greatly disappointed,' Lady Helen said, her body tense with indignation. 'I go away for a couple of weeks and when I return all manner of things have happened: Mr Massey falling into a machine and nearly losing a foot, Mr Stainthorpe ill in hospital, and now I hear they want to close the school.'

'It has been pretty eventful,' agreed Elisabeth.

'Well, don't you worry, my dear. We will fight them all the way. My grandmother was a suffragette, you know. Always chaining herself to some railing or other and throwing bricks through butchers' windows.'

'That might be a little excessive,' said Elisabeth.

*   *   *

Later in the week Lady Wadsworth made her grand entrance at County Hall. She had booked an appointment to see the Director of Education and had dressed for the encounter in her brightest tweeds and heaviest brogues and decorated herself with a variety of expensive-looking jewellery. From her wide-brimmed hat escaped a wave of bright copper-coloured hair. Her lipstick was as thick and red as congealed blood.

As she was shown into his office, Mr Preston rose from his chair behind the large mahogany desk, came to the door to greet her and proffered her a hand.

'My dear Lady Wadsworth,' he began, with the polished smile he had perfected.

'Don't Lady Wadsworth me, Mr Preston,' she retorted, waving away his hand and plonking herself down straight-backed in the nearest chair. Her gaze was so level and her expression so mocking that the Director of Education was uncharacteristically thrown off balance. 'I am extremely angry!' she exclaimed.

'I am assuming you are here to see me about Barton-in-the-Dale school,' said the Director of Education, retreating behind his desk and sitting down.

'You assume correctly,' she replied frostily, continuing to look at him pointedly with the severe expression. 'It is quite outrageous that you are contemplating closing the school which my grandfather founded and endowed.'

'I assure you, Lady Wadsworth,' replied the Director of Education, 'I very deeply regret having to go down this road.'

'Well, why go down it then?' she asked bluntly.

'The Education Department has to cut costs and—' he began, but was interrupted.

'Mr Preston,' Lady Helen said, holding up a gloved hand, 'the school is at the very centre of village life. It's used by the WI, the local choir, the Brownies and the Cubs, the flower-arrangers and I don't know what else. Furthermore, the new head teacher, Mrs Devine, is a most accomplished and hard-working woman and—'

'I am well aware of that and I do fully appreciate—' the Director of Education attempted to intervene.

'Please allow me to finish, Mr Preston. I am not used to being interrupted. The new head teacher, Mrs Devine, is a most accomplished and hard-working woman,' she repeated, 'and has transformed the school since her arrival and I do not use that word lightly. I find it amazing that you should appoint her and then decide to close the school.'

'Nothing has been finally decided yet, I assure you, Lady Wadsworth, and I should say—' the Director of Education began.

Ignoring him, she continued: 'The village school has become highly successful and greatly regarded and it is inconceivable that you should think of closing it.'

The Director of Education would have given any other person who berated him so in his own office short shrift, but he was aware that he was speaking to one of the most influential and well-connected personages in the county. He gave a faint smile, cleared his throat several times, locked his fingers and placed his hands on the desk. He would need all his diplomatic skills to pacify this virago who sat before him with a face like Medusa's.

'I am merely an officer of the local authority, Lady Wadsworth,' he told her. 'It is the councillors on the Education Sub-committee who decide on the schools earmarked for closure. I just carry out their directives.'

'On your advice,' said his visitor sharply.

'I beg your pardon?'

'The councillors act on your advice, do they not? They are guided by you. It is you who recommend which schools should be closed and which should remain open. I assume that that is one of your functions.'

'I do give my advice but, of course, it is not always acted upon and—'

'So I take it you did not recommend that Barton-in-the-Dale should close?' she asked brusquely, 'and that I need to take this matter up with the chief executive and the leader of the council?'

'I am not in favour of any school closing,' he

337

replied evasively.

'I am pleased to hear it.'

'But sometimes needs must.'

Lady Wadsworth curled a lip. 'Mr Preston, let me be perfectly clear. If you decide to go ahead with this outrageous proposal you will face massive opposition. I do need to point out a consideration of which you and the members of the council may not be aware. Should the school close, God forbid, then the buildings and adjacent land revert to the Limebeck Estate. There is a codicil in the endowment document to that effect. So, if the councillors think they can sell the building and the land in the misguided belief that they can raise money, then they are very much mistaken.' She stood. 'I bid you good day, Mr Preston, and trust you will think on.'

At her departure an angry Director of Education reached for the telephone.

'Tell Mr Nettles I wish to see him immediately!' he shouted down the receiver.

CHAPTER SEVENTEEN

Elisabeth knew why Dr Stirling had called at the school that morning. He stood outside her classroom door looking tired and ill at ease.

'Excuse me for a moment, children,' she told her class. 'I have to pop out. Please get on with your reading quietly. Best behaviour, please.'

She joined her visitor in the corridor. Dr Stirling rested a hand on her arm. She didn't need to be told. 'It's Danny's grandfather, isn't it?' she asked.

She knew what the answer would be.

'Yes,' replied Dr Stirling, 'he died this morning.' Elisabeth gave a great heaving sigh. 'Are you all right?' he asked.

'Not really,' she replied. She looked through the small window in the classroom door at Danny, who was sitting by the window reading quietly. 'I guess it falls to me to tell him,' she said quietly.

'I think it would be best coming from you,' he said. 'I'll stay if you wish.'

'Thank you, I would appreciate that, but this is not the best time to tell him. Perhaps you could call back at lunchtime and we'll see him then. It will also give me time to think of the words I have to say.'

'You'll be much better at it than I,' he said. 'Having to tell someone that the person they love is seriously ill or has died I find the most difficult part of being a doctor. I've never been particularly good with words and what I say always seems so inadequate.'

'I'll tell him,' said Elisabeth. 'He knew that his grandfather had little time left, not that that makes it any easier. I promised his grandfather I would take care that Danny was well looked after, but I really don't know what will happen to the boy now. Since he has no family I suppose he'll end up in care, although it's so difficult to place a child of his age with foster parents. I can't imagine him settling in a children's home. I do so worry about him. Anyhow, I'll let Social Services know. I guess they will need to make arrangements.'

'Children are surprisingly resilient,' said Dr Stirling. 'They learn to cope.'

Some don't, though, thought Elisabeth. Take his

own son, for example. James had still not been able to come to terms with his mother's death, though it had been two years now since her tragic accident.

'Danny has had to face some tough things in the past,' Dr Stirling continued. 'He'll be all right, I'm sure.'

'I hope so,' said Elisabeth. 'I hope so.'

Returning to the class, Elisabeth found Chardonnay waiting at her desk. 'Miss, Ernest Pocock has done this for Mr Stainthorpe,' she said. She held out before her a large colourful card with a country scene on the front and the words 'Get Well Soon.' 'It's good, isn't it, miss?'

'It is,' agreed Elisabeth.

'Miss, we've all signed it,' said the girl. 'Will you put your name on it, miss, and Danny can take it with him to the hospital when he sees his granddad tonight.'

'Thank you, Chardonnay,' replied Elisabeth, taking the card from the girl. 'That was a really nice thought. I'll sign it later. Now you get on with your work.' As she looked at the card tears came to her eyes.

'Are you all right, miss?' asked Chardonnay.

'I'm fine thank you,' Elisabeth replied. 'I'm fine.'

At lunchtime Dr Stirling returned and joined Elisabeth and Danny in her classroom. The boy looked utterly wretched, for he knew why they had asked to see him and it was confirmed when he saw the expressions on their faces.

The boy had known that his grandfather had only a short time to live, for the old man had explained how things stood the previous week as Danny sat by his bedside.

'We've allus been straight with each other,

340

Danny,' the old man had told him. His face had been pale and his eyes filmy. 'We've allus been able to speak us minds and tell each other things, 'aven't we?'

'Yes, granddad,' the boy had replied, sniffing.

'Well, lad, there's summat I have to tell thee. I thowt abaat t'different ways of tellin' thee, but I reckon it's best to just come straight out wi' it.'

'Please, granddad,' the boy had pleaded, wiping his eyes. 'Don't tell me tha not goin' to get better. Please don't tell me that.' His face had crumpled.

'Nay, Danny lad, I'm not gunna get better and that's the way of it,' he had told him quietly between shallow breaths. 'I'm dying and there's no two ways about it.'

The boy had buried his head in his grandfather's arms and sobbed. 'No, no, granddad, don't tell me that.'

The old man had stroked the boy's hair gently and then had lifted up his face, wet with tears.

'It's best you know t'truth,' he had said, wiping the tears away. 'I've never in my life kept things from you—good and bad—and I don't intend startin' now. I'm not frightened. I knew my time was comin' up an' I've 'ad a good life.' He had cupped the boy's head in his hands and looked at the tear-stained face. 'I need to tell you, Danny, that you've been everythin' to me. Best thing what's ever 'appened in my life when you came to live wi' me. Like a breath of fresh country air you were. 'Appy little lad with a sunshine smile. There's never been a granddad who's loved 'is grandson as much as I 'ave loved you. You're a grand lad and tha'll grow up into a fine young man.' The boy's body had heaved with his sobbing. 'Now I don't want

341

you to tek on so. I want you to be brave, and when I'm gone remember all them 'appy times we've 'ad together. Be a good lad and do as Mrs Devine and Dr Stirling say. They'll mek sure tha'll be all reight. They've told me that. They'll tek care of you. Now, I wants you to dry your eyes and get off home and you can come and see me tomorrow. Mrs Devine's waitin' outside. You don't want to keep 'er waitin'.'

'I don't want to leave you, granddad,' the boy had wept, clinging to the old man.

'I know. I know. But I'm a bit on t'tired side. You go now and come and see me tomorrow. There's a good lad.'

'Danny,' said Elisabeth now, a hollow feeling in her heart, 'I'm afraid I have some very sad news.' The boy began to cry. She put her hand around his shoulder and held him to her.

*   *   *

Elisabeth arrived at Forest View on the following Saturday afternoon. She found John sitting at his favourite table by the window, rocking gently backwards and forwards and staring intently at a large coloured poster on the wall. When she sat next to him he held out his hand, which she grasped and squeezed.

'Oh, I see that you're in the mood to hold hands today, are you?' she said. 'I'm sorry I couldn't make it this morning. I had somewhere really important to go to. Mr Williams tells me you were a model pupil this week on the trip to see the Christmas lights at Clayton and is really pleased with the way you've been this week. It's very cold now. Lots of frost about and icy winds. The garden looks very

342

bare and bleak at the moment. Danny's put some little wire cages in the trees, full of nuts and seeds for the birds. He's a good boy.'

This would be his first Christmas without his grandfather, she thought. It would be a sad time for him. That morning she had been at his grandfather's funeral. The crematorium had been packed and the Reverend Atticus's homily had moved his congregation to tears. 'I reckon there will be snow before too long,' said Elisabeth now. 'Do you remember how you used to like the snow? I remember your face when you first saw those big flakes falling from the sky and how you loved to scoop them up when they had settled and watch them melt in your hands. We built a snowman, remember? I've decided what I am getting you for Christmas but it's going to be a surprise.' John, not looking at her, continued to rock. 'School is still as hectic as ever and I'm still waiting to see if the school has a future. I suppose I'll find out soon enough.' The boy stopped rocking and examined a tiny insect that scurried across the table. He touched it gently with his finger. 'I never imagined that this job was going to turn out like this,' continued Elisabeth. 'Apply for a post at a quiet country school in a picturesque little village, I thought, lovely scenery, lots of peace and quiet, no worries and no problems.' She sighed. 'Still,' she said, trying to sound cheerful, 'I'm able to come and see you as often as I want now and that's the main thing.'

'Well, that is good to hear.'

Elisabeth turned to find the head teacher standing in the doorway.

'How long have you been there?' she asked.

343

'Not long,' he said. 'I'm sorry, I couldn't help but eavesdrop. For what it's worth, I think you made the right decision. It's been really good seeing you in school. You know, I look forward to your visits as much as I hope John does.'

'I don't know what benefit there is for him,' said Elisabeth, 'me rattling on out loud like this, but I should like to think he understands something of what I say and I find it therapeutic. He's the only one I can be really honest with and share all my hopes and fears and feelings. It's quite a change to talk to someone and not be interrupted or disagreed with.'

Mr Williams looked at her for a moment. He had liked this attractive, intelligent, good-humoured woman from their first meeting a few months ago, he realised, when she had brought her son to the school.'I'm a good listener,' he said, 'and I promise not to interrupt or disagree with you.'

'I wouldn't want to burden you with all my problems,' she replied.

'Well, if ever you feel you do, give me a call.'

'I will.'

'So how did the public meeting go?' he asked.

'It's hard to tell,' she replied. 'Mr Preston is a very clever and persuasive man and very adept at charming an audience. He gave those who attended the impression that nothing had been decided and that he would consider any objections carefully, but I am afraid I don't trust him as far as I could throw him.'

'No, he's a skilful operator is our Director of Education,' agreed Mr Williams, 'but I think you may be misjudging him. He's under a deal of pressure to make savings in the education budget.

It can't be easy for him. Actually, I wanted to have a word with you about something which has arisen.'

'Is it about John?' she asked.

'No, no, he's doing fine. It's on another matter. Could you call into my office on your way out?'

Later Mr Williams explained his own worry. 'The head teachers of the special schools were called to a meeting with Mr Preston last week,' he told Elisabeth, 'and it looks likely that your school is not the only one to be threatened with closure. They have to make quite stringent cuts and it appears they want to shut one of the special schools. I have an idea that it might be this one. Being a very specialist place and expensive to maintain, I think we may be first in the firing line.'

'Oh, please don't tell me that,' said Elisabeth.

'Well, I thought you should know.'

'But no other school could cater so well for my son's or the other children's needs. John's barely started here and settled in. I've never seen him so contented. It would be enormously disruptive for him to move schools again and get used to a new environment. And I moved schools so I could be near to him and able to visit him regularly.'

Mr Williams sighed. 'I know that. It will be a great upheaval for many should the school close.'

'It can't close!' cried Elisabeth angrily. 'It just can't!'

'I assure you that I shall fight until my last breath to resist any moves to close the school, but they are keen on integrating children with special needs into mainstream schools.'

'But John couldn't cope in a mainstream school!' she exclaimed.

'I know that,' he replied, 'but in their view it's

a more cost-effective option. The children would receive some classroom support. It's all to do with money, I'm afraid. With children who have severe disabilities, like John, I assume they will be found places in other specialist residential schools outside the county. I am sorry to have to add to your worries, Elisabeth, but I felt you ought to be aware of the way things stand.'

'But you received such an outstanding inspectors' report. Doesn't that count for anything?'

'It appears not. Fine words butter no parsnips, as my mother would say. We will just have to hope and pray that they change their minds.'

'I imagined that nothing else could possibly add to my worries,' she said.

'This news makes my other problems seem trivial.'

'Nothing may come of it, of course,' Mr Williams reassured her, 'but if it does and I end up in the same boat as you, with a proposed closure on my hands, I would appreciate your support.'

'That goes without saying,' she replied.

'Thank you, I appreciate that,' said Mr Williams. 'And if you do want to talk anything through with me I should be delighted to listen. Perhaps I might take you out for a drink one evening?'

'That would be nice,' she replied smiling but not really listening.

*　　　*　　　*

Later that afternoon Elisabeth found Danny leaning against the horse-chestnut tree. He held his ferret in his hands and was stroking the long sleek body. The needle-eyed, furry creature wore a small

346

coloured collar on which was fastened a tiny silver bell.

'Hello,' she said gently.

''Ello, miss,' he replied, trying to force a smile.

'You shouldn't be out here in this weather. You'll get your death of cold. Come into the house and I'll make you a warm drink.'

'No, you're all reight, miss. I like it out 'ere. I don't mind t'cold.'

'Dr Stirling will be worried about you. I had better give him a ring and let him know where you are.'

''E knows where I am, miss,' he told her. 'I telled 'im I wanted to be by missen for a bit, to think things ovver.'

'Do you want me to go?' asked Elisabeth.

'Naw, you're all reight, miss.'

'I see you've brought your ferret.'

'Aye.'

Elisabeth stood next to him and put a hand on his shoulder. They remained there for a while in silence.

'I used to go ferretin' with mi granddad,' said the boy suddenly. 'We'd stretch a bit o' string netting across t'openings to t'rabbits' burrows. Then we'd put t'ferret down and 'e'd chase rabbits out and then they ended up in t'net. 'Course sometimes if there were a big buck down there t'ferret could get a nasty kick. They can grow reight big can bucks. Granddad used to say that it's a gret sport is ferreting, all that fresh air and free meat and it keeps t'population of rabbits down. This is reight time o' year for doing it. Best time is when it's cowld. If it's too mild rabbits stay down and sleep. Difficult for a ferret to shift 'em then. You only

347

have to half-feed a ferret.' There was a tremble in the boy's voice. 'Keep 'im too 'ungry and 'e'll stop down t'burrow an' eat what 'e kills. Feed 'im too much and 'e dunt bother. I miss my granddad. I miss him so much.'

'I know, Danny,' she said.

The boy sniffed. 'I like it 'ere under this tree.' He looked up. 'That big branch wants lopping off. It might come through your roof if there's a bad storm. It were lightning what did it, splitting t'branch like that. I remember when it 'appened.'

'I'll get it seen to,' said Elisabeth.

It was now getting dark and they watched together in silence as the garden underwent a magical transformation. The lawn glittered with frost, frozen plants creaked in a gentle wind, the prickly holly hedge sparkled and in the sky stars winked and a cold white moon shone between clouds of frozen breath.

'You know, Danny,' said Elisabeth, 'on nights like this one could almost believe in Father Christmas.'

'It were a good funeral for mi granddad, weren't it miss? All them people turnin' out and t'vicar sayin' all them nice things about 'im being an 'ero.'

'It was a wonderful funeral. You were very brave this morning, Danny.'

The boy nodded.

'Your grandfather was a very special man. He was loved and respected and he will be missed greatly by all of us who were fortunate to know him. And I know he'd have been really proud of you the way you coped at the service.'

'I loved him, miss,' said Danny sniffing. 'I really loved him. I don't know what I shall do now he's gone.'

The boy's arms were suddenly around her and he held her close, burying his head in her coat. He began to cry, great shuddering sobs, and she cried too and they remained holding tight to each other and crying until eventually Elisabeth wiped away her tears and bent down to face him.

'Your grandfather would want you to keep being brave and remember all the things he told you and did for you and all the happy memories you've had. He brought you up to be a fine young man, Danny.'

'Mrs Devine, do you think they'll let me take mi ferret with me when I go to live somewhere else?'

'I should think so.'

'If they won't, do you think Dr Stirling will let James look after 'im for me?'

'Of course, and you can come and visit to see how's he's getting on and call in to see me.'

'They say that t'school's gunna close,' he said.

'That's what they say,' said Elisabeth, 'but I don't intend to let it happen.'

'I like school now,' he said. 'Never used to. Miss, do you think I might 'ave to move to another school?'

'That depends on where you go to live,' she replied.

The boy thought for moment. 'Mrs Devine, could I still live here?' he asked. 'I could stay in t'caravan. I'd be all right and I wouldn't be any bother and you could keep an eye on things.'

'I don't think that's a very good idea, Danny,' she said.

'Aye, well, it were worth askin'. Well, I'd best be off.'

'Goodbye Danny,' she said and watched the sad

little figure climb the wall and walk slowly across the field towards the village.

*   *   *

The three women, attired in black and with suitably cheerless expressions, sat in the 'parlour' at the rear of the village store. Mrs Sloughthwaite had closed the shop for the day 'as a sign of respect', but the more cynical in the village viewed such an action as more to do with the shopkeeper not wishing to miss Les Stainthorpe's funeral, to see who attended and to hear all the gossip. As everyone was well aware, Mrs Sloughthwaite was a person who liked to be fully in the know, and she would hardly miss such an event.

'It was a lovely funeral, so it was,' observed Mrs O'Connor, taking a sip of tea.

The shopkeeper responded with appropriate solemnity, nodding her head dolefully. 'It was,' she said. 'He had a lovely send-off.'

'Well, the poor man has gone to his reward now, God rest his soul,' sighed Mrs O'Connor, crossing herself.

'I prefer a church service myself,' pronounced Mrs Pocock. 'I told my husband that if I go before him, they'll take my coffin into that crematorium over my dead body.'

'No, I feel the same,' agreed the shopkeeper. 'You get a much better send-off in a church. It's more historical and the atmosphere's a lot better. Did you notice the flower display in the entrance at the crematorium, by the way? I thought to myself, they should have had roses or lilies, not red hot pokers. Very unfortunate choice. And did you see

350

the sign on the door: "The Management wishes all visitors a warm welcome." Very inappropriate, to my mind.'

'Well, I thought the sign for the fire exit could have been a bit more discreet,' added Mrs Pocock. She helped herself to a salmon paste sandwich.

'The vicar was very good,' observed Mrs O'Connor.

'Except that nobody understood much of what he said,' observed the shopkeeper. 'Too highbrow and academical for my liking. I mean he's a nice enough man, don't get me wrong, but my goodness his sermons could put a glass eye to sleep.'

'I was surprised at the tunes they had,' Mrs Pocock said, reaching for another salmon paste sandwich. 'I like a good hymn myself.'

'Well, Les Stainthorpe wasn't a religious man,' said Mrs Sloughthwaite. 'I've never see him inside the church and, to my knowledge, I don't think that grandson of his was ever christened.'

'I felt sorry for the poor wee lad,' said Mrs O'Connor, 'sitting there at the front crying his little eyes out.'

'Yes,' nodded Mrs Pocock, 'it's a bleak future got him, destined for the children's home.'

'It was good of Mrs Devine and Dr Stirling to look after him at the funeral,' said Mrs Sloughthwaite meaningfully. 'Quite a little family group, it was, sitting together on the front pew.'

Mrs O'Connor knew what the shopkeeper was up to, fishing for information about the relationship of the head teacher and the village doctor. She reached for a sandwich.

'Yes,' she said non-committally, then quickly changed the topic of conversation. 'I thought it was a very nice touch having music that was popular during the war. My goodness, that brought back memories.'

'I never knew Les Stainthorpe was an old soldier,' said Mrs Pocock, 'until the vicar started on about him being a Dunkirk veteran and all and having all those medals.'

'Neither did I,' said Mrs Sloughthwaite. 'Never said a word to anyone. He was a dark horse and no mistake. You can bet he's left a tidy sum. I've seen it before. They go through life as if they hadn't a penny to rub together and when they've gone it's discovered they've left a small fortune. Probably squirrelled it away in that caravan of his. I made that Bakewell tart myself, by the way.'

'And very nice it looks too,' said Mrs Pocock, reaching for a slice.

'I have to admit I shed a silent tear when Vera Lynn started singing "We'll Meet Again",' remarked Mrs O'Connor.

'I got quite choked too,' nodded Mrs Sloughthwaite, 'although I thought the choice of the second piece of music was not really appropriate, being in a crematorium and all.'

'Oh, I don't know,' said Mrs Pocock. 'I think it was very appropriate, the deceased being an old soldier, and I've always liked "Keep the Home Fires Burning".'

'I thought it was a bit rich Fred Massey making that grand entrance and hobbling down the aisle like Long John Silver on his crutch,' said the shopkeeper, 'and plonking himself down at the front. It's not as if he was Les Stainthorpe's friend.'

'Probably felt guilty,' remarked Mrs Pocock.

'Would anyone like a Venetian chocolate

biscuit?' asked the host, holding up a plate.

Her two guests shook their heads simultaneously and replied, 'No thank you.'

'Last time we were at the crematorium was for Mrs Pickles' funeral,' said Mrs Pocock. 'I think you were on a pilgrimage at the time, Mrs O'Connor.'

'And what a fandango that was,' added Mrs Sloughthwaite.

'Oh no, I had a lovely time,' said Mrs O'Connor. 'We went on a coach trip to Knock. It was very spiritual.'

'I meant the funeral,' said the shopkeeper. She looked at Mrs Pocock, who was nibbling at another slice of Bakewell tart. 'Don't you remember? Mrs Pickles had requested in her will that when she passed on she wanted that Judy Garland number from *The Wizard of Oz* played. You know the one, "Somewhere Over the Rainbow".'

'And?' asked Mrs O'Connor.

'Well, they put the wrong track on, didn't they, and the coffin disappeared behind the red velvet curtain to: "Ding, Dong, the Wicked Witch is Dead!"'

'No.'

'Yes.'

'And that's not all,' added Mrs Pocock. 'When they tried again, the tune changed to "I'm Off to see the Wizard, the Wonderful Wizard of Oz". I mean, you couldn't help smiling.'

'Well, you know what my owld Grandmother Mullarkey used to say,' said Mrs O'Connor, 'There's no marriage where there is no weeping, and no funeral where there is no laughing.'

'Is someone getting married then?' asked Mrs Pocock, leaning forward.

'Not as I know of,' replied Mrs O'Connor.

Mrs Sloughthwaite rolled her eyes. 'Another slice of Bakewell tart, anyone?'

*   *   *

Miss Brakespeare's mother sat straight-backed, enthroned in her armchair by the window, her face tight and pale above her grey dress and grey cardigan. She wore her usual martyred expression. 'You are going where?' she asked.

'I said I am going to France, Mother,' replied her daughter. Her hair had been freshly done and she wore a new lavender-coloured woollen suit and black patent leather shoes.

'Don't be ridiculous, Miriam. Why ever would you want to go to France?'

'To join the Folies Bergère,' she told her mother flippantly.

'What?'

'Mrs Devine has arranged a school trip to France and she's asked me to go.'

'Oh, not that woman again,' interrupted Mrs Brakespeare. 'Mrs Devine this and Mrs Devine that. I'm heartily sick and tired of hearing about her. It was a sad day when that woman with all her airs and graces came here.'

'No, Mother, it was not,' retorted her daughter sharply. 'Quite the contrary, in fact. You have not met her and therefore are not in a position to judge her.'

Mrs Brakespeare looked at her daughter with some displeasure. She had never spoken to her in that sharp tone of voice until 'that woman' had become head teacher of the village school. 'I hear quite enough about her from you and about all the changes she has been making. You talk about nothing else these days.'

'Well, if you are tired of hearing about her, then in future I shall not bore you with the details about what goes on in the school. I assumed that you would be interested.' It was sad, she thought, that her mother found the world such a harsh and unloving place. Since the death of her husband Mrs Brakespeare had become increasingly miserable and disapproving, almost revelling in playing the martyr and finding fault with most things her daughter did. Of late her offhand manner and critical comments had become more noticeable, and her daughter was wearying of it.

Mrs Brakespeare eyed her daughter curiously. 'Go to France, indeed,' she mumbled to no one in particular.

'Yes, mother, go to France.' Miss Brakespeare's eyes shone with the excitement of it all. 'I shall be accompanying a group of the older children to Brittany early next year. I have seen precious little of the world and this is an opportunity I do not intend to pass up.'

'If the school is here next year,' observed her mother pointedly.

'Oh, it will be here all right,' replied Miss Brakespeare, not rising to the comment. 'And of course, if the school does close then I shall be redeployed somewhere else in the county and shall, no doubt, have to move to live somewhere near the school.'

'Move! I don't want to move.'

'Then let us hope the school doesn't close,' said her daughter.

Her mother looked chillier than ever. 'And who will look after me while you're gallivanting in France?' she asked, putting on a pained face.

'You can either stay in Oakview, the residential home at Urebank, for the week or—'

'A residential home!' snapped her mother. 'Over my dead body! Living with all those senile old women sitting around the television all day and old men snoring in their armchairs.' She wore the miserable expression habitual to those who feel themselves badly done to in life.

'You can either stay in the residential home for the week,' repeated her daughter, 'or I will arrange for a carer to call in each day.'

'Well, I never thought I would hear a daughter of mine say that. I suppose that is what I've got to look forward to now, is it—pushed into a home or with other folk looking after me? I might as well be dead.' She began to sniff theatrically and dab her eyes with a small handkerchief which she had produced from the sleeve of her cardigan.

'Please, Mother, you are talking foolishly,' said her daughter. 'I am not pushing you into a home, and as for other people looking after you, it would only be for a week.'

'You've become very selfish and ungrateful, Miriam,' moaned her mother. Her face was mutinous, like a spoilt child's.

'No, I have not,' replied Miss Brakespeare, looking directly at her. 'If anyone is selfish and ungrateful, it is you. It seems that there is no pleasing you. Whatever I say or wear or do you always manage to find fault. I am going to France and there's an end to it. I have a life outside this house. I am happy to cook and clean and get

356

your medicines and I do try to make your life as comfortable as possible as well as hold down a full-time job, but I am no longer prepared to be at your beck and call all the time. Now would you like some fish for tea?'

'I'm not hungry,' said her mother. Her voice was stiff. 'I couldn't eat a thing.'

'In that case, I'll just get myself something,' said her daughter, leaving the room.

*   *   *

James was waiting outside the staff-room door the following Monday morning.

'Hello, James,' said Elisabeth.

He gave a small smile.

'Did you want to see me?'

He nodded.

'Let's go into the entrance where it's quiet and we won't be disturbed and then you can tell me what's on your mind.' They sat on the small bench beneath the brass plaque. Elisabeth took a small notebook and a pencil from her handbag and gave them to the boy. This was the means by which the boy communicated with her in class. 'Now you can write down what you would like to say,' she said.

The boy shook his head and passed the notebook and pencil back.

'You don't want to write things down?'

He shook his head again.

'Right, well, I suppose I shall have to ask a few questions to find out what it is. Let me see. Is something upsetting you?'

He nodded.

'Is someone picking on you, calling you names? Are you being bullied?'

He shook his head.

'Are you unhappy about something?'

He nodded.

'Well, you know, James, I can't help you unless I know what it is that's making you unhappy. Why don't you write down what's worrying you?'

The boy, looking at his feet, thought for a moment. She could see him struggling to speak, twisting his small fingers and mouthing words. Then he took a deep breath and whispered, 'It's Danny.'

'Danny,' Elisabeth repeated. 'Are you worried about Danny?'

He nodded.

'I see. Well, I'm worried about Danny too. He's had a very difficult time lately and I know how upset he is about his grandfather, but we are doing our very best for him and we'll see he is all right. He's got a lot of people, like you and your father and me and many other people, looking out for him.'

The boy shook his head. He struggled to find the words. 'He doesn't want to leave,' he whispered, still looking down at his feet. He began to tremble. He raised his voice. 'He wants to stay here. He doesn't want to go away. I don't want him to go away.'

'James,' said Elisabeth. 'I don't want Danny to go away either, but he will need to be looked after and it may mean that he is going to go to a family that lives away from here. I know he doesn't want to leave the village and the school, but there's nothing I can do. I wish I could change things, but I can't.'

The boy looked up and stared at her for a

moment. Then he gripped her arm. 'Please,' he said.

CHAPTER EIGHTEEN

After school, Elisabeth called at Dr Stirling's. The last time she had visited the large stone villa at the end of the long gravel drive, it had been in darkness. Now, in daylight, she saw how neglected it was. Thick green ivy climbed up the walls and covered part of the two bay windows at either side of the door, and some of the blue slates on the roof were missing. The garden was overgrown. Weeds grew amongst the rough spiky grass which had once been a lawn, and the borders were clotted with a thick mass of dead roses, thorns and holly bushes. The trees with their intricate mesh of smaller branches had grown wild.

She was shown into the dark narrow hall by Mrs O'Connor and followed her into the sitting room.

'Look at the state of this place,' said the housekeeper, tut-tutting. 'I wish he'd let me give this room a good going over but he says he likes it the way it is. Excuse the mess, Mrs Devine.' She moved a pile of medical journals off a chair and brushed the material with the back of her hand. 'Doctor's not back from the surgery yet, but he'll be here any moment. You make yourself comfortable and I'll get you a cup of tea.'

'That's kind of you, Mrs O'Connor,' replied Elisabeth, 'but it might be better if I called back.'

'Sure, he won't be long. He's usually in by this

time. You sit yourself down and rest your legs.' She waddled off to the kitchen.

Elisabeth sat by the window and looked out over the neglected expanse, thick with weeds and overgrown bushes. It was like the garden at the cottage when she had first moved in—wild and abandoned—but with some care and attention it could be restored to its former state. She glanced around the room. Like the garden it was uncared for. It had a dusty, stale smell to it. The carpet was a muddy brown and the pale walls had a few dull prints and an insipid watercolour of a mountain and a lake. A bookshelf was crammed with books, journals and papers, and on a large oak desk were an old-fashioned blotter, a mug holding an assortment of pens and pencils and more papers stacked untidily. Near her, on a small walnut table, several photographs in small silver frames had been arranged. One showed Dr Stirling with his arm around a striking-looking woman, another was a more formal portrait of the same woman posing before a horse. Elisabeth picked up the photograph and looked at the happy face. She replaced it quickly on the table when Mrs O'Connor bustled through the door with a tea-tray.

'Now I've mashed it nice and strong, just the way the doctor likes it. My owld Grandmother Mullarkey couldn't stand the sight of weak tea. It should be strong enough to trot a mouse across it, she would say.' She chuckled. 'And that's the front door now. I told you he wouldn't be long.'

'Oh, hello,' said Dr Stirling, coming into the room.

'I've just made Mrs Devine a cup of tea,' the housekeeper informed him. 'Upstairs has all been cleaned, ironing done and the boys have been fed and your dinner's in the oven. Now I'm off.'

'Thank you, Mrs O'Connor,' he said, as she shuffled through the door.

'I'm sorry if I've called at a bad time,' Elisabeth began.

'No, no, not at all. Would you like a cup of Mrs O'Connor's tea? She must use half a packet. I must warn you it's like treacle.'

'She said you like it strong.'

'Not quite as strong as this,' he said, pouring a cup.

'I have some good news,' Elisabeth told him.

'They are not going to close the school!' he exclaimed.

'No,' she replied. 'I'm afraid things have gone very quiet in that direction. It's about James.'

'James?'

'We had a conversation this morning.'

'He spoke to you!' He put down the cup with a clatter, causing the tea to spill over on to the saucer. 'Good gracious. Whatever did he say?'

'It was Danny, in effect, who prompted him to speak. James came to see me to tell me how unhappy Danny was about leaving the village and the school. I think he felt that speaking to me rather than writing it down as he usually does would have greater effect.'

'That's wonderful news,' said Dr Stirling. 'I can't tell you how happy that makes me feel. I mean about James speaking. That's something of a breakthrough, isn't it?'

'It is. James asked me,' she said, 'if I could do something to get Danny to stay in the village but I had to tell him that I couldn't.'

361

'But I can,' said Dr Stirling, smiling. 'James had the same conversation with me yesterday and told me what I guess he told you. I said very much the same as you to him, but then I got to thinking and this morning I got in touch with Social Services and asked if it was possible for Danny to stay here on a more permanent footing, for me to become his foster carer initially but, if things work out, to adopt him.'

'Adopt him? You mean you would adopt him?' She was stunned.

'Don't you think it's a good idea?' Dr Stirling asked. He looked worried.

'Yes, yes, I think it's a wonderful idea,' she said, 'but—'

'But what? You don't look all that convinced.'

'Michael, it's a very big step to take,' said Elisabeth. 'Perhaps you ought to think about it for a while.'

'I have thought about it,' he told her. 'I've got quite attached to the boy since he's been here. He's a frank, good-natured lad and I know James likes him around.'

'I can see that,' agreed Elisabeth. 'Danny is a very likeable and considerate young man and he obviously gets on well with you and James. It's just that maybe you should give it a little more thought.'

Dr Stirling looked peeved. 'Really, Elisabeth, I should have thought that you would be all for it.'

'I am, of course I am,' she said. 'It would be ideal for Danny to have a stable home and he's clearly very happy here, but have you looked into exactly what adoption involves?'

He looked irritated. 'Of course I have. It might appear a spur of the moment decision to you, but I have discussed things pretty thoroughly with Social Services.'

'And what did they say?'

'They thought it was an excellent idea. They usually like to place children with couples, of course, but they said it was really hard to find homes for adolescent boys. Most people want babies. To be honest, I'm really excited about having him here and I don't think I'll make too bad a father.'

'You'll make a great father and you know it.'

'There will be a sort of trial period,' Dr Stirling explained. 'It's quite a long process. At first, as I said, I become his official foster carer and, after a period of time when we have both got to know each other, then Danny can become my adopted son, that's of course if he agrees.'

'Oh, he'll agree all right,' said Elisabeth.

'You think so?'

'Of course,' she said. 'Well, I really hope things work out. After all he's been through Danny deserves a good home and I know he'll get it here.'

'Good.' Dr Stirling gave a big smile. He ran his hand through his untidy hair. 'I know Mrs O'Connor will be pleased. She's been fussing around him like a mother hen since he arrived and moaning to me like a banshee about "the poor, wee orphan child" who has nowhere to go. I've not mentioned anything to Danny or to James yet, because there are a few formalities that have to be taken care of before it is agreed. They also need to speak to Danny, to make sure he's happy about the arrangement. I meant to phone you to let you know I'll be going to the children's department at County Hall with Danny tomorrow to sort things out. So

Danny won't be at school. I think they might want a reference from you.'

'Of course,' said Elisabeth. She felt like reaching over and hugging him. You're a good, good man, Michael Stirling, she thought.

*   *   *

The next morning Danny stood in the hall looking clean and smart in a crisp white shirt, tie, grey jumper and polished black shoes.

'Well now,' said Mrs O'Connor, brushing the boy's shoulder with a hand, 'don't you scrub up well?' She looked down at the sad face. 'Cheer up now, Danny, sure 'tis not the end of the world.' She kissed his cheek. 'You look as if you've lost a shilling and found a penny.'

He gave a weak smile. 'Thank you for looking after me, Mrs O'Connor,' he said. He looked like someone on his way to his execution.

'It's been a pleasure,' she replied. 'And whatever it is you're worried about, sure it may never happen.' She looked at Dr Stirling and winked. He had acquainted her with his intention to have Danny stay with them but had asked her not to say anything to the boys.

'Will I need to pack my things?' the boy asked.

'Not for the moment, darlin',' she said.

'What about Ferdie?'

'James will take care of him,' she said. 'Don't you go worrying your head about that.'

'Well, come along, young man,' said the doctor cheerfully. 'Let's be off.'

In the car Danny was very quiet and twiddled his hair nervously. 'Will I meet the people who are going to look after me today?' he asked after a while.

'Maybe,' said Dr Stirling evasively. He smiled inwardly.

'Have you met them, Dr Stirling?'

'In a manner of speaking.'

'Are they nice?'

'Very nice.'

Miss Parsons, senior social worker, came out of her office to meet them. She was a handsome woman with bright eyes and light sandy hair tied back to reveal a finely structured face. 'Good morning, Dr Stirling,' she said shaking his hand. She turned to the boy. 'Hello, Danny.'

'Hello, miss.'

'Dr Stirling, I would like to have a little chat with Danny on his own, so if you wouldn't mind waiting. We won't be that long.'

Danny followed the woman into her office and was introduced to her colleague, Mrs Talbot, a small, smiling woman with short cropped white hair. The boy sat nervously on a hard wooden chair facing the desk, his hands locked beneath him. He felt a tightness in his chest and he was close to tears. He bit his bottom lip.

'Now then, Danny,' said Miss Parsons, giving him a reassuring smile, 'don't look so frightened, I'm not going to eat you. We're just going to have a little chat.' She sat behind her desk. 'I was very sorry to hear about your grandfather. He sounded like a very special man.'

'He was,' Danny replied, a tremble in his voice.

'And I know how difficult it is for you at the moment, wondering what will happen to you and where you will go.'

Danny nodded.

'How are you getting along at Dr Stirling's?' she asked.

'OK, miss,' he replied in a small voice.

'Just OK?'

'Well, no. I really like it there.'

'What's the best thing about living at Dr Stirling's house?' she asked.

'Well, there's my best friend James there and Mrs O'Connor.'

'She's the housekeeper.'

'Yes, she looks after Dr Stirling, cooks and cleans and that. She's really nice is Mrs O'Connor. Dr Stirling's really nice as well. And I can keep mi ferret in t'back garden.'

'A ferret. Don't they bite?'

'Sometimes, but not if you know 'ow to 'andle 'em.'

'Aren't ferrets rather smelly creatures?' she asked.

The boy suddenly became animated. 'A lot of people think that, but they're wrong. If you feed 'em rabbit and meat like that, they do smell, but if you get t'special food from t'pet shops they don't. They're very clean and friendly animals.'

'You seem to know a lot about ferrets, Danny,' said Miss Parsons.

'I reckon I do,' he replied. 'I used to go ferreting wi' mi granddad. I'd put t'ferret down t'rabbit 'ole and 'e'd chase out t'rabbits. Ferret that is, not mi granddad. Then mi granddad would catch t'rabbits in t'net an' chop 'em on t'neck sharpish like. I got a pound a rabbit when I sold 'em to t'butchers in t'village.'

'You're quite the little businessman,' said Miss

366

Parsons.

The boy nodded.

'And what about Dr Stirling?' asked Miss Talbot. 'How are you getting on with him?'

'I like 'im.'

'And he's been looking after you?'

'Yes, miss.'

'So you've been happy there?'

'Yes, miss.'

'Better than OK?'

'Yes, miss.'

'What about school?' asked Miss Parsons. 'How are you getting on there?'

'I like it now. I didn't used to, but we got this new 'ead teacher and she's really good. She dunt shout at you an' she's been really kind.'

'This is Mrs Devine,' she said, looking down at some papers in a folder.

'Yes, miss.'

'She says some nice things about you too. She says you're a very cheerful and well-behaved young man.' Danny didn't say anything. 'So you are pretty settled then?'

He nodded. 'I suppose so, miss.'

'Is there anything you want to tell me, Danny?' she asked.

'I'd like to stay in t'village if I can and at t'same school, but I know I probably can't. And if I do move somewhere a long way away I'd like to tek mi ferret wi' me.'

'Well, we'll see what we can do. Let's get Dr Stirling to come and join us,' she said, rising from her chair. Dr Stirling was asked to come into the office and he sat down next to the boy.

'Before you came in this morning, Mrs Talbot

367

and I had a discussion about where you should go, Danny,' Miss Parsons told the boy. 'We want to make sure that you will be well looked after, happy and secure and have a supportive home life. Do you understand what I'm saying?'

'Yes, miss,' said the boy.

'Now, Danny, at the moment you are being fostered by Dr Stirling. Do you know what I mean by the word fostering?'

'No, miss.'

'It means that someone looks after a child or young person until they can go back to their parents. In this case, it would have been your grandfather. Well, sadly you can't go back to your grandfather, so we have to make other arrangements.'

The boy's eyes were brimful of tears and his face became twisted in anxiety.

His small body looked as loose and floppy as a puppet. 'Where will I go?' he asked, his breath coming with difficulty.

The senior social worker reached across the desk and patted the boy's hand. 'Well now, Danny, I have had a talk with Dr Stirling,' she continued, 'and he thinks it would be a good idea, as you do, that you should stay in the village and at the same school. That's right, isn't it, Dr Stirling?'

'Yes, it is,' agreed the doctor.

'Well, we think the same.'

Danny looked up quickly, then turned to Dr Stirling and rubbed his eyes.

'Dr Stirling wants to continue to foster you, Danny,' Miss Parsons told him.

The boy's bottom lip began to tremble and his eyes began to fill up again. He bit the inside of his cheek and hugged himself tightly, locking his arms around his chest.

'And if it works out and you are happy there, he wants to adopt you. Do you know what that means?'

Danny sniffed and rubbed his eyes. He tried to speak but the words wouldn't come.

'It means he wants to bring you up as his own son,' said Miss Parsons.

'Would you like to stay with me and James?' Dr Stirling asked him, resting his hand gently on the boy's shoulder.

'Stay with you?' Danny asked quietly, 'You mean come and live with you and James and not go anywhere else, not never?'

'Not never,' said the doctor. 'So what about it? Do you want to stay with us?'

Danny looked at Dr Stirling for a moment and began to cry. His small body shook and tears bubbled from his eyes.

'Good gracious,' said Dr Stirling, feeling tears welling up in his own eyes. 'I didn't think the thought of living with me and James would have this effect.'

'I'm just happy,' sobbed the boy.

*   *   *

Elisabeth was walking around the playground and came across Danny sandwiched on a bench between Chardonnay and Chantelle. The two girls were muffled up in thick gloves, bobble hats and scarves, and sported bright rubber boots. Danny was just wearing a school jumper under his coat.

'Danny Stainthorpe!' Elisabeth exclaimed. 'What

are you doing out here without a scarf? It's bitterly cold. You'll freeze to death.'

'I'm all reight, miss,' the boy told her. 'I don't mind t'cold.'

'He's dead tough, isn't he, miss,' said Chardonnay, squeezing Danny's arm.

'And the cold makes his cheeks dead rosy,' added Chantelle.

The boy winced.

'It's good to see you a whole lot happier these days,' said Elisabeth.

'I am, miss,' he said. His eyes were dancing. 'Now I can stay wi' Dr Stirling and James, stop at t'school and keep mi ferret, I'm dead chuffed.'

'Well, I'm really pleased it's turned out so well for you,' she said.

'I'm glad you're staying, Danny,' said Chardonnay, edging closer to him.

Danny wrinkled his nose as if there were a faintly unpleasant odour.

'And I am,' said Chantelle, fluttering her eyelids.

Danny sighed and looked heavenwards. ''Course, there are some things I could well do wi'out, miss,' he grumbled.

'Excuse me, Mrs Devine.' Oscar had marched across the playground. 'I think you ought to know that there is a man in a car at the front of the school. He looks to me like a suspicious character and you can't be too careful these days.'

'Thank you, Oscar,' Elisabeth replied. 'That's very observant of you. I shall go and see what he wants.'

'I think that would be a very good idea,' said the boy.

The man in the car was in the entrance hall when

370

Elisabeth arrived back in the school, staring at the brass plaque on the wall. Tall and precise-looking, he was dressed in an expensive light grey suit, silk tie and wore highly polished shoes.

'Mr Preston,' said Elisabeth.

'Good morning, Mrs Devine,' he said, putting on his professional smile. 'I trust it is not an inconvenient time for me to call.' He was perfectly courteous but his voice was slightly flat.

'Not at all. I am very pleased to see you. Perhaps you might like to look around the school and meet the staff and pupils.'

'Thank you, no. I have a very busy schedule this morning. Perhaps another time.'

'If there is another time,' said Elisabeth.

The Director of Education gave the faintest of smirks. 'I don't think there is any doubt about that. Could we perhaps go somewhere a little more private?'

In the classroom Mr Preston sat in the teacher's chair and rested his hands on the desk. 'The reason for my visit is to tell you that the decision to close this school has been deferred.'

'Deferred,' repeated Elisabeth.

'That is correct. The Education Sub-committee has, on my advice, decided to put on hold any closure plans with regard to Barton-in-the-Dale. I have examined the inspectors' report and the various representations from those in the community and have recommended that the school remains open for the foreseeable future. I am sure that news comes as a very pleasant surprise.'

'Am I to understand,' asked Elisabeth, 'that this is just a postponement and that the future of the school is still uncertain?'

371

'It is possible that the school might close at some future date, but that is highly unlikely as things stand. For the moment it will remain open.'

'I see. It's rather like the sword of Damocles dangling over us then, isn't it?'

'Hardly that, Mrs Devine,' said the Director of Education. 'The Education Sub-committee has reconsidered and agreed, as I have said, to leave things as they are for the time being with regard to this school. Sadly, your good fortune is another school's misfortune.'

'I see.'

'And should Barton-in-the-Dale continue to be the successful school it clearly has become,' he said, 'and numbers continue to increase, then I have no doubt it will remain open for a long time to come.'

'I have your assurance on that?' she asked.

He regarded her steadily. 'Of course,' he said, his eyes revealing nothing of the thoughts which lay behind them.

'That is very good news,' said Elisabeth. 'Thank you for taking the time and trouble to tell me personally.'

'You have achieved a great deal since you arrived,' said the Director of Education. 'A great deal. It always amazes me how good leadership and management can transform a school in the way that you have done. The inspector's report was very positive and I have received some very supportive correspondence about the changes you have made.' He thought of the latest letter. It appeared that everyone and anyone was getting in on the act. Now the Bishop of Clayton was lobbying him.

'Thank you,' Elisabeth said. 'Now that there is every likelihood that Barton-in-the-Dale will remain open for some time to come, can I assume that the two teachers here will be offered permanent contracts?'

'Yes, of course.'

'And the desks will be replaced?'

'I shall ask Mr Nettles to see to it.'

'And the damp?'

'It will be dealt with.'

'And we can have a library?'

'Mrs Devine,' said the Director of Education, holding up a hand. 'It will be considered all in good time.'

'Thank you,' said Elisabeth.

'I shall leave it to you to inform your Chairman of Governors and you will no doubt wish to tell the staff and parents.' He stood. 'By the way, you might be aware that the post of head teacher has come up in the north of the county in a large purpose-built school. It's an excellent salary. You might consider applying.'

'No, Mr Preston,' she told him. 'I am more than happy here.'

There was a knock at the door and Oscar entered. He eyed the man sitting at the teacher's desk.

'I'm sorry to disturb you, Mrs Devine,' he said, 'but the black car which is parked at the front of the school is on double yellow lines and is blocking the entrance. I think it would be a good idea if it was moved.'

*   *   *

'"How beautiful upon the mountains are the feet of him that bringeth good tidings",' trilled the

Reverend Atticus.

'I beg your pardon?' asked the shopkeeper.

'The news, my dear Mrs Sloughthwaite, the good news,' the cleric replied. 'Should we not rejoice at the decision of the educational mandarins not to close our village school?' He looked heavenwards and clapped his hands like a child at a party. 'Is it not joyous news?'

The vicar had called in at the village store with a list of provisions given to him by his wife and which he was commissioned to collect. He had received a call that afternoon from Elisabeth, acquainting him with the details of the conversation that had taken place that morning with Mr Preston. He was therefore in a particularly cheerful mood.

'It is good news, vicar,' agreed Mrs Sloughthwaite, thinking to herself that the vicar was a tad over-enthusiastic, 'but then I always thought they wouldn't go ahead with it.'

'I wish I had shared your confidence,' he replied. 'I think they were hell bent—pardon the expression—on closing the school and had it not been for the dedicated efforts of the head teacher, I do believe they would have most certainly proceeded.'

'We all did our bit, vicar,' retorted Mrs Sloughthwaite, sounding peeved.

'Indeed we did.'

'I'm not saying that Mrs Devine was backward in coming forward, but there were a lot of people in the village, me included, who worked behind the scenes, so to speak.'

'Of course,' said the vicar. 'A great many people were opposed to the proposal, I am fully aware of that, and they were wonderfully supportive. Indeed, the bishop was in touch with the Director of Education to express his disapproval, and I believe Lady Wadsworth petitioned too. What it has done has brought our small community much closer together—the true fighting spirit of the British so evident during the war. It is something which has unified our village.'

The shop bell rang, and like the entrance of the wicked fairy at the christening, Miss Sowerbutts made her entrance and limped slowly towards the counter. She carried a substantial walking stick and for once the battered canvas shopping bag she always carried was not in evidence. One arm was in a sling. She was wearing thick gloves, a heavy scarf, a shapeless woollen coat around her shoulders, large crêpe-soled boots and the silly knitted hat.

'Good morning, Miss Sowerbutts,' said the vicar cheerily.

'Good morning,' she replied curtly, limping to the counter.

'I was sorry to hear about your unfortunate accident.'

'In my experience, vicar, all accidents are unfortunate,' she replied.

'Quite. Well, I was saddened to hear of it.'

'If those lazy and irresponsible assistants at the supermarket in town will leave the floor dangerously wet, it is no wonder someone will eventually slip.'

'I always make sure my floor is safe and dry,' announced Mrs Sloughthwaite from behind the counter.

Her comment was ignored.

'And the wait to be seen at the hospital was intolerable,' Miss Sowerbutts told the vicar, in an aggrieved tone of voice. 'And the doctor was cursory.'

'It must have been most distressing for you,' the Reverend Atticus commiserated.

'It was indeed.'

'But it could have been a whole lot worse,' he added sympathetically.

'In what way?' she asked.

'You could have broken your neck,' remarked the shopkeeper over-emphatically.

Her comment was again ignored.

'It should not have happened in the first place,' Miss Sowerbutts told the vicar.

'Well, I am pleased to see you are on the mend,' he said solicitously.

'On the mend?' she repeated. 'I am still in a great deal of pain and it is extremely inconvenient.'

'Well, I guess you'll be in for some compensation,' remarked Mrs Sloughthwaite. Her face hurt with the false smiling.

Miss Sowerbutts turned to face the shopkeeper with a contemptuous expression on her face. 'That is not the point,' she said brusquely, 'but I shall, of course, be pursuing the matter.'

Yes, I bet you will, thought the shopkeeper. 'Well, what can I get you?' asked Mrs Sloughthwaite, not lowering her gaze and staring hard into the cold hooded eyes.

'I have a list,' she replied. 'Since I shall no longer be giving the supermarket at Gartside my custom after my accident and I am unable to get into town, I shall have to shop here.'

Mrs Sloughthwaite bristled and pursed her lips but said nothing. She folded her arms under her substantial bosom and stared across the counter.

'I would like these delivered,' said Miss Sowerbutts, leaning her stick against the counter and reaching into her coat pocket. She passed a slip of paper across.

The shopkeeper left the paper where it was and adopted again the artificial smile she had perfected over the years.

'I'm sorry, but we don't do deliveries,' she replied.

'Not do deliveries!' Miss Sowerbutts exclaimed, her eyes narrowing.

'There's no one to do them,' the shopkeeper told her. 'You could perhaps ask the supermarket to deliver them,' she said pointedly, 'or maybe one of your former pupils could collect them for you. I am sure that Malcolm Stubbins would welcome the chance of earning a bob or two and, of course, him being expelled from Urebank, he has time on his hands at the moment.'

'I should be only too pleased to drop off your provisions,' said the vicar, good-naturedly.

Slightly mollified, Miss Sowerbutts managed to mouth a 'thank you'.

'We were just saying before you came in,' said the shopkeeper, casting a triumphant smile in the woman's direction, 'how very happy everyone is in the village now that they have decided not to close the school.'

Miss Sowerbutts glared venomously at her. If looks could maim, Mrs Sloughthwaite would at that moment have ended up on crutches.

*   *   *

'I have decided,' said Lady Wadsworth to Elisabeth

377

down the phone the following lunchtime, 'to endow the library in the school. It can be called the Lord Wadsworth Memorial Library, and I shall commission a plaque to be displayed on the wall outside the room.'

'That's most generous of you,' replied Elisabeth.

'I cannot tell you how delighted I was to receive the news about the school,' she said. 'Of course, I gave that Mr Preston a piece of my mind when I went in to see him and I should like to think that I did my part.'

'You went in to see him?' said Elisabeth. 'I never knew.'

'Oh yes,' Lady Wadsworth informed her. 'I made an appointment to visit the Education Office and told him in no uncertain terms how appalled I was at the plans to close the school.'

'Well, it certainly did the trick,' said Elisabeth.

'Oh, I take but little credit, my dear,' she said, not for one moment believing that. 'It was a concerted effort from all those in the village. I know the vicar was very proactive, as indeed were the other governors, and then the bishop got involved and you made a formidable adversary. Well, I must go. Gordon needs worming.'

Elisabeth put down the receiver in the school office.

'That was Lady Wadsworth,' she told the school secretary. 'She is to pay for a new library.'

'More good news,' replied Mrs Scrimshaw.

'But she wants to put up another plaque.'

'Oh dear. That will not please Mr Gribbon.'

'I suppose we can't object,' said Elisabeth. 'She is footing the bill, after all, and she has been very supportive.'

'You must be very pleased, Mrs Devine, with all the support and good wishes you have received.'

'I am. It's been such an anxious and unpredictable time. I've been overwhelmed with all the encouragement. Well, I had better go and see my visitor.'

'If it was me,' said the secretary, 'I'd make her wait after all the carry-on the last time she came into school.'

'No, I'll see her,' said Elisabeth. 'Such is the mood that I am in this morning, Mrs Scrimshaw, I would see the devil himself.'

Mrs Stubbins was sitting in the teacher's chair in the classroom, her sullen-faced son standing next to her. She made a move to get up when Elisabeth entered.

'No, no, Mrs Stubbins, don't get up,' said Elisabeth, recalling the last time she had seen the woman and how uncomfortable and comical she had appeared—such a large woman overflowing on one of the small desks used by the children.

'Thank you for seeing me, Mrs Devine,' said Mrs Stubbins obsequiously. Gone were all the anger and bluster and finger-stabbing Elisabeth had witnessed when the woman had come into the school the last time.

Elisabeth stood by the teacher's desk and looked down at her visitor, her hands clasped before her. 'What can I do for you, Mrs Stubbins?' she asked.

'The thing is, Mrs Devine, he never settled at Urebank. Did you, Malcolm?'

'No,' grunted the boy.

'Quite apart from all the travelling backwards and forwards,' said the woman, 'he was very unhappy there. Weren't you, Malcolm?'

'Yeah.'

'He was picked on by the other kids and by the teachers something dreadful. You was, wasn't you, Malcolm?'

'Yeah, I was,' grumbled the boy.

'As he was here,' remarked Elisabeth.

'Beg pardon?'

'I do recall you telling me, Mrs Stubbins, that you felt that I picked on your son.'

'Well, no, not in the same way. You were much nicer about it.' She smoothed an eyebrow with a little finger and shuffled uncomfortably in her seat.

Elisabeth wondered how one could be nice about picking on someone, but she let it pass.

'So I'd like Malcolm to come back here,' Mrs Stubbins said.

'I see.'

'You want to come back, don't you, Malcolm?' his mother asked the boy.

'Yeah.'

'He's better off here. So he can start next Monday or after the Christmas holidays, if that's all right with you, Mrs Devine.'

'The thing is, Mrs Stubbins,' she was told, 'I am really not inclined to have Malcolm back.'

'What?'

'You were very critical of this school, refused to cooperate and you ignored my advice by sending Malcolm to Urebank. Furthermore, you said some rather unkind things about me. I don't feel it would be a good idea to move him again and I suggest that your son stays where he is.'

'Oh, don't say that, Mrs Devine,' pleaded the woman. 'He was excluded from Urebank and now they've gone and expelled him. They won't have

380

him back. I've been in touch with the Education and they say that if no other school will have him, he might end up in one of these special schools, a referral unit or some such place, for unruly kids.'

'You refused to support me when he was disobedient and badly behaved,' Elisabeth told her.

The woman's bottom lip began to tremble. 'I know what I did was wrong and if I'd have known then what I know now, I wouldn't have done what I did when I did it. I want him to come back here. I'm sorry for what I said. Everyone says that it's a really good school now, and I know for a fact other parents are wanting to move their children from Urebank and who can blame them? The head teacher's like Hitler. Everyone said that they're not going to close this school now and people are queuing up to get their kids in.'

'A bit of an exaggeration,' Elisabeth told her, 'but the school is not closing and is doing well.'

'Malcolm's been under my feet. It's driving me to destruction, it really is. I just can't be doing with it.' She sniffed loudly and wiped a tear from her cheek.

'And what do you have to say, Malcolm?' Elisabeth asked the boy.

He jumped sharply, as if he had been jabbed with a cattle prod. 'Me?'

'Yes, you,' said Elisabeth. 'Do you want to come back here?'

'Yeah, I do.'

'Pardon?' snapped Elisabeth.

'I mean, yes miss, I do,' he mumbled.

Elisabeth turned her attention back to the boy's mother. 'You see, Mrs Stubbins, since Malcolm's departure, things have been a whole lot better in the school. It's been a more peaceful and a happier place. There has been less disruption because your son has not been here to distract and to pick on the other children.'

'I know he can be a bit of a handful at times, Mrs Devine,' said the woman, 'but he's a good lad at heart. He just needs a bit of discipline.'

'I couldn't agree with you more,' said Elisabeth.

'And if he was to come back, he'd be as good as gold. Won't you, Malcolm?'

'Yeah,' muttered the boy.

'Please have him back, Mrs Devine.'

Elisabeth thought for a moment. 'If I do have Malcolm back, it will be for a trial period to see how he behaves himself, and there will be a few ground rules. Firstly, of course, he will need to complete the tasks I set as a punishment after the fight with Danny Stainthorpe. Secondly, I shall see him every week in my classroom to hear how he is getting on. Thirdly, I do not wish to learn of any bullying or misbehaviour. Finally, I expect to receive your full support, Mrs Stubbins, and should Malcolm step out of line, I shall contact you immediately and ask you to take him home.'

Mrs Stubbins cheered up. 'That's very good of you, Mrs Devine,' she said. 'Does that mean he can come back?'

'So, Malcolm,' said Elisabeth, turning to the boy, 'did you understand what I have just said to your mother?'

'Yes, miss.'

'And you are going to be on your best behaviour if you return?'

'Yes, miss.'

'Then I shall I expect to see a very different boy walk into school next week.'

'Yes, miss.'

'Say thank you to Mrs Devine,' said Mrs Stubbins, poking her son.

'That hurt!' he cried, rubbing his arm.

'Shut up,' she told him, 'and thank Mrs Devine.'

'Thank you, Mrs Devine,' he said unenthusiastically.

'We do have a place on the football team, if you are interested,' said Elisabeth.

The boy suddenly came to life and his face lit up. 'In the team?' he cried.

'If you are interested.'

'You bet!' exclaimed the boy.

'Well, we will leave it there, Mrs Stubbins,' said Elisabeth. The woman shuffled in the chair but made no effort to move. 'Is there something else?'

'Well, there is actually,' said the woman, her round face becoming flushed with embarrassment. 'I can't get out of the chair. I'm stuck!'

CHAPTER NINETEEN

When Mrs Stubbins, with help from Mr Gribbon, a screwdriver and a hammer, had finally extricated herself from the chair and departed, Elisabeth went to the school office to phone Urebank school.

'I think you're a saint,' observed Mrs Scrimshaw as she watched Elisabeth pick up the telephone, 'having that ne'er-do-well back. I would have told that Mrs Stubbins where to get off.'

'I have an idea young Malcolm will be a changed boy when he returns,' Elisabeth told her. 'I think he's learnt his lesson.'

'Let's hope so,' said the school secretary, looking unconvinced.

'Children have to be educated, Mrs Scrimshaw,' Elisabeth told her, 'even the difficult and demanding ones.'

'Repellent, more like,' mumbled the secretary as Elisabeth dialled the number for Urebank school.

'Robin Richardson, the headmaster, speaking,' came a voice down the line.

'Good afternoon, Mr Richardson,' Elisabeth said pleasantly. 'This is Elisabeth Devine here, from Barton-in-the-Dale school.' There was a silence. 'Are you still there?'

'Yes, I am still here,' he replied coldly.

'I wanted to let you know that I have just seen Malcolm Stubbins and his mother.'

'Oh yes?'

'And I have agreed to take the boy back. I understand he has now been expelled from Urebank and I am sure you will agree that it's not really a good idea to have a child sitting at home all day and missing his education.'

'As I explained to you, Mrs Devine,' he said haughtily, 'the boy was a most difficult and disruptive pupil. Had I known this, I should never have considered taking him.'

'So you will no doubt be pleased that he is returning here,' she said. There was another silence. 'Well, that is all I wanted to say.'

'One moment, Mrs Devine,' came the sharp voice down the line. 'I was intending to get in touch with you. I am extremely angry about the situation.'

'The situation,' said Elisabeth, feigning ignorance.

'The situation of parents, against my advice,

384

sending the children from my school to yours. I gather several other parents are considering taking their children away from my school. It is just not acceptable.'

'I have had a number of enquiries,' Elisabeth told him.

'Indeed. I have impressed upon these parents how disruptive it is to move a child from a school and the detrimental effect it will have on their children's education.'

He never mentioned that when he first spoke to me, thought Elisabeth, he was all too ready to accept children from this school. 'Well, it's not as if they are midway through an examination course, and it is a fact that children sometimes do have to move and are better suited at another school.' She was not being lectured to by this man.

'Well, I do not think it is at all acceptable,' he retorted.

'I believe that most of the children involved were originally at this school,' Elisabeth told him, 'and that they live in this catchment area. So, technically, they should be here.'

'Some are,' he told her, 'but there are other parents who have been in touch whose children are not. These pupils live in *my* catchment area and should by rights go to *my* school. I trust you will not entertain any further requests should a parent get in touch with you.'

'Do you recall our conversation over the matter of parents choosing to send their children to another school, Mr Richardson?' asked Elisabeth.

'No, I can't say that I do,' he replied.

'Well, let me remind you. I think we agreed that one has to accept that parents have the right to send their children to another school if they so wish. As you said yourself, if they are insistent then there is very little one can do about it.'

'So I take it you are encouraging parents of pupils in my school to send their children to your school.'

'That is not what I said, Mr Richardson,' replied Elisabeth, knowing full well that he had been guilty of this very thing he was accusing her of before her arrival at Barton-in-the-Dale. 'It would be highly unprofessional of me to do that.' She stressed the word he had used in his letter to her. 'What I meant was that if parents wish to send their children here, then it is up to them and I do not intend to turn these children away.'

'I see. Well, I have to say, Mrs Devine, that I find your attitude at the very least very surprising and at most unprincipled,' he said angrily, 'and I shall be contacting the Education Office over this matter.'

Elisabeth remained calm and courteous. 'Well, that of course is up to you, Mr Richardson,' she said. 'Good afternoon.'

'That's telling him,' said Mrs Scrimshaw, smiling gleefully as Elisabeth replaced the receiver. 'He doesn't like it when the shoe's on the other foot. He was all too willing when the children were queuing up to get into his school to go poaching. Not so happy now that they all want to come to ours.'

Mr Gribbon entered the office. 'I've fixed the chair, Mrs Devine,' he told Elisabeth with a grim expression on his face. 'I've reinforced the bottom and mended one of the arms. It was the devil's own job getting that woman out of it. She was like a cork in a bottle.'

Elisabeth and the secretary burst out laughing.

'We're just giving your garden a last tidy-up before winter sets in, aren't we, James?' said Danny.

His friend nodded.

It was Saturday morning and Elisabeth was off to see her son at Forest View as usual. She was dressed in a smart camel-hair coat and green woollen scarf and matching gloves. She smiled with pleasure at seeing the two boys so obviously happy.

'You look nice, miss,' he said.

'Thank you, Danny,' she replied. 'My goodness, you two are up bright and early,' she said.

'Aye well, miss,' replied Danny, 'there's a fair bit to do. We've got to start fettlin' 'is dad's garden after this. It's in a reight old state. Weeds everywhere, briars and brambles, trees what want prunin', 'edges what want trimmin'. Jamie's mam used to do all t'gardenin', so it's not been looked after for a while. 'Course, 'is dad's too busy to do it so we said we'd tackle it. I don't know where to start.'

'Well, don't you go overdoing it,' Elisabeth told him.

''Ere, it's grand news abaat t'school, in't it miss?' said Danny. His face lit up.

'It is,' she agreed.

'Things often turn out all reight in t'end. That's what mi granddad used to say.'

It's certainly turned out well for you, she thought. 'A wise man, your granddad,' said Elisabeth.

'Aye, he was,' the boy said thoughtfully.

'Well, I'll be off,' she said. 'Goodbye, you two.' Elisabeth had turned to go when James spoke.

It was a quiet, hesitant voice but she heard him clearly enough. 'Are you going to see your son, Mrs Devine?' he asked.

Elisabeth's heart missed a beat. This was the first time she had heard the boy speak since he had been to see her about Danny. She was also startled to hear him mention her son.

'Yes, I am,' she replied, turning back to look at him and trying to conceal her surprise.

The boy stared at her with wide eyes and a serious expression. 'You have a son at Forest View,' he said.

'I do,' Elisabeth replied.

'My father told me. He visits the school. He's there this morning.'

'I didn't know you had a son, Mrs Devine,' said Danny in a loud and cheerful voice.

'Yes, I have a son, Danny. His name's John and he's about your age. He has special needs. I go to see him every Saturday.'

'My father said he doesn't speak,' said James shyly.

'No, he doesn't, and sadly, he probably never will.'

'I'm sorry about that, Mrs Devine,' he said. There was a genuine concern in his voice.

'Fancy you 'avin' a son, miss,' said Danny putting his hands on his hips. 'I was only saying to James last week that you'd make a super mam.'

Elisabeth smiled at the small boy with his floppy fringe of mousy hair, small pointed chin and bright brown eyes. It was good to see him so happy. 'You're a little charmer, Danny Stainthorpe,' she said, 'and when you grow up you'll have all the girls running after you if you start flattering them like that.'

The boy screwed up his face. 'I don't want any lasses running after me,' he said. 'I'm 'appy as I am wi' mi ferret. You know where you are wi' ferrets. There's them two lasses at t'school who won't leave me be. Everywhere I go there's that Chardonnay, and t'other 'un, Chantelle, is allus sending me notes. They're drivin' me barmy.'

'You'll have to introduce them to your ferret,' said Elisabeth laughing. 'That might put them off, but I don't want it bringing into school again.'

'Danny Stainthorpe!' came a voice from the track down the side of the cottage.

'Hey up, miss,' said Danny tilting his head to one side, 'it's Mester Massey. I wonder what 'e's after.'

'Danny Stainthorpe!' shouted the man again. 'I wants a word with you.' The boy ambled over to the gate. 'Now then, young fella-me-lad, I hear you've got a ferret.'

Danny eyed him suspiciously. 'I might have,' he replied.

'Well, is this any good to you?' He pointed down to a fancy-looking cage.

'For me?' asked Danny.

'Well, I don't reckon Mrs Devine has much use for it unless she keeps ferrets. Do you want it?'

'Yes please,' said Danny. 'Thanks very much, Mester Massey.'

'And if you've a mind, you can come up to the farm. I've a few jobs wants doing. You can help my Clarence out. He needs it. Paid work, mind you. I don't want owt for nowt.' The old man wiped his nose on the back of his hand. 'He were a grand man was your granddad. I can't say as how we always saw eye to eye, but he was a grand man. I wouldn't

389

be here now if it weren't for him.' He waved at Elisabeth. 'Now then Mrs Devine, I was glad to hear that the school's stopping open,' he shouted. 'You'll be pleased to know I'm here to move my sheep from your paddock.'

'About time as well,' muttered Danny, walking towards Elisabeth. 'Should have shifted 'em ages ago.'

'You sound just like your granddad,' Elisabeth told him.

The boy grinned.

James followed Elisabeth as she headed for the cottage. She stopped. 'Is there something else you wanted to say, James?' she asked.

The boy nodded.

'What is it?'

He touched her hand and looked up into her eyes. 'Thank you,' he said.

*　　　*　　　*

The Reverend Atticus sat at his desk in his study that afternoon. His half-finished sermon had been put aside and he was in a thoughtful mood. The theme of his homily was self-interest and the unwillingness of some people to see the other's point of view. He felt a twinge of guilt as he thought of his wife and her desire to move to the city, something he had refused to contemplate. He had been obdurate in turning down preferment, he thought, never even considering the bishop's offer of having his name submitted for the dean's position. He had been deceitful in not mentioning it to his wife, knowing full well that had he done so she would have persisted endlessly in trying to

390

pressure him into being considered for the position.

He pressed his fingers to each temple like a mind reader. Perhaps he should have agreed. With hindsight, he felt he had failed in his obligation to his wife. It had been selfish of him, he thought, to deny Marcia the life she craved, a life she had been so used to in the cathedral city where she had grown up, with its narrow medieval streets, the jade green river curving beneath the ancient walls, the pale stone cathedral with its vivid stained glass, a beautiful, tranquil place. The more he thought about life at the cathedral the more attractive it sounded. He had been so wrapped up in his own life, he thought, that he had neglected hers; he had been so concerned with tending to his parishioners' needs and fighting their battles that he had failed to give attention to the one he should have cared for the most, namely his wife. Were the situation to present itself again, he thought, he would agree to have his name put forward, but it was unlikely that the opportunity would arise. Dr Peacock was a relatively young man and would, no doubt, remain as dean for many years to come. He sighed and turned his attention back to his sermon.

Then, as if in answer to a prayer, came the telephone call from the bishop.

When he heard what his lordship had to say, the vicar did not have to 'give the matter some serious thought' or 'talk it over with his wife'. He was told by the bishop that his name had been put forward as the most suitable candidate for the position of archdeacon.

Bishop Bill was surprisingly complimentary.

'A man of your abilities, Charles,' he was told, 'with a firm grasp of ecclesiastical law, a deep knowledge of theology and someone who has great experience at the parish level is most acceptable to myself, the dean and chapter and all at the cathedral. You are a man of strong principles and an inspiration to us all and you are greatly respected and admired, just the sort of person to take on such a demanding role. Indeed your name has been mentioned to me so many times I have stopped counting.'

'My lord,' the Reverend Atticus replied, 'I am, of course, deeply honoured that you should deem me suitable—'

'Now, don't go turning this down, Charles,' the Bishop interrupted sharply. 'I won't hear of it. We need someone of your calibre, so I want you to give the matter some serious thought and to talk it over with your wife.'

'My lord,' the vicar replied, 'I don't need to give it any serious thought. I should be honoured to accept.'

'Really?'

'Yes, indeed.'

'Splendid,' said the bishop, rather taken aback at the speed of the vicar's acceptance. 'I shall be in touch. Oh, by the way, I sorted out the matter of the school closing. I had a word with the right people.'

'We are all very grateful, my lord,' said the Reverend Atticus.

The sermon could wait, the vicar told himself. He needed to tell his wife the good news.

Marcia Atticus was arranging some flowers when he entered the drawing room. She looked in a particularly good mood and was humming to herself.

'Oh, there you are, Charles,' she said brightly. 'I think these will be the last of the roses. Sermon finished?'

'Not quite,' her husband replied. 'My dear, I wanted to have a word, if I might,' he said.

'Before you do, let me tell you my good news. I would have told you earlier when the post arrived, but I know how you don't like to be disturbed when you are writing your sermons.'

'Good news?' repeated her husband.

'I have just received a letter from St John's College informing me that I have been accepted to do teacher training. Isn't that wonderful?'

'Congratulations,' said the vicar, bending to peck at her cheek.

'I'm really quite excited about starting,' she trilled, 'and I must go into the city on Monday to get the books on the reading list. I didn't think I would ever take to teaching, but the days I have spent in the village school have convinced me that I would be a good teacher and would enjoy it. Indeed, Mrs Devine said that if I succeeded in gaining a place at St John's, I could do my teaching practice at the village school. It's all worked out so well. You know, you were quite right, Charles, going into the village school each week has given me a new lease of life. I have felt useful and valued.' She linked her arm through his. 'I know I go on about you being more ambitious and assertive but I have come to realise that I have been rather selfish.'

'No, no, not at all, my dear,' began the vicar. 'In fact—'

She placed a finger over his lips. 'Yes, Charles, I have,' she said determinedly. 'I now realise that

393

being a country parson is your vocation and it is what you are so good at. I know how very well regarded and respected you are in this community and that you would be very unhappy with all the politicking and social gatherings at Cathedral Close. So, in future, I won't go on about you not becoming a dean or an archdeacon or a bishop. I know that it wouldn't suit you. You would be like a fish out of water.'

'Thank you, Marcia,' said the prospective Archdeacon of Clayton, with a wan smile.

'Now, you wanted to speak to me about something.'

*　　　*　　　*

Elisabeth was leaving Forest View after visiting her son when the head teacher approached.

'I was hoping to catch you before you left,' he said.

'Nothing's wrong, I hope?'

'No, no, it's just that I wanted you to be one of the first to know. I had a telephone call from the Education Office yesterday and they have decided on the special school they are intending to close.'

'It's not this one?' Elisabeth asked with a sinking heart.

'No, no, we are safe, thank goodness.'

Elisabeth sighed, 'What a relief.'

'And I hear you have a reprieve too?'

'That's right. Mr Preston came to see me personally. Any decision on the future of Barton-in-the-Dale has been put on the back burner.'

'You must be very pleased.' Mr Williams beamed.

'More than I can say, but I am even more pleased that this school is not going to close and that John is going to stay on here.'

'Perhaps . . .' started Mr Williams, 'er . . . perhaps you might like to take me up on that offer.'

'Offer?' Elisabeth repeated

'For a drink—as a way of celebrating our two pieces of good news. You mentioned that you would allow me to take you out. Perhaps this evening?'

'Well, I—' she began.

'Of course, you may be busy and—'

It seemed churlish of Elisabeth to refuse. 'Well, yes,' she replied.

'You're busy?'

'No, I should like to go for a drink. Thank you.'

Mr Williams smiled widely. 'Excellent. Shall we say seven-thirty? I could drive over and meet you in the Blacksmith's Arms in Barton, or the other pub.'

'I should prefer somewhere outside the village, if you don't mind,' said Elisabeth.

'Yes, of course. What about the Royal Oak at Gartside?'

'That would be fine,' said Elisabeth. He was a pleasant enough man was Mr Williams, good-humoured, chatty and a dedicated and hard-working head teacher. He was easy to talk to and good company. She knew that after his divorce, he had moved to live alone near the school and must sometimes feel lonely. What harm could there be, thought Elisabeth, in having a drink with a colleague?

*　　　*　　　*

Those standing at the public bar stopped talking when Major C. J. Neville-Gravitas breezed into the Blacksmith's Arms that Saturday lunchtime.

'Good day, one and all,' he said cheerfully.

There were a few nods of response from the men at the bar.

'Your usual, major?' asked the landlord.

'Just the ticket,' he said, 'and make it a double. And one for yourself, my good man.' He stroked his moustache and looked around smiling.

'Thank you kindly, major,' said the landlord, getting the single malt which was the major's tipple.

'And how are you, landlord, on this bright, crisp and beautiful day?' asked Major Neville-Gravitas.

'I'm fine, thank you, major. How about you?'

'Tip-top.'

'Ready for Christmas?'

'As ready as I'll ever be,' the major replied. 'Cheers.'

'It's good news about the school,' said the landlord.

'Yes, great news that it is to stay open,' replied the major approvingly. He stroked his moustache again. He was in a particularly buoyant mood.

'No thanks to you,' observed Fred Massey, who had been watching the major with a sour expression on his face.

'I don't follow your drift, old man,' said the major, turning in the speaker's direction.

'Well, you were all for the school closing, from what I've heard,' said Fred.

'Not at all,' replied the major irritably. 'I exercised discretion. Being the chairman of the governing body, I felt it appropriate in the first instance to abstain from the vote.'

'Running with the hare and hunting with the hounds, you mean,' said Fred.

'Meaning?'

'Sitting on the fence.'

'I did not sit on the fence!' the major told him forcefully. 'I took a neutral position, not that it is any of your business.'

'Same thing,' said Fred.

'It is not,' said the major angrily. 'And having assessed the situation and seen how successful the village school has become and how well regarded is its head teacher, I campaigned strongly in favour of keeping the school open.'

'Well, you were last in the village to do so,' said Fred, 'and you only did it then because you saw the strength of feeling.'

'Don't you tell me what I did and what I didn't do!' exclaimed the major.

'Well, I'll tell you this—' began Fred mulishly.

'She's a very good head teacher,' said the landlord, trying, by changing the subject, to cool a situation that was getting increasingly heated.

'Aye, she is,' agreed Fred Massey, 'but what I want to ask the major here—'

'Hang on, Fred,' interposed Albert Spearman, tapping his arm, 'you've changed your tune. You hadn't a good word for Mrs Devine a few weeks back.'

'Aye, well,' replied Fred impatiently. 'She's mellowed. It's true we didn't start off on the right footing but we get on right well now. We've come to some accommodation about that track and she says I can keep my sheep on her paddock. Anyway, what I want to ask the major here,' he continued obstinately, 'is this.'

397

'How's your foot then, Fred?' asked the landlord, in a vain attempt to distract him.

'Bloody painful. What I wanted to ask the major here—' he started again, turning to the object of his vilification, but Major C. J. Neville-Gravitas had downed his whisky and left the pub.

'He went without paying for his drink,' said Albert.

'Typical,' said Fred.

'What were you going to ask him anyway?'

'I was going to ask him if he'd signed the petition,' said Fred. 'You can bet your life his name's not on it, fence-sitter that he is.'

'I've told you before, Fred Massey,' said the landlord, 'you have a nasty habit of driving my customers away.'

'You said it were a talent before,' said Fred chuckling. 'Any road, you were asking me about my foot.'

'Oh, don't start that again, Fred,' groaned Albert.

'Well, I've been asked and I'm telling him. It was a terrible ordeal,' Fred said, raising his voice so those inclined to listen could hear. 'I could have lost a foot, nay, a leg or even bled to death. As it is I lost two toes and half my heel. The doctor at the hospital said it was a wonder I didn't go into shock. He said it was me remaining calm and not panicking what saved my life.'

'That and Les Stainthorpe,' added Mr Spearman.

'Oh yes, he came to the rescue right enough and very grateful I am to him too.'

'So, who's looking after the farm until you're back on your feet?' asked the landlord.

'My nephew, young Clarence. And if I don't

watch him like a hawk he makes a pig's ear of everything he touches. I don't know, youngsters these days. He's not got a brain cell in his head. Doolally most of the time. He has about as much gumption as a dead fish.'

'Well, there's a real vote of confidence for the lad,' said the landlord sarcastically.

'He tries his best, I won't deny that,' said Fred, 'but he has no common sense.'

Albert Spearman gave a knowing look in the direction of the landlord. The speaker did not display much common sense, he thought, sticking his leg down a machine used for cutting up sugar-beet, but he said nothing.

'I mean,' continued Fred, 'take what happened last week. I got the vet out to look at six of my cows which were down with rampant diarrhoea.'

'Must you?' groaned Albert, a pork scratching poised before his mouth.

'Anyway, the vet arrives, that young one who's wet behind the ears and thinks he knows everything, and he says they've eaten some sort of weed that didn't agree with them and hence the diarrhoea, which was all over the field.'

Albert stared for a moment at the pork scratching before returning it to the bag.

'Young Clarence had put the cows into yonder field with all these weeds and that's what brought on this diarrhoea.'

'Must we go there?' asked Albert, who had been looking forward to his substantial Saturday lunch.

'Let me finish, let me finish,' said Fred. 'So the young vet tells me it's bovine diarrhoea and he'll give the cows these Dutch pills which will sort them out. He asked for a bucket of hot soapy and disinfected water—I couldn't see why, to be honest—which I fetched and then he gets out from his bag this long rubber tube and a box of pills. Clarence brings in the first cow and blow me the vet heads for the rear end. "What are you doing down there?" I asks from where I was standing at the beast's head. "Pills aren't going in that end," he says, pointing to the back end, "they're going in this." So he washes this rubber tube in the bucket and inserts it up the back of the cow.'

'Oh dear, oh dear,' moaned Albert. 'Do we need to know this?'

'Then he puts one of these Dutch pills in the end of the tube,' continued Fred undaunted, 'nips the end, puts it to his mouth and gives the tube an almighty blow and up goes the pill. "Now," he says, "you have to do this to every cow first thing in the morning and after the cows have been milked in the afternoon." I says to him, I says, "I'm not right keen on doing that and I'd as sooner you do it." Well, he tells me, he'll do it all right but it'll cost me for every cow he treats and he tells me how it'll be a long business and he'll want paying by the hour. I said, "Not bloody likely. Give me the tube." Well, Clarence brings in the second cow. I does what the vet did and pops this pill in the tube, nipping the end and inserting it up the back of the cow. I tells Clarence to keep the animal steady because I don't want anything coming down that tube when I've got it in my mouth.'

'I can't be doing with this,' said Albert, finishing his pint and ready for off.

'No, no, I've nearly finished,' said Fred.

'Another time,' Albert told him, walking out of the pub.

Fred turned to the landlord. 'So Clarence holds the cow's head and I take hold of the rubber tube,' he told the landlord, 'and I gives the end a blow. Then what happens?'

'I can't imagine,' said the landlord.

'The pill gets stuck half way up the tube. "No, no," says the young vet, "you've got to give a really big blow." "Well, I'm not up for this," I tells him and I asks Clarence—he's a big lad as you know and has plenty of puff—to finish it off and give it another blow. Well, you'd never guess what the dozy lad did?'

'I can't wait to hear,' said the landlord wearily.

'Clarence comes down the rear of the cow, takes out the tube, turns it around the other ways and sticks it back in. Then he blows like billy-o. "What did you do that for?" I asks him. "Why did you turn the tube round the other way?" "Well," says he, "I'm not having it my mouth after it's been in yours."'

'Well, thank you for sharing that with me, Fred,' said the landlord. 'You've now managed to clear all the public bar.'

CHAPTER TWENTY

Miss Sowerbutts rarely received any letters, but that Saturday afternoon four dropped through her letterbox. The first was from the hospital confirming her next visit to the orthopaedic department. The second, the contents of which made her curl a lip, was from the supermarket manager, apologising profusely for the wet floor and hoping she was 'on the road to recovery'. He had enclosed some gift vouchers. If he believed that a few paltry gift vouchers would settle the matter, she thought, he had another think coming. The third letter was from her nephew saying that he was spending Christmas with his wife's family that year and therefore could not invite her to spend the festival with him. This did not unduly upset Miss Sowerbutts, for she never enjoyed spending the day with him and that fussy little wife of his, eating overcooked turkey, watching inane television programmes and having to endure the noisy children, who received far too many presents for her liking and ate far too much. She was relieved also that they hadn't the time to visit her. She looked over to her cabinet with its collection of cut glass and china and recalled the time one of the children had taken out the porcelain figurine of Marie Antoinette and broken the head off. Miss Sowerbutts treasured her possessions more than she did people, so she was not amused when her nephew pointed out that the unfortunate queen did, in fact, lose her head. She was pleased that she would not have to put up with the endless noise, the sticky fingers and the perpetual demands for the attention of her great-nephews and nieces. The fourth letter brought a smile to her thin lips. It was from her solicitors, Smith, Hartley & Wellbeloved, informing her that her claim for compensation for her supermarket injury had been lodged and she could expect a sizeable payout.

Although a little early, Miss Sowerbutts decided to celebrate with a large glass of extra dry sherry. She took a large gulp. With the windfall, she would go on a cruise over Christmas, she thought, well away from this incestuous little village and its

402

parochial inhabitants, and when she returned she would put her cottage up for sale and move to an apartment in the city, one overlooking the river and the cathedral. There was nothing now for her in Barton-in-the-Dale. All she seemed to hear about in the shops, the doctor's, the dentist's and the chemist's was how happy everyone was that the village school would not now be closing and how wonderful was the new head teacher, that pushy woman in the red shoes. Even the mousy little Miss Brakespeare had been converted.

'I am well out of it,' she said aloud, finishing her drink and pouring another generous glass.

Miss Sowerbutts took her sherry and gazed out of her French windows and over the neat little garden. She peered through the glass and then her face assumed its familiar sour and pinched expression. Her manicured lawn was covered in small dark mounds of earth.

'Moles!' she exclaimed, screwing up her face. 'Moles!'

*   *   *

'Where are we going?' demanded Mrs Brakespeare.

'I've told you, Mother, we are going into town for tea,' replied her daughter, looking at herself in the hall mirror. She was dressed in the grey cashmere sweater, pillarbox-red woollen coat and shiny black leather boots she had recently treated herself to.

'Why?' Mrs Brakespeare asked suspiciously.

'Because I wish to take you out for afternoon tea. We'll be going to the Rumbling Tum tea shop in the high street,' said her daughter. Life seemed to hold few pleasures for her mother these days, and she had perhaps been rather sharp with her of late, so Miss Brakespeare had decided to give her a treat. There appeared little enthusiasm for the idea from her mother.

'It's Saturday,' her mother told her. 'You know how crowded it will be at this time of year, all those Christmas shoppers rushing about.'

'I've booked a table. You can sit in the window and listen to the Salvation Army band. They always play in the square the Saturday before Christmas.'

'You have never taken me out on a Saturday afternoon before.'

'Yes I have, Mother,' her daughter replied wearily. 'You forget.'

'I can't remember,' her mother groused.

'Well, I am taking you out now.'

'I can't walk far,' grumbled her mother. 'Not with these legs.' She assumed the mantle of suffering so effectively that it was clear she was enjoying it.

'I'm not expecting you to,' said her daughter. 'I have a taxi ordered. It will collect us in an hour.'

Her mother sniffed. 'A taxi!'

'So you need to get ready,' she told her.

'Why are we going into town? You're not telling me something.'

'We're going to call in somewhere.'

'I knew it,' cried her mother, with that 'I-told-you-so' expression she wore when she was proved right. 'You're taking me to look around one of these old folks' homes.'

Her daughter laughed. 'Stuff and nonsense,' she said.

'I know what you're up to. I'm not daft, Miriam. I'm being institutionalised.'

'Don't be silly, Mother.'

'You want to stick me with all these old folks out of your way. I knew it. Ever since—'

'Mother!' interrupted Miss Brakespeare. 'I am not taking you to see an old folks' home.'

'Don't come the innocent with me, Miriam,' said Mrs Brakespeare. She reached into her handbag and brought out a glossy piece of paper, which she waved in the air. 'What's this then?'

'What's what?' asked her daughter.

'I found this in the hall. I know what you've been up to. Don't try and pull the wool over my eyes.'

'I have not the slightest idea what you are talking about,' said her daughter.

'It's a brochure,' announced Mrs Brakespeare. 'I found it on the hall table.'

'You are not making any sense,' said her daughter.

'I'll read it,' announced her mother. ' "Placing an elderly relative in a care home can be a complicated and confusing time. Why not call Anita Edwards, our friendly care adviser, today with no obligation, for a free support and advice pack to help you find the perfect placement for your loved one." '

Miss Brakespeare laughed.

'You may laugh, Miriam,' said her mother, her eyes filling with tears, 'but to think it has come to this.'

'Mother,' Miss Brakespeare told her, putting her arm around her parent's shoulder and kissing her cheek, 'I am not putting you in a home and I never shall. That's just another circular they put through every door. We are going into town for afternoon tea and then we are calling in at the travel agent's.'

'Why? Are you thinking of sending me abroad?'

'We are calling in at the travel agent's,' explained

her daughter, 'because I am going to book a week's holiday over spring bank holiday at a hotel at Scarborough and I want you to help me choose.'

'Who's it for?'

'For both of us, of course. Who else would it be for? I thought it would be a nice little break for us, and I know how you loved Scarborough when we visited when Father was alive.'

'A holiday,' said her mother. 'I don't know about that, what with my condition.'

'I have spoken to Dr Stirling and he says it will do you a power of good.'

'Does he?'

'Yes. He does.'

'You're not putting me in a home, then?' asked her mother in a childish voice.

'Of course not.'

'It must be twenty years since I was last in Scarborough,' said Mrs Brakespeare. 'I bet it's changed for the worse.'

'The sea and the sand and the promenade won't have changed,' said her daughter, remaining cheerful. 'A week away in a hotel being waited upon and with all that fresh sea air will be good for us both.'

'Well,' said her mother, raising a small smile, 'maybe so. Do you think that Max Jaffa will still be playing at the Spa?' she asked.

*   *   *

Mr Preston, the Director of Education, sat behind his large mahogany desk in a thoughtful mood. He stared out of the window at the uninterrupted view over the high street, busier and noisier than ever with Saturday afternoon traffic. It was not his practice to spend any part of his precious weekends in his office, but he had two important things to attend to before Monday morning.

The first job was the short-listing for the post of Deputy Director of Education, which had arisen with the imminent retirement of the present incumbent. Mr Preston smiled wryly when he saw the application at the top of the pile. Mr Nettles, the man with the round smiling face and whining voice, who had recently been moved to school meals, had had the temerity to apply; this man, who had an inflated and entirely undeserved opinion of his own meagre talents, was overly optimistic to think he could ever be considered for such a post. Mr Preston placed the application at the bottom of the pile.

Having completed the selection of the five candidates to be called for interview, he yawned, stretched and leaned back expansively in his leather chair. He then applied himself to his second task: to write his formal letter of resignation. Only that morning he had heard that the post of Chief Executive for a town in the Midlands and for which he had applied some weeks before, had been offered to him. He would, of course, say in his letter how he had found his present post as Director of Education challenging and fulfilling and that he was profoundly sorry to leave, which was being rather economical with the truth. He would also ask if he might waive the two months' notice he was required to give and take up the position rather earlier. He was, of course, content to relinquish his present position and leave behind all the problems and discord that would inevitably arise now that the list of schools for closure had become public. That troublesome little village school in Barton-in-the-Dale, which would now remain open following the inordinate pressure that had been exerted, had set a dangerous precedent. All schools threatened with closure, such as the one at Urebank, would no doubt follow suit and object in the strongest possible way. No, he thought to himself, he was well out of it. Of course, after Christmas he would have to deal with the pressing matter of Councillor Smout's expenses claims and the unaccounted-for receipts.

*   *   *

'Don't you think it a little excessive, my lady,' remarked Lady Wadsworth's butler, peering over the shoulder of his mistress.

'Excessive!' she repeated sharply. 'Certainly not! I think the appropriate word to describe it would be impressive.'

'It is rather on the large side, your ladyship,' commented the butler. 'Some might say a little ostentatious.'

'Watson, really,' she retorted. 'As my grandfather often said, if a thing is worth doing, it is worth doing properly.'

The room which she was at present occupying was indeed a testimony to her grandfather's pronouncement. To describe it as grandiose would be something of an understatement. Everything exuded comfortable opulence, from the heavy burgundy velvet drapes to the highly polished oak floor covered by a huge Persian silk carpet, from the delicately moulded ceiling to the deep armchairs and inlaid tables. Two walls were panelled in highly polished mahogany shelving and crammed with leather-bound books; the others were covered in a soft green patterned Chinese paper. Above the impressive carved marble fireplace, bearing the Wadsworth coat of arms, a huge Chippendale mirror caught the light from the shimmering chandeliers.

Lady Wadsworth was sitting in the library of Limebeck House in a huge plum red upholstered armchair beneath an enormous portrait in oils of her grandfather, the second Viscount Wadsworth, attired in his scarlet robes. He stared self-importantly from the canvas and bore an unnerving resemblance to the lady of the house. Through small gold-rimmed spectacles, she was examining the sketch, spread out before her on a small desk with gold tasselled drawers, of the plaque she was intending to have commissioned for the village school library.

'But it is a small school library, your ladyship,' observed the butler. 'Might not such a large plaque appear rather out of place? Perhaps a small brass plate would be more suitable.'

'A small brass plate!' exclaimed her ladyship. 'Like they have on the top of a coffin? I think not.'

'But perhaps something a little more discreet,' suggested the butler.

'Watson!' snapped Lady Wadsworth, 'I merely asked for an opinion, not a full-blown criticism. If I am endowing the new library at the village school, I think it should have an eye-catching commemorative inscription to commemorate the opening.'

'But your ladyship—' began the butler.

'No more,' she commanded, raising a hand. 'The discussion has ended.'

'As you wish, my lady,' the butler said, bowing slightly.

'I have to say,' said Lady Wadsworth, raising her eyes to the huge portrait of the mutton-chopped figure staring from the picture, 'that my dear late grandfather would be most pleased, were he alive, at the decision not to close the school he founded and endowed.'

'Indeed, my lady.'

'Of course, it was largely by my good offices that it came about.'

The butler raised an eyebrow.

'Had I not spoken to the Director of Education and had a small word in the ears of the Lord Lieutenant and the High Sheriff, the village school would undoubtedly have been no more. It is always the best thing to go right to the top in matters like this and I do pride myself in still having some influence in the community. Mrs Devine has written me an extremely nice letter of thanks.'

'I am sure Mrs Devine and the teachers are very pleased,' said the butler. 'Speaking of Mrs Devine, your ladyship, might it not be appropriate to show her your plans for the proposed plaque?'

Lady Wadsworth shook her head like her tetchy terrier. 'I think it is time for afternoon tea, Watson,' she said.

*   *   *

Mr Gribbon, hands clasped behind his back, toured the school premises like a lord of the manor inspecting his estate. He was not required to come into school on Saturday afternoons, but liked to ensure that those who had been playing football on the fields that morning had left the place as they had found it. The payment for overtime was also very welcome. Mrs Devine's stern warning in assembly each Friday that the football would be cancelled should there be any litter found or the building left in a poor state, had clearly been heeded, for the place was indeed as Mr Gribbon had left it: clean, tidy and litter-free.

He was surprised to see the school secretary in the office.

'What are you doing here, Mrs Scrimshaw?' he asked, poking his beak of a nose around the door.

'I forgot to mail the letters on Friday,' she told him, 'and I've just called in to collect them. What with all those books arriving for the new library and having to check all the invoices, it slipped my mind to take them to the post.'

'I nearly did my back in lugging all those boxes,' said the caretaker, pulling a face and stretching theatrically. 'It's playing up again. It's not been right since I moved them bins. Then it took a turn for the worse getting that ruddy plaque back up on the wall. I sometimes can't get out of bed in the morning, suffering as I do.'

As you keep reminding me, thought Mrs Scrimshaw.

'And then I'll have to put another of them big heavy brass plaques up outside the new library. That won't be an easy job either.'

'Yes, well, I shall have to make a move in a minute,' said the secretary, not wishing to prolong the conversation about the caretaker's many medical problems. 'I have a WI meeting this

411

afternoon. Mrs Cockburn is talking to us about creative things to do with the Christmas leftovers.'

'And very smart you look too, if I may say so,' Mr Gribbon remarked, jangling the keys in his overall pocket.

'Thank you, Mr Gribbon,' she said. 'One has to make a bit of an effort. I have just been elected as the president of our local group so I want to look my best. We've finally managed to dislodge the last president. It's been so difficult having Mrs Bullock in the chair, what with her not being able to hear much.'

'Well, you look very colourful,' he told her, thinking that the scarlet jacket with wide lapels edged in the sort of black braid one sees on lampshades was way over the top.

'So how did the match go this morning?' the school secretary asked.

'Match?'

'The football. Who won?'

'We did,' said the caretaker. 'Three-nil. That's four wins in a row. The Stubbins lad scored all the goals. I can't say as how I like him, big, surly lump that he is, but by the heck he's a good footballer. You wouldn't believe with all the bulk he's carrying that he could be so light on his feet. I reckon he'll end up playing for some big club in the Premier Division and driving a fancy sports car by the time he's twenty.' He sighed. 'Such is life.'

'He's been a different boy since he returned, has Malcolm Stubbins,' observed Mrs Scrimshaw. 'Of course, he's been put on a trial period by Ms Devine and should he step out of line, he's out the door.'

'I don't forget when he used a can of spray

412

paint on the back wall of the school,' grumbled the caretaker. 'It took a full morning to clean off the mess. 'Course he denied it and got away with it but I knew it was him. If it had been up to me—'

'Look, I must go,' said the secretary, 'I shall be late. I'll see you on Monday, Mr Gribbon.' Mrs Scrimshaw negotiated the desk, headed for the door and scurried off down the corridor, her high heels clacking on the polished wooden floor.

'Well, I'll be—' said the caretaker out loud as he saw her exit though the door at the entrance to the school.

The school secretary was wearing red shoes.

* * *

Elisabeth arrived at the Royal Oak that evening to find David Williams waiting for her at a corner table in the lounge. The place was crowded and noisy. She looked her usual immaculate self, dressed in a white satin blouse and tight blue skirt with her blonde hair swept up in a tortoiseshell comb.

'Good evening, Elisabeth,' he said, rising to his feet to greet her. He had an easy, confident smile.

'Good evening.'

'You look very nice,' he said, pulling out a chair for her to sit.

'Thank you,' she replied. 'So do you.'

He coloured a little. 'I'll get the drinks in. What would you like?'

'Just an orange juice for me,' she said.

'Nothing stronger?'

'No, an orange juice will be fine.'

Mr Williams headed for the bar.

'How do, Mrs Devine,' came a loud and cheerful

413

voice from the public bar. She looked up to see the weather-reddened face of Fred Massey. He waved.

'Hello,' she shouted back, then closed her eyes and sighed. He was heading in her direction.

'Out on the town, I see,' he said.

She gave a small pained smile. It was just her luck that Fred Massey of all people should be there. It would be around the village now like wildfire.

'I didn't know this was your local, Mr Massey,' she said.

'It ain't, but I've been barred from the Blacksmith's Arms for getting in a barney with Albert Spearman. He must think my brains are made of porridge trying to pull a fast one. He sells animal feed and the last lot he tried to load off on me was duff. It was Clarence, my nephew, who took delivery. If I'd have been there Albert Spearman wouldn't have got away with it, I can tell you. He's looking after the farm is Clarence until I'm back on my feet. Well, supposed to be, but he's more trouble than he's worth. Anyway, Albert Spearman palmed him off with a load of rubbish. Didn't think I'd notice. Well, I did, and we had a set-to in the pub and I've been barred.'

'I see,' said Elisabeth, trying to look interested.

'Things got a bit heated when he made a clever comment about my accident—said I were like Long John Silver and I was as much a pirate as he was. I didn't prod him very hard with my crutch. Anyway, the landlord won't have me in the pub so I come here now.'

Mr Williams returned with the drinks.

'How do,' said Fred, eyeing the man up and down.

'Good evening.'

414

Elisabeth decided not to introduce her companion, but Fred Massey was determined to discover as much as he could.

'I'm a neighbour of Mrs Devine's,' he explained, smiling and revealing a set of misshapen yellow teeth. 'Fred Massey's the name. I have a farm in Barton.'

'I see.'

'Welshman, are you?'

'I am indeed.'

'My grandmother was Welsh. She was called Tudor, descended from a long line of kings so I was told.'

'A very fine Welsh name,' said Mr Williams.

'And you are?' he asked.

'Williams. David Williams.'

'And might I ask what do you do for a living, Mr Williams?' asked Fred.

'I'm a head teacher,' he replied, surprised at the man's bluntness.

'Well, we've got here the best head teacher in Yorkshire, bar none,' said Fred Massey, nodding in Elisabeth's direction.

'I'll not disagree with you there.'

'Well, I'm pleased to meet you. 'Course when I was at school, head teachers—'

'It is good to see you, Mr Massey,' interrupted Elisabeth. 'I'll let you get back to your pint.' She gave him a tight smile of dismissal.

'Aye, well, good to see you too, Mrs Devine, and to have met you, Mr Williams. I hope you both have a very pleasant evening.' With a smile on his face and a flash of the yellow teeth, he departed.

*   *   *

Elisabeth Devine sat in an easy chair by the window in the sitting room later that evening after David Williams had gone. She looked out across the garden, illuminated by a bright moon. Danny had done a grand job. She was in a thoughtful mood. The person most on her mind was Michael Stirling.

The evening with David Williams had not gone well. With hindsight, Elisabeth thought, she should never have accepted his invitation to join him for a drink. It would have been far better to keep their relationship strictly professional. In the Royal Oak they had been observed for the whole evening by Fred Massey and by several other customers who, no doubt, had been given a blow-by-blow account of who she was. The old farmer would of course be relaying information to those in the village. She could visualise Mrs Sloughthwaite leaning ponderously over her counter in the village store regaling her customers. Elisabeth had wished to leave the pub as soon as possible and had invited David Williams back to her cottage for a coffee, which in retrospect was another thing she now regretted. He had sat on the sofa, his hands cradling the cup, and had suddenly launched into a most unexpected and deeply embarrassing speech.

'I'm so glad I have this opportunity of speaking to you,' he had said. 'My office at Forest View is not the best place to broach such a matter.'

Elisabeth had felt her stomach lurch. She had prayed he was not going to say what she imagined he would.

'I know we have only known each other for a relatively short time, Elisabeth,' he had continued, 'ever since John came as a pupil to the school.'

'That's right,' she had said in a small voice.

'But I feel I know you. It's as if I have always known you. When my wife and I divorced,' he had continued, 'I went through a very bad patch. We'd been married for twenty years, Susan and I. It wasn't the most perfect marriage by any means but we never squabbled or disagreed and I thought she was happy enough. It came as a shock when she left. Evidently she'd been having an affair with her boss for some time. I suppose I was so wrapped up in my work I didn't notice anything.'

'I'm sorry,' Elisabeth had said.

'I've felt pretty lonely these last few years, as I guess you have too.'

'Well, I—' she had begun.

'I have a great admiration and respect for you, Elisabeth, and have so much enjoyed your visits to the school, but more recently my feelings for you have grown and—'

'David,' Elisabeth had interrupted, 'please don't say any more. You know how much I appreciate all you do for my son. I think a lot of you and—'

'I guess there's going to be a "but" at the end of this sentence,' he had said sadly.

'I'm afraid there is,' Elisabeth had told him.

'I see.'

'I'm sorry—' she had begun.

'If you need a little time?'

'No,' she had said firmly. 'I would not wish to give you any expectation. I am afraid I don't share for you the feelings you may have for me.'

'I see.'

'We can remain friends?' she had asked.

'But of course.' He had looked down, deflated, and replacing the cup on the table had stood up. 'Well, I guess I should be going. I shall see you as usual at Forest View next week.' He had reached forward and shook her hand. 'Goodnight, Elisabeth.'

'Goodnight, David,' she had said, and when the door had closed behind him she had taken a deep, deep breath.

*　　*　　*

'Do you know who the mystery man is then?' asked Mrs Pocock when she called into the village shop the following day.

'Mystery man?' the shopkeeper repeated.

'Him who was out with the new head teacher last night. I've just seen Edith Widowson on her way to chapel and she said Mrs Devine was out with a man last night. Fred Massey told her.'

Mrs Sloughthwaite leaned over and rested her substantial bosom and chubby arms on the counter. 'I don't know why everybody in this village thinks that I'm the foundation of all knowledge.' Mrs Pocock raised an eyebrow but didn't say anything. 'As you well know, I'm not a one for tittle-tattle, it's just that people insist on telling me things. I've always been a very good listener. It has been said that I should be one of these Samaritans that listen to other people's problems on the telephone, but I haven't the time what with running the post office and the shop. Anyway, I've no idea who he is.'

'Well, I was only asking,' said Mrs Pocock, sounding peeved.

'All I know is that Fred Massey come in here for his Sunday paper this morning and told me he'd seen Mrs Devine sitting at a corner table in the

Royal Oak at Gartside with this man and very cosy they looked too.'

'Do you think it was the husband?'

'No, this chap's name is Williams. He's a Welshman. Her name's not Williams, is it?'

'Well, I haven't seen him in the village,' remarked Mrs Pocock.

'Who, the husband?'

'No, the fancy man.'

'He's a head teacher by all accounts,' confided the shopkeeper.

'Really?'

'About the same age as her and friendly enough, according to Fred Massey.'

'Do you think he's married?'

'Couldn't say, but it struck me as a bit furtive, them meeting in the corner of a pub in another village.'

'Imagine.'

'Well, good luck to her, that's all I say,' said Mrs Sloughthwaite.

'I bet it was a blind date and she's met him through one of these dating agencies. They're all the thing these days.' She chuckled. 'You ought to think about it yourself and get fixed up with somebody,' she said flippantly.

'Not on your life!' exclaimed Mrs Sloughthwaite. 'I had enough trouble with the last one. My Stan, God rest his soul, was a good man but as lazy as Fred Massey's dog. It has to lean against the barn door to bark. I'm better off on my own. You know what Mrs O'Connor says: there are three kinds of men who fail to understand women—young men, old men and middle-aged men.'

Mrs Pocock nodded sagely. 'Well, you've met my

other half,' she said glumly.

'Least said,' observed the shopkeeper.

The topic of their earlier conversation walked through the door.

'So as I was saying, Mrs Pocock,' said Mrs Sloughthwaite, deftly changing the subject, 'the Venetian chocolate biscuits are on special offer this week. Oh, hello, Mrs Devine.'

'Good morning, Mrs Sloughthwaite,' said Elisabeth. 'Good morning, Mrs Pocock.'

'Morning, Mrs Devine,' said the other customer.

'I've just called in for my order,' said Elisabeth.

'It's all ready for you,' said Mrs Sloughthwaite, making no effort to get it.

'And to thank you for all the support you have given over the proposal to close the school,' added Elisabeth.

'It's nice to be appreciated, I'm sure,' said the shopkeeper. 'We're all very pleased with the outcome.'

Elisabeth turned to Mrs Pocock. 'The governors, of course, have been splendid. I think your petition had a massive influence in changing their minds at the Education Office. Thank you for all your hard work and sterling efforts.'

Mrs Pocock gave a self-satisfied smile, nodded appreciatively and then exchanged a glance at the mention of a certain word.

The shopkeeper began her interrogation.

'It was good of Dr Stirling to take on young Danny, wasn't it?' she asked.

'It was,' replied Elisabeth.

'He's a very compassionate man is Dr Stirling.'

'Yes, he is.'

'And a very good doctor.'

'Indeed.'

'It was tragic when his wife was killed.'

'Yes,' agreed Elisabeth, 'it must have been very hard for him.'

'It was. Mind you, it's been two years now since the accident.'

'Really?'

'Time can be a great healer,' added Mrs Pocock.

'Indeed,' said Elisabeth.

'It's a pity that he's never got married again,' remarked Mrs Sloughthwaite.

'I suppose so.'

'From what his housekeeper tells me, Clumber Lodge needs a woman's touch about the place.'

'Well, I'll be on my way,' said Elisabeth. 'If I could have my order.'

Mrs Sloughthwaite disappeared behind the counter and reappeared with a box full of provisions. 'Goodbye, Mrs Devine,' she said. 'Have a nice day.'

CHAPTER TWENTY-ONE

That afternoon Michael Stirling sat in an easy chair by the window in the sitting room, looking out across the garden. The boys had done a grand job pruning, weeding and tidying. He should be happy, he told himself. The battle to keep the village school had been won, young Danny had found a home, and his once quiet and distant son was coming out of his shell and looked much happier of late. But he was miserable. The medical journal he had been reading had been set aside and he was in a thoughtful mood.

The person most on his mind was Elisabeth Devine.

Mrs O'Connor appeared at the door.

'Will you be wanting a cup of tea, doctor?' she asked.

'Yes, thank you, Mrs O'Connor, that would be very welcome,' he replied.

'I'll put the kettle on.' The housekeeper paused at the door and heard him sigh. 'You look miles away. Is there something wrong?'

He sighed again. 'Not at all, everything is fine.'

'Well, as my owld Grandmother Mullarkey often used to say, a happy heart will often sigh.'

'Tell me, Mrs O'Connor,' said Dr Stirling, raising a smile, 'does this amazing Irish grandmother of yours, who likes giving everyone the benefit of her homely advice, actually exist or do you make up these words of wisdom?'

'Dr Stirling!' she cried in mock horror. 'Sure, my sainted grandmother is spinning like a whirling Dervish in her grave at this very moment.'

He laughed and shook his head. 'And is everything fine with you, Mrs O'Connor?'

'Well, you might have a word with young Danny about that weasel of his.'

'Weasel?'

'That long, furry, smelly creature he has with him. He never seems to go anywhere without it.'

'Oh, the ferret.'

'Weasel, ferret, it's all the same to me,' said the housekeeper. 'It puts the very fear of God into me, so it does, when I see it scuttling about with them sharp teeth and all.'

'What has Danny been doing?'

'He keeps taking it into his bedroom. I can't be doing with it. It's a horrid animal at the best of times and a bedroom is no place for it. I had a nasty shock when I found it in the bath.'

'In the bath?' repeated the doctor. 'Not with him, I hope.'

'No, he was washing it,' the housekeeper told him. 'There it was poking its pointed little head out of the soapsuds as large as life and twice as natural.'

'I'll have a word with him.'

'Thank you, Dr Stirling.'

'Danny seems to have settled here very well, all things considering,' said the doctor.

'Oh, he's a fine lad. It's as if he's lived here all his life. Apart from that weasel creature, he's no trouble at all.'

'I'm very pleased to hear it.'

'It was very good of you to take the lad in, Dr Stirling,' said the housekeeper. 'You're a decent man, so you are.'

He smiled. 'I don't know about that, Mrs O'Connor,' he said. 'I'll let you get the tea.'

The housekeeper was not yet ready to depart, for she had things to say. 'I saw Mrs Devine today,' she said casually.

'Oh yes,' replied Dr Stirling, equally casually.

'She's a lovely woman, to be sure.'

'Yes, she is.'

'And such an attractive, good-natured and intelligent woman. What a blessing it was when she came to the village.'

'A blessing indeed.'

'From what Mrs Sloughthwaite says she's got a gentleman friend.'

Dr Stirling took a sudden interest. 'Has she?'

'Another head teacher. A Welshman. Quite the dapper man, so I heard.'

423

'I see.'

'Well,' said the housekeeper, 'I shouldn't think she'll be short of admirers.'

'No, I suppose not,' said the doctor.

Having sown the seed, she said, 'I'll get the tea,' and left the room.

His housekeeper had put an idea into his head which made Michael Stirling feel more wretched. So Elisabeth Devine had an admirer in David Williams. The man was good, clever, generous and obviously attractive to women, and he also had that facility with words often possessed by the Welsh, something he, the village doctor known for his taciturnity, clearly lacked. The couple had so much in common, too. He now recalled sadly the many occasions when the head teacher at Forest View had brought Elisabeth into the conversation, speaking of her in glowing terms. The man was clearly keen on her.

Mrs O'Connor returned with a large brown-glazed teapot, a china cup and saucer and a jug upon a tray. She poured the thick black liquid. 'Why don't you give her a ring?' she asked.

'I'm sorry?'

'Mrs Devine,' said the housekeeper. 'Why don't you give her a ring? Call her up on the phone.'

'And why would I want to do that, Mrs O'Connor?' he asked.

'A fire in the heart makes smoke in the head, as my owld Grandmother Mullarkey used to say.'

'I'm sorry,' said Dr Stirling, 'I don't quite know what your Grandmother Mullarkey meant by that.'

Mrs O'Connor gave a small smile. 'Oh, I think you do, Dr Stirling,' she said, leaving the room. 'I think you do.'

 *   *   *

As Elisabeth sat in her sitting room now, thinking over the events of the evening before, the telephone rang shrilly.

'Hello.'

'Hello. It's Michael Stirling here.' His mouth was dry. 'I'm not disturbing you, am I?'

'No, not at all,' replied Elisabeth. Her heart missed a beat. 'You must be a mind reader. I was just thinking about you and was intending to give you a call.'

'Thinking about me?'

'Yes.'

'Nothing bad, I hope.'

'Pardon?'

'About me, nothing bad.'

'Of course not.'

'So how are you?'

'I'm fine.'

'Good, good.'

'How are the boys?'

'They're fine.'

'And you?'

'I'm fine too.'

'Well, then everybody appears to be fine.'

He took a breath. 'I was wondering if you might . . . if you are free, that is . . . that you might consider letting me . . . coming out . . . that is . . . with me . . . for a meal.' He sounded nervous and embarrassed. His heart was thudding. 'Of course if you have something planned—'

'I'd love to,' Elisabeth replied quickly.

'Pardon?'

'I said I would love to.'

'You would?'

'Of course. I was going to invite you around for a meal as a thank you for all your support over the last few weeks.'

'Well, I thought we might go to a restaurant.'

'I shall look forward to that.'

'Well, goodbye then.'

'When have you in mind?' said Elisabeth before he could put down the receiver.

'Sorry?'

'When have you in mind to go out for the meal?' she asked.

'Yes, yes, sorry. Er . . . what about tonight?'

'Tonight?'

'Yes, tonight,' he said quickly. 'Of course, if you've something on, I—'

'Tonight will be fine,' Elisabeth told him, her heart too beating like a drum in her chest. 'I shall look forward to that. Where shall I meet you?'

'Oh,' he said, trying to catch his breath. 'I'll collect you at about seven.'

'Right,' she said.

'Right,' he replied.

'I'll see you then.'

'Fine.'

He put down the receiver and flopped back in his chair.

*   *   *

'It's very good of you to look after the boys for the evening,' Dr Stirling told Mrs O'Connor later.

'It's a pleasure,' she replied. 'Anywhere nice?'

'Pardon?'

426

'Are you going anywhere nice?'

'Frederico's, the Italian in Limebeck.'

'With anyone special, or shouldn't I ask?' She gave a knowing smile.

'Yes, Mrs O'Connor, I am going out with someone very special.'

'Well, do give Mrs Devine my best wishes, won't you.'

'And how do you know it's Mrs Devine?' he asked.

'Oh, come along, Dr Stirling, I do have eyes in my head. I've seen the way you look at her.'

'Is it that obvious?'

'Has the Pope got a balcony?' she asked.

'Do you think she—'

'Feels the same about you?' Mrs O'Connor finished the sentence. 'Of course she does. I've seen the way she looks at you as well, and as my owld Grandmother Mullarkey was wont to say—'

'Oh please, spare me another of Grandma Mullarkey's words of wisdom,' said the doctor, laughing.

'As my Grandmother Mullarkey was wont to say,' Mrs O'Connor continued, as if he hadn't spoken, 'faint heart never won fair lady.'

The two boys appeared at the door.

'Where are you going?' asked James.

'Just out for a meal,' replied his father. 'I shan't be long.'

'Can we come?' James asked.

'No, not tonight,' said his father, smiling and ruffling the boy's hair.

'You look very smart,' said Danny. 'Doesn't he scrub up well, Mrs O'Connor?' he added, with a cheeky grin on his face.

'Sure he does, darlin'. Doesn't he look the bee's knees.'

Dr Stirling smiled and shook his head. 'Would you two not talk about me as if I'm not here,' he said good-humouredly.

'You've got your new suit on,' said James, frowning. 'And you're wearing aftershave. I can smell it. Who are you meeting?'

'All these questions,' said Dr Stirling, colouring a little. 'I've already been interrogated by Mrs O'Connor. I'm just meeting someone for a quiet meal, that's all.'

The two boys looked at each other and Danny whispered in his friend's ear. They both giggled. Then Danny nudged James and winked at him before turning to the doctor.

'Give Mrs Devine our best wishes, won't you, Dr Stirling,' he said, another great smile filling his face.

*   *   *

It was the last day of term at Barton-in-the-Dale village school. Over the two weeks leading up to Christmas, the staff and pupils had been busy decorating the building in celebration of the very special festival. Down the corridor and on classroom walls the children's poems and stories were enhanced by pictures of vivid winter scenes depicting great white peaks, forests of dark green pine trees, rolling fields and rocky outcrops hidden under a dusting of snow. Ernest had painted a large, smiling Santa riding on a golden sleigh pulled by prancing, mud-coloured reindeers and laden with presents. Mrs Atticus had supervised the transformation of the entrance hall, where the children had stuck different shapes of coloured tissue paper on the windows to give it the effect of stained glass. Mr Gribbon had made a wooden crib that housed small polished wooden figures of the Holy Family, the angels, the Magi and the shepherds, and Lady Wadsworth had donated a large fir tree from the Limebeck estate which had pride of place at the front of the hall.

The air was icy fresh that day. Great flakes of snow began to fall in the morning and soon walls, paths, trees, road signs, letterboxes and rooftops were shrouded in white. The whole area around the small school was a vast silent sea. Rays of watery winter sunlight pierced the high feathery clouds, making the snow glow a golden pink. The scene was magical.

Of course the school caretaker was not in the best of moods as he surveyed the scene from the school office.

'I hate this weather,' he moaned to Mrs Scrimshaw. 'It's like the bloody Arctic Circle out there. I've been out since dawn chucking sand and salt all over the path and shovelling mountains of snow, and as soon as I've shifted one lot another lot falls. And this cold gets into my bones and what with my bad back—'

'Happy Christmas, Mr Gribbon,' interrupted the school secretary cheerily.

'Beg pardon?'

'What a lovely time of year it is,' she said, maintaining her overly cheerful demeanour. 'A time of peace and goodwill, when everyone sounds happy and full of good cheer and enters into the spirit of the season.'

'What?' he asked, missing the sarcasm in her voice.

She changed her tone. 'For goodness' sake cheer up. You're like the Prophet of Doom. It's the end of term and it's nearly Christmas. You can rest your back and your bones over the next two weeks.'

'Fat chance,' he grumbled. 'We've got the relations coming. You don't want to hear what my brother-in-law's like.'

'No, I don't,' she said quickly. She gave a great sigh and returned to the letter she was typing. She could think of nothing more to say and hoped that the caretaker might go, but he remained, jangling the bunch of keys in his pocket and staring dolefully out of the office window.

A small voice could be heard in the corridor.

'Excuse me, Mr Gribbon, I'm sorry to interrupt your conversation but may I have a quick word with Mrs Scrimshaw?'

The caretaker breathed through his nose like a horse and moved away from the door to let a small boy into the office.

'Oh, it's you, Oscar,' said the school secretary, looking up. 'What is it you want?'

'I was just checking we are up to speed for this afternoon.'

'Up to speed?' she repeated.

'As you know, I am the narrator at the Nativity play and I just wanted to make sure that the carol sheets are ready to put on the chairs. If they are, I could do that at lunchtime if you like.'

'That won't be necessary, Oscar,' said Mrs Scrimshaw. 'Everything is in hand.'

'Tip-top,' he said.

'Shouldn't you be in your classroom doing some

work instead of wandering around the school?' asked the caretaker.

'Miss Brakespeare said I could pop out,' the boy told him.

'Well, you want to pop back in,' said Mr Gribbon. 'Go on, off you go.'

'Actually I'm glad I've seen you, Mr Gribbon,' said Oscar, ignoring the instruction. 'I've noticed that the path leading up to the school entrance is covered in snow again.'

'Have you indeed?' The caretaker stiffened.

'I nearly slipped and I could have hurt myself,' continued the boy.

'Well, you should look where you're going then, shouldn't you?' the caretaker replied brusquely.

'It's just that if someone does slip and fall over, they could break a bone and the school could get into a lot of trouble. I think it would be a really good idea, Mr Gribbon, if you did a bit of shovelling.'

The caretaker opened his mouth to reply but the boy smiled widely and said, 'Well, I must press on.'

'Goodbye, Oscar,' said the school secretary, a quiet little smile appearing in her face.

'Oh, goodbye, Mrs Scrimshaw,' he replied. He turned to the caretaker. 'Goodbye, Mr Gribbon, and you won't forget about that snow on the path, will you?'

The children were to perform the Nativity play that afternoon and it promised to be a very large turnout from the village. There was a lively chatter in the classrooms and, being the end of term, the teachers were rather more indulgent about the noise. Elisabeth, however, had to confiscate a sprig of mistletoe brought to school that day by

431

Chardonnay, who pursued poor Danny across the playground at morning break in the hope of getting a kiss. When the girl at last cornered her victim, she closed her eyes and puckered her lips in expectation.

'Clear off!' Danny told her, his face red with embarrassment. 'I'm not into that sort of thing.'

Not one to give up easily, Chardonnay approached him later on in the classroom as he pored over his reading book. Leaning close to him, her hair falling about her face, she dangled the mistletoe above the boy's head and pouted.

'Miss!' shouted Danny. 'Will ya tell 'er?'

'Miss,' Chardonnay announced, 'everyone kisses under the mistletoe. It's an old custom at Christmas.'

'I am well aware of that,' said Elisabeth, trying to stop herself smiling, 'but the person you wish to kiss under the mistletoe has to want to be kissed, and by the looks of it Danny isn't all that keen. Give it a couple of years, Chardonnay,' she told the girl, 'and it will be him chasing you for a kiss.'

The girl grinned. 'Do you reckon, miss?' she said.

'Dream on,' said Danny under his breath.

And so the sprig of mistletoe ended up on the teacher's desk.

It seemed that the whole of Barton-in-the-Dale had turned out for the Nativity play, for the school hall was packed that afternoon. Mrs Sloughthwaite, Mrs Widowson and Mrs O'Connor arrived early and commandeered seats in the centre of the front row. The shopkeeper had closed the village store early so she could attend. Mr Gribbon, who had observed the threesome trail muddy water across his parquet floor, muttered to himself and mopped it up in their wake. He approached them, clutching the mop to his chest like a spear.

'Those seats are reserved for Lady Wadsworth and other VIPs,' he told them, thrusting out his jaw. 'You'll have to move.'

'You don't say?' replied Mrs Sloughthwaite curtly, making no effort to rise from her chair. She gave a superior little sniff before adding, 'They should have reserved notices on if they was reserved seats, so we're not moving.' Then she pointed to a puddle beneath her feet. 'You've missed a bit,' she said. Mr Gribbon departed muttering again.

The Reverend Atticus, the prospective Archdeacon of Clayton, arrived rubbing his long hands together and smiling widely and joined the three women on the front row. He was soon followed by Lady Wadsworth and the major.

'It's so good to have the Nativity play performed again in the school,' remarked the cleric. 'As I recall, Miss Sowerbutts was not that keen when I broached the matter with her.'

'She was not very keen on anything which involved any extra work,' observed Lady Wadsworth.

'I was once in a Nativity play, you know,' remarked the major. 'When I was a kiddie, of course.'

'Really?' said the lady of the manor. She could not have put less enthusiasm into a single word.

'Yes, indeed,' the major told her. 'I was the ass.'

Mrs O'Connor glanced in the direction of Mrs Sloughthwaite, who as was her wont had been eavesdropping, and caught the look in her eye.

'Yes, I was the donkey,' continued the major. 'I had to wear a *papier-mâché* head.'

433

The vicar raised an eyebrow but didn't respond.

Soon there wasn't an empty seat in the hall. Mr Tomlinson took up his position at the piano, and the school choir, smart in their white shirts, with grey trousers or skirts, filed in and stood beneath the small stage. Silence descended. Dr Stirling, who had been called out on an emergency, arrived just before the performance began and joined Elisabeth, who was standing at the rear of the hall. From behind the makeshift curtains could be heard the excited whispering of the children. Oscar, dressed in a dark blue blazer with a red bow tie, slipped through the curtain. He cleared his throat several times and then, tilting his coloured glasses slightly on the bridge of his nose, announced: 'We would like to welcome you all to our Nativity play. Before the performance commences you need to be familiar with the exits in case there is a fire or a bomb scare and you have to vacate the building.' Then, like an airline steward, he indicated the various exits before disappearing behind the curtain. The lights dimmed and Oscar re-emerged.

'Tonight the children of Barton-in-the-Dale village school will recreate the scene in Bethlehem two thousand years ago when a very special baby was born, a baby who grew up to be someone who transformed the world with his teachings.'

The curtain opened to reveal the Virgin Mary, a small girl from the infants. She was a pretty little thing of about six, and was busy bustling about the stage, wiping and dusting. Oscar began to narrate the story. 'Many years ago there was a young woman called Mary. One day an angel appeared to her.' Chardonnay entered stage right wearing a white frilly nightie, large paper wings and sporting a crooked tinsel halo. She stretched out her arms dramatically.

'Hail Mary, full of grace,' she said, 'the Lord is with thee. Of all women you are the most blessed and soon you will have a baby and his name will be Jesus.'

'Oh,' said the Virgin Mary, blushing. 'Thank you very much.'

'In a town called Nazareth,' continued Oscar, 'there was a carpenter called Joseph.' A smiling little boy with apple-red cheeks strode on to the scene and positioned himself behind Mary. He was dressed in a tartan dressing-gown with a coloured towel on his head and had a cotton-wool beard gummed on to his chin.

'The angel appeared again,' said Oscar.

'Hail Joseph,' said Chardonnay, 'the Lord is with thee. He has sent me from Heaven to tell you to marry Mary, for soon she will have a baby and His name will be Jesus.'

'Oh,' said Joseph blushing. 'Thank you very much.'

'Now we will all stand and sing "Once in Royal David's City",' announced Oscar. When the hymn had ended and the audience had sat down he continued.

'And it came to pass, that a decree went out from Caesar Augustus, the Emperor, that the entire Roman world should be taxed. Joseph took Mary from Galilee to the city of David which was called Bethlehem, in Judea from where his family came. Long and tiring was their journey but they finally arrived at an inn looking for somewhere to stay.'

Malcolm Stubbins strode on to the stage wearing

a blue and white striped apron. He raised a hand.

'Before you ask,' he told them sharply, 'there is no room in the inn. There's the stable around the back. It's warm and dry and you can stay there for the night.'

'Thank you very much,' said Mary.

'Thank you very much,' repeated Joseph.

The narrator took up the story. 'And so Mary and Joseph had to sleep in the stable, for there was no room in the inn that night. Now nearby, in a distant dale, two shepherds were tending their sheep and watching over their flocks.' Danny and Ernest entered accompanied by a group of infant children dressed as sheep, wearing white woolly jumpers and cardboard masks. 'And the Angel of the Lord appeared again.' But the Angel of the Lord did not appear again. 'I said!' Oscar shouted, 'then the Angel of the Lord appeared again.' Chardonnay, her halo askew and one of her cardboard wings bent, rushed on to the stage.

'Sorry about that,' she told the audience.

'Hey up!' said Danny. 'Who are you?'

'I am the Angel of the Lord,' replied Chardonnay, 'and I bring you tidings of great joy.'

'What's that then?' asked the second shepherd.

'There's a baby boy been born this very night in a stable in Bethlehem. He is the Son of God, the Saviour of the World, Christ the Lord, the Messiah. So leave your sheep and follow yonder star and worship Him.'

The narrator stepped forward. 'And suddenly the sky was filled with a host of heavenly angels. Remain seated please. This carol will be sung by the choir only.' Mr Tomlinson struck up the piano and the children sang lustily 'While Shepherds

Watched their Flocks by Night'.

As the angels and shepherds left the stage, the Three Kings arrived on the scene.

'Now far far away in a distant land, three kings, wise men from the East, saw a bright shining star high in the dark sky which foretold of the birth of the new-born king,' said Oscar. 'Could you all stand for the next carol: "We Three Kings of Orient Are".'

Someone had really gone to town on the costume of the first king, for he was resplendent in a gold cape and silver pants. He wore a large bejewelled cardboard crown that shone brilliantly under the stage lights and trainers that lit up and flashed as he walked.

'I am Melchior, king of the north,' he announced loudly before kneeling before the manger and laying down a brightly wrapped box. 'I bring you gold.'

The second wise man, played by Chantelle dressed in a very fetching blue cloak, strode forward carrying a blue shampoo bottle. She too boomed out his words: 'I am Gaspar, king of the east, and I bring you myrrh.'

The third wise man was James. He was dressed in a velvet cloak made from a faded red curtain that still had the hooks in it and he was sporting a cardboard crown that covered half his face.

Elisabeth turned to see the expression on Dr Stirling's face. He moved his head forward, his eyes straining as he looked intently at his son. James shuffled nervously to the centre of the stage and stared around him wide-eyed and frightened, as if lost in a busy shopping street. There was a long silence. The children in the choir turned their heads

437

and the other two kings looked at each other and shrugged. Oscar, feeling he should take charge of the situation, moved forward and was about to speak, but he stopped when he saw James hold up a hand. The boy closed his eyes for a moment, then he took a deep breath and in a loud and confident voice he spoke.

'And I am Balthazar, king of the west, and I bring frankincense.'

When he had delivered his lines a flash of pure pleasure lit up his face. With his eyes shining, he looked over the heads of the audience to where his father was standing and smiled a triumphant smile.

The curtains closed and Oscar took centre stage.

'And on that holy night, when the stars were shining brightly, in a humble stable in Bethlehem, Jesus Christ was born and the Three Wise Men and the humble shepherds, the angels and the beasts of the fields, worshipped Him, for He was the Son of God, the most wonderful, the King of all Kings and the Light of the World.'

The curtains opened again to reveal a tableau at the centre of which stood Mary, cradling a large plastic doll. Chardonnay moved forward and the children knelt as she sang.

'O holy night! The stars are brightly shining,
It is the night of our dear Saviour's birth.
Long lay the world in sin and error pining,
'Til He appear'd and the soul felt its worth.
A thrill of hope the weary world rejoices,
For yonder breaks a new and glorious morn.
Fall on your knees! O hear the angels' voices!
O night divine, O night when Christ was born;
O night divine, O night, O night Divine.'

And that afternoon, as great flakes began to settle and form a thick carpet along the pavements, a lone figure, walking with thin rigid steps, made its way back to the cottage at the end of the village. Miss Sowerbutts, her pale face as blank as a figurehead on the front of a ship, heard the high, clear voice that filled the air as she paused at the gate of the school. And as she heard the divine singing a bitter despairing loneliness swept over her.

And as the snowflakes landed and melted on the window-panes in the school hall and the lights on the Christmas tree winked, Dr Stirling stared at the stage. But it was not the singing angel whom he saw, nor the innkeeper in his striped apron, nor the shepherds in their coloured dressing-gowns nor the little figure in blue cradling the plastic doll in her arms. It was the small boy in the faded red velvet curtain, the boy with his face glowing and his eyes shining. And when the choir of angels sang 'O night divine', he wiped the tears from his cheeks.

*　　　*　　　*

That evening a white moon lit up the landscape, luminous and still. Cars growled along the road through the soft snow, throwing cascades of slush in their wake. Lights twinkled and flickered in windows and there was the smell of pine in the air. No wind blew, no birds called, no animal moved and, save for the sporadic soft thud of snow falling from the branches of the towering oak tree which stood before the school, all was silent.

Elisabeth sat at her desk in the classroom.

Everyone had gone home and the school was silent. There was a stillness, as if life itself had been suspended.

A figure appeared at the door.

'I saw the light on,' said Dr Stirling.

'I wasn't quite ready to go home yet,' Elisabeth told him. 'I'm just having a quiet few moments, unwinding before tidying things up.'

'It was a wonderful Nativity,' he said, coming over to the desk. She could smell the cologne on his collar.

'Yes, it was. I was very proud of the children.' She looked down at her hands, almost afraid of meeting his eyes. 'And what about James? Didn't he do well?'

'He did,' replied the doctor. 'I was very proud of him. And you must be very proud of what you have achieved since you started at the school.'

'I am,' she said.

'Elisabeth,' he began after a moment, but stopped, searching for the right words to use, unsure how to begin. 'I . . . I . . . wanted to say . . .'

Then, seeing the sprig of mistletoe on the desk, he reached out and picked it up.

'One of the girls who has a bit of a crush on young Danny brought it into school,' Elisabeth told him. She chuckled. 'She chased the poor lad around the yard but he was having none of it. Then in the classroom she—'

'Happy Christmas, Elisabeth,' interrupted Dr Stirling, leaning forward and holding the mistletoe above her head.

She looked at him for a moment, then smiled. 'Happy Christmas, Michael,' she said, lifting up her face.